Praise for *Compulsion*

"Boone's Southern Gothic certainly delivers a compelling mystery about feuding families and buried secrets, not to mention a steamy romance."
—*Booklist*

"Mixes dark spirits, romance, feuding families, and ancient curses into the perfect potion."
—*Justine Magazine*

"A paranormal Southern Gothic with decadent settings, mysterious magic, and family histories rife with debauchery."
—*Kirkus Reviews*

"Skillfully blends rich magic and folklore with adventure, sweeping romance, and hidden treasure . . . An impressive start to the Heirs of Watson Island series."
—*Publishers Weekly*

"Eight Beaufort is so swoon-worthy that it's ridiculous. Move over, Four, Eight is here to stay!"
—*RT Book Reviews,* RT Editors Best Books of 2014

"A little bit *Gone with the Wind*, a little bit *Romeo and Juliet*. . . ."
—*School Library Journal*

"Even the villains and not-likable characters were just so engrossing. I have to say I've already put the sequel on my TBR shelf."
—*USA Today Online*

"Darkly romantic and steeped in Southern Gothic charm, you'll be *compelled* to get lost in the Heirs of Watson Island series."
—Jennifer L. Armentrout, #1 *New York Times* bestselling author

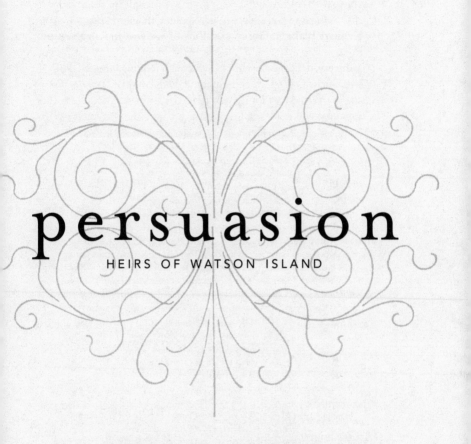

persuasion

HEIRS OF WATSON ISLAND

MARTINA BOONE

Simon Pulse

NEW YORK   LONDON   TORONTO   SYDNEY   NEW DELHI

SIMON PULSE

An imprint of Simon & Schuster Children's Publishing Division
1230 Avenue of the Americas, New York, New York 10020
First Simon Pulse paperback edition August 2016
Text copyright © 2015 by Martina Boone
Cover photographs copyright © 2015 by Trevillion Images (room) and
Getty Images/Corey Jenkins (couple)
Also available in an Simon Pulse hardcover edition.
All rights reserved, including the right of reproduction in whole or in part in any form.
SIMON PULSE and colophon are registered trademarks of Simon & Schuster, Inc.
For information about special discounts for bulk purchases, please contact
Simon & Schuster Special Sales at 1-866-506-1949 or business@simonandschuster.com.
The Simon & Schuster Speakers Bureau can bring authors to your live event.
For more information or to book an event contact the Simon & Schuster Speakers Bureau at
1-866-248-3049 or visit our website at www.simonspeakers.com.
Cover designed by Regina Flath
Interior designed by Hilary Zarycky
The text of this book was set in Granjon LT Std.
Manufactured in the United States of America
2 4 6 8 10 9 7 5 3 1
The Library of Congress has cataloged the hardcover edition as follows:
Boone, Martina.
Persuasion / by Martina Boone. — First Simon Pulse hardcover edition.
p. cm. — (Heirs of Watson Island ; [2])
Summary: When a mysterious man wielding a fatal spell appears at the Watson plantation, claiming the key to the Watson and Beaufort magical gifts and the Colesworth curse lies beneath the mansion, Barrie and dreamy Eight Beaufort struggle to make sense of the escalating danger and their growing feelings for each other.
[1. Families—Fiction. 2. Love—Fiction. 3. Supernatural—Fiction. 4. Blessing and cursing—Fiction. 5. Orphans—Fiction. 6. Islands—South Carolina—Fiction.
7. South Carolina—Fiction.] I. Title.
PZ7.1.B667Pe 2015   [Fic]—dc23   2014043183
ISBN 978-1-4814-1125-7 (hc)
ISBN 978-1-4814-1126-4 (pbk)
ISBN 978-1-4814-1127-1 (eBook)

To the survivors.

For all those who suffer from PTSD, and for the victims of violence, persecution, and marginalization all around the world.

For anyone who has been "persuaded" against their will.

May the world become a kinder, safer place.

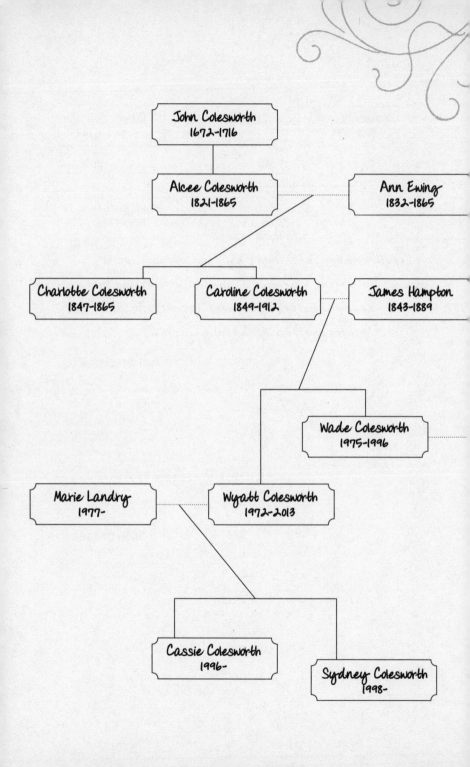

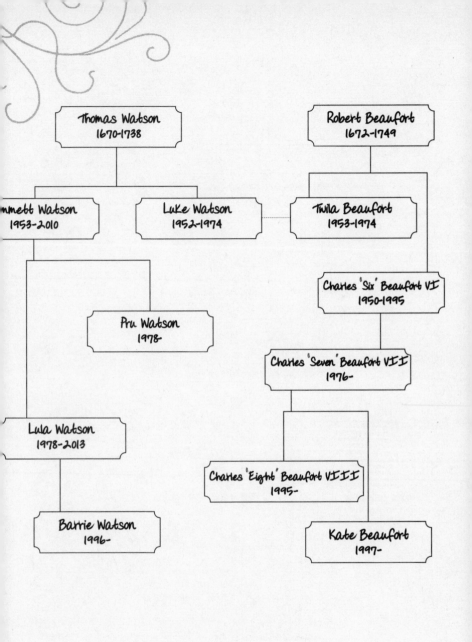

CHAPTER ONE

The last miles of the journey stretched eternally, and Watson's Landing pulled more and more on Barrie's finding gift. The ache at her temples had never been absent since she and Eight and Seven Beaufort had flown out to San Francisco to retrieve her godfather's ashes. Now the pain swelled to a pounding pressure.

Seven turned the Jaguar off the bridge from the mainland onto Watson Island. Slitting her eyes, Barrie tried to avoid the afternoon sun slanting through the oaks that shadowed the road along the water's edge. The blackwater Santisto River surrounded three sides of the island, but the Atlantic Ocean on the Eastern side added a familiar tang of salt to the tannin-scented air and made her more eager still. A few miles later, the car clattered across the smaller wooden bridge spanning the creek that separated the Watson property from the other half of the island, and a historical marker stood at the edge of the high wall that skirted the rice plantation Barrie's family had owned since 1692. Beyond the bricks lay the Watson woods, with the Fire Carrier's Scalping Tree at their heart. The thought both drew Barrie and repelled her.

"There, you see? Almost home." From the backseat behind her, Eight reached over and lightly touched Barrie's shoulder. "You'll feel better in a second, Bear."

Barrie smiled absently in the passenger seat, tightening her grip on the boxed urn she held in her lap. She braced herself as Seven swung into the driveway. The car stopped in front of the wrought-iron gate decorated with its ornate gold *W* and swirling hearts.

Perceptions were fickle things, as formless as smoke and just as dangerous. Weeks ago, when Barrie had first seen the plantation her mother had run away from in her teens, the light clawing through the haunts of Spanish moss along the avenue of ancient oaks had seemed ominous, and the down-at-the-heels mansion beyond the trees had appeared forbidding.

So much had changed since then. The things Barrie had considered "safe" at first had tried to kill her, and the spirits and the landscape that had frightened her initially were part of what she'd missed the most these past four days.

Leaning forward, she waited for the gate to open. It occurred to her only as the sticky heat blasted into the car from Seven's lowered window that the entrance shouldn't have been shut at all—not on a Sunday afternoon in tourist season. Trying and failing to tamp down a twinge of panic, she turned to Seven, who had reached out to press the intercom button set into the thick brick pillar.

"Why is the gate closed?" Barrie asked.

Seven didn't answer, and in the backseat, fabric rustled across the leather as Eight shifted and slid his eyes away. Not that their evasions delayed the truth for long.

The Watson gift for finding lost things had continued to grow stronger since Barrie's mother's death. A tug of pressure pulled her toward the answer, which was hidden from view by Seven's shoulder. Craning her head around him, she discovered that someone had taped a sheet of yellow paper over the plaque on the gatepost:

> *Tearoom and gardens*
> *closed to the public*
> *until further notice.*

"All right, what's going on?" Fighting to keep her voice level, Barrie skewered Eight with a glare. "What happened? Did Pru hurt herself? Where is she?"

"Your aunt's okay," Eight answered at the same moment Seven said, "Pru's just fine."

Barrie looked from one to the other, but it was Seven who had spent the most time on the phone with Pru. "Out with it," Barrie commanded. "What are you hiding?"

In the rearview mirror, Eight and Seven flicked each other looks that acknowledged guilt.

"There's been a bit of trouble with reporters and ghost hunters since the story broke about the explosion," Seven hastened to say. "Nothing to worry about. Pru and I decided it was better to close up in an abundance of caution."

"You and Pru decided . . . ," Barrie repeated. "Why didn't anyone tell me?"

Seven's face smoothed into the typical Beaufort *for your own good* expression that drove Barrie nuts. He jabbed the intercom button again, and Barrie aimed an expectant and disapproving eyebrow in Eight's direction.

"Well?" she asked.

A hint of red spilled across Eight's cheeks. "Come on, Bear. You were already dealing with packing up the rest of your mother's things." Losing his usual confident calm, he waved a hand toward the box on Barrie's lap. "Not to mention Mark."

Grief didn't make Barrie fragile. She would have told Eight that, but the intercom crackled, and her aunt's voice came across the wireless system.

4

"Hello? Who's there?" Pru asked.

Seven's expression softened as it did whenever he spoke to Pru. "Just us," he said.

"Well, thank God for that. Hold on, and I'll buzz you through."

It was so good to hear the honey-slow pace of her aunt's South Carolina drawl that Barrie's train of thought evaporated briefly. But then the exchange only heightened her sense that the situation was worse than the Beauforts let on. Turning in her seat, she studied them. They were a matched set in their pastel oxford shirts, with their stubborn-jawed faces and their hair lightened by the sun.

She wasn't sure which of them frustrated her more. They both had the infuriating bossiness that came with the Beaufort gift of knowing what people wanted and being compelled to give it to them. Seven even more so, as Barrie had discovered the past few days. But Eight? He was supposed to be on *her* side. He shouldn't have kept things from her. Not about Watson's Landing.

Technically, the plantation still belonged to Pru, but it was Barrie who was bound to the land by blood, magic, and inheritance. The house, the gardens, the woods where the Fire Carrier disappeared each night, and the spirits of the *yunwi* that the ancient witch kept corralled on the island with his nightly ceremony of fire on the river were all Barrie's responsibility.

Responsibility.

The word felt right as Barrie thought it. She *was* responsible. Because who else could be? Pru barely had the Watson gift at all; she had never been the true heir. As the younger twin, younger than Barrie's mother, Lula, the gift had touched Pru only incidentally, and she couldn't see the spirits or feel the land as strongly as Barrie did. And how was Barrie supposed to protect the *yunwi* or keep Watson's Landing safe if no one let her know what was going on?

She had every intention of telling Eight exactly why he was wrong and what kind of betrayal it was to keep secrets from her, but before she could open her mouth to speak, he leaned closer with his uncanny green eyes intent on hers.

"You're right, we should have told you," he said, echoing her thoughts the way the Beaufort gift so often let him. "But what was the point of worrying you? You couldn't do anything while we were away."

"Can't do much even now. The Santisto's a public river," Seven said.

Barrie swung her attention back to him. "What does this have to do with the river?"

"There are a few boats using it to watch what's going on here. Reporters and people hoping to see the Fire Carrier." Seven pushed the car back into gear. "Don't worry. The excitement will die down after your cousin's hearing and

Wyatt's funeral. Everything will go back to normal."

In front of them, the black iron gate trembled and began to slide. A dozen or more knee-high figures with mischievous, childlike faces rushed through the opening toward Barrie's side of the car. Their shadow-shapes were hard to see because of the daylight and the speed with which they moved, but their eyes etched dim trails of fire and gold into the air behind them. Barrie smiled and rolled down the window to stretch out her hand.

A movement on the six-foot wall beside the gatepost made her pause.

There was a man sitting up on top. He was dark from head to toe, dressed in a black suit with a sheen that blended into his skin and an aubergine silk shirt, and he was reading a newspaper so casually, he could as easily have been sitting at home on his sofa. He turned and looked dead at Barrie. Thick rows of dreadlocks swung past his shoulders, and when he lowered the newspaper, something white flashed in sharp contrast against his wrist.

Barrie shaded her eyes, and he smiled . . . and vanished. Between one blink and the next, the top of the wall was empty except for a large raven sitting in the spot where the man had been. The bird peered at her with its head tilted considerably.

"Bear? Are you all right?" Eight grasped Barrie's shoulder. "What happened? You've gone as white as a sheet." He managed to avoid the five-day-old stitches where a piece of her uncle's exploding speedboat had sliced into Barrie's muscle as she'd tried to swim across the river, but she flinched anyway, and shivered.

"There was a . . . ," she began, but before she could mention the man she had seen, she couldn't remember what she had meant to say.

Eight's forehead creased into worried lines. "There was a what? A person? Another reporter? Someone snooping around?"

Barrie tried to focus. She was supposed to remember something. . . . Her thoughts were sluggish, as if she were trying to think through quicksand. What had she been looking for? Why was she staring at an ordinary raven on the wall?

"Sorry. Nothing." She shook her head to clear it. "It was nothing."

The look Eight threw her was as sharp as it was reproachful. "One of your 'nothings' usually means there's something. You're not going to start keeping secrets again because we're back, are you?"

"Pot, kettle, black, baseball guy. You're the one keeping secrets."

She watched the raven fly away until it was only a smudge of receding darkness. She was going crazy; that was all there was to it. Not that it was any wonder, with everything that had happened and the migraine that hadn't let up in days.

Seven had stopped to look around instead of driving through the gate, which wasn't helping any. Rubbing the ache at her temple, Barrie nodded toward the entrance. "Can we please just *go*?" she asked.

The relief was instantaneous. The moment the car tires crunched on the white oyster shell and gravel of the avenue between the oaks, the Watson gift released its grip, as if Barrie had merely been another lost object that she was compelled to return to its proper place.

She sagged into her seat and filled her lungs with air scented by jasmine and magnolia. Fingers of moss hanging from the oak canopy overhead swayed in the breeze from the river, and the graceful old mansion at the end of the drive glowed white and gold in the waning sun. For once, all the dark green shutters hung straight and properly in place.

Ghost hunters or not, it was a relief—a joy—to be back. Barrie took in the wide lawns and the maze of hedges between the house and the Watson woods where the ground sloped gently toward the river that formed the boundary between Watson's Landing and the Beaufort and Colesworth plantations on the opposite bank.

But a blue-canopied speedboat and two smaller craft marred the view.

Barrie wasn't prepared for the way the sight felt wrong.

The boats staked out beyond the rippling expanse of marsh grass made her muscles tighten as if her whole body had turned into a charley horse and needed to be unclenched.

She wasn't afraid; the claustrophobic feeling wasn't one of her usual panic attacks, which, thank goodness, were becoming rare. This was something different, an anger that came from an urge to protect Pru and Watson's Landing. Barrie wasn't even sure how much of that emotion came from a natural sense of violation on hearing about the intruders, and how much stemmed from the magical binding that connected her to Watson's Landing more strongly day by day.

With a glance at the *yunwi* running alongside the car, she drew the box with Mark's urn closer to her chest. "Those are the boats you were talking about, the ghost hunters? How does anyone know the Fire Carrier was involved? Eight and I never told the police—or anyone."

"You didn't need to mention it." Seven's voice and eyes had both grown cold. "Enough people have claimed to see the flames on the river over the years, or at least they've heard the legend of the fire at midnight. Someone was bound to put two and two together when Wyatt's boat exploded at that time of night—"

He broke off abruptly, but it was too late. Tears pricked Barrie's eyes, and the memories swept in before she blinked: the face tattooed on the back of Ernesto's skull, the strength of his grip, the ache of his booted feet connecting with her ribs. None of it had faded from her nightmares yet, but it was her uncle's voice that haunted her. Wyatt's voice ordering her into the boat so they could take her out to kill her.

She couldn't be sorry that he and Ernesto were dead.

She refused to be sorry.

A muscle ticked along Eight's jaw as he read her, and he leaned toward her in concern.

She shook her head and turned back to Seven. "There isn't anything you can do about the boats? There has to be some way to get rid of them."

The instinct to protect Watson's Landing was so new, she didn't understand it herself. She didn't expect Seven to mirror her outrage, but his eyes flashed, something real and raw sparking behind them before he seemed to get hold of himself. Then he rubbed his head with an exhausted wince, as if Barrie's migraine had been contagious.

"Better to let the interest die down on its own," he said. "Anything we do is only going to create more publicity. Your aunt's put up NO TRESPASSING signs around the dock and shoreline, and so far that seems to be working. She hasn't seen anyone coming ashore here the way the treasure hunters have done at Colesworth Place—"

"Treasure hunters?" Barrie's voice was sharp. "I thought we were finally done with Cassie's imaginary treasure."

Seven swerved to avoid the white peacock and pair of peahens that had strayed too close to the road. "The treasure might not be so imaginary after all. One of the reporters found an old newspaper article while he was snooping around. Alcee Colesworth took up the family tradition of privateering during the Civil War—"

"Piracy," Barrie said. "Call it what it is."

"*Privateering* sanctioned by the Jefferson Davis government," Seven corrected, "at least in this instance. Although, in typical Colesworth fashion, Alcee never shared his last prize with anyone. His ship sank outside Charleston Harbor, and by the time they managed to raise it, the gold had disappeared. It's not a stretch to assume he kept it for himself."

Not long ago, Barrie would have argued Seven's assumption. She would have said it was unfair to jump to conclusions merely because of the feud that had existed between the Colesworths and the Watsons and Beauforts for three hundred years. Barrie was, after all, a Colesworth, too, on her father's side. But she had learned the hard way that the feud existed because the Colesworths weren't capable of being honest with anyone, or of accepting a hand offered to them in friendship. Why her mother had ever run off with one of them, Barrie would never understand. But Lula had spent the remainder of her life paying bitterly for that mistake.

The idea that Cassie had actually told the truth about the

treasure . . . about anything? Barrie didn't believe that, and what her finding gift had sensed at Colesworth Place hadn't felt like gold or money.

She stared through the trees to the dark water of the Santisto, gleaming with the dull sheen of tarnished silver. On the opposite bank, the jagged columns and shattered chimneys that were all that remained of the ruined Colesworth mansion stood atop a shallow rise. As always, the sight made Barrie thankful that Watson's Landing was still intact. A little frayed at the edges, like one of her aunt Pru's well-worn sundresses, but perfect and beautiful and familiar.

Only the boats were wrong. Barrie shivered as she remembered the last boat the Fire Carrier had encountered, and her breath came easier once the river was out of sight.

The Jaguar crawled to a stop in the circular drive below the columned portico. At the top of the wide front steps, one of the double doors flew open, and Barrie's aunt hurried down to meet them. Barrie was barely out of the car before Pru was there, flinging her arms wide and then squeezing hard enough to make Barrie's stitches groan.

"Lord, I've missed you! It seems like a month since you left." Pru stood back to look at Barrie critically before giving Seven a baleful frown. "Didn't you feed this child while you were gone, Seven Beaufort? She's likely to disappear on us." Leaning forward, she kissed Barrie on the forehead. "Now, don't you worry, sugar. We'll get you straightened out in no time. I'm making a beef roast with sweet potatoes for supper, and I've got bourbon chocolate cake for dessert. That's the only upside to having the tearoom closed: there's plenty of time for cooking."

Barrie shifted the box to her other arm and gave a reluctant nod.

Pru eyed the box a little wildly. "Is that . . . Oh, honey, have you been holding him all this time?"

"I couldn't put him in the luggage." Barrie was pleased her voice didn't tremble.

"Do you want any help finding a place to put . . . him?" Pru turned helplessly to Seven, but he was watching her as if she were a slice of his favorite whoopie pie cake and he wanted to eat her up.

Barrie couldn't help an inward smile. "You and Seven go do whatever you need to do in the kitchen." She held her hand out to Eight as he popped the trunk to get the suitcases. "Eight can come and help me."

Apart from needing to find a safe place for Mark, she and Eight hadn't had a moment all day to be alone.

CHAPTER TWO

The box slipped in the crook of Barrie's elbow. It grew heavier the longer that she held it. How was it possible that with all the rooms at Watson's Landing, all the Sheraton cabinets, Hepplewhite sideboards, and Chippendale tables, there didn't seem to be a nook or cranny where Mark would fit? None of the antiques were as too-perfectly preserved and off-limits as those that Barrie's mother had collected, but none of them felt like Mark.

The library wasn't any better. Pausing on the threshold, Barrie took in the new bowl of flowers Pru had put on the table between the wingback chairs and the new chintz curtains hanging in the windows. It was a beautiful room, but no amount of cleaning or redecorating could erase the fact that it had been the inner sanctum of a man who had murdered his own brother. The fog of his sins seemed to fill the room.

Murder. The word was still impossible to process. Barrie was related to murderers both on her Colesworth side and on her Watson side.

"Maybe we should try in the front parlor again," she said, turning to go.

"Bear, we've been in there twice already." Gently, Eight folded her free hand into his. The rough baseball calluses were familiar and comforting against her skin, and his grip was steadying. "You have to let him go," he said.

I can't. Barrie wanted to scream the words.

She had thought she was doing all right, surviving the blows one at a time. Discovering the skeletons of Luke Watson and Twila Beaufort in the tunnel and being locked in the tunnel herself by her cousin Cassie, that had shaken her. But she had held herself together. She had managed to escape when Ernesto and her uncle Wyatt had tried to kill her after she discovered their drug smuggling operation. The same smuggling operation that years before had made Wyatt set the fire that had killed her father and left her mother scarred.

With Eight's help, Barrie had survived the whole long, awful night and finding out that Mark had died. She had made it through the trip to San Francisco and sorting through the last of Mark and Lula's things. But how was she going to survive saying good-bye to Mark? How was she supposed to let him go? She didn't have the strength for that.

"Let me do it." Dropping a kiss on her nose, Eight removed the box from her hand. After he set it on the corner of the desk and took the urn out, a piece of paper fluttered to the Oriental carpet.

Barrie stooped to pick it up, but she knew what it said by heart.

Isn't this a hell of a thing, baby girl? The damn cancer is growing faster than I thought, so I better write down everything I don't have the courage to tell you on the phone.

Don't you ever, ever forget that I love you, all right? Raising you is the best thing I've done. You're my legacy, so remember your promise to put mileage on those fabulous shoes for both our sakes. And if that number Eight of yours is what's going to make you happy, go after him with a pitchfork.

Now, baby girl, here's the hard part. I'm leaving it to you to decide what to do with my ashes. You'll probably hate me for that awhile, but you're the one who is going to need the ceremony. I'll be okay with anything you decide, and anyway, I'm planning on sticking around to watch what you make of yourself. Make it interesting for me, would you?

Make me proud.

There was no salutation or signature. No closing. No closure.

"I need to find the right place. It's the one last thing I can do for him." Barrie smoothed the crumpled paper and put it back into the box. "You don't have to wait with me."

"I'm not going anywhere." Eight studied her with his eyes drawn and worried. Then he caught both her hands. "Bear, I'll be here for however long it takes you to find the perfect spot for Mark. You know that, but this indecision isn't about a place. You couldn't find anywhere that felt right in San Francisco, either."

"Mark deserves respect. He deserves *everything*."

"Of course he does." Eight's jaw grew even more square and stubborn, and he held his palms out, the rolled-up sleeves of his oxford slipping down to catch at the crooks of his elbows. "What about putting him in the glass case here for now, where he'll be safe? At least, until you find someplace permanent that speaks to you. Do you know where Pru put the key?"

"It's probably on the key ring in the center drawer." Barrie pointed to the desk.

Eight gave her the kind of grin that always made her heart catch against her ribs. "There. That wasn't so hard, right? It's a good spot, and you have to admit, from everything you've told me about Mark, he would have gotten a kick out of invading your grandfather's space and giving Emmett a big up-yours."

18

Smiling when she wouldn't have thought it was possible, Barrie picked the urn up from the desk while Eight retrieved the key. She traced the seams of gold in the dark blue lapis. They had reminded her of the *kintsugi* pottery she and Mark had seen at a museum once, simple vessels repaired with gold so that they were all the more beautiful for having broken. That was Mark. He had been the gold that ran through her life and made it whole.

She moved to the cabinet as Eight fitted the key into the lock, but raised voices from down the corridor behind her made her pause. The kitchen door creaked open, and determined male footsteps echoed on the mahogany floorboards. Barrie listened for her aunt's kitten-heeled tread escorting Eight's father out, but Pru didn't leave the kitchen.

Barrie clutched the urn to her chest and blinked at Eight. "You want to go see what they're fighting about?"

"Not even a little bit. Stop trying to distract me." He unlocked the cabinet door and held it open.

Barrie instructed herself to move, to place the urn on the shelf, but her muscles seemed to belong to someone else.

The problem was, Mark couldn't be gone.

"Bear?" Eight's voice was gentler. "Do you want me to do the honors?"

"I can manage." She succeeded in pushing her feet forward, raising her arms. Each of the mechanical motions that should have been automatic required thought and force. She set the urn in position, stepped back to study it, and moved it one shelf up before putting it back again where she had originally set it.

Eight waited to see if she would change her mind again. Then he shut and locked the cabinet and stood jiggling the keys in his palm as if he couldn't decide what to do with them. As if he were contemplating appropriating them to save Barrie from herself.

That would be exactly like him.

"You can put the keys back in the drawer," she said. "I'll stop being neurotic."

"Don't make promises you can't keep." With another teasing smile, Eight leaned in and kissed her. A light kiss, that was how it started, but she cupped his face in both hands to hold him close. He pulled back and gave her a searching look, and then his lips met hers with the kind of hunger that sent goose bumps up her spine and made her cling to him while she still could before he left her.

She wished he weren't going to school in California. She wished he would stay, because then she might have a chance to make things work with him. At USC, he would meet lots of girls. With his looks, and charm, and baseball scholarship, they would be all over him. How could she compete?

He pulled away, and she felt lost again. His expression was

dark and serious. "This is a pause, not a halt. I don't want to start something more when Pru might come in, so I'm putting a bookmark right here." He tapped her lip with his index finger. "I refuse to wait until after dinner to tell you what I need to say."

"I want to talk to you, too. About the boats and what's going on."

Eight's eyes gleamed in anticipation. "Me first," he said.

CHAPTER THREE

A whisper of wind down the oak-lined avenue cooled Barrie's cheeks as Eight led her out the front door and around to the right side of the house. The shadow shapes of the *yunwi* crowded around her, surging ahead and darting impatiently back. She struggled to keep her footing in the strappy high-heeled sandals she had chosen that morning because they were a perfect match to her dark denim jeans.

"Where are you dragging me, caveman baseball guy?" Barrie asked, forcing a smile because Eight was taking her somewhere, and because she was home, and because she hadn't truly felt like smiling since the night Mark had died.

"Haven't you been to this side of the house?" Eight paused, his head tipping as he considered that. "I guess I keep forgetting that you haven't had time to just wander around this place."

"I've been a little busy."

"Well, come on then. It's out of sight of the river, and we won't be interrupted by Pru or anyone else."

"There is no one else. The tearoom's closed."

Eight shook his head at her, took her hand, and started walking. They cleared the side of the house and crossed the lawn toward a row of ruined outbuildings covered in vegetation. Although Barrie had seen the slave cabins and restored kitchen, icehouse, and chapel at Colesworth Place, she hadn't so much as asked herself whether any of those structures still existed at Watson's Landing. They weren't visible from her room, standing as they did level with the main house, away from the path to the river.

There weren't any slave cabins, thank goodness. The closest building was a stable. A laced web of wisteria, resurrection fern, and Spanish moss decorated the bricks, making it eerily beautiful, an impression that was only intensified as a shadow flew over Barrie's head and a raven landed in a nearby oak.

At first glance, the stable complex looked neglected. Closer up, though, the masonry stood solid, and there was a structured harmony to the moss and vegetation that wasn't truly wild. Even the wooden floors inside appeared intact when Barrie peered through a window. A heavy, heart-shaped iron padlock barred her entry, and the wooden door barely budged on its hinges when she shook it.

"Is there any way inside?" she asked Eight across her shoulder.

"Leave it for now. There's something else I want you to see."

He bypassed the stand-alone kitchen and some other structures. The chapel was the only ruin. Charred by fire and roofless, it stood at the center of a fenced cemetery, with a congregation of angels, crosses, and tombstones of every possible size and shape, rank after rank of them, mourning above the silent graves outside its walls. Inside the chapel, an oak tree had taken root and spread its branches wide overhead to create a living ceiling.

Eight paused beside the fence. "Beautiful, isn't it? In the winter, when the leaves are off the trees, it's visible from my room. I've always wanted a chance to come over and poke around."

"So basically, wanting to kiss me was only an excuse?"

"Other way around." Eight stepped closer and his eyes focused on her lips. "I'll use any excuse to kiss you."

Instead of kissing her, though, he grinned and took her hand again to help her clamber over the waist-high fence. His touch lingered on her skin as he led the way through the empty arched entry into the chapel, where light filtered through the oak canopy to create streaks across the grassy floor. He grabbed the top of the doorway and leaned forward, rocking slightly on his toes as if he were testing the strength of the building.

Nothing moved, not so much as a trickle of mortar crumbling from between the centuries-old bricks.

How much of that preservation was due to the *yunwi*, and how much was due to the same sort of protection magic that had kept the tunnel beneath the river in perfect repair? There was still so little about Watson's Landing that Barrie understood. The word "magic," though—the *idea* of magic—still ran through her with a rush. Her gift had always been part of her, so much so that she'd never really thought of it as something special. Now, knowing that magic existed, and she was part of it, filled the world with possibility.

"We have to find a way to get rid of the people on the river," she said. "*All* the reporters and ghost hunters." She turned back to look at Eight after slipping past him through the doorway. "It seems wrong for people beyond Watson Island to know about the Fire Carrier. Like too many people knowing will spoil it, the way you're not supposed to tell a wish when you blow out a candle."

"I'd buy a billboard in Times Square if that was all it took." Letting his hands drop from the doorway, Eight crossed the threshold.

Barrie's eyes widened. "You'd really get rid of your gift?"

"You wouldn't? Think about it. You wouldn't have to deal with migraines, and you'd be free of Watson's Landing." He gave an easy one-shouldered shrug, as if it didn't matter.

"I don't want to be free of Watson's Landing."

"Things would be a whole lot simpler."

"'Simpler' doesn't mean 'better.'"

"Don't let's argue." Eight caught Barrie's hand and led her deeper into the chapel to where a waist-thick branch of the oak hung low and then snaked up and out through a glassless window. Leaning back against the branch, he pulled her toward him.

"Don't you hate people knowing about our gifts? About *him*?" Barrie whispered.

"There's no harm in a myth. That's all people will assume the Fire Carrier is. Practically every plantation in the South has a white lady walking around in a nightgown, and every lonely road has a hitchhiking specter. So what if we have ghostly fire? Let people believe it or assume it's a hoax, whatever they want. It doesn't change anything for us."

"Tell that to Mary." Barrie sniffed indignantly. "You realize she's worked here most of her life, and now with the tearoom closed, she doesn't have a job? And what if someone tries to sneak into the woods and the Fire Carrier hurts them? What happens then?"

"He never has so far."

"He killed Wyatt and Ernesto!" The words came out so fast, it was as if they'd been bottled up in Barrie's throat since the night of the explosion. Maybe they had been.

Eight's brows sloped inward as he studied her, but after a moment, he adjusted his hands at her waist and drew her even closer. The heat of his fingers burned through her synapses, making it harder to be afraid.

"You listen to me, Bear. Wyatt and Ernesto, that was not your fault. Running drugs and trying to kill you were choices they made all on their own. The same applies to anyone who trespasses in the Watson woods. You can't be responsible for people's stupidity. You worry too much as it is."

"Worrying is what you do when you have strangers camped on your doorstep. And what happens to the restaurant we were going to open? You'll be going to school in a month, so if we have to wait much longer, you won't be able to help. Tourist season will be over soon after that. If we don't open in July, there's not much point starting until next summer. Wait, why are you turning away?" Barrie broke off as Eight's eyes slid away from hers.

It took a while to process what his silence meant; there were still too many thoughts flying at her all at once. "You knew," she said, feeling stupid and kicking herself. "All the time we were in California talking about recipes we wanted to try for the restaurant and I was babbling on about tables by the fountain and candles in the water, you knew the tearoom was closed and our plans weren't going to happen."

"You *wanted* to be distracted. Dad and Pru thought—"

"What? That I couldn't handle it?" Heat spilled across Barrie's cheeks. She tapped him on the chest with her finger, wishing he could read her feelings or her *reasons* instead of just what she wanted most, because she wasn't positive she could explain. She had never been good at explanations.

"The restaurant was going to be here for you whenever you came back," she said, tiptoeing through the words. "It was the career you said you wanted after baseball, and you've been so focused on wanting to get off this island for so long, I wanted to give you a reason not to run away. Maybe that was silly. Or hopeless, I don't know. It was also something Pru and I could do together. Something that would connect us all to Mark."

"I know all that." Eight looked at her as if he saw *her*, as if he did understand.

Barrie hated that she couldn't sort out how much of that came of caring for her, and how much was due to the Beaufort gift. Either way, it did horrible things to her concentration and her confidence. Suddenly she didn't want to talk at all.

"You mentioned something about a bookmark," she said, her voice sounding small over the too-loud drum of her pulse. She wished she could bat her eyes flirtatiously without making a fool of herself. Wished she was good at the kind of charming seduction that Cassie had probably nailed before she was five years old.

Eight pulled his hands from her waist. His fingers grazed

her cheeks, making her breath expand and catch in her lungs. Her eyes fell closed, as if he were stealing her control until it was impossible to think about anything but that moment.

The chapel smelled spiced and warm, and his lips came down slowly enough that energy had time to arc back and forth between them and build and build.

Barrie's lips felt swollen and her fingers tingled when she finally came up for air, but the worst damage was to her throat. The words came out a rasp when she tried to speak. "I wish we had more time," she said.

"We do have time," Eight said. "That's what I've been trying to tell you. I've changed my mind about going to USC, and I emailed the baseball coach this morning and gave up the scholarship."

"What?" Barrie blinked at him, certain she had heard him wrong.

"Going to California was a way to prove something to my dad, but there are more important things than pride. You, for one." He paused and raised his head. "Hey, I figured you'd be happy. Why aren't you?"

She wanted to be happy. After all, she was getting what she wanted.

But wasn't that the problem?

"Are you staying because you want to stay, or because I want you to?" she asked.

"It's not going to matter. I sent out emails this morning to the local schools. I've already heard back from the coaches at the College of Charleston and Charleston Southern, but I'm still hoping to hear from the University of South Carolina. Columbia is only an hour away, and it's got a great athletic program. I may have to wait a semester, but I don't need a scholarship anymore. Dad was only refusing to pay for school to get me to stay here, and now I'm staying."

He watched her, puzzled, and so obviously still waiting for her to be happy that it made her feel even worse. The longer she waited, the more his eyes darkened.

The late afternoon light had spotlit a spider's web in the corner of the chapel. It looked gossamer thin, but webs were always stronger than they seemed.

"You've spent your entire life wanting to get off the island," she said.

He stared off past her shoulder in the direction of the river. "You weren't here then."

"Pretend I'm not here now. What would you do if you weren't compelled to give me what I want?"

"The gift doesn't quite work like that." His smile was odd and almost wistful.

"So you admit it's the gift making you want to stay?" Barrie asked.

"Don't put words into my mouth. And who cares why I

want what I want? I would be away from you all year, for four whole years."

"What kind of a person would I be if I wanted someone who didn't want me back?"

"I *do* want you."

"Do you want me for *myself*?" Barrie forced herself to meet his eyes, to let him see how much it mattered. "Choosing is the whole point of a relationship—the fact that someone picked *you*, the whole you, the good and bad, the awful secret things as well as the good parts you want the world to see. That's the only way you can know a relationship is real."

"You're saying it's too fast?"

"No." Barrie wrapped her arms around her waist, holding herself together. "You can know some people in days more than you can know other people in years or decades. A night spent fighting for your life with someone teaches you more about them than a year of talking ever would. But if I let you give up your scholarship because of what I want from you, then how will I ever know whether you would have picked me on your own? I can't let you make decisions that will change the course of your life when you can't be certain that you . . ." She stopped herself and shook her head.

"You can't even think the word, can you?" There was a current of tension in Eight's voice, a live wire that threatened to give off sparks.

She was hurting him, pushing him away when she really wanted to hold him close. It made her shiver until her teeth chattered. She was coming apart, shedding pieces of herself. First her mother, then Mark, now Eight.

"People throw the word 'love' around like it doesn't mean anything," she said. "But they don't know what it's like not to have it. Before I came here, I'd only ever heard it from one person in all my life."

Eight raised his hand and brushed her cheek. "You're asking for guarantees, and there's no such thing when it comes to feelings."

"How can you sound so sure?"

"Faith is what gives any relationship a chance. That's the difference between us, Bear. I happen to know you're worth it."

She wanted to believe him, of course she did. But wasn't believing *in* him a bigger part of the equation? If she believed in him, then she was being selfish for wanting him to stay. Wanting what *she* wanted was his compulsion. She couldn't let him—make him—do it.

Stepping back again, she put distance between them until she had almost reached the arched doorway and the path to escape. It would be impossible to say no when his skin burned on hers.

"Give me logical reasons why the University of South Carolina is better for you than the University of Southern

California," she said, "and make me believe you aren't giving up your scholarship just for me."

The last traces of Eight's smile fell away. He lapsed into the expectant stillness that she had come to know. It was as if when he needed to concentrate, he channeled all of his kinetic energy into thinking. Seeing the hurt written across his features, an apology dropped onto Barrie's tongue, ready to let him off the hook. She bit it off and made herself stand there waiting.

Dammit, she wasn't going to cry.

But not crying got harder the longer he was silent. The longer he looked like he didn't have a clue what to say.

"You know what?" She managed to keep her voice steady. "Never mind. That's my answer. I hope you can undo whatever you've done with the scholarship, because I can't let you give it up. Not on my account."

Wrapping the last scraps of her dignity around herself, she walked out of the chapel before she could burst into tears. Before she could change her mind.

CHAPTER FOUR

It was only when Barrie had passed the stables that she let herself look back. Eight had emerged from the chapel doorway. Cloaked in shadows with his shoulders hunched and his hands in his pockets, he seemed hesitant, as if he wasn't sure whether to follow her or let her go. He looked miserable.

Barrie couldn't allow herself to care. The stables blurred as she strode past, and the caw of a bird swooping overhead was the sound of her own silent screech of rage. Not at Eight. Rage at the circumstances. At his gift. At herself. At the way the blows kept coming.

Rushing around the corner of the house, she stepped off the lawn and her heels bit into the gravel. A low breeze hit her knees, drawing her attention to the shadows milling in front of her. There was something agitated about the way the *yunwi* pushed at her, as if they wanted her to go back the way she'd come. Their silent whispers, sound without sound, hummed in her ears:

Caution. Caution. Beware, they seemed to say.

Heart already revving, Barrie brought her head up to scan the circular drive, but there was nothing unusual.

"What are you up to now?" she asked the *yunwi*. But they didn't answer.

A faint finding tug pulled her attention to a green object on the ground directly in front of her. It was about the size and shape of a poker chip, and it stood out starkly against the white gravel surface.

The disk couldn't have been there earlier. Barrie would have had to step right over it on the way to the chapel with Eight. It was possible she'd been too engrossed in Eight to see it, but she would have felt it, because clearly it was lost.

She bent to retrieve the token. "Who'd you steal this from?" she asked. "And I thought you weren't going to do that anymore?"

Only the word "beware" came back to her.

The wooden disk was silken against her fingers, in that way old wood grew soft, but the underside was sharply etched with a design. When she turned the token over, a raven peered back at her, its expression so vivid that it seemed intelligent and alive. The bird reminded her of something she needed to remember. But what?

The returning portion of her gift kicked in. Pressure, faint but insistent, pulled her to the flowerbed beside her. Barrie bit her lip, because that couldn't be correct.

For the first time in her life, the returning sense had failed her. There wasn't anyone in the flowerbed.

No one. Not at first. And then . . .

The same man she had seen on the wall was there, the same dark suit and aubergine shirt shimmering like an oil slick in the afternoon light, the same dreadlocks snaking over his shoulders. Like the disk, he hadn't been there before. He hadn't been there, and now he was, leaning back so casually against the house, one foot propped against the white-painted bricks, that he might have been standing there for hours.

"I'm glad I saw that for myself," he said in a voice that sounded foreign and deep, as if it had started with a growl inside his barrel chest. He flashed her a smile full of gold and white enamel. "I wouldn't have believed the gift could have survived so long."

Barrie's heart gave a nasty jump. "Who are you? How did you get in here?"

He peeled himself away from the house and moved toward her with an eerie, gliding gait that seemed too smooth for human motion. "No need to be afraid of Obadiah, *petite*. Not you."

The *r* in "afraid" was rolled in the back of his throat, but along with the French, there was a musical hint of the sea island Gullah that Barrie was learning to recognize. It should have been a pleasant combination, but there was a harshness to his voice, something too clipped and careful.

Fear as sharp as vinegar welled up in Barrie's throat. "You're trespassing. You need to leave."

"I will soon enough."

"My friend is around the corner. He'll be here in a second if I scream."

The man smiled still more broadly. "Will he, now?"

Opening her lips to yell, Barrie felt her tongue and cheeks go dry, as if her mouth had filled with sand. Sand that poured down her throat.

She couldn't scream and she couldn't breathe. Panic punched her like a fist.

Obadiah reached out and touched a fingertip to her forehead.

The sand was gone. The panic stilled.

Why had she been thinking of screaming? Everything was fine.

"There. You see, little one? No need to bother with any foolishness. It's only us here, you and me, and we're friends now, aren't we?" Obadiah spread his palms out to show her they were empty. "I'm not here to hurt you, and the Beaufort boy isn't needed. Let's leave it between us two."

"Who are you?" Barrie fought to push words through a cotton-wool padding of indifference she knew she shouldn't feel.

He winked at her. Winked, for Pete's sake. "I couldn't help overhearing your argument," he said.

The wink and the amusement in his voice helped clear some of Barrie's fuzziness away. "How? You couldn't have overheard."

"'How' is never the most important question. You see? Already I've given you a lesson to show we can help each other."

"Help each other do what?" Barrie forced her feet back a reluctant step; they felt weighted down as she waded through the false calm that enveloped her. But fear was the shoreline. Fear was safety. She should have been afraid. "*Why* are you here, and what do you want?" she asked.

His laugh was harsh, but genuine amusement lit his eyes and lightened his expression. "'Want' is an interesting concept, isn't it? The one your Beaufort boy doesn't know how to answer. Human want is an onion, layer upon useless layer of it. The more you *have*, the more you *want*, until before long you've lost touch with what little you really need. The boy wants his gift gone, and I can take it away for him. Easy as pie. All I need is a small favor in return."

Hearing him mention Eight again, Barrie finally got her

throat to work. She filled her lungs and screamed for him. Where was he, anyway? How was he not there?

Her voice came out a strangled screech, instead of the words that she intended.

A muffled rustle and a rush of air pulled her attention back to Obadiah, but he was gone. Just gone. There was an empty flowerbed where he had been, and emptiness all the way to the corner of the house. Emptiness to the front steps in the other direction.

That was impossible.

Wasn't it?

"Bear?" Eight rounded the corner at a sprint and stopped beside her. "What's wrong? What happened?"

A piece of Barrie clicked back into place when Eight touched her, the finding gift homing in on him in the Watson version of magnetic north. For the moment, their argument ceased to matter.

"You're as white as that old peacock over there." Eight grasped her hands and held them. "Tell me what's going on."

The albino peacock was, as usual, perched on the hood of Pru's ancient black Mercedes, more proof that no one had run away in that direction. Obadiah wasn't anywhere. Had he been there at all?

"Th-there was a man." She fought to get the words out. "Obadiah. He was here a second ago."

"Where? There's no one." Eight scanned the same empty flowerbed and vacant drive that Barrie had searched already.

She tried to summon up a picture to describe who she'd seen, but her memories were smoke. The more she tried to catch them, the harder it was to recall what she was trying to remember.

She had found something, hadn't she? A green disk of some kind?

Thinking of the disk brought everything flooding back. Uncurling her fingers, she held her palm out, ready to show Eight the reason she had turned and seen the man in the first place. Because he had used it to test her finding gift.

Except the disk, too, was gone.

She stared at her empty palm. The imprint of a raven's head was pressed into the heel of her hand where her fist had clenched around the token, and then that, too, disappeared. She opened her mouth to tell Eight to look, but the words slipped away. What had she meant to say?

"Why are you gaping like a fish, Bear? What happened? Who was the guy? What did he say?"

"I don't know. I don't remember." Barrie dug her fingernails into her palms, hoping the twinge of pain would clear the strange fog from her head. "Maybe there wasn't anyone." She shook her head. "No, I'm sure. There wasn't anyone."

Eight's lips paled as they tightened. "You're scaring me.

Focus. You said the guy's name was Obadiah. You didn't make that up. Where did you see him?"

The name brought a brief tug of memory. Barrie pointed at the flowerbed, but a moment later, she couldn't remember why. She followed close behind Eight as he stepped onto the loamy soil. She barely avoided a collision when he stooped to examine a footprint that had sunk deep into the ground a few inches from the house.

At the sight of the footprint, the image of Obadiah snapped back into focus. He had stood exactly there, in that spot, all of his weight resting on one leg while he'd propped the other foot against the wall.

Why hadn't Barrie been able to remember that? He had walked toward her, walked right past where she was standing now, and the *yunwi* hadn't liked it. . . .

"Bear? Are you okay?" Eight straightened, and she looked up.

Everything went fuzzy again, then blank. She nodded. "I'm fine."

"No, you're not. Someone was here, obviously, but I don't understand how there's only the one footprint. I really need you to think. What did he say? Did he hurt you? Did he threaten you? Is that why you don't want to tell me?"

"I'm trying to tell you." Frustration fluttered in Barrie's stomach. "But you never listen."

With a pained sigh, Eight wrapped his arm around her waist, radiating heat back into her body where she'd gone cold. "All right. Look, I'm sorry," he said. "Let's get you inside."

She stared up at him while the *yunwi* wove slowly around the bushes and the driveway as though they, too, were hunting for something or someone. "I'm not crazy," she said. "I don't make people up."

"I know." Eight cast another glance around the yard before he ushered her up the stairs and back into the house. "I really wish I thought you did."

CHAPTER FIVE

In the dim light of the foyer, with the front door safely closed behind them and the grim portraits of Watson ancestors watching Barrie from the walls, it seemed ridiculous to have been so shaken.

"Don't say anything to Pru, all right?" She tugged the rolled-up sleeve of Eight's shirt and coaxed him to a stop. "I don't want to worry her about nothing."

"This wasn't nothing. I need to go back out there to look around."

"If you're going, then I'm going with you."

"Whoever was out there disappeared when I showed up, which means you're the one he was after. You'd be safer in the house with Pru."

Barrie hated when he was logical.

Catching her hand, Eight hurried toward the kitchen with its 1970s avocado-colored appliances and lack of anything remotely modern. The warm scent of roasting beef and herbs hung to dry in the window mingled with the perfume of fresh-cut roses in the bowl laid on the crisp cloth draping the kitchen table. If love had a scent, this was it: food and flowers and herbs and warmth. Coupled with the sight of her aunt slicing tomatoes at the counter beside the sink, it instantly made Barrie feel more grounded.

"Now, where did you two get to?" Pru turned with a smile. "I went to see if you wanted some tea after Seven left, but you had disappeared." Her smiled faded as she took a closer look at Eight. "What's wrong? Did something happen?"

"Not at all," Barrie said.

Eight sent her a sideways glance, but continued undeterred: "There was someone trespassing out front. A man. He tried to speak to Barrie."

"One of those ghost-chasers from the river?" Pru's voice went tight, and the tendons in her neck stood out, as taut as strings beneath her skin. "I swear, I've had it up to here with them. One of them came sneaking up past the fountain this morning. I had to tell him to clear out."

"I'm not even sure I saw anyone," Barrie said, sending Eight a fearsome glare. "It could have been a shadow, for all I know. If someone was there, he's long gone by now."

Pru turned to Eight for confirmation. "I don't understand. Was there someone or wasn't there?"

"He left a footprint in the flowerbed," Eight said without looking at Barrie.

"Which could have been there last week, for all we know," she pointed out.

Eight tilted his chin at her. "It looked pretty fresh to me."

"Because you're suddenly an expert on footprints?"

"Oh, I am so tired of these people!" Pru wiped her hands and tore off her apron. "Why can't they let us have some peace and quiet? Seven should have forced the sheriff to arrest a few of them days ago, and then we wouldn't have trespassers roaming around thinking they can do whatever . . ." She stared at the floor, and then her head came back up.

Eight watched her with concern. "Want me to call Dad and get him to come back here?"

"No. I'll do it." Lips pursed, Pru threw the apron onto the counter before marching toward the square, black phone on the wall near the back door that led out to the porch and upper terrace. She picked the receiver up to dial.

Eight poured himself the last glass of sweet tea from the pitcher and dropped into a chair. "Want this?" he added as an afterthought, holding the glass out to Barrie as if nothing had changed between them. As if one little worry wiped away their entire argument.

"No, and for someone who knows what I want, you pay zero attention. Why are you making such a big deal out of this?"

"Why *aren't* you making a big deal out of it?" Folding his arms, Eight studied her, taking her apart and putting her back together. "You're the girl who used to hate having strangers wandering around here when the garden was open. Now some random guy shows up and you aren't even scared? That makes no sense."

He was right. Barrie should have been scared. She should have been panicked.

Why wasn't she?

Eight seemed to believe she had mentioned a man named Obadiah. Not only did she not remember saying the words, she didn't remember why she would have said them. As if the memories themselves had been plucked from her brain, leaving behind empty spaces.

Pru half-turned away to speak into the telephone, winding and unwinding the loopy black phone cord around her finger as she talked to Seven in a voice designed for Barrie and Eight not to overhear.

When she finally hung up, she came back to the table. "Seven's coming back over now. And, Eight? He told me to remind you that Wyatt Colesworth had some unsavory friends. Regardless of how it turns out with Ernesto, you shouldn't go out there by yourself." She caught Eight's eye and held it a moment as if there were more to the message than the words.

Barrie's stomach knotted and she gripped the edge of the table. "What do you mean, 'turns out with Ernesto'? I thought the police assumed that his body swept out to sea or the alligators got him? He's dead."

"Of course." Pru and Eight exchanged another look. "This close to the ocean, they might never recover the remains," Pru said. "But it never hurts to be cautious. The point is, he and Wyatt weren't smuggling drugs alone. There had to have been other people involved. Quintero Cartel people, not to mention locals—Colesworths, most likely—helping them on the boat. It'll be months before the police untangle all of that."

The smile she gave Barrie was meant for reassurance, but the best Barrie could manage was a stiff nod in return. Pru didn't push the point. Averting her face as if she were the one who needed time to collect herself, Barrie's aunt crossed to the butler's pantry and disappeared. Barrie dropped into the chair beside Eight's and kicked his ankle beneath the table.

"Ow." He gave her a wounded look. "What did you do that for?"

"You know exactly why, you jerk. You didn't tell me the police were still investigating Ernesto. Also, I told you not to upset Pru about Obadiah."

"She's not that upset. Anyway, what about *me*? Here you are, talking about a guy who disappears into thin air and then telling me he wasn't there and acting like *I'm* the crazy one for being worried." Eight's eyes were grave, and despite his teasing tone, he was clearly more shaken than he let on.

Lifting the empty pitcher of tea from the table, he sloshed the ice around in the bottom, and then poured the last few drops of liquid out into his glass as Pru came back into the kitchen. She was carrying a large bowl filled with raw sweet potatoes, which she proceeded to peel at the sink in a flurry of flying skins. A Band-Aid-size strip of potato skin hit the backsplash behind the sink and slid slowly down the tiles.

Barrie watched it, oddly mesmerized. Then she gave Eight's ankle another tap. "Right. Clearly Pru's not upset. At all." She pushed her chair back, then crossed over to the sink. "Want me to peel those potatoes for you, Aunt Pru?"

"That's all right. I've got it. I need something to do with my hands anyway." The furious peeling paused, and Pru plucked the skin off the counter and threw it into the sink.

"Speaking of doing something . . . I think I'll go check to make sure all the doors and windows are locked." Eight got up from the table.

Pru cast him a narrowed look. "With everything that's been going on, I've made sure every one is closed up tight, believe me."

Barrie thought of Pru alone in the house, alone without even Seven nearby to call, and people creeping around the property at night. It upset her all over again. How could the Beauforts have kept that secret from her?

"What about installing motion detectors along the water-line and dock?" she asked. "We had them in San Francisco. I'm not sure if animals or the *yunwi* would set them off—the *yunwi* might think that was fun—but it might be worth a try."

Pru tilted her head as she considered. "It's not a bad idea. You could explain to the *yunwi*. They seem to listen to you, so maybe they'd leave a system like that alone. On the other hand, we do have raccoons wandering in from the woods, not to mention gators and birds, so we could ask whoever installs the system to adjust the sensitivity. Darrel down at the hard-ware store ought to know who I could call for that."

As Pru returned to the phone, Barrie opened the cabinet and took down four Blue Willow plates. The sense of famil-iarity that came from seeing the same pattern she had used all her life at her mother's house was comforting.

For the first time, it occurred to her that maybe it had been more than nostalgia that had made her mother try to re-create Watson's Landing in the San Francisco house, from the style of the house itself and the furnishings down to these same Blue Willow plates.

The Watson gift had already been exerting its pull on Lula the night she had run away after finding the entrance to the Watson tunnel. After having taught his daughters that the gift was evil so that they wouldn't discover Luke and Twila's bodies, Emmett must have been scared and furious. And how had Lula felt when she ran away from that rage? She had rowed across the river with some romantic notion that Wade Colesworth was going to save her, envisioning a Romeo and Juliet romance. Instead, she had stumbled across Wyatt smuggling drugs, and then spent her life exiled from Pru and Watson's Landing while her gift did its best to pull her back.

The thought of Lula grasping for childhood things, longing to have a part of Watson's Landing with her, even after all those years in San Francisco, made Barrie feel like she was trying to breathe underwater. When it came to her mother, her emotions were still too raw. How was it possible to both love and hate someone more after they were dead?

She still needed to read her mother's letters, but . . . Not yet. Not if she wanted to be fair to Lula while she read them.

Returning to the table with the stack of plates, she found Eight leaning back watching her, his legs stretched out in front of him. The last bits of sun through the window cast his face in shadow, and he looked like an unfinished statue, perfect and maddeningly *im*perfect. Barrie's heart filled with ache and want.

"What?" He folded his arms across his chest as Seven's master-of-the-universe tread sounded on the porch outside.

"Nothing," Barrie said, turning away. "Nothing at all."

Eight glanced at his father through the glass-topped back

door, and stood up in one graceful move. "I know you're mad because I made a fuss." He stepped in close to whisper into Barrie's ear. "But the other night I thought I'd lost you before we even had a chance. That's not going to happen again. It's not about you not being strong enough. Watson's Landing is yours—I get that. And everything else? School? All that? We'll figure it out."

Figure it out. That was Eight's solution for everything. He was so sure about things that had no surety, as if he could simply will things to turn out all right, while Barrie had to fight for each scrap of conviction.

"Please tell your dad not to scare Pru about the man I saw," she whispered back. "There's no point making her more upset, and whoever it was has long since gone."

"Maybe, but it's worth looking around to figure out where he came from. And if we don't find him, I'll stay until the motion detectors are installed. It's not like there aren't extra bedrooms."

Barrie bit her lip, holding back the refusal that would only lead to another argument. The idea of having Eight think he needed to spend the night, of thinking that she and Pru weren't safe in the house, of not being able to keep *themselves* safe . . . No. That wasn't acceptable.

After they'd said good-bye, she waited on the porch until Eight and Seven had reached the bottom of the terrace steps. Then she marched through the kitchen and pushed open the swinging door that led out into the corridor.

"Where are you going?" Pru demanded, running after her and hitting the door with the heels of her hands to keep it open.

"To see the footprint. I need to remember what happened."

"What do you mean 'remember'?"

Barrie pulled up short a few feet from the foyer. It hadn't been something she'd considered consciously, but now that the words were out, she realized they were exactly right. She needed to see the footprint, see something of Obadiah's, to make the memories clearer.

"It's just a figure of speech," she said.

"Don't go out there by yourself. At least hold on a second, and I'll come with you." Pru disappeared back inside the kitchen before Barrie could answer, and when the door swung open again, she marched out like vengeance in a sundress, carrying a shotgun and stuffing brass-topped red gun shells into her pocket.

CHAPTER SIX

A search of the flowerbed didn't so much as raise a ping from Barrie's finding sense. Her memories of Obadiah returned when she saw the footprint, then swirled away into fog again each time she moved her eyes away. She kept reminding herself she was looking for an intruder, for a man named Obadiah, and at least that fact stayed with her.

What was wrong with her memory?

And how had Obadiah vanished? There hadn't been time for him to get to the other side of the house, and if he'd ducked around toward the chapel, Eight would have seen him. That left the oak avenue that led out to the gate.

With Pru beside her, she headed across the gravel driveway. They had almost reached the first of the thick tree trunks when Eight and Seven came back around the side of the house from the maze.

"Oh, Lord. Now we're in for a lecture," Pru said as Seven approached with long, angry strides that kicked up dust.

"I thought I told you to stay in the house," he said before he'd even reached them. "You trying to give me a heart attack, woman? Traipsing around here with a shotgun. Do you even know how to use that thing?"

The color in Pru's cheeks deepened, and her chin came up. "I hear it's pretty self-explanatory, actually." She adjusted the gun in a way that said she knew exactly how to use it. "And if you don't want me to put a load of buckshot up your backside to prove it, I'll thank you not to talk to me like that. Barrie thought that this would have been the most logical place for someone to duck out of sight in a hurry. It made sense to come and look. Did you find anything out back?"

"No sign." Seven's voice was grim, and he turned back to Barrie. "What was the guy wearing? Could he have waded ashore? Were his clothes wet? Can you give us any sort of description?"

Barrie stared blankly, digging down into her brain, but the harder she tried to remember, the more her thoughts turned to mist.

What in the hell was wrong with her?

"It's okay. Don't stress about it." Eight touched her shoulder, and that small contact made her calmer.

Seven glanced from her to Eight and back. A gust of evening wind blew his hair into his face, and he pushed it aside without taking his eyes off her. Barrie fought to keep herself from squirming—being read by two Beauforts at once was exponentially worse than when Eight was the only one doing it.

"All right." With a disconcertingly easy smile, Seven turned and spoke to Pru. "Seeing as how you have the gun, why don't you and Eight go around toward the chapel and check if there's any sign of anyone down that way. Barrie and I can walk up toward the gate."

Pru arched her brows at Barrie, who gave a shrug and started plodding toward the plantation's main entrance with a wary glance at every tree and bush along the way.

Twilight was turning the sky a bruised lavender as the last rays of the sun spilled over the river behind the house. Shadows darted across the lawn and chased one another up the lane, and the stillness gave a sense of time passing at a pace different from that of the world beyond Watson Island. Touching one of the ancient trunks that stood at the edge of the grass, Barrie absorbed the hum of energy beneath her fingers and closed her eyes.

She opened them again as Seven stopped beside her. "I'm not

going to apologize for not cowering inside," she said. "Pru and I are the ones who have to live here. I hate that I feel like I am constantly having to fight everyone to have my opinion matter."

"Of course it matters—but you're not invincible. Or infallible." He sighed and steepled his fingers in front of his lips as though searching for words, which was something that Barrie imagined happened very rarely. "I understand what a struggle all this is for you. You're still grieving and settling in. You and Eight have spent virtually all your time together since you got here, and I can see why you wouldn't want to say good-bye. But he just told me about turning down the scholarship. You have to make him change his mind."

"Why?" Barrie braced herself against the oak tree and stared at him. "You didn't want him to leave in the first place—that's why he had to get the scholarship."

"My objections were never about the scholarship—or even about playing baseball." Seven took two steps toward the gate and stopped with his back to her. He ran a hand across the back of his neck. "All I wanted was for my son to choose to stay here and practice law. To decide he *wanted* to do that, before he found out he had no other options. I thought if he decided for himself, he wouldn't feel as trapped. After almost losing him . . . I realize that was a mistake. He deserves the chance to experience life away from the island while he can."

Barrie stared hard at his back, but he refused to turn and

look at her. "While he *can*? Are you trying to say that Eight's bound to Beaufort Hall the same way I'm bound to Watson's Landing?"

"Not exactly. Not until after I'm gone and he inherits."

The words defied comprehension. Yet the signs had all been there when she and Seven and Eight had been together in San Francisco: the way Seven rubbed his head, his irritability, his eagerness to get back. Barrie had assumed that was all due to his missing Pru . . . How had she missed making the right connection?

Probably because, even though Eight knew about the headaches that came on every time Barrie left Watson's Landing, he had never mentioned that his father had them.

"Eight doesn't know about your migraines, does he?" she asked. "Or about the binding?" Her voice wobbled, and she stopped and took a breath before she continued. "He didn't understand why I was getting headaches any more than I did when I first got here. Which means you've never told him—"

"Is that so wrong?" Seven turned and frowned down at the fine, white shell dust that coated the toes of his burgundy wing tips. "Try to understand. All I want is for him to have a semblance of a normal life. None of the heirs ever have real choices—our lives are mapped out for us by decisions that were made three hundred years ago. I've resented that since I first found out that was what was waiting for me. I wanted

Eight to have at least the illusion of having chosen. I swore I would find a way to make it different for him."

"That's still you choosing *for* him. He doesn't want to be a lawyer. Don't you know him at all?" Remembering the bleak expression on Eight's face when he had told her about his dyslexia, she wished for the first time in her life that Mark had taught her something more useful than how to pick out a great pair of shoes. A solid right hook, for instance, would have been great for waking Seven up.

She fought to keep her voice steady. "Eight's learning disability makes him self-conscious. Instead of telling him you're proud of him for who he is, though, and saying you'll support him no matter what he wants, you've tried to force him into a mold he was never going to fit. He thinks that means you're disappointed in him for not being more like you."

That was a worse betrayal than anything Lula had ever done. Lula might not even have known about the binding. Since Emmett had wanted the gift buried and forgotten, Barrie had to assume he had never explained it to Lula any more than he had to Pru. But also, Lula had been Lula. She'd never made any pretense of being up for a mother-of-the-year award.

"You have to tell Eight. Warn him." Pushing away from the tree, she walked to where Seven stood. "You should have warned *me* when I first came."

"Pru wasn't sure you even had the gift, and she didn't want us saying anything in case you didn't. At least until you'd settled in." Seven placed both hands on Barrie's shoulders. "Honestly, I wasn't sure how to tell you until I knew you better. But I do know Eight. His happiness obviously means a lot to you. Think about it. Wouldn't you keep a secret to keep him happy?"

Barrie shook her head. "Not this secret. It isn't mine to keep. Or yours. And he's going to do what he wants about going out to California, regardless of what I tell him."

"Is he?" Seven's face was pinched with regret. Barrie tried to picture what she would have done in his shoes, but she couldn't say. Seven's good intentions didn't change the fact that hiding something this important from Eight was wrong. All that did was set him up for an even bigger trauma later.

Seven glanced toward the corner of the house to see if Eight and Pru were returning yet, but they weren't. Digging into his pockets, he jiggled his keys or loose change—something that sounded like raw nerves jangling.

"I love Eight," he said simply. "Thanks to the Beaufort gift, that fact alone makes it painful for me to refuse him anything. On the other hand, I'm also his father, which means I have responsibilities beyond what the gift urges me to do. Eight thinks he knows what the compulsion to give people what they want feels like. He has no idea how much worse that will become, and I won't tell him and spoil his happiness. But that's why you have to let him go. You have to *want* him not to stay, and you can't tell him about the binding."

"How do I make myself want something that I don't really want? I can't," Barrie said.

"You will if you care about him at all." Seven's eyes softened into sympathy, but he averted his face almost immediately as if he realized how much she didn't want his pity. Of course he realized. He *knew*.

"With all that's happened since you arrived," Seven continued, "I've finally come to see that, to Eight, baseball is much more than a sport. It's who he is. Don't you see? These things that we Beauforts and Watsons refer to as 'gifts' are as much curses as anything the Colesworths have to bear. The 'gifts' keep us bound here so tight, we don't even bother dreaming. You've already given up on wanting to go to art school. But you at least had the chance to consider what you wanted. Beaufort heirs have always stayed here and practiced law, so that was what I was going to do. I never even let myself think about other options when I was growing up. Dreams shape the kind of human beings we become. Not having a dream gave me a smaller future and made me a smaller person. It would be selfish for me not to want more than that for my son."

Until that moment, Seven had always been a little larger than life to Barrie. He'd always seemed so self-possessed and intimidating that she'd never imagined that he could look so . . . undone.

"Eight will still have to abandon whatever life he has built for himself once I'm gone," Seven said, "but at least he will come back to Beaufort Hall knowing that he has done his best to live the kind of life he wanted. That's why you have to let him go."

"How am I supposed to do that?" Barrie asked in a strangled voice.

"By realizing there's no scenario in which you two can have a future together. You are bound to Watson's Landing, and Eight will be bound to Beaufort Hall. The distance across the river might not seem very far, but it would always be there between you. One or the other of you would always be in pain. That would only get worse. The bindings will force you back to your responsibilities, and people in both families have gone crazy from the pain of that. They've committed suicide to escape it. If you let Eight give up his scholarship when you have no hope of a future together, he'll have given up his dreams for nothing."

He finished speaking, and Barrie heard the staccato rush of her own heartbeat in her ears. An hour ago, she wouldn't have let herself think about marrying Eight. The idea that she couldn't, though, made her realize how much heartache she was in for.

CHAPTER SEVEN

While she was alone upstairs, the quiet of the house wrapped around Barrie like a comfortable shirt. Comfortable, not comforting. She had too much pent-up frustration to let herself be consoled.

Emerging from the shower in a billow of steam, she felt weighed down by gifts and obligations, by fear and loss and fury. She needed to try to speak with the Fire Carrier again. What Seven had told her made it even more important than before that she find a way to understand what was expected of her and what the binding meant.

Wrapped in a towel, she stopped at the balcony door on her way to get her clothes. It was almost midnight, but several of the boats were still there, bobbing in the moonlight that reflected across the water. The scene was too similar to her memory: a boat and the Fire Carrier approaching, flames shooting across the water, the boat exploding, the smell of fuel burning, Wyatt and Ernesto screaming.

Logically, Barrie knew there had been other boats before and the Fire Carrier hadn't done anything to them. Logically, she knew he had saved her. But logic didn't trump the memories.

She'd had days to come to terms with how she'd seen him that night, not as the shadowed spirit of an ancient Cherokee witch but as something more. As someone real. And all along, he'd had something he wanted to tell her that he didn't know how to communicate.

Since that night, she'd been thinking about trying to speak to him again, but thanks to the boats and Eight, who was asleep in the room beside hers, the Fire Carrier would have to wait. After dressing hurriedly, she slipped outside to the balcony. Treading lightly to avoid the creak and groan of weathered wood, she crossed to the railing.

The darkness whispered with night birds calling and insects droning, and the air settled around her, heavy with the sweetness of honeysuckle and magnolia and damp, cloying heat. All these things had been here when she'd first arrived at Watson's Landing. Since the night the spirit in the fountain had bound her, though, sight and smell and hearing, all her senses, were more intense, as if her skin had melted away and left her raw and beating in time with the landscape.

She didn't need the chime of the grandfather clock downstairs to warn her.

Orange tongues of flame appeared in the woods, the flickering glow marking the Fire Carrier's progress to the river. He emerged in the marsh with the sphere of fire in his outstretched hands. Bending low, he unraveled it a thread at a time until the entire surface of the water had ignited and the blaze ran upriver the length of the island, and down to the creek on the far side of the Watson woods.

Barrie held her breath, waiting for the boat to catch, to explode and send up a spray of smoke, fumes, and sharp fiberglass shards. She let the memories hit her, and they came in waves and waves.

Nothing exploded. The boats on the river never moved, and whoever was in them showed no sign of being aware that anything magical was happening around them.

The Fire Carrier turned to face Barrie. He gave her a silent nod, and she raised her hand and waved.

"What does he look like?" Speaking behind Barrie, Eight made her jump.

He stood in the doorway, shirtless with his golden skin shining with moon and flame. His hair fell across his forehead, making Barrie want to reach over and brush it away. Brush away all her doubts and the things she wished she didn't know.

She concentrated very hard on *not wanting to talk about any of that*.

"He's our age," she said. "Your age, maybe. Wearing a red-and-black mask of war paint and a dark feathered cape. Not what I'd expect a witch to look like."

"Then maybe he's a warrior. Or a war priest, or one in training." Eight's lips kicked into a lopsided smile. "Yes, I've been trying to read up. The Internet's a wonderful thing."

"What does your dad say about him?"

"Nothing much except that he's yours. You're supposed to protect the island and keep it safe, which is why you see him, and we're supposed to know what people want so that we can guess their intentions and keep our side of the bargain."

"What kind of bargain?"

Eight gave a tight and impatient shrug. "Dad claims that's all he knows."

"Do you believe him?"

Eight turned to look at her more fully. "What do you mean?"

Barrie took a moment to choose her words, because family relationships were like rubber bands, liable to snap back against anyone who tried to stretch them. And despite the questionable choices he had made, Seven was still Eight's father.

"The gift has never been interrupted in your family," she

said. "So why wouldn't all the knowledge and the reasons—the whole instruction manual for the bargains the Fire Carrier made—have been passed down to Seven? Since Pru doesn't know anything, your father is our best chance for finding out the truth."

"Don't you think I've tried to get him to tell me? He doesn't want me to know."

"You're not a kid. Maybe it's time you stopped asking, and demanded that he give you answers."

Eight had gone still again, that uncanny stillness he wore like a mantle. The silence filled with the too-loud sounds of frogs and insects and the drum of Barrie's heart. She waited for him to speak, to yell at her, to tell her to mind her own business.

Instead, he said, "What is it that you are trying so hard to hide? I can't get a read at all—except that there's something you don't want to tell me."

He crossed the balcony and leaned down beside her. With his forearms braced on the railing and his shoulder brushing hers, they were millimeters and miles apart. When she looked up, his eyes shone green and deep.

Barrie couldn't tell him. She had already said too much. On the other hand, the fact that he couldn't read her gave her a little hope. Evidently, she couldn't lie to him about what she wanted, but she could mask her wants, or at least layer them with other things she wanted.

She turned back toward the river.

"There are these things called boundaries," she said. "From now on, if I don't want to tell you something, maybe you could try respecting that. You clearly accept it with your dad. And maybe I don't even know what I want. People frequently don't."

"I can't help knowing, any more than you can help feeling something lost. What you want is just *there*, like seeing colors when some people are color-blind."

"You told me once that you don't like your dad's sense of ethics. That he manipulates people—"

"I'm not manipulating you—"

"That's not what I'm trying to say." Barrie picked at a shard of cracking paint on the balcony railing and watched the boats drifting on the water. "You told me once that you didn't want to live the way your father does, using the gift to bend the rules and maneuver people into doing what you want. I know he doesn't do anything illegal. But what if he did something bad in another way, something you didn't like, except he did it for good reason?" She made herself watch his reaction. "Could you forgive him?"

"What's this really about?" Tugging the chain of her necklace, he pulled the three Tiffany keys from beneath the baby-doll tee Barrie had thrown on with her sleep shorts. He used the chain to draw her closer. Then he slid his arms around her waist. "What did my father say to you while you walked out to the gate together?"

"What if it was *me* who'd done something you didn't like?" she said a little desperately. "Would you forgive me?"

"Are we still being hypothetical?" Eight tipped his chin toward him and pushed her hair behind her ear, smiling to soften the words. "I suspect I could forgive you almost anything, but you were right earlier about being honest with each other. I should have told you about what was going on here when I found out. That wasn't fair. I'll try to be more open with you, and I hope that whatever you've got going on in your head—whatever happened between you and my dad—you'll trust me enough to tell me."

Down on the river, the Fire Carrier had recalled the flames from the surface of the water, reeling them in and spooling them back into a fiery ball. He didn't glance up toward the balcony again. Barrie held her breath, and felt like her lungs were burning, too. As the Fire Carrier turned to go back into the Watson woods, she used the excuse to get away from Eight. Moving to the end of the balcony, she watched while the wavering orange glow of spirit fire lit the trunks of cypress and oaks that soared toward the star-pricked sky.

Eight came up beside her and pulled her down to sit against his lap. With his chin resting on her hair, he waited quietly while she watched the light moving deeper into the woods. Long after it had vanished and the boats on the river were all that remained to disturb them, she still didn't want to move, or speak, or do anything to break the beauty of sitting there with Eight. Their breath came in sync, and even their hearts beat together, as if Eight could sense how hers sped up whenever they touched like this.

She knew if she brought up Seven again, it would ruin things. Maybe it was wrong not to tell Eight, but maybe she had already said enough to make Eight go back to get answers from his father. It couldn't hurt to wait another day and see whether that worked before she told him about the binding.

Eventually, they both returned to their rooms.

In the small hours of the night, Barrie woke to find flashlights moving on the shore near the charred remains of the Colesworth dock. But Cassie's treasure was the last thing that Barrie wanted to worry about. She rolled over and went back to sleep.

CHAPTER EIGHT

All the boats were gone the next morning when Barrie and Eight set off to meet Seven for Cassie's hearing. They climbed into the *Away*, Eight's pretty sailboat, with her sleek lines and the name that was a promise of his intent to get out of Watson's Landing. Eight started the motor for the trip to Watson's Point. A short distance below the creek, a bald eagle plummeted from the sky to snare a fish in his talons, then flew off in a rush of wings and bubbling water. Barrie imagined she knew how the fish felt. In addition to the usual migraine, she had the same sense of impending doom at the thought of seeing her cousin.

"Don't worry about the hearing," Eight said after ten minutes of making small talk and getting one-syllable answers. "Dad says the judge will ask us a few questions about how

Cassie left us locked inside the tunnel and how we feel about her going to jail versus getting community service. We'll tell him jail is good, and then we're done."

Barrie would have preferred not to be going at all. Pru had remained at Watson's Landing to have the motion detectors installed, and Barrie would much rather have stayed to help.

After tearing off the faded orange life vest, she stowed it into the storage compartment beneath the seat. Eight bumped the *Away* gently against the floating walkway in the marina. He jumped out to tie off the line, and the boat rocked wildly. Barrie grasped the mast, but her fear of the water wasn't as overwhelming anymore. The small flash ebbed as quickly as it had come, and her brief gasp was drowned in the cry of a pair of gulls squabbling over a french fry a few feet away.

"I'm sorry." Eight caught her hand and helped her out. His arm slipped around her waist, circling her in warmth that felt good in spite of the scalding temperature of the mid-June morning. They passed a pair of old men with faded eyes and faded T-shirts stretched tightly over rounded bellies. Each man stood with one foot braced on the gangplank of a rust-dribbled cabin cruiser that stank of fish.

"Morning, Eight. Barrie." One smiled while the other nodded.

"Morning," Eight said, which Barrie echoed, even though she'd never seen the men before. Their curiosity followed her as she passed, but it seemed no more avid or hostile than it had felt when she'd first arrived in town. Barrie really missed the cloaking fog and anonymity of San Francisco.

"What Emmett did has nothing to do with you," Eight said, reading her with his uncanny accuracy. "You aren't him."

"He's my grandfather as much as Cassie is Wyatt's daughter—and actually, the Colesworths are my family, too. You should be afraid of my genes." Barrie scowled down at the weathered boards of the floating dock peppered with seagull guano and occasional bleached fish bones as fine as needles. "Maybe you *should* go to California."

"Are we really doing this again?" His face crinkled adorably into a question mark.

They climbed the stairs to Seven's office, and the lavender-haired receptionist in an iron-gray suit rose from behind the MS. CONLEY sign on her desk to stop Eight from pushing through into the inner office. The way she put herself between him and the door, Barrie got the impression she would have defended it to her dying breath.

"He's on the phone," she said.

Eight's expression darkened faster than Barrie had ever seen it. "We're supposed to be in Charleston at eleven."

"Half an hour." Ms. Conley's lips pursed in disapproval as Eight let out a groan. "He promised."

"It's always half an hour," Eight said, "and he always

promises." Turning to Barrie, he added, "We may as well sit down. If we're both really good, maybe we can get a cookie while we wait. They're amazing cookies."

He winked at Ms. Conley, who hurried to her desk. "I didn't think to bake any—it's been so long since you or Kate had to wait after school. But I think I have a granola bar in here somewhere."

Barrie had a sudden image of a little-boy Eight, with a cowlick and missing teeth, kicking his heels against the quiet chairs and white sofa with its don't-touch-me vibe that made her want to break out her most violently brilliant pens and crayons.

"Let's go wait at that bakery across the street," she said, thinking of Mark's chocolate-and-coffee-can-fix-anything-broken philosophy. "I don't know about you, but I'm dying for chocolate." Grabbing Eight's wrist, she spun him away and shoved him out the door and across the street before he had a chance to argue.

She watched his reflection in the glass of the SeaCow Bakery as they approached, observing the gradual release of tension as he got farther from his father's office and the ghosts of his childhood faded. The realization that there was a shadowy figure of a man reflected between them in the window, as if he were walking very close behind them, came so gradually that Barrie couldn't say when he had appeared or whether he had been there all along.

She recognized him. The glossy dreadlocks snaking below the dark shoulders of his suit, the dark eyes as avid as a bird's, his head slightly tilted as he watched her curiously.

Obadiah.

The name swam out of the mist in Barrie's mind and dropped onto her tongue, but before she could turn or even say it, he was gone.

Wait. Who was gone?

She tripped on the sidewalk as she whipped around to look for something out of place, and she ground to a halt as Eight steadied her.

"You all right?" he asked, a hand gripping the top of each of her arms.

Blinking at him owlishly, she couldn't find the words to explain, so she simply nodded and shoved open the bakery door still feeling disoriented.

Taking a deep breath of chocolate, coffee, and comfort, she paused at the edge of the room, feeling an odd sensation of having escaped from something she couldn't remember. An immediate rustle of fabric brought a flush to her cheeks. Heads turned and whispers fell into an unnatural hush punctuated by the espresso machine's hiss and gurgle. Everyone quickly looked away, as if embarrassed to be caught staring, except for a big man in a sand-colored T-shirt pulled tight across massive shoulders.

He sat alone, which surprised Barrie, because he looked like the sort of guy who usually had a girl on his arm, the kind who spent half the time in the gym and the other half watching himself in mirrors and store windows. He stared at her until she squirmed and threaded her fingers through Eight's and towed him toward the counter.

The coffee menu was stenciled on an old-fashioned chalkboard overhead, and the huge selection of desserts was labeled on folded rainbow-colored index cards in front of each item. Eight leaned a hand on the counter and turned to Barrie. "What sounds good to you? Pretty much everything they bake here will make your toes curl."

They both ordered, and by the time the server had plated their pastries and left to prepare their coffees, the smell and thought of chocolate made it impossible for Barrie to resist breaking off a small piece of the Mississippi Mud Brownie that looked big enough to serve six people. It turned decadently gooey in her mouth.

"Damn, that's good," she said.

The server handed the drinks to Eight and smiled at him. "Hey, I heard you might be going to school in Charleston. You going to play ball there?"

Barrie blinked at how fast the news had traveled, but Eight smiled affably enough. "Haven't decided between Charleston and Columbia yet. I'm meeting with one of the coaches tonight." He slapped down a twenty, took their tray, and waited while the server gave him change.

At a booth halfway down a wall hung with hundreds of photographs, Mary stood and waved. After meeting them partway, she wrapped Barrie in a hug, then stepped back and laid both palms briefly on Barrie's cheeks.

"You're a sight for sore eyes, and that's the truth."

Dressed in a bright turquoise shirt and white slacks, Mary looked both worried and thinner, and a wave of impotence over the closing of the tearoom hit Barrie all over again.

"It's good to see you, too. You doing okay?" she asked.

"I'm mad as hell, but there isn't anythin' I can do about it. I can't figure people out. Imagine huntin' for ghosts, when what folks ought to be doin' is runnin' away just as fast as they can. Let's hope they all give up before much longer. Now, look at you!" She turned back to Eight. "What'd you feed the girl out there in California? Bean sprouts and lettuce?"

"She ordered a brownie and a pound of truffles to take home to Pru. She'll be all right," Eight said.

Glancing behind her to the table she had left, Mary waved to the pretty girl in a pink-and-brown SeaCow server's apron who was there nursing a cup of coffee. "You haven't met my granddaughter, have you? Come on over here, Daphne."

Daphne grinned when she arrived, revealing a deep dimple in her left cheek and a front tooth that was badly chipped. "I'm glad I get to meet you finally. I wasn't sure when I would, with the tearoom closed and all this mess."

Eight waited until they'd finished the introductions, then nodded at Daphne's uniform. "I thought you only worked on weekends," he said.

"Just picking up some extra hours."

Mary squeezed Daphne's shoulder. "Girl won a scholarship, and now she's tryin' to cover the rest on top of it. Always feels like she's got to do all the heavy liftin' by herself."

"I wonder who I get that from?" Daphne smiled at Barrie and Eight, and both she and Mary excused themselves.

Barrie turned to follow Eight to the table. Across the aisle and two booths down, she found the same guy still staring at her over the rim of his cup. Reddening, she looked away.

"What's Mary doing now that the tearoom is closed?" she asked as she slid in across from Eight. "Can she get another job? Pru and I could give her money."

"She wouldn't take money. As for work, there's not a lot of that in a town this size, and the summer jobs are all taken. With three grandkids to care for, she can't leave the island, so it's a problem."

"Three grandkids?" Ashamed she hadn't known already, Barrie fiddled with her watch. "Where's their mother?"

"A drug house somewhere, probably." Eight shrugged, but his voice vibrated in a way that said he cared more than the gesture suggested. "She'll show up in a few years with a new baby for Mary to raise, promising to go straight. Then she'll take off again a month after that. That's how she usually does it."

More shame settled into Barrie's stomach. "Then we'll open the tearoom back up. To hell with the ghost hunters."

"And the second some idiot wanders into the woods and steps on a copperhead, you're going to have a lawsuit. It's too dangerous. Pru and Dad were right. People can't go traipsing around unsupervised when you don't know what they're after. Look at that Obadiah guy."

"I'm starting to hate being a Watson."

Eight's jaw softened, and his lips tipped upward. Not quite a smile, but close. "It's not all bad. I know you're worried about what Emmett did to Luke and Twila reflecting on you, but the Watsons have done a lot of good on this island over the years. That still means something. And you—you're a hero as far as the people in this town are concerned. There have been rumors about Wyatt smuggling drugs, but no one suspected one of the big cartels could be involved. That's over because of you. So don't worry. No one is thinking less of you. Give people a chance and they'll meet you halfway."

"Careful. You might fool someone into thinking you *like* this place."

Eight reached across the table to take her hands. "I never said there weren't things here to like."

Kitty-corner from them, the big, dark-haired man levered himself out of the booth. His eyes were still locked on Barrie beneath lowered brows, and he made a point of bumping their table in passing. She tried smiling at him, meeting him halfway, as Eight had said.

"Bitch," he said loudly enough for the whole room to hear.

Barrie's face flamed, and her eyes watered. For an instant that felt too long, the walls tunneled in, and her heart pounded too fast.

Eight jumped out of his chair, but she tightened her grip on his hands and refused to let go. "Sit back down," she hissed. "We don't want any more drama. Especially not here."

His cheeks blotched with rage, Eight watched the man's retreating back. Finally, he dropped into his seat and sat back so that Barrie had to release her hold. Their only contact was his legs against hers beneath the table, and she was grateful to have that much.

Eight leaned forward with his forearms on the table. "Ignore that guy. Don't even worry about him. Ryder Colesworth is just the idiot who proves the rule. He used to work with Wyatt—they're cousins. But he's so crazy that even Wyatt wouldn't have anything to do with him anymore. Nobody's going to listen to anything Ryder says."

"You know, I need an app on my phone to tell the Colesworths apart from everyone else. Or maybe they could wear black hats so I'd be warned when I saw them coming. That would be helpful."

Eight grinned as she'd intended, but he sobered quickly. After plucking the last bite of his maple bacon cupcake from the wrapper, he popped it into his mouth as he stood up. "Watson Island is no different from anyplace else," he said. "There's no such thing as a pure white hat or a pure black one. Everyone comes in different shades of gray. Give it all a little time. With Cassie in jail and Wyatt dead, maybe the feud will finally die down."

Snatching the bag of truffles from the table, he headed toward the door. Barrie smiled at everyone, pretending not to notice the sympathetic and embarrassed glances on the faces she passed. Having lost her appetite, she tried to hand the rest of her brownie over to Eight as they exited the building, but he shook his head.

"Don't make me throw out chocolate," she said. "That's sacrilege."

"I'm full. And anyway, I like my desserts more layered and subtle. I think we've discussed this before. Someday, I'll give you a rundown on my philosophy about cakes, women, and complexity."

Despite her anxiety, Barrie's blood gave a zing of pleasure at the look in his eyes, and she wanted to hug him for it. "Apparently, you like cookies, too."

Eight looked both ways then crossed the street back toward Seven's office. "Mostly I liked that Ms. Conley took the time to make them for us."

"So I guess you and Kate spent a lot of time waiting for your dad," Barrie said.

Eight's expression darkened. "Pretty much every day after Mom died." Instead of climbing the full length of the outside staircase that led to Seven's office, he sat down on the fifth step up. "Dad used to promise he would drop us at home any minute, and then we'd wait, and wait, and wait. Looking back, I don't think he wanted to go home to the memories."

Thinking of families, looking across at the bakery, and smelling the chocolate brought an idea bubbling to the surface of Barrie's mind. She braced her elbows on her knees and turned her head to look at Eight.

"Remember I told you how Mark and I used to re-create restaurant recipes?" she asked. "There was a place we went once that had a lottery where they picked random people to come when the restaurant was closed. They pushed all the tables together, and by the end of the meal, we felt like we'd been part of a family. At least, I imagine that's what a big family feels like. It was the first time I had seen Mark hold a crowd. Sort of like Cassie. You know how she can make everyone in the room, in the building, disappear until she's the only one you see? Like she blinds you to everyone else."

"Except that Mark used his superpower for good," Eight said. "I'm assuming."

"Mark *was* good."

Was. The ugliest word in the English language.

Barrie could see the night in the restaurant as clearly as if she had painted it into her memory. A violinist and a cellist playing Bach, the click of cutlery, and the low moans of foodie pleasure, and then the wrong note—the waiter dropping a plate, spilling sticky cream into Mark's lap and shattering the dish. Into the mortified frenzy of cleanup, the chef had brought out homemade hazelnut truffles and coffee, and Mark had laughed and said, *Dessert and laughter are better than glue. There's not much broken that they can't fix.*

"I think I know how we can have the restaurant," she said, "without having people going where we don't want them to go."

CHAPTER NINE

The pretrial intervention hearing wasn't in a vast room full of people as Barrie had feared. No doubt as a courtesy to Seven— or more likely thanks to his ability to maneuver around what people wanted—it took place in the judge's chambers. Apart from Barrie, Eight, Seven, and the judge, who looked a little bit like God-as-played-by-Morgan-Freeman, there was the prosecutor, the court reporter, the defense attorney, and Cassie herself. But Barrie's cousin seemed to fill the room. With her combination of near-black hair and deep blue eyes, Cassie was always the focal point, but today it was more than that. Slouched in her chair, she gave off waves of resentment, glaring at Barrie until her attorney poked her in the ribs. Even then, Cassie didn't bother sitting up.

Judge Abrams studied everyone from behind his desk. "All

right, now. Y'all understand why we're here? This isn't a trial. Not yet. Ms. Willems"—he nodded at Cassie's attorney—"has asked the prosecutor to have the case kicked over for pretrial intervention, and Mr. Allgood"—he nodded to the prosecutor—"feels disinclined to agree, seeing as he wants the defendant tried for kidnapping, which wouldn't be an eligible offense. The case has been sent up here to me after a bit of arguing back and forth." He slid his glasses down his dark, freckled nose and pinned Cassie's attorney with a stare that made the woman squirm.

"You two"—he waved a hand first at Barrie and then at Eight—"are here because making amends to the victims is a key part of the PTI process. You being the kidnappees, as it were, I want to hear what you have to say."

Cassie's attorney half-rose from her seat, her deep auburn hair bouncing in a low ponytail. "Your Honor, if you'll look at the facts of the case, you'll see that the charge of kidnapping isn't warranted. All my client did was slam a door closed. At worst, that's a matter of—"

"Is your client admitting to unlawful confinement, Ms. Willems?" The judge leaned forward. "Because if I remember the law, and I believe I do, that's pretty much the definition of kidnapping here in South Carolina."

"Your Honor!" The attorney was young and attractive, although unlike Cassie, she didn't seem to do anything to try to use that in her favor.

Not that, for the moment, Cassie was using either her looks or the charm she could so easily turn on and off. The realization made Barrie sit up in the round-armed chair and study her cousin. The Cassie she knew would have been leaning forward, watching the judge with wide blue eyes, looking innocent and beautiful and lost. This Cassie, on the other hand, showed almost no interest in the judge. She sat there, pale and hollow-eyed, still slouched and rubbing her temples, squinting against the light that shone through the open blinds in the window behind the judge.

Barrie knew that body language. She'd lived with her mother's migraines, and she suffered them herself. She'd managed to ignore Seven's symptoms in San Francisco, but that had been before she'd known he was bound to Beaufort Hall the way she was bound to Watson's Landing. Now she noticed how often he squinted and rubbed his temples when he thought no one was watching.

The Fire Carrier had given magic to all three families. The oldest direct descendant in both the Beaufort and Watson families was bound to the land in addition to having a stronger version of the gift than anyone else.

Why *wouldn't* Cassie be bound to Colesworth Place? It made perfect sense. Wyatt dying in the explosion had left Cassie the heir to the Colesworth curse. Gift, curse—did it matter?

Between the angle and the light shining through the

blinds, Seven's face was hard to read as he sat beside Barrie. She scooted toward him in her seat and tapped him on the leg.

"Last night in the lane, you said none of us has a choice," she whispered. "Did you mean only Watsons and Beauforts, or does that include Cassie, too?"

"Now is neither the time nor the place for this conversation." Seven kept his profile to her, his eyes locked on the judge.

"Is Cassie having migraines because she's in jail?" Barrie insisted.

"She's not in jail yet. She's in juvenile detention. Now stop. Pay attention." Seven's eyes had gone from light green to glacial. He looked hard, the kind of hard that had to come from a lifetime of being pushed, in spite of yourself, to give people all the petty, stupid, senseless things that humans always wanted.

The set to his jaw, a defensive mulishness, clued Barrie in. "You're deliberately avoiding the question," she said, "which means you either know or you suspect and you don't want to know." She paused and gathered her thoughts. "The judge said something about the prosecutor *wanting* to try Cassie for kidnapping. Does that mean what I think it means? Did you manipulate him? Use your gift to read what he wants and use that to your advantage?"

Seven's nose flared and his brows snapped together. "You and Eight could both have died in that tunnel."

Barrie pulled back. Away from him.

Stated so baldly, the words conjured the clang of the door and the stench of death that had seeped into the air after all those years that Luke and his fiancée had lain forgotten in the tunnel. Barrie fought to block the memories of the long, awful night and stuff them back into the locked compartment in her mind, where they belonged.

She hoped Cassie had felt half as terrified in jail as she and Eight had felt in the tunnel, when they'd thought they would die down there and no one would ever find their bodies. Still, Barrie remembered how much the migraines hurt. Remembered what they had done to Lula. Seven had said they'd made people commit suicide to get them to stop.

"Excuse me." The judge turned in their direction. "Are we disturbing y'all? Because I wouldn't want this proceeding to be an inconvenience to you, Mr. Beaufort."

"We're very sorry, Your Honor." Seven turned a gimlet eye to Barrie, and then looked past her to Eight, who had leaned in closer.

Barrie swallowed what felt like a throatful of bitterness, and it settled in her stomach, heavy and impossible to digest. Shaking her head at herself, she couldn't believe what she was about to say.

She had no choice.

Leaving Cassie in prison with the same migraines that had

made Lula go half-crazy, the kind of migraines that didn't let up, *that* was cruel. It amounted to torture.

If dreams changed a person, as Seven had suggested, then so did cruelty. The sort of person who could turn her back, knowing Cassie would be in pain every day, wasn't the person Barrie wanted to become. She hated what she was going to say, but she would hate herself more if she didn't say it.

"Can I speak, Your Honor?" Her voice came out too soft, and she cleared her throat and scooted forward in her chair to try again. "Is it okay if I ask a question?"

"Sure, what the hell. Why not?" The judge pushed back the yellow tablet he had in front of him and clicked the end of the pen as he sat back. "What do you have to say, young lady?"

"If Cassie can make some kind of amends, I think she should get to do that." Barrie ground to a halt as she felt both Eight and Seven staring at her, but she refused to look at them. She especially couldn't look at Eight. "I'm not going to make excuses for Cassie, and if the amends can include me never seeing her again, I'd be happy with that. I'd have a hard time living with myself, though, if I thought she was in jail with people who had done a lot worse than lock a door and walk away. I don't want to be the reason her life is ruined."

The judge glanced at Cassie, who had looked up at Barrie with sullen eyes and very little reaction. What he saw didn't seem to impress him. "That's very commendable of you," he said, "but you didn't make the choices for your cousin."

Barrie nodded and held his gaze longer than was strictly comfortable. "I know that, Your Honor."

He finally looked away. "What about you, Mr. Beaufort?" he said to Eight. "Is that what you want?"

Bracing for the betrayal she was going to see written on Eight's face, Barrie turned with her eyes stinging. For once, she was glad he had his gift to urge him to agree with her. On the other hand, his gift also pushed him to want what Seven wanted. Did that mean Eight would feel pain no matter what he told the judge?

Eight gripped the armrests of his chair. "I want what Barrie wants," he said with only a hint of bitterness. "If she wants Cassie to make amends instead of going to jail, then I'll go along with that."

CHAPTER TEN

Barrie and Eight turned into the marina and threaded their way along the narrow labyrinth of floating walkways among the berths, boats, and empty water. It was another of the between places in the world that became addictive to contemplate, ships loaded with hope as they set off to fish or search for adventure, coming back with dreams fulfilled or empty holds. Either way, there was something innately optimistic about the kind of people who were always ready to set out in search of something *more*.

There was nothing optimistic, however, in the set of Eight's profile as his boat shoes and Barrie's sandals slapped in time along the boards. He had barely looked at her on the long drive back in Seven's car. When they reached the *Away*, he helped Barrie into the boat before he threw off the rope and jumped down to head toward the motor.

"Are you not going to talk to me at all?" Barrie dropped onto the seat beside him and rubbed her aching head.

"I'm waiting until I figure out what I'm going to say to you," he said, pulling the cord on the outboard until it sputtered to life. "Or until you can explain to me why the hell you did that. Without even asking me. Without even giving me a heads-up first." Shading his eyes, he guided the boat cautiously out of the marina and past the no-wake zone before speeding up. Glancing over at her, he shook his head. "And put on your life vest."

Barrie kept her center of gravity low as she went to get the vest and slip it over her head. It was odd how things changed. Fears and perspectives. A week ago, she had been terrified of being on the water, but she had come about as close to drowning as a person could get. That wasn't her biggest fear anymore. She had been terrified of Eight going to California, but that was only a geographical loss. A temporary loss. There were things far harder than geography to overcome.

Explanations, for example. It wasn't up to her to explain to Eight that his father had lied to him all his life.

Eight opened up the motor a bit and steered across the short stretch of ocean that stood between the harbor and the point, guiding the boat past the sandbars where the dark Santisto River emptied into the frothed Atlantic like tea spilling into nonfat milk. The *Away* hit the top of a wave and slammed down again, jarring Barrie in her seat.

"The letter that Mark left for me with Lula's lawyer asked me to choose what to do with his ashes," she said.

Eight glanced at her, then looked back out toward the lighthouse they were approaching on their left. "I know that."

"He also told me that I was—I am—his legacy. I've been thinking about that. Thanks to what he gave up for me, I'm all he has to show for his life. I figure that means it's my responsibility to do the kinds of things he taught me by example. To be the kind of person he was."

The boat slammed down again, and her heart thundered in her ears. Not with anxiety. Or not *only* anxiety. Blood and adrenaline and need made her tingle in every finger, every toe, and against all logic, it made her feel alive. Out loud, no-holds-barred alive. She looked at Eight, and he was watching her without a smile, but still with the kind of focus that made her feel like the only girl in the world.

She hated Seven then. Seven and Cassie and the Beaufort gift.

"Have you ever been to a drag show?" she asked him.

He eased the motor back to slow the boat. The tails of his shirt whipped against his pale chinos, so he looked like the last kind of guy to go to a drag show. Still, she could picture him cheering for Mark.

Mark would have loved him.

"A drag show?" he repeated. "No, I've never been."

"I used to beg Mark to do his Gayle Force act for me. He'd sing 'I Can't Stand the Rain' as Tina Turner, and 'Heat Wave' as Diana Ross, 'Rain' as Madonna. Then for the finale he would do himself—Gayle—belting out 'It's Raining Men.' He was better than the Weather Girls or any of them. He always said he never minded giving up performing to take care of me. He said that's what you did for people you cared about. But I always seem to be on the receiving end when people give things up. First Mark, and now you with your scholarship, and Cassie losing her freedom."

"I wondered where you were going with this."

Barrie swiveled her knees around and tucked her hands beneath her thighs so she wouldn't reach for him. Not until he met her partway. "Cassie getting herself locked up might not be my fault, but I don't want to look back and regret it, either. The amends thing makes sense. It gives her a way to fight back from the hole she dug for herself."

"I hated even seeing her in the same room with you after what she and her father did." Eight shook his head. "She didn't seem like she even gave a damn. If she had apologized, or even looked at you like she realized what she had done—"

"She's an actress. I respect her more for the fact that she didn't put on a show." This time, she did reach for Eight's hand. Slipping it between hers, she folded his fingers around her own.

The world slowed down to details. The hardened skin that kept him from feeling pain. The white scar of an old injury across the backs of his knuckles. A wisp of cloud parted, and the sun slashed through, making his green mosaic eyes look darker. She painted him in her mind, fixing him there permanently. He smelled familiar and important, rumpled cotton and sunshine with undertones of salt and his particular cherries-and-root-beer scent.

She turned back out to look across the water. "Do you believe in karma?" she asked. "Because I think I do. I don't know about heaven or hell or reincarnation or any of the rest, but I believe that what we do comes back to us one way or another. If I can be generous to Cassie, whether or not she deserves it, maybe I'll deserve a little generosity back."

Really, it came down to that.

She had never agreed to keep Seven's secret, but somehow that was what was happening. Eight would be hurt and furious if he ever found out she had kept the knowledge from him. To avoid that, Barrie was going to need every ounce of good karma she could get.

CHAPTER ELEVEN

Two small motorboats were anchored near the mouth of the creek by the time Eight guided the boat toward Watson's Landing. The pair of paunchy middle-aged men in the first of the craft were chatting with each other, but the lone guy in a checkered short-sleeve shirt and a camouflage fishing hat in the other boat had a rod and reel set to dangle fishing line into the water. He didn't seem very interested in catching anything except Eight and Barrie.

He stood up and waved as the *Away* approached. "Hey, are you the Watson girl? You live here, right? Can I ask you some questions?"

"No," Barrie and Eight answered simultaneously.

Barrie averted her eyes, but that brought her attention to the charred boards of the Colesworth dock. Memories are powerful things; a whiff of the burned wood, and she was right back in the midst of that night, smelling the smoke, heat licking her skin, water closing over her, and the lack of oxygen searing her lungs.

"Is your shoulder hurting?" Eight asked.

She hadn't realized she was rubbing it. "Not much," she said.

He swung out toward the Beaufort side of the river to go around the other boats, then returned to cross the midpoint and nose the *Away* back toward the Watson side. Barrie had a brief moment to realize that at some point in the future, that spot, the midpoint between Beaufort Hall and Watson's Landing, might be the only place where she and Eight could meet without one or the other of them being in pain. Then the surge of returning hit her like she imagined a dose of ecstasy or some designer drug must feel—like a shot of Alice's "much-ness" infused into her veins. The boat bumped against the pilings on the dock, and Eight jumped ashore to tie the line.

"You don't have to walk me to the house," she said. "Isn't your sister coming home from camp today? It's already bad enough your dad won't be there, and if you're meeting with the coach from Charleston later, you'll want to spend some time with her."

"Kate is self-sufficient. Five minutes after walking through the door, she'll have grilled the housekeeper like a backyard cookout and wrung every piece of news out of her. Trust me, I'm going to be a low priority."

Barrie hesitated, glancing back at the intruding boats, then gave a shrug. Hooking his hands into his pockets and watching the ground beneath his feet, Eight fell in step beside her. They passed a fresh line of NO TRESPASSING signs along with several gray-green boxes that hadn't been there earlier that morning. Which probably meant that the perimeter control system had gone in—or at least part of it had.

Eight scanned the woods on the way to the house, only stopping a few feet from the terrace steps, where they were out of sight of the kitchen and the rooms above. The look he gave Barrie was like a physical touch, curious fingers probing her thoughts.

"Are you done being mad at me yet?" she asked.

"I don't like you being generous to Cassie when she doesn't deserve it. But that's who you are, and since who you are is what I happen to like about you, it wouldn't make sense for me to blame you for it."

"Does that mean you don't?"

"It means I'm working my way out of it." Leaning forward, he stole a kiss before she could decide whether they were still in a kissing sort of relationship anymore. Her lips made the decision for her; she couldn't help responding. When he pulled away, his grin held a smugness that should have made her want to grind her heel into his instep.

"I'll call you as soon as I'm done with the coach and I know what Dad has planned for tonight," he said. "He's probably going to want to take Kate out for dinner. It's what we usually do, but I'm sure she's dying to meet you, so maybe you and Pru—"

"No. Your sister should get you to herself for one night. Anyway, I need to tell Pru about Cassie and the restaurant. Plus I still have unpacking and sleep to catch up on. I think I could sleep for a week now that I'm back."

The stir of the wind in the trees and the splash of the fountain seemed louder as he reached back over and pulled her toward him. He hadn't bothered to shave that morning, and the stubble was dark against his tanned skin, a contrast to his sun-lightened hair. His eyes stood out, as bright and green as the little tree frogs that congregated near the river.

He kissed her more slowly, a permission-asking kind of kiss, a glad-we're-back kind of kiss. "Are we okay now?" he asked. "I'm not mad at you, and you're not mad at me?"

Barrie's eyes filled and her throat clogged, and she hated Seven and magic and gifts for making it all too complicated. "Yeah," she said. "We're fine. Good luck with the coach."

Taking the steps two at a time, she fled into the kitchen and shut the door behind her. Fingers pressed against her lips, she watched Eight through the window above the sink. In spite of what he'd said, he walked with his head bowed and shoulders hunched, looking as close to defeated as she had ever seen him look.

Not that she could blame him. He had given up something he had wanted badly, and neither of the two people he had expected to cheer for him had given him anything but grief.

Before she could stop and think, she threw the door open again and ran after him, but he had reached the *Away* before she came level with the fountain. She couldn't bear the idea of shouting across at him and having strangers listening and judging from the boats on the river, so she stopped and waited, hoping he would turn and look back.

He didn't.

The sun beamed down relentlessly. *Yunwi* chased one another along the rows of hedges, and the pulse of Watson's Landing thrummed beneath her feet, echoed in the hum of the earth's energy, the whisper of marsh grass, the warbled conversations of the birds, and the low, incessant drone of insects. Across the river, Beaufort Hall sat on the opposite bank, and she could't help wondering if the binding and connection felt the same to Seven.

She turned back toward the house. A shadow crossed above her with a rush of wings, and another raven alighted on the edge of the fountain basin. Cocking its head, the bird studied her curiously, its ink-oil wings glistening with purple highlights in a way that made her think she should be remembering something.

She found herself thinking of Obadiah, and with the name on the tip of her tongue again, she wondered how many Obadiahs there could possibly be. Thousands probably. Hundreds of thousands. Still, she dug her phone out of her pocket, opened up the web browser, and typed in *O-b-a-d-i-a-h*, hoping she had spelled it right.

A voice spoke behind her as the browser began to think. "Careful, little one. Names are powerful. You don't want to call for things you can't control."

Barrie's heart jumped. Hand at her throat, she felt the thud, thud, thud of it beating in triple time. She turned and found Obadiah himself sitting on the edge of the fountain in the precise spot where the bird had been. Stepping back to put distance between them, she ended up in a flowerbed with her legs pressed against a boxwood hedge.

Obadiah didn't come toward her, though, only watched her with mild amusement. The more she looked back at him, the more he seemed raw and out of focus, like a modernist painting come to life. She blinked, and the impression cleared. He was just *there* again. Present instead of absent.

"I wasn't aware Google was magic," she said, trying to sound anything but petrified.

Obadiah raised his eyebrows, and the slight flicker of his

eyes suggested he was laughing. "I suspect more people believe in Google magic than in my particular kind."

"What kind is that?" Barrie asked, trying to decide whether he had actually been a bird, or whether the bird had only been an illusion of some kind. Or hypnotism, maybe?

Around her, the *yunwi* were converging from every corner of the garden, rushing as if they hadn't had any warning he was coming, either. As they neared the fountain, they bent to scoop bits of gravel and oyster shell from the ground, which they flung at Obadiah before stooping to pick up more.

A shell pierced Obadiah's wrist. Blood trickled and dripped to the ground.

When Barrie had dropped her blood-soaked socks on the night the water spirit had appeared in the fountain and bound her to Watson's Landing, the *yunwi* had fallen on the blood like dogs in a feeding frenzy. Now their eyes grew dull in their faces.

"Who *are* you?" Barrie locked her knees to keep herself from running.

How could she have forgotten anything about this man? From the high cheekbones to the long dreadlocks and the expensive cut of his black silk suit, everything about him was memorable. His shirt was a dark, shining green instead of eggplant like before. That was the only difference.

"What is it you want from me?" she asked.

"A favor. A small one, and in exchange, I'll give you what I offered you before."

"Which is what?"

"Truth," he said. "And freedom, if you want it." Obadiah's teeth slithered from behind his lips. "You wish to know if the Beaufort boy loves you for yourself. You want assurances and choices. I can give you all of that."

Barrie's brain lagged sluggishly behind his words. She caught herself about to ask how he could possibly know anything about her, but really, the answer was obvious, wasn't it? If the man could turn into a raven and back again, listening to a conversation would be all too simple. If he could turn into a raven, what else could he do? What *couldn't* he do?

Her world shifted on its axis with the force of a seismic quake. It was one thing to accept the Fire Carrier and the family gifts, to believe in Cherokee witchcraft and voodoo on an ancient level. Seeing magic standing before her in the shifting shape of a man who could turn into a bird and back . . . That was fierce and fearsome. And wonderful. It meant there was more magic at large in the world than she had ever imagined, and that opened up countless possibilities. If that kind of magic existed, what else was real?

"You're not afraid anymore." Obadiah watched her with open curiosity. "Why not?"

"Should I be afraid?" Barrie asked.

He cocked his head and walked around her slowly, and without his changing his expression at all, she had the impression he was laughing at her. She spun in place to follow his progress, but the alarm that had been growing in her subsided as fast as it had risen. She had no reason to be alarmed.

When he had walked all the way around her, Obadiah stopped and leaned back against the fountain. "Have you figured it out yet, *petite*?"

"Figured out what?"

"Honestly, I had hoped you would be more intelligent." He trailed an idle finger in the basin. The water spat at him with a hiss of the pipes. He snatched his hand away. "Your handsome friend across the river might not be suited for magic. The gift is a responsibility, and he told you himself he doesn't want it. Your problems would be solved without it. You would have answers about how he feels. He could come and go as he pleased. No binding. No restrictions."

In the basin, the water level rose until it threatened to spill over the fluted marble lip, the way it had the night the spirit had appeared to bind Barrie to Watson's Landing. Barrie eyed the water warily, expecting that any minute it would assume the liquid shape of a woman, but Obadiah passed the flat of his hand above the basin, then clenched his fist. The bubbling subsided in a low, rippling moan that was echoed by a screech from the *yunwi* as if they were in pain.

The flurry of shell bits and gravel being pelted at Obadiah grew thicker.

Obadiah flexed his hand again, raised it in the air.

"Leave them alone!" Barrie yelled. She grabbed his arm in both of her own, and held on with every ounce of her strength.

He easily shook her off. "Enough of this. I'll make the choice simpler for you. Choose whether you want to keep *your* gift or lose it."

"*My* gift?" Barrie's hands went numb and cold as if she were slowly freezing from the inside out. "We were talking about Eight."

"We were," Obadiah said, "but I've offered twice to remove the Beaufort gift. You don't seem willing to cooperate."

CHAPTER TWELVE

Barrie's ears rang with the silent screech from the *yunwi* in the wake of Obadiah's words. "You can't take the Watson gift away," she said.

"I can't?" His smile held no amusement. "Or I shouldn't? Because it might require a bit of time, but I assure you, it *can* be done. You have something I need, so consider it a bargaining chip."

"You haven't even said what you want. Anyway, I can't agree without asking Eight."

"In your shoes he wouldn't hesitate," Obadiah said.

Remembering what Eight had told her the day before, Barrie wasn't sure Obadiah was entirely wrong.

"What I'm asking is not so difficult," Obadiah continued with the air of someone who had already won a bet. "There's a lodestone buried on the Colesworth property that binds the curse to the family and the family to the plantation. I need you to find it for me."

Barrie stared at Obadiah, taking in the too-steady way he watched her. It struck her as evasive. He was lying, or hiding something. "Did Cassie send you? Is that what this is about?"

"No one sent me. My ancestor laid the curse on the Colesworth family. Finding the stone would let me try to break it." Obadiah sighed and shook his head. "Dark magic rebounds on the caster. What you wish on someone else, you reap in return. The same way the curse passes from generation to generation in the Colesworth family, the karmic price of casting it has passed from mother to child in my family ever since. I'm tired of seeing them suffer."

A chill crawled up Barrie's spine. "Why now?"

"Because you're here with your gift. You can find the stone, and when the Colesworths finally pay their debt, I can break the curse."

"What debt?"

"Blood and years and lives. Which isn't the point." Obadiah's voice took on a soothing tone. "You have no reason to care about the curse as long as it doesn't affect you or Watson's Landing. Compared to the curse, removing the spell that created the Beaufort gift would be child's play. *If* you want it removed. That would be your choice. You would only have to find that lodestone, too." His smile turned oily and smooth, and he held his hands out, palms open, as if to show he was holding nothing back. "You see? I can be generous as well. I may not know where the other stones are buried, but the Scalping Tree is a landmark no one can miss."

Barrie turned instinctively in the direction of the enormous oak at the center of the woods where the Fire Carrier emerged and disappeared each night. Local legend said braves had once hung the scalps of their enemies on it in tribute to the ancient spirit, and she had felt the pull of something lost emanating from it the moment she'd first arrived at Watson's Landing. That had turned out to be from the keys to the tunnel, which Emmett had hidden in a recess beneath the trunk. But she and Eight had retrieved those already.

"There's nothing else lost in the woods. I would feel it if there were," she said, but even as she spoke, she acknowledged to herself that there was *something*. She had attributed it to the Fire Carrier himself.

"The Watson and Beaufort lodestones aren't lost. Thomas Watson and Robert Beaufort buried the stones themselves as part of the Fire Carrier's bargain. I may not be able to find the others, but the area around the Scalping Tree is not so large that I wouldn't eventually find it myself. I'm not above a bit of revenge, *petite*." Obadiah's lips twisted, and he blinked a little too slowly, as if he were seeing something about himself he didn't like. "Given a choice between my family and yours, make no mistake which I'll choose."

There was something in the way his eyes shifted that made Barrie not entirely sure she believed him, but the *yunwi* seemed to have no such doubts. Their soundless shrieks of fury made Barrie wince. They rushed at Obadiah, and the handfuls of shell and gravel they had been throwing swelled to a barrage.

Several slivers of shell bounced off Obadiah's cheek. His face shimmered under the onslaught, like a holographic projection losing power. For an instant, Barrie wasn't sure what she saw there, a man Mark's age, or someone older, different.

He put his finger up to wipe his skin, and it came away glistening with drops of red. Frowning at the droplets, he circled his finger in the air. The flurry of pebbles and white shards stopped and hung, suspended. Then in a rush of air they swirled and spun, faster and faster, climbing skyward until they vanished.

Barrie's hair whipped into her face. All around her, the *yunwi* darted behind the low hedges of the maze, and whimpers sounded in the wind, barely audible and more felt than heard.

"You're hurting them. Stop it!" Pivoting back to Obadiah, Barrie grabbed his finger, pulled it toward her, and let go only when the air stopped churning.

"They're a nuisance. Now, are you going to help me?" Obadiah flicked a piece of shell from a crease in the dark fabric of his suit. There was a hard edge to the way he watched Barrie that turned the question and the motion into a threat.

It struck Barrie then how helpless she was. In the face of Obadiah's power, how could she stop him from doing anything he wanted?

As if he'd heard the thought, Obadiah extended his finger and tilted her chin up to make her look at him. Her fear fled and left her blinking.

Why would she want to argue? She should *want* to help Obadiah. Feeling disconnected from the movement, she found herself nodding.

"That's good. There, you see." Obadiah smiled darkly. "I have no need or wish to harm your pets, little one. You come with me to find the lodestone. I remove the Colesworth curse, you keep the Watson gift, and everyone is happy. Then you can choose whether you wish to find the lodestone at Beaufort Hall."

There was something off about the logic, something wrong. It niggled at the back of Barrie's brain the way a tickle in the throat demands that you cough, even when you can't. But it was hard, impossible, to think through the sludge of hot insistence that overwhelmed her objections. Of course she had to protect the *yunwi* and the Watson magic. That was her responsibility. Giving Eight the chance to live without the Beaufort gift was an added bonus.

Relationships never came with any kind of guarantee, but Barrie couldn't imagine that she would ever feel indifferent to Eight. There would always be warmth or pain, and having to live with the Santisto between them would be either too much distance or too little.

"What if I—*we*, because this isn't my decision alone—tell you to go ahead?" she asked. "If you remove the Beaufort gift, is there any danger to Eight and Seven?"

"Think of all the magic here like it's a layer cake. It's harder and more dangerous to remove the middle or bottom layers than it is to remove the top. I need to break the Colesworth curse before I can safely reach the Beaufort gift. Of course, I'll also need the Beaufort lodestone, but it must all start with the curse."

Barrie glanced across the river, first at Beaufort Hall, and then at Colesworth Place. "I'll talk to Eight, but first you have to promise you won't put anyone in danger. And no matter what happens, you don't get to take my gift," she said. "You don't get to touch the *yunwi* or the Fire Carrier or anything or anyone at Watson's Landing. Not ever. Those are the terms."

Obadiah changed. Not a change of expression: a more fundamental, physical transformation of features into someone kinder and more familiar. Someone beautiful. He looked . . . not like himself.

Rationally, she knew it wasn't real, but he looked like Mark.

Mark, who would never, had never, hurt anyone in his life.

"No harm will come to you or anyone you care for, but there is no 'we' in our bargain," he said. "This is between you and me and the Colesworth girl. Leave Eight Beaufort out of it."

Barrie looked up sharply. "You never mentioned Cassie."

"The curse is bound in blood. It requires blood to remove it. A prick of the finger, no more than that."

"Take mine, then. I'm a Colesworth, too."

"That wouldn't satisfy. You aren't bound by their curse." Obadiah's smile dropped away. "Listen, *petite*. Nothing is sure in life except for death, and even that isn't as certain as you might think. You don't know me well enough to trust my promises, but I'll give one to you anyway. Keep your bargain, and I'll keep mine. The last thing I want to do is add more blood or pain to the burden my family bears."

He spoke with such sincerity that Barrie couldn't help believing what he said. And really, the choice was simple. If Obadiah took away the Beaufort gift, Eight would never need to know about the headaches and all the things his father had never told him. He would have his dream and the escape he had wanted all his life.

He could choose to go play baseball. He could choose anything, or anyone.

When you set someone free, they could choose to fly. But they could also choose to leave you.

"All right," she said reluctantly. "I'll help you. I'm not sure about the logistics, though. Even if I can get Cassie to agree, what about her family? Not to mention there are still ghost hunters and treasure hunters and reporters hanging around. Someone is going to see us and wonder what we're doing. I can't get over there unless Eight takes me—I don't have a boat or a driver's license—"

"I already told you to leave Eight Beaufort out of it." Obadiah leaned forward, his nostrils flaring with a sudden intake of breath. "Tell no one about our bargain, or I'll consider it the same as if you refused. As for the boat, I'll take care of that and any unwanted attention. You just find a way to get the Colesworth girl to cooperate, or I will do it less pleasantly. And don't wait too long to call me."

"Call you how?" Barrie asked, thinking of the way he had appeared out of the blue.

He pointed toward her fist in answer, and something cold and hard dug into her palm. The green disk was back. At the center of it, the raven ruffled his feathers and blinked up at her, and she let go as if he'd pecked her skin. The disk clattered to the gravel. The raven stilled, became an etched image and nothing more.

Barrie raised her eyes back to Obadiah. "What does that have to do with calling you?"

"Pick it up." He lifted his brows and regarded her with clear amusement.

She used two fingers to lift the disk, and found a phone number etched in gold on the other side. A laugh escaped her; she couldn't help it. In one way, a phone number didn't seem at all like Obadiah, but on the other hand, it hinted at a sense of humor.

When she looked up again, Obadiah was gone.

This time, though, she remembered all too clearly that he'd been there.

CHAPTER THIRTEEN

Pru wasn't in the kitchen when Barrie rushed through the door. That relieved Barrie only slightly more than it disappointed her. She couldn't mention Obadiah, but there was no alternative to confessing what she'd done at Cassie's hearing.

After checking the butler's pantry, she peered into the silent tearoom and found that empty, too. The shining glass of the windows caught the sunlight, but fallen petals and a dusting of pollen lay scattered around the cut-glass bowls on the starched white tablecloths, as if Pru hadn't had the heart to remove the dying flowers yet.

Barrie turned away. She hastened through the kitchen and out into the corridor, where the door swinging shut behind her gave a deep and echoing groan.

"Is that you, Barrie? I'm in the library." Pru's voice drifted toward her.

Pausing on the threshold of the room a few moments later, Barrie found her aunt rifling through the contents of several drawers, which appeared to have been emptied onto the surface of the desk.

"Are you looking for something in particular?" Barrie asked. "Maybe I could help."

"You haven't seen the keys that were in the top drawer here, have you?" Curled wisps of Pru's hair had escaped her ponytail, and she brushed a hand back distractedly to smooth it. "I've arranged for a local auction company to come out to take what you and I sorted from the attic, along with the furniture that we're going to replace with Lula's pieces that the movers are bringing out from California. But there are bound to be things on the trucks that we won't have room to keep. Walking past the stable building last night reminded me that it might be the perfect place for temporary storage. I'm pretty sure the key was on that ring."

Barrie's cheeks heated at the thought of how she and Eight had distracted each other while he'd still had the keys in his hand. "Eight must have forgotten and slipped the ring into his pocket after we put Mark's ashes in the cabinet," she said.

She and Pru both glanced at the blue-and-gold *kintsugi*

urn on the shelf, and grief crept into the room. Then Pru rammed the desk drawer shut.

"You know, I'm tired of waiting for Beauforts. There's bound to be a way to open the padlock. I probably have something in the toolbox that will break it."

She carried the whole toolbox out, and Barrie followed her around the corner of the house, peering into the shadows for any sign of Obadiah and checking the trees for ravens. For the moment, at least, everything was quiet.

Even the *yunwi* didn't seem concerned. They hung back while Pru tried to find a way to break open the heart-shaped iron lock holding the arched doors to the stables in place, but once Barrie simply removed the screws and threw it—hasp and all—into the toolbox, they cheerfully pushed open the door and surged inside.

Daylight swept in to flood the wide concrete aisle. A closed room on either side preceded neat rows of polished mahogany stalls with wooden doors carved into graceful reverse arches at shoulder height.

Pru looked around with an expression that reminded Barrie of Mark talking about his drag-queen glory days, and then she stopped beside the nearest stall and traced the empty name plate. "Some of my happiest moments were spent in here," she said. "Here and on the back of a horse."

Her shoulders had hollowed, but she stiffened when Barrie

went to hug her, as if she didn't want to be touched. Crossing briskly to the door on the right, she threw it open to reveal what had clearly been a tack room. Neatly buckled bridles coated in thick layers of dust hung beside a few cloth-covered saddles that still sat on racks mounted to the wall. Beneath each saddle, a tack trunk held the name of a long-dead horse engraved in large script letters: *Cordelia, Yorick, Claudius, Orlando, Hermione* . . .

Barrie smiled at that. "Hermione?" she asked.

"From *The Winter's Tale*," Pru said. "Watsons have been naming their horses after Shakespeare's characters since before the American Revolution, so my choices were limited. But she was a wonderful mare. I wish I'd had her longer."

Barrie braced herself for an answer she wouldn't want to hear, but she couldn't help asking. "What happened to her?"

"My father." Pru backed out of the room. "He sold all the horses after Lula left." Standing in the aisle again, she hugged her arms around her waist and stood staring longingly at the rows of empty stalls. "I shouldn't have let him do that. I should have stood up to him, stopped him. You know, I watch you and the way you quietly go do whatever you think needs doing . . . It's frustrating to think that sneaking out with Seven on a few dates was the biggest act of rebellion in my entire life, and I stopped even that when Lula left. Maybe if I hadn't . . ." She shook her head once, slowly, and then looked hard at Barrie.

"On the other hand, maybe I need to be a little bit more like my father."

There was no way in which Pru wanting to be more like Emmett could ever bode well. "What do you mean?" Barrie asked.

"Isn't there something you want to tell me?" Pru crossed her arms, and her expression was closer to stern and implacable than Barrie had ever envisioned it could appear.

"Seven told you about Cassie's hearing," Barrie said, closing her eyes. She didn't even bother to pretend it was a question. Of course Seven was going to call Pru the second Barrie's back was turned.

"The question is, why didn't *you* tell me? I've been waiting for you to bring it up, to explain. Or better yet, you could have tried talking to Seven about it before you went and said something to the judge. Or spoken to me. Honestly, we're not trying to smother you. I don't want you to feel like that, but it is our job to keep you safe. I'm not your mother, and Lord knows I don't have any experience mothering anyone, but I thought we were friends. I hoped you knew that you could come and talk to me if you were trying to work something out for yourself."

The sunlight slanting in through the open doorway suddenly felt too bright, too revealing. Something small and cold hardened in Barrie's chest, as if the lump in her throat had sunk down to her heart when she swallowed, because Pru's voice had trembled when she'd said she wasn't Barrie's mother. And it occurred to Barrie that Emmett's refusal to let Pru see anyone after Lula had run away had cost Pru not only the chance of a future with Seven, it had taken away any children that Pru and Seven might have had together.

Her first instinct was to tell Pru everything. Tell her about what Seven had done to Eight, and about Obadiah and the lodestones, and the chance that maybe Obadiah could remove the Beaufort gift and set both Eight and Seven free. But Obadiah's instructions had been very clear. Even the thought of mentioning Obadiah made Barrie's mouth feel oddly dry.

"Did you know that Seven gets the migraines, too?" she asked softly instead. "So does Cassie. That's why I did it."

"I'm sure you meant well—that's not the point." Pru went to the door across the aisle and pushed it open into a room that held nothing but dust, a few dried wisps of hay, and a stack of empty burlap feed sacks. "But one way or another, you're letting your cousin rope you in again, and that's going to land you right back in trouble. I can already see it coming."

Barrie shook her head emphatically. "I promise that I'm not falling for any more of Cassie's sob stories, but this is a question of fairness. It's not fair for her to suffer from migraines every day she's in jail. That would be a bigger punishment than a judge or jury knew they were giving her."

"How is it *fair* for her to get away with what she did?"

"She's not getting away with it. She still has to make amends in the pretrial intervention program." Casting a smile at Pru, Barrie tried to coax her to see the humor in the situation. "Honestly, can you picture Cassie in an orange jumpsuit, picking up trash on the side of the road? For her, that will be a worse punishment than just about anything else they could give her."

"You'd be safer with her in jail." Pru refused to be distracted. Without waiting for Barrie to answer, she closed the door on the empty room and walked out of the stable building with her back as stiff as an exclamation point. Barrie shut the double doors outside and retrieved the toolbox before running to catch up.

On the front steps of the house, Pru stopped and turned abruptly. "I've been trying my hardest not to be upset with you ever since Seven called and told me what you did. I've tried, and I'm failing. What upsets me most is that being mad makes me a lesser person than I hoped I was. Logically, I understand that having Cassie out of jail doesn't necessarily mean she'll have an opportunity to hurt you again. But I know how that family winds people around their fingers." With a sigh, she rubbed her hands together, coming about as close to wringing her hands as anyone Barrie had ever seen. "I admire you for trying to be fair, but at least promise me you won't have anything to do with her. Can you do that much?"

Barrie wanted so much to promise. Her head felt too

heavy on her neck as she shook it. "I'm sorry, but I think I need to go to Wyatt's funeral, Aunt Pru."

Pru stared blankly, and then looked up at the sky, as if Barrie had exhausted her patience. "What in heaven's name *for*?"

"I need . . ." Barrie let her voice trail off. Various possible answers swirled around like kaleidoscope images while Barrie searched for a way to answer without actually uttering a lie. What *did* she need?

She needed to convince Cassie to let Obadiah do whatever he wanted to do at Colesworth Place, but the more she thought about that, the more she realized she still didn't know exactly what that would be. She needed time to talk to Cassie, which Cassie wasn't likely to give her on the phone. She also needed to convince Cassie to listen, which wasn't Cassie's strength at the best of times.

"Before Cassie locked us in the tunnel," Barrie said, "she told me that no matter what I did in my life, people would always forgive me because I'm a Watson, like they would always blame her because she's a Colesworth. She was right. People were still nice to me in town today." The image of Ryder Colesworth knocking into their table surfaced, but she pushed it firmly away. "I'm not saying I can forgive Cassie, but we can't keep fueling the feud without expecting the fire to burn us all to pieces."

"You can't be the only one trying to make peace, either," Pru said. "People like Cassie take advantage of that."

"Wyatt and Emmett are both dead," Barrie said, and her lips felt stiff on the word. "They were the ones who hung on to the feud. Don't you see? Going to the funeral would be a gesture for Cassie and Sydney. A chance to show the whole town that we can forgive and we don't have to go on the way the Watsons and the Colesworths have for the past three hundred years."

"I could ground you." Pru snatched the toolbox away from Barrie.

"You could. But I hope you won't."

"You're not playing fair. How am I supposed to argue against kindness?"

"Hopefully, you're not supposed to," Barrie said.

A faint smile squeezed the corners of Pru's eyes for a moment before it died. "Cassie and her mother aren't likely to want you at the funeral."

"I know, but at least I'll have made a gesture."

Pru walked through the foyer and stopped at the closet beneath the stairs. She set the toolbox back inside, then closed the door hard enough for the sound to echo off the ceiling before she turned back to Barrie.

"All right," she said. "On one condition. If you're going to insist on going, I'll take you myself. Unless you want to see more of that smothering in action, I also suggest we don't mention the funeral to either one of the Beauforts until well after it is over."

CHAPTER FOURTEEN

At the entrance to Colesworth Place, Pru swerved to avoid a pothole the size of a swimming pool. The black Mercedes groaned and quivered in its old age, and Pru's hands tightened on the wheel.

"Not to speak ill of the dead," she said, "but you'd think with all the drug money Wyatt Colesworth spent fixing up the plantation outbuildings, he could have spent a little to fix the road."

"Different things matter to different people," Barrie said, staring out the window.

"What on earth possessed him to put in an asphalt driveway in the first place? It was criminally stupid. Not to mention historically inaccurate. Hubris, that's all it was, you mark my words. Every Colesworth has more than enough of that to go around."

"Maybe it had something to do with smuggling drugs. Gravel makes noise and dust. Asphalt is quieter. I'd guess he'd have to have been thinking about those kinds of things."

Pru sent her a worried glance. "Are you positive you want to do this?"

"Of course," Barrie fibbed. But thanks to Obadiah, she had no choice.

Just being at Colesworth Place scraped her nerves. Driving through the open gate with its oak canopy of weeping moss, she couldn't help remembering being there to watch Cassie's performance of *Gone with the Wind*, after which Eight had peeled out onto the main road as if the devil were behind him. That had been the first time Wyatt had threatened Barrie.

Still, the memories weren't all bad. Driving to the beach afterward with Eight, kissing him, talking quietly as they sat together on the moonlit sand . . .

How was Barrie going to keep Eight from finding out she'd come to the funeral behind his back? He would be furious when he realized. Then there was Seven's confession, and Obadiah. Too many secrets.

She directed Pru toward the parking lot, which was empty except for a sedate beige Toyota with a GOD ANSWERS KNEE-MAIL bumper sticker. After parking alongside the car, Pru sat with her hands tight on the wheel, fixedly staring down the path that led toward the modern house and the outbuildings Wyatt had painstakingly restored.

"We can't be the only ones here, can we? Did we get the time wrong?" Barrie opened the door to slide out onto the sweltering asphalt. She rubbed her temple and studied the empty lot.

"This is what was in the paper. Even if no one came for Wyatt, I'd have thought they'd be here for Marie—that's Cassie's mama." Pru got out of the car and pushed the straps of her big white purse up to the crook of her elbow in a movement that suggested she was girding herself for battle. "Marie's got three sisters, and all of them are married with children. Then there's *her* mama, Jolene Landry, not to mention the folks on the Colesworth side. Maybe they all parked beside the house?"

From her tone, Pru wasn't convinced, and when they emerged from behind the line of trees that hid the parking lot from the rest of the property, there were no other cars parked anywhere.

"Well, that's a shame," Pru said. "Might not be such a bad thing you and I came, after all. It'd be a shame for folks to punish Marie for Wyatt's mistakes. She's got to be feeling bad enough for marrying him in the first place. Much less staying with him all these years."

"Maybe she couldn't figure out how to get away," Barrie said. "Or maybe she didn't want to leave if it would hurt Cassie and Sydney. We can't know what she was thinking." Barrie was coming to realize that trying to understand a family when you weren't right there with them was like looking through a window into a darkened house.

She and Pru skirted the Colesworth cemetery, which was enclosed by wrought-iron fencing. A pull of loss seeped out of it and made her wince. Cemeteries were full of loss, but they had never *felt* lost to her before. They'd always been a place people went to find those who had left them behind. Maybe the open grave was what made the difference, like a hole in the earth that symbolized the hole in the world that someone left behind.

Metal chairs and a white canvas awning stood alongside the hole, and all around, crosses and slabs and marble angels gave testament to long-past sorrows. Soon Wyatt Colesworth would be one of them, nothing but a marker above a coffin pinned into place by thousands of pounds of earth.

A tide of panic swept over Barrie so fast and so viscerally that it made her stumble and lose her breath.

Pru reached out to steady her. "You all right?"

"Just caught my heel." Barrie took a gulp of air.

The thought of being buried . . . Too clearly, she remembered wondering if she and Eight would die in the tunnel when Cassie had locked them there. She remembered how the dirt and bricks had taken on weight and presence, closing in until she had felt she couldn't breathe. They had escaped; it had all ended well. But human memory clung to pain and terror so much harder than it grasped at joy.

Collecting herself, Barrie forced the thought aside and hurried to catch up with Pru. They reached the path leading to the restored shell of the old brick chapel.

Set back beneath the oaks a hundred yards from the defiantly broken columns of the old Colesworth mansion, the building was a barren contrast to the overgrown and lovely chapel at Watson's Landing. If it was due any deference as a place of worship, Cassie refused to acknowledge it. Looking bored and sullen in a bright red shirt and matching slacks that set off her roses-and-cream skin and the long, dark waterfall of her hair, she stood outside the door with her mother; her younger sister, Sydney; an elderly woman; and a thirtysomething African American minister.

In a somber navy dress, Sydney was a pale and more sedate reflection of her older sibling. She, at least, was listening politely to what the minister said, and that fact didn't seem to be lost on the elderly woman, who, judging by the family resemblance, was obviously Cassie's grandmother. The narrow-eyed disapproval she threw at Cassie, however, along with the salt-and-pepper hair scraped back into an austere bun, and the deep creases of grimness from nose to mouth, made Jolene Landry appear about as far from grandmotherly as it was possible to get. She was the one who first noticed Pru and Barrie. Stopping midsentence as Barrie and Pru trod up the path, she elbowed Marie Colesworth in the ribs.

Marie rushed forward. "Pru Watson! Isn't it kind of you to come? And Barrie, too. Thank you." She clasped Pru's hand in both of hers and offered Barrie a smile that managed to be both sad and happy at once, but then she bit her lip and gave a furtive glance around. "You'll have to pardon the lack of attendance. I'm sure everyone will be along directly. Unless I managed to tell them all the wrong time or day of the week. I swear, I've been about as useful as a wig on a porcupine the past few days."

Her own hair was as stiff as a wig, teased and sprayed and held back with an alligator clip, and the expertly applied makeup couldn't disguise the deep bruises beneath her eyes. She seemed worn down and worn out, and Barrie wondered how on earth you managed to look yourself in the mirror after discovering that the man you'd been sleeping beside for twenty-odd years was a drug dealer and a murderer. Or had she known all along?

Pru didn't seem to know what to do, but good manners came to the rescue. "I'm truly sorry for your loss, Marie. I know it'll be hard on you and the girls without Wyatt here."

Barrie hadn't even thought what she would say about Wyatt's death. How did she express regret she didn't feel?

Abruptly, she felt ashamed for being there under false pretenses. All she'd been thinking about was how to find a way to speak to Cassie about Obadiah. *That* task had seemed impossible enough. Now here was Cassie's mother beaming at her, as if everything Barrie had told Pru in the stables was true and not some made-up excuse.

"I'm sorry, too," she mumbled.

As a statement, it was hopelessly incomplete. There were so many ways she could have finished that sentence:

I'm sorry your husband was a son of a bitch.

I'm sorry your husband killed my father.

I'm sorry your husband burned my mother and ruined her life.

I'm sorry your husband tried to kill me.

Pressing her tongue into the roof of her mouth, she stared at the small gold cross that hung in the V of Marie Colesworth's stark black dress.

After releasing Pru, Cassie's mother reached down and clutched Barrie's hands. "The lawyer told me what you did, speaking to the judge for Cassie. I know she doesn't deserve your generosity after what she did. But I'm grateful. We're all grateful." She glanced back at the door, where Cassie had half-turned away, still pretending boredom, while the minister, Sydney, and Jolene Landry made an obvious effort toward polite conversation. "Cassie, honey, come on over here and say 'thank you.'"

Standing three feet from the wall of the chapel, Cassie still managed to give the impression that she was leaning nonchalantly, observing the scene as if it had nothing to do with her. At first when her mother called her over, she didn't respond at all, and then she approached very slowly and offered up one of her dazzling Scarlett O'Hara smiles.

"Imagine seeing you here, Cos," she said. "You didn't have anything else to do today?"

"Cassie!" her mother snapped. "You owe Barrie a debt of gratitude, not to mention an apology. I know you're sorry for what you did."

"Do you?" Cassie gave her mother a look simmering with amusement. "Well, if you say so, then I *must* be sorry."

Marie's hand flashed toward Cassie's face. She stopped the motion and lowered the hand without connecting to Cassie's cheek, glancing from Barrie to Pru before dropping her eyes.

Barrie's face heated until it felt close to the deep red of Cassie's low-cut T-shirt. She remembered all too vividly how Wyatt had hit Cassie on the night of the play. She'd felt so sorry for her cousin then. She stared hard at the ground to avoid glaring at both Marie and Cassie, wishing she could just turn on her heel, grab Pru's hand, and head for the car.

She couldn't. Not with Obadiah's threat still hanging over her.

"I'm ashamed of you, Cassie. The least you could do is

meet people halfway when they're generous to you." Marie's voice wobbled, but whether that was frustration or embarrassment, Barrie couldn't tell, and she made no effort to pull Cassie aside or speak to her in a way that would keep everyone there from hearing. Turning her back on Cassie, Marie moved up and started reaching for Pru's arm. She stopped before actually making contact, and the gesture turned into an oddly helpless wave instead. "Why don't y'all come and say hello to the others?" she suggested. "Barrie, I think you've met Cassie's sister, Sydney, haven't you? But you may not know Pastor Nelson or my mother, Jolene Landry, yet."

Herding Pru and Barrie to where the minister, Sydney, and the elderly woman were all deep in conversation, Marie stopped at the chapel door. Barrie peered inside during the introductions and wasn't surprised to find no one else was there.

Only the brick walls, floor, and roof of the old structure had been restored. To soften the starkness of the space, someone had dyed four bedsheets a mottled black and hung them from the bare-bulbed light fixture at the center of the ceiling. Each sheet was bunched with white lilies and yards of ribbon and fastened to the walls to form drapes that hung low above several rows of metal folding chairs, and a plain pine coffin stood in the puddled light flowing in from the empty windows.

"Pru Watson," the minister said in a hearty, deep bass

voice. "I might have known you'd be the first person to hold out an olive branch. Thank you for coming out. It was a very generous thing to do."

"It was all my niece's idea, I'm ashamed to say." Nodding back, Pru pushed her handbag higher up her arm, and the minister turned to Barrie with a smile.

"Please call me Jacob," he said. "I don't like to stand on ceremony."

"Jacob's father," Pru continued with a nod, "was the minister at the Baptist church in town back when I was still in school."

The pastor's approval made Barrie feel like the worst kind of fraud, and she was glad all over again that Eight wasn't there with her. He would have instantly known what a hypocrite she was. Edging closer to Pru, she linked her arm through her aunt's.

"It's a pleasure to meet you," she said as cheerfully as she could manage.

"I must say, it's nice to see the families coming together. Isn't that right, Cassie?" The minister slid a glance at Barrie's cousin as Cassie stopped alongside her mother, but then his gaze slid past Cassie along the path and locked on something that made his eyes dilate with surprise—or shock or some even less-pleasant emotion. Adjusting his wire-rimmed eyeglasses on his nose, he schooled his expression into polite indifference.

"Ryder," he said, nodding first at the man Barrie had seen at the bakery, and then at a weedy, thatch-haired guy who looked like he hadn't slept in half a week. "Junior."

Cassie jumped at the sound of the names. Whipping around, she simultaneously stepped backward, lost her balance, and fought to keep from stumbling. The movement left a scrape of red on the gravel that looked like blood, and for the first time, Barrie noticed that the soles of Cassie's cheap heels were red. Painted red.

Her throat aching suddenly, Barrie looked down at her own expensive red-soled Louboutins. Then her hands tightened into fists. Because feeling sorry for Cassie was the very last thing she could afford to do. She had made that mistake once already, and it wasn't as if painting the shoes came from a need for acceptance or a boost of confidence, not for Cassie. It came from the same self-centered jealousy that had driven her to steal Barrie's necklace—the kind of jealousy that had nothing to do with the Colesworth curse. Shoes had been far from Barrie's deepest desire the past few days. Or ever. Shoes were *shoes*. Fabulous but dispensable.

Fuming about the shoes distracted Barrie, and by the time she realized she'd lost track of what was going on, Cassie had slipped inside the chapel and out of sight. That left Marie to step in front of the two men who had come up the path.

"What are you doing here?" Cassie's mother ignored the

hand Ryder held out to her. Her voice was at least twenty degrees closer to frostbite than it had been before.

"Junior and I figured we'd pay our respects. Least we could do. I'd have sent flowers, but Wyatt wasn't the kind to hold with all that." Ryder's hand shook as he lowered it, but he nodded politely to the pastor and Jolene, who seemed to approve even less of him than she did of Cassie. Then his gaze landed on Barrie with an intensity that made her want to squirm. His eyes remained locked on her even as he continued speaking to Marie.

"Whatever's past is past. Colesworths ought to stick together," he said. "You let me know what you need around here, and I'll be round directly to take care of it. Mowing, fixing potholes, or shoring up the buildings, helping out any way I can."

"What makes you think anyone wants your help?" Jolene stepped up beside Marie. "You haven't been welcome here in years, so you turn right around and get out."

Marie put her hand on her mother's shoulder. "No, Mama. Ryder's right. Whatever disagreement he and Wyatt had, it's gone and done." Glancing through the doorway into the silent chapel, she shook her head, then turned back to Ryder and Junior with a smile that wasn't likely to fool anyone into thinking she meant it. "We're in no position to turn away friends or family, so you're welcome here," she added. "Both of you."

The pastor didn't look happy, either, but he cleared his throat. "I suppose we'd better get started, since we're running late."

Inside the chapel, he helped Marie to a seat in front of the casket. The mottled black swathes of sheeting added to the gloom, and it wasn't until her eyes had adjusted that Barrie thought to wonder where Cassie had gone. She found her pressed tight against the wall beside the door, staring forward at the coffin with her cheeks streaked with tears. Sydney was there, too, talking to her in a voice too low to hear. When Cassie didn't answer, Sydney took Cassie's hand and gently pulled her across the chapel to sit next to her mother.

Kicking herself, Barrie took a seat beside Pru in the row behind them. She should have realized that Cassie's rudeness had come from grief.

Shivering, Cassie sat staring toward the casket as if she was determined to block out everything except the reason for the funeral. Then Ryder Colesworth dropped into the chair on Cassie's right and leaned in to whisper something into her ear. She flinched away, jarring Sydney, who sat between her and her mother. In three-quarter profile Cassie's face was so pale, it had taken on greenish shadows, and Junior, the skinny, thatch-haired man who had come in with Ryder, gave a nervous giggle that made the minister turn with a frown as he took his place.

The service itself was short, the kind of send-off given to a man about whom one could say nothing good. Barrie couldn't help comparing it to her mother's service and the service she wanted to have, needed to have, for Mark. By the time the minister had concluded, she had been dragged back down into her memories a hundred times. Her hands hurt from holding them pressed together tightly enough to keep them from shaking in her lap.

The pastor closed the Bible, and the sound echoed off the chapel's walls. "I think we can go ahead and go," Pru whispered. "Marie's been through enough already without us sticking around for the interment."

Barrie would have liked nothing better than to have been gone already, but leaving without getting the chance to speak to Cassie would have defeated the whole purpose of coming. "Wouldn't that be rude?"

Marie Colesworth rose in the front row and dropped a crumpled Kleenex into her open purse. Whether by chance or because she'd heard Barrie's questioning, she leaned across the back of her chair. "Thank you both again for coming. I can't tell you how much it means to me to have you here."

Pru nodded without saying anything, and looked relieved when the minister came to confer with Marie about carrying out the coffin. Marie moved to speak with Ryder and Junior, who went to stand at either side of the casket, with Junior on the far end in front of Sydney. Cassie was still sitting in her chair.

"Cassie! Get up, girl. We're all waiting on you." Marie shook Cassie's shoulder, but Cassie barely flinched. Marie glanced back at Pru with another helpless flush, and it was Sydney who came and took Cassie's hand again, pulling her into place in front of Ryder. Cassie's movements were defiantly wooden and disengaged.

The minister exchanged a look with Marie. "I swear I don't know what's wrong with that girl," Marie said apologetically.

"Grief and embarrassment and a bit of shame, most likely," the minister said. "It's a difficult time to lose a parent. Not that there's ever a good time for that."

He and Marie both helped the four pallbearers carry the coffin. Outside, the temperature had climbed from sweltering to sixth-circle-of-hell in the brief time they had all been inside the church. There was no opportunity to leave gracefully, so Barrie and Pru followed the procession into the cemetery, where the pallbearers slid the coffin onto the rack draped in satin. Leaving it there, they went to take their seats in the row of chairs, and Pru and Barrie reluctantly did the same. Only Cassie lagged behind, standing beside the coffin while the tarp overhead crackled in a thin breeze that failed to dispel the hum of rogue mosquitoes. Seeing her sister still standing there, Sydney went to get her and led her back to sit beside their mother.

Cassie's head came up as she passed Ryder's chair. She looked as if she wanted to say something to him, but he lifted a finger to his lips in a gesture that made her go pale with fury. Sydney pushed her into her seat, and Cassie sat stiff and unmoving throughout the pastor's service. When it was over, Sydney had to nudge her up again.

Barrie understood grief. She still felt the numbness that refused to accept an impossible good-bye, and her own grief for Mark and Lula hit her at random moments. In this, she felt for Cassie. It was possible to both love a parent and hate what they had done, or miss them and realize you had never known them at all. But Cassie had set herself at center stage without so much as thinking that her mother, or even her little sister, might have needed *her* help and support. It was such typical Cassie behavior that it took away any sympathy Barrie might have felt, along with any compunction she might have had about bringing up Obadiah right after the service while Cassie was grieving.

Unfortunately, Pru seemed inclined to make talking to Cassie impossible. Rising the instant the graveside service ended, Pru collected her purse and nudged down the empty row of chairs behind the Colesworth family.

"Come on, sugar. Let's leave the family to their good-byes."

Without waiting for Barrie to respond, she turned back toward the moss-covered archway that marked the opening in the wrought-iron fence. Barrie couldn't think of any reason not to follow, so she walked very slowly.

"Wait!" Marie Colesworth called from behind them and hurried to catch up. "Ya'll can't go yet! Come on up to the house for a bit. Please? I swear, I've got food enough to feed six armies, and no one to come and eat it."

CHAPTER FIFTEEN

Marie's face was pale enough to reveal a spray of freckles across her cheeks and the bridge of her nose. They, along with the faded blue eyes and the gray strands beginning to thread through her hair, made her seem even more vulnerable. Catching Pru's questioning glance, Barrie gave a sedate nod she hoped would hide her relief at having an excuse not to leave.

"We can't stay too long," Pru said, "but we'd love to come."

Looking up, Barrie found Ryder and Junior staring at her as they approached. She moved off the path to let them pass, but they stopped beside Marie instead, and Ryder watched Barrie with his chin lowered and his arms folded to show biceps that had clearly spent too much time lifting dumbbells. He made her want to take a shower.

"Those two creep me out." She fell into step beside Pru on the way to the single-story home the Colesworth family had built to replace the mansion burned by Union soldiers in the Civil War.

"Best to stay as clear of them as you can," Pru said.

The whole house wasn't much bigger than the restored one-room chapel. Inside, though, antique furniture and bric-a-brac crowded every square inch of floor space apart from a narrow path that snaked across the room. Paintings hung on the walls from waist height to the ceiling. Expensive paintings.

Cramped as the house was, it wasn't quite a hoarder's lair. There was nothing out of place, no sense of haphazard, throw-away-nothing disarray. There was merely too much of everything, much too much, so that it left Barrie with the impression that she had crawled down Alice's rabbit hole.

"Come in, come in." Cassie's mother wended past an inlaid teak chest, an elaborately carved settee upholstered in indigo velvet, and several dozen lamps and tables that all stuck at odd angles into the path, making it hard to walk. After pausing at a side door, Marie invited them through into the kitchen.

There, they might as well have been in a different house. The counters were empty apart from a solitary coffeepot, and the walls around the table, refrigerator, and old-fashioned stove were bare of so much as a photograph.

Marie gave a small and self-conscious shrug. "I expect

you're shocked at the difference, aren't you? We don't get many visitors, so I forget how it must seem to people sometimes."

"It looks very nice," Pru said kindly.

"It doesn't. The emptiness just makes the rest more awful, but at least it gives me one place in the house where I can breathe." With a wry twist of her mouth, Marie crossed to the refrigerator and began clattering platters of mini sandwiches, a cheese plate, and a watermelon bowl out onto the counter as the minister and the others filed in behind them. Barrie and Pru helped Sydney move the platters to the table.

Jolene dropped into a chair and fanned her sweat-sheened face with her hand. "You'd think with all the money that man spent 'collecting' for the 'big house,' he could have bought a damn ceiling fan. Or air-conditioning." She nodded at the remaining chairs at the table and gestured for Pru, Barrie, and the minister to sit.

Marie popped her head up from behind the refrigerator door. "There wouldn't have been any room for the air-conditioning to circulate anyway, so there would have been no point."

Jolene offered empty plates to everyone and took one for herself. Leaning forward, she selected several dainty sandwiches from the platter and sat back again, waving her hand to indicate that Barrie and the others should help themselves.

"How many times," she said, speaking to Marie after taking a delicate bite, "did I tell you Wyatt needed to see a shrink? Not sure whether it was an obsession or a delusion, all this 'collecting,' but either way, they have drugs for that. And not the kind of drugs he was selling, either. When I think how useless it all was, squandering money fixing up chapels and slave cabins and buying antiques for a house he couldn't afford to rebuild . . . Now what's going to happen to you and the girls? The police'll haul all the expensive things away, and how are you going to sell this place? That's what I want to know. Who's going to want to buy it?"

Marie glanced uncomfortably from Pru to Barrie to the minister, narrowed her eyes at her mother, and then nodded her chin in Ryder's direction. "Mama, that's a conversation for another day . . ." she began, pausing as several car doors slammed simultaneously in front of the house. "Now, who on earth is that?"

The doorbell rang. Marie pushed past Ryder and Junior, hurrying from the kitchen and leaving a moment of suspended sound and movement in her wake that was broken as the kitchen door swung shut. Jolene sat a moment, then rose and followed Marie as curiosity got the better of her.

"Here's our excuse to go," Pru mouthed.

Barrie nodded, hoping that in the commotion, she could finally get in a word with Cassie as she said good-bye. Winding her way through the stacked furniture toward the front door, though, she couldn't find Cassie anywhere. She caught Pru's hand and hung back as they approached the door.

Standing in the doorway, a clearly agitated Marie was pointing her finger at an elderly man with a deeply tanned face shaded beneath a wide-brimmed hat. "I don't suppose Cassie thought to mention that we were burying my husband today?" Marie said with her voice rising. "The last thing I want to worry about is whether to let some archaeologist dig up my front yard."

"I apologize. That was my mistake." The man swept off his hat to show pale skin above the line where his brim had been. "When your husband turned me down after the tunnel collapsed, I never dared hope to have another chance, until your daughter called. It broke my heart to have to tell her I was already committed elsewhere, so she didn't know I was coming. *I* didn't know I was coming until I spoke to Andrew here"—he waved to one of the two men beside him—"and he told me he was willing to head up the excavation."

Andrew was younger than the man with the hat, late twenties maybe, and the guy beside him was obviously still a student. They both stepped forward, and Andrew held out his hand. "Andrew Bey, ma'am. I'd be very pleased to work on this for Dr. Feldman, and I'd be honored—"

"You're not honored, just greedy," Jolene stepped forward

and cut him off. "You're after the gold in the newspaper, same as everyone. Well, it doesn't exist. It's a figment of Cassie's imagination. I swear, that girl is as crazy as her father."

"All right, Mama." Marie nudged Jolene aside and smiled grimly at the older archaeologist. "I'm sorry y'all came all the way out here for nothing, but there's no point starting any kind of an excavation with everything up in the air like it is. That tunnel has been down there for three hundred years. It's not going anywhere anytime soon, so I can't imagine what got into Cassie to make her say you had to start right away. Now, where's she got to? She can apologize to you herself." Glancing around, she shouted, "Cassandra Marie Colesworth, you get over here right this minute! Where are you?" When there was no answer, she turned back to Sydney. "Where's your sister?"

"Back at the cemetery. She told me to leave her alone." Sydney's round face looked pale and worried. "She's been—"

"I don't care what she's been. Go and get her."

"I'll find her!" The words were out of Barrie's mouth before she'd even thought them through, and she slipped outside through the collection of people crowded around the doorway before Pru could stop her. She didn't look back. She knew Pru's expression would show betrayal, or confusion, or fury. Or all of the above.

"Mind if I come with you?" A male voice spoke beside her

as she reached the cemetery fence, and Barrie looked over to find the guy who had stood beside Andrew Bey. She hadn't heard so much as the crackle of a leaf while he'd been catching up.

She gave him a dubious smile. "I'm sorry. I need to talk to my cousin alone. It's why I came out here, honestly. No offense."

"None taken," he said automatically and politely.

He didn't look much like an archaeologist. He was probably only a few years older than Eight, but those extra years had etched white creases into the sun-browned skin around his eyes. His hair, in contrast, was white blond and cropped so close to his head in a military-style cut that it was barely longer than the stubble on his chin and cheeks. There was a sure and lethal cleverness, a sharpness, about him that Eight didn't have even after a lifetime of living with the Beaufort gift.

Sharp and clever was the last thing Barrie needed then, but the guy didn't seem to have gotten the message; he wasn't leaving.

"Can I help you with something?" Barrie stopped beside the low iron gate.

"I was hoping Cassie would answer some questions for me. Or you would."

"What sort of questions?" Barrie glanced back toward the house. Pru hadn't come outside yet, and Marie and the other two archaeologists were still deep in discussion.

"We could start with what's going on here, for one thing. I'm curious why someone would call and ask for an archaeological excavation when she should have been more concerned about her father's funeral. And why she would forget to mention there was probably seven or eight million dollars in gold buried down there. We had to read about that in the local paper."

Which were both damn good questions. Barrie reached for the gate and pulled the latch, saying, "I'm about the last person on earth who can explain why my cousin would do anything."

"You might be the perfect person, since you clearly don't get along." His hand shot out, and he held the gate in place.

Barrie turned slowly toward him. "Who did you say you were again?"

"I'm one of the archaeology students who's going to be working on the dig with Andrew." He grinned, and his smile was gap-toothed and probably charmed every girl he used it on.

It made Barrie more suspicious. "You don't seem like an archaeology student," she said.

"Well, to be fair, I've been other things besides a student." He didn't volunteer anything more except his name. "My name's Berg Walters, by the way."

"Barrie Watson," Barrie said automatically, wondering

how to get rid of him. "Listen, it's nice to meet you, and I really hope you can work things out with Cassie, but—"

"Watson? As in Watson's Landing?" Berg's focus sharpened as Barrie nodded, and he grinned a little sheepishly. "Andrew and Dr. Feldman would both kill me if I didn't ask if we could have a look at the tunnels on your side of the river. Andrew's called your aunt several times, but she hasn't called him back. It would be a big help to see the tunnels intact before we start excavating."

"*If* you start excavating, and you'd have to talk to my aunt," Barrie said, making a note to make sure Pru had no intention of agreeing. Even the thought of anyone crawling around in the tunnels beneath the house made Barrie feel exposed and vulnerable.

She was concentrating on getting away from Berg, so she didn't realize at first that Cassie was right in front of her. Halfway to the folding chairs set up by the grave site, Cassie sat huddled at the base of the moss-covered statue of an angel with an upraised fist.

Cassie was visibly trembling, rocking back and forth. Her eyes were fixed on the ground while tears streaked down her cheeks. Barrie ran forward automatically to help—and then she stopped. This was *Cassie*, who had fooled her. Lied to her. Manipulated her one too many times. Cassie, who was lying to the archaeologists now. Cassie, who lied to everyone.

Barrie took a sledgehammer to the wave of sympathy she had felt. "There are archaeologists here to see you," she said coldly. "They found out about the gold, and your mother is mad as hell. Also, I need to talk to you. Privately."

Cassie acted as if she didn't hear, as if Barrie didn't exist. She didn't even turn her head.

Molten rage swelled in Barrie's chest and throat until she was feverish with it.

"Stop it, you damn drama queen. We all get it. You're grieving. Well, other people are grieving, too. Your mother and your sister, for instance. You don't always have to be the center of attention." She reached out to shake Cassie, but Berg caught her hand before she could.

His eyes had softened, but his jaw and his voice had both gone tight. "Wait," he said. "Don't touch her."

CHAPTER SIXTEEN

Berg dropped into a squat beside Cassie, visibly concerned. "Cassie, can you hear me?" he asked. "You're safe. You're in your family's cemetery." He spoke softly and paused to give Cassie time to answer, but Cassie only continued rocking forward and back, her arms clutching her knees as if they were a lifeline.

Barrie bit off a snort of exasperation. "Of course she can hear you. She's faking."

"She's not reacting to us at all and her breathing is rapid. Her pupils are dilated—"

"She's an actress. You don't know her." Disgust stiffened Barrie's tongue and made the words come out thick and slow. "Trust me when I tell you that this is all a show for your benefit."

"I was in the Marines. I know a flashback when I see one," Berg said sharply. Then he turned his attention back to Cassie and reverted to the soothing tone he'd used before. "I need you to listen, Cassie. Just listen and focus and know that everything right now, in the present, is fine. My name is Mason Walters. Berg, they call me. I'm a student who came out with Dr. Feldman to talk about excavating your tunnel. You remember calling Dr. Feldman, don't you?"

Cassie was still rocking back and forth. Mascara had stained her cheeks, but her face was smooth and expressionless, as beautiful as ever. The tears brimmed and fell, eerily silent, designed to evoke Berg's sympathy. Barrie's sympathy.

Barrie refused to let them. She *refused*.

Easing back and looking thoughtful, Berg draped his hands across his knees. "Does your cousin do this often?" he asked Barrie. "Do you know what happened to her?"

Barrie felt the exasperation building. "She's a brilliant actress. That's what happened," she said, more as a reminder to herself than for Berg's benefit. "She's decided her usual tricks won't work, so she's trying something different."

She reached for Cassie's shoulder to shake her, but Berg put his hand on her wrist. "Don't." Shifting back onto his heels, he frowned as he studied Cassie. "Just speak to her. Talk about something she likes, something familiar. Ground her back in the present. I don't know her well enough."

Barrie didn't know Cassie at all. Not really. She knew too little and too much, and she couldn't think of what to say. Feeling sorry for Cassie just made her furious again.

How stupid *was* she? She couldn't fall for any more of Cassie's tricks. She'd promised Pru and Eight, but most of all she'd promised herself. She wasn't the same naïve idiot who'd let Cassie play her when she'd first arrived. How many times had she already let Cassie fool her?

Berg's expression grew tighter at her silence. Finally, he looked away.

"You don't usually see angry angels in a cemetery," he said to Cassie, using the same sure and quiet tone that Mark had always used on Barrie when she had a panic attack. "Did you sit by her because she happened to be here, or did you pick her because you like her? Focus on the angel, Cassie. Let her bring you back to the present, to the cemetery." He leaned in a little closer. "Is it all right if I touch you? I just want to remind you where you are."

Shifting forward, he very gently touched a fingertip to Cassie's waist, but she flinched and trembled harder, turning her face to him with expressionless eyes. He glanced at Barrie, who felt the full weight of his condemnation as if whatever was going on were somehow her fault.

How was Cassie making Barrie the bad guy here? And wasn't that just typical?

Berg turned back to Cassie. "I used to hate cemeteries when I was growing up," he said. "My parents are both archaeologists, and they would drag me around with them every summer. I spent most of that time thinking how stupid it was to spend your life digging around in the past. But the more I see of the world, the more I realize the past always sucks us back. Either we return to it voluntarily to study it and understand it, or we're doomed to repeat it. One way or the other, we can't escape." He paused, and Barrie couldn't tell whether he was giving Cassie time to respond or whether he was lost in his own dark thoughts. Then he sighed and looked back up at the statue above Cassie's head.

"My mother has a whole philosophy on funerary angels," he continued. "She claims that it's the angels who say the most about who the people really were. Maybe she's right. Anyone can write 'beloved' on a gravestone, but whoever put this angel here understood what it means to scream at death. To rage and let out all that anger no one wants to hear because it's too messy or too embarrassing."

Barrie studied the angel statue. The name and dates on the pedestal had long since worn away, and the marble features had been softened by storms and moss and years. But despite that, the angel's upturned face and defiant fist held a heaven-cracking fury.

The raw, awful loss that came from near the old mansion

made other losses hard to pinpoint at Colesworth Place. Coupled with the constant headache of being away from Watson's Landing, it played havoc with Barrie's gift. Looking at the statue, though, she realized the grave beneath it, not the open grave set for Wyatt, was the source of the pull she felt within the cemetery enclosure.

Probably the lack of an inscription had something to do with that.

Obadiah had mentioned that names were important. Barrie supposed everyone needed to be acknowledged, in life and in death. It was why the *yunwi* had needed her to find the skeletons in the tunnel beneath the river so that Luke and Twila wouldn't remain unburied and unacknowledged. Thinking of Luke and Twila, of Mark's unburied ashes in their urn, and of her own mother, whose request to have her ashes scattered had left her without a place of mourning, Barrie found her cheeks were wet again.

Berg was still talking steadily, but Cassie's rocking had begun to slow. Her head came up an inch. An instant later, her eyes focused. Seeing Berg right in front of her, she scrambled backward.

"It's all right, Cassie. You don't need to be afraid," Barrie said, intervening in spite of her resolution not to let herself get sucked back in. "Berg's trying to help you. He's one of the archaeologists who came out to talk to you about the excavation."

At the sound of Barrie's voice, Cassie turned her head. Her eyes were glassy and dead, both more and less present than when she'd been crying a minute ago, dead as if everything behind them had been burned away. They slid from Barrie to Berg, and then, predictably, the creases in her forehead smoothed. Wiping her cheeks with the backs of her thumbs, she schooled her face into one of her Scarlett O'Hara smiles. That was a kind of magic in itself, that ability to make the mascara streaks unnoticeable and make herself beautiful again with just a glance. There was a difference, though, from the Cassie that Barrie remembered. The dead eyes remained unchanged.

"Archaeologists?" Cassie focused her attention all on Berg. "I thought Dr. Feldman couldn't help me?"

If Berg was surprised by her response, he didn't show it. "He couldn't. He still doesn't have the time himself to excavate, but one of his grad students offered to supervise. Andrew's dying to dig here. We all are. So Dr. Feldman brought us out to talk to you about that and the gold."

"Oh, Lord." Cassie jumped to her feet. "Mama doesn't know anything about Dr. Feldman. I didn't get a chance to tell her." She took three running steps toward the house, but then as she saw the crowd by the front door, she stopped. The color bled from her face again, and she started to shake.

Berg was instantly beside her. "Don't go away on us again.

Focus on breathing and the sound of my voice. You're here and you're safe. You're standing in the cemetery, and your family is right there, a few steps away."

Cassie took a shaking breath. "I'm fine," she said, then her eyes closed and she shook her head. "God, what's wrong with me? It's like a movie, right there all over again, and I'm a deer in the headlights, frozen and useless."

Berg waited for her to go on, but she didn't. "You haven't had flashbacks before?"

"Flashbacks?" Cassie seemed to test the sound of the word, drawing it out before her expression abruptly hardened. "You know what? I've been through a lot the past few days." She sent a glare at Barrie. "My father is dead, remember? And I'm worried about keeping my house, and—"

"And you've just gotten out of jail," Barrie said. "I'm sorry about the house and your father, but don't make it out like you're the victim here. You're the one who locked me—and Eight—in the tunnel."

"You think *that's* what it's like to be locked up?" Cassie shuddered, as if even the mention of the word was more than she could bear. "Every little thing that happens is earth-shattering to you, isn't it? You have no idea what it's like to have your world destroyed. My father is dead. Do you get that? He might have had his problems, but he kept us safe. At least, he did his best." Her voice shook, and she turned away.

"Just go away, would you?" She stumbled back to the angel statue and slumped down with her back against it.

Berg went and crouched beside her again, leaving Barrie reeling. She was desperate to walk away from the unfairness of Cassie's words. From Cassie herself, because who needed more proof that Cassie was awful? But she couldn't leave. Nothing that had happened changed that.

Berg was still offering Cassie sympathy. "It's normal to want to lash out when you feel like this. Do you have someone you can call? Someone who can help?"

"'Someone'?" Cassie gave a bitter smile. "You mean like a shrink? Someone who'll *talk* to me? You know what would *help*? Having everyone give me some space. That would be fantastic. Can you make that happen?" She looked toward the house, and her mouth snapped closed on anything else she might have been going to say. "The best thing you could do for me is ask Dr. Feldman to start right away. In fact, if he wants to dig here at all, tell him he has to start tomorrow, or I'll find someone else."

"You'll have to deliver that message yourself." Berg watched Cassie steadily. "Anyway, you can't stay here alone. Whatever happened to you—"

"Nothing happened to me! Nothing that matters." Cassie raked both hands through her hair and pushed it out of her face.

"You don't have to tell me about it, but you shouldn't keep it in—"

"Keep it in? I've kept it in for *four years.*" Cassie laughed, a harsh, ugly sound. She stopped abruptly, as if only then realizing what she'd said, and she glanced from Berg to Barrie and back again before nervously licking her lips. "I was kidnapped, all right? But it was only for a couple of days, so it was no big deal. I've been fine. I am fine. I don't know why I'm even thinking about it."

"Did you see something that reminded you about what happened?" Berg asked.

"Reminded me? The whole day. Everything." Cassie sighed, looking genuinely confused and overwhelmed—as much as anything about Cassie was genuine. She cut another look at Barrie, and her chin quivered. She turned back to Berg. "I'm sure everyone in the whole state has heard that my father worked for a drug cartel. Everyone thinks they knew him, but he wasn't in it for the drugs. He needed money, and once you start working for the cartel, you don't ever get out. Daddy tried. Four years ago, when the tunnel collapsed, he told them he wanted out. They took me and kept me in a basement until he agreed he wouldn't quit."

Barrie thought back to the way Cassie had simultaneously controlled her father and feared him. The way Cassie had dismissed Wyatt at the Resurrection Tavern when he had intruded on their girls' night out because he couldn't resist coming to quiz Barrie on how much Lula had said about him. The way Wyatt had hit Cassie when he'd found out that she had invited Barrie over to find the treasure without his approval. The way he'd let Cassie come after Barrie to apologize for him so that Barrie wouldn't go to the police.

Watching Cassie shake off the hand Berg offered to help her up, Barrie couldn't help feeling a grudging drop of admiration for her cousin's strength.

Which made Cassie's breakdown even less believable.

It simply wasn't real. It was some angle that Cassie was playing. The performance might have been directed at Barrie, or it could have been for Berg's benefit. Either way, Cassie wanted something.

"I think you're exactly right," Barrie said to Berg. "Cassie needs someone to talk to. Why don't I give it a try?"

CHAPTER SEVENTEEN

Berg's expression was protective as he measured Barrie, as if Cassie were the one in danger. Which was the biggest joke of all. Not that Barrie could laugh about it.

He turned back to Cassie before he straightened. "You're sure you're all right?"

Cassie's hand tightened on the stone folds of the angel's gown. Her voice sounded tired. "Yeah. I'm just fine."

Berg turned and walked away. His footfalls were silent on the grass and weeds that had already grown too tall in the week since Wyatt's death. Everything about Berg was eerily quiet and controlled.

Barrie waited until he was out of earshot. "Cassie, I don't know what you're cooking up to cheat the archaeologists. That's your own business, and it's going to backfire soon enough. What I came to tell you is that I've found someone who can remove the curse."

Cassie's head shot up. "What do you mean 'remove the curse'?"

"I met a m-m-ma . . ." Barrie began, intending to tell Cassie about Obadiah, but the words to explain him wouldn't come. Her mouth felt as dry as sand, and her tongue felt too thick to form the word "man" or "magician" or even "guy." How was she supposed to convince Cassie if she couldn't explain? With a growl of frustration, she lowered herself to sit beside Cassie on the base of the angel statue.

Cassie scooted over. "Are you planning to say something anytime soon or do you expect me to wait all day?"

"Who's buried here?" Barrie asked while she furiously tried to think.

"Are you trying to stall? What are you up to?"

"I'm curious."

Cassie touched the same fold of the angel's gown that she'd been holding earlier. "Her name was Charlotte," Cassie said. "But she isn't actually buried here. She disappeared when the house burned down, and no one knows what happened. It's a romantic story, really. She was the most beautiful girl in three counties, and she promised to wait here for her fiancé to come back from serving with the cavalry. I guess she did, because the family never went away, even when they knew the Yankees were coming.

They say she was the inspiration for *Gone with the Wind*."

"*They* say, or you say?" Barrie dropped her gaze to the ground, where the rocks had faint flecks of red from the painted soles of Cassie's shoes. "See, this is the problem. You make it impossible to believe anything."

"You're the one who asked. And you're wasting time. You're supposed to be telling me about the curse, so talk fast, or I'm going to decide you don't have a thing to say that I'm interested in hearing."

Rising to her feet, Barrie dusted off her pants. "You know what," she said, "forget I said anything. You go ahead and keep the Colesworth curse. Enjoy it. I don't even know why I thought you would want to get away from here. You're going to have such a fabulous future."

She walked toward the gate, but as she'd suspected, Cassie didn't let her go five steps before jumping up to follow. "Wait," Cassie said. "Who is this guy you say you met?"

Barrie focused all her energy on getting the words out. "H-he says he's descended from the slave who cast the curse."

"It wasn't the slave who did that. John Colesworth got a slave from the West Indies to trap the Fire Carrier, and it was the Fire Carrier who cursed us."

"Or maybe the slave never told John he was the one who did it. Or, gee, here's a stretch—maybe one of your ancestors *lied* about how it happened."

"Or your guy is the one who's lying. My family has been trying to get rid of the curse for three hundred years."

"Maybe you've asked the wrong people all along. I've also heard that asking *nicely* works wonders."

Cassie peered at Barrie as if Barrie were the one who went around locking people in tunnels and stealing from them. "Why would I believe you even want to help me? You could be after the gold for yourself."

"I have no interest in helping you," Barrie said, taking the last couple steps to the gate, "but I want you to go *away*. Unless the curse is broken, I can either make sure you stay in jail suffering, or I can spend the rest of my life never knowing when I'm going to run into you at Bobby Joe's or the Resurrection."

Cassie recoiled, and then she laughed, a cackle that had nothing to do with her usual silvery peal of amusement. "Bless your heart, *Cos*. You've finally found the guts to be honest about what you want."

"You know what? You being stuck in jail is starting to sound not so bad to me right now." Barrie reached for the gate.

Cassie grabbed her arm, seeming to sense that Barrie's patience had run out. "All right, I'm sorry," she said. "It's hard for me to apologize when I mean it. And I do mean it. Locking you in the tunnel was wrong. I snapped, seeing you and Eight happy together—you both have so much already, and I don't have anything. The curse used to make me want to leave here, when leaving here—going anywhere else—was what Eight wanted most. I was all right with that because I wanted to go to Hollywood anyway. But then you came, and the thing *you* want most is to stay—and to be with Eight.

"Now suddenly I want to stay, and I want Eight, and I know that neither of those is what *I* really want, but knowing that in my head doesn't change what I feel. Do you understand how awful that is? It's like being possessed by someone else's emotions. On top of that, I'm stuck here on this stupid property because I get these headaches that make me want to die, and I might not be able to stay because we have to sell the place. And then today . . ." Cassie bit her lip and bowed her head.

Back at the house, the archaeologists were now clustered around the Prius in which they'd arrived, having what looked like a heated conversation among themselves. Cassie's mother and grandmother had Pru cornered just inside the front door, and Pru, looking like thunder, was staring fixedly in Barrie's direction.

"I'm going to have to go soon," Barrie said.

"Please." Cassie put her hands together to reinforce the word. "I can't leave Colesworth Place. If you know how to break the curse, then tell me. Help me. What did the guy say?"

Pleas had always poured out of Cassie's mouth too easily. In the past, Barrie had given in too easily.

"He says the curse is anchored in some kind of a lodestone that's buried here," Barrie said, relieved that she didn't have to try to say Obadiah's name. "If I find it, he says he can remove it—but it has to be done at night."

"Buried . . ." Cassie's expression hardened. "Are you stupid? He's after the gold."

Barrie's lips parted, but she couldn't deny it. It was a possibility. A probability.

Still, even if Obadiah *was* after the gold, it changed neither the carrot he had dangled in front of her nor his threat. She'd had a taste of his power, and a taste had been enough to convince her he could do as he'd warned.

"I've told you from the beginning that what's buried here doesn't feel like money," she said. "The loss I feel is darker and more personal than that, so it doesn't matter what he wants. Even if he is after the gold—"

"Hang on." Cassie snapped her fingers. "You're right. It doesn't matter. We don't even need this guy. The archaeologists are already here. You find the lodestone, and I'll tell the archaeologists that's where the gold is buried. Once they've dug up the lodestone, you can point them to the place where the gold is really buried. . . ."

Barrie's jaw hung slack. "Aren't you listening to me at all? I don't know where the gold is, and I'm not interested in finding it for you. As far as the lodestone goes, do you even know what it is? What it looks like? Because I don't. What if it's just some ordinary-looking rock and the archaeologists cart it off, or bury it again? Even if we could get it out, you would still need someone to remove the curse. Problem is, I'm not sure removing it would begin to cure what's wrong with *you*."

Thrusting the gate open with a creak and letting it bang shut behind her, Barrie left the cemetery and walked toward the house.

"All right! All right, you win," Cassie called after her. "We'll try it. Bring your guy over."

Barrie stopped walking, but instead of feeling victorious, she felt as if a noose had tightened around her neck and was cutting off all her air. And the thought of getting in a car or a boat with Obadiah by herself didn't help.

"He wants to do it soon," she said. "You'll have to come bring your boat over to get us."

"Tell him tomorrow night, then—eleven thirty. We'll have to wait until my mother's asleep, and you'll have to find your own way here." Cassie twitched up the hem of her wide red slacks to reveal a gray rubberized ankle monitor attached to a bulky three-inch box. "I get to wear this stylish new piece of jewelry until the final hearing, so all hell would break loose if I tried to get across the river."

CHAPTER EIGHTEEN

"Have you completely lost your mind?" Pru stalked toward the car, her handbag clutched tightly to her side. "I asked you to promise me you weren't going to have anything to do with Cassie, but here you are right back to trying to be her friend again."

"Going after her had nothing to do with friendship." Barrie had to hurry to keep pace as Pru skirted the cemetery back toward the parking lot. "I'm sorry I left you, Aunt Pru. I am, but I felt claustrophobic in the house with all those people arguing and all that furniture pressing in on me. Plus, didn't you see Cassie at the funeral? She was completely freaked out and no one noticed. They didn't even realize she wasn't in the house."

"She told Sydney to leave her alone," Pru said, more sharply than she had ever spoken to Barrie before. "I defy anyone to argue with Cassie, much less her poor sister who seems to want to do nothing except keep the peace in her family."

"Fine, but Cassie was having some kind of a breakdown when I got to the cemetery." Barrie was still convinced Cassie had been putting on an act, but the statement was true enough. Then she found herself adding another truth she hadn't realized she'd accepted. "I don't know what happened in jail, but it was something bad," she said. "Cassie also mentioned that the drug cartel had kidnapped her to force Wyatt to keep working for them. They locked her in a basement, and being locked up in jail, I guess it brought it all back up."

"That's awful if it's true. But I don't believe it for a second. You see?" Pru stopped and spun to look at Barrie. "This is exactly what I told you. You're falling right back into Cassie's web. What's she going to convince you to do for her next, hmm? I'm sure there's something." She peered at Barrie with spots of angry color high on both cheeks.

"What if it *is* true?" Barrie began, then held her palms up as Pru stepped forward. "No, hear me out. What if it really is the curse making the Colesworths do all these things? How do we know where something like that starts and where it ends? What's magic and what's the poison in the soul or the blood that warps the person and makes them change?"

"I don't know where it begins," Pru said. "What I do know is that plenty of other people are tempted to want what other people have, without locking their relatives in tunnels or holding them at gunpoint with plans to kill them." Not waiting for an answer, Pru marched to the car and threw herself inside.

Barrie got in more slowly. The heat from the scalding leather seats seeped into her skin, even through her somber clothes, and sweat ran in a rivulet down her temple as Pru turned the ignition over. Barrie rolled down the window and fanned herself with her hand while Pru backed out of the parking space.

"God, it's sweltering in here," Barrie said.

"Maybe we'll finally get some rain tonight." Pru rammed the gearshift forward and turned the wheel. "Now, don't try to change the subject. Trying to distract me with weather, not to mention kidnappings and curses. I have every right to be upset about you running right back to Cassie."

"I know you do."

"Do you? I'm not so sure, or you'd have stayed away." Pru lapsed into silence again. At the end of the drive, she turned the old Mercedes west onto the oak-shaded road that led along the river and back up toward the highway.

Barrie tried to catch a glimpse of Beaufort Hall as they passed the entrance a few minutes later, but there was only the wide white-iron double gate that rose in a graceful arch. Beyond it, another lane of stately oaks disappeared into the shimmer created by the heat and distance.

"Sugar, are you even thinking about what I said?" Pru's tone was a little calmer, but not much, and she was still flushed an angry red as Barrie's eyes met hers. "I honestly thought this was all over when Cassie went to jail, and here we are again. Today was a classic example of what that girl is like. She's barely even out of the detention center, and she's calling archaeologists to come and do what her father refused to let them do. Without telling her own mother. On the day of her father's funeral."

"I get that that was bad, but—"

"But nothing! She didn't even bother to tell the archaeologists *why* she was calling them. Imagine how they felt when they read in the paper it wasn't only a collapsed old tunnel but millions of dollars in missing Union gold."

"Not that the paper is necessarily right."

"In this instance, it happens to be exactly right. Checking historical records is the first part of any kind of an archaeological project. They checked the shipping manifests and the military records, all of it. Which you would know if you had stuck around instead of haring off the way you did."

"Honestly, I *am* sorry, Aunt Pru. I wish I'd never heard of any of the Colesworths, all right?" Catching herself about to admit her own frustration, Barrie stared straight ahead through the windshield. "Can we please not talk about it anymore right now? I have an idea that I wanted to tell you about. Something good for a change."

"I'm not sure my heart can take any more of your ideas." Pru ran her thumb along the steering wheel, then shook her head. "You know what? I don't want to argue with you today. Clearly I'm not going to convince you, and I have an idea, too." She sent Barrie a smile that was as close to brewing with mischief as Pru was likely to ever get. "I hate to admit this, but I've been thinking about this ever since we walked into the old stable yesterday, and seeing the buildings all fixed up over at Colesworth Place cemented it. What would you say if we got a couple of horses? Alyssa Evans always has a few for sale, so we could go have a look tomorrow and see what we think. Might even keep you out of trouble for a while."

"Horses? Really?" Barrie scarcely held back a squeal, but then she sobered. "Wait. Tomorrow? I've thought of a way to do the restaurant so we don't have to wait for the fuss to die down. That's what I was going to tell you. With that and the furniture coming, we wouldn't have time right now—and horses would be a lot of work."

Pru's smile took on the pre-Christmas-gift-giving glow that was even better than getting presents. "*Life* is a lot of work, if you live it right. The point is, you said something yesterday about choosing how we live our lives. So far, all I've done the last twenty years is wait and mark time and give up the things I loved and wanted. I've played it safe. I'm tired of doing that. I'd rather feel the wind in my hair. Wouldn't you?"

"Sure, if I thought it would be the wind and not the pile of manure I'm likely to fall into."

"You're still young enough that a few falls won't hurt you much." Pru gave the steering wheel a delighted little tap. "Good. That's settled then."

"At least wait until you hear my idea." Barrie pressed her palms tight against the seat. "Please? We could let Mary get back to work. And the restaurant was something you wanted, too, wasn't it?"

Pru turned onto the highway, guided the car onto the river bridge west of Watson Island, and then glanced over at Barrie. "All right. Tell me what you have in mind."

"What if we have dinners by invitation or lottery, where people sign up and we pick who gets to come? It would be more like a private dinner party, and we could bring guests in by boat and keep them from wandering around and sneaking into the woods or getting in trouble." Barrie turned in her seat, pushing away the seat belt that cut into her shoulder. "What do you think?"

"If they come by boat, the gate wouldn't even have to be open. We could still have dinner in the garden, as long as we keep an eye on everyone." Pru's eyes narrowed thoughtfully on the road. "Mary does need to get back to work. She won't take help, but I know she's worried."

Barrie grinned and flopped against the seat, letting her

head fall back. Then she sobered. "I'm sorry about the horses, Aunt Pru. I'd love to do that after the movers come and everything has settled down."

"Oh, doing the restaurant doesn't change what I want to do with the horses, sugar."

The highway ran along the north bank of the Santisto before turning north toward Charleston. Pru slowed to let a Walmart truck go past before she merged into the right lane to turn off onto the bridge that would take them back onto Watson Island.

"Like I said, I've been waiting my whole life for the things I want. Some of them I can't control," Pru said, "but bringing horses back to Watson's Landing is one I can manage. Don't you worry about how we'll find the time. Mary was looking forward to helping with the restaurant, and between all of us, we'll work out the details." Tipping her head, she raised her brows at Barrie. "The thing I don't understand is how, considering you're so damn dumb about Cassie, you can be so smart about other things."

CHAPTER NINETEEN

The downside to setting things in motion was how quickly they snowballed out of control. Pru was so excited about the restaurant that she insisted on calling Mary the moment she and Barrie got back to Watson's Landing. The three of them spent forty minutes on the phone, Pru and Barrie taking turns shouting into Barrie's cell phone while they made sheet after sheet of scribbled notes about tasks that needed to be done. Between that, a few tentative menus to be priced out, and their own dinner to prepare and eat, it was past ten o'clock before Pru retired to bed and Barrie finally managed to find some peace and quiet to call Obadiah.

Given how much the *yunwi* hated him, she hadn't dared leave the disk where they could find it. Standing in the relative privacy of her own room, she pulled the disk from her pocket and made herself ignore the way the *yunwi* immediately darted under the canopied bed and peered at her from beneath the bedskirt. A wordless screech vibrated in the air.

"I'm doing this to protect you," Barrie said. "So don't nag at me. What happens to you and Watson's Landing if Obadiah takes away the gift?"

Turning her back to them, she studied the disk and half-expected the raven to cock its head at her again, or to fly out from the disk to peck her hand. It didn't move, and after a wary moment, she flipped the coin over and felt both relief and dread on finding that the phone number hadn't disappeared.

She dialed, and eerily, Obadiah picked up before the phone had even rung. "You were running out of time, pretty girl. 'Soon' means soon. I was afraid you needed a better demonstration of why it wouldn't pay to cross me. You don't need a demonstration, do you?"

"No, but 'soon' means when it's *possible*." Barrie felt her nerves slip away, to be replaced by a strange calm at the sound of his cold, crisp voice. Obadiah seemed more human now that she was speaking to him during the semblance of a phone call. More normal.

Too normal. It didn't pay to forget he wasn't.

"What are you?" she asked, lowering herself onto the edge of the bed and gripping the carved post until it dug into her fingers. The slight pain helped to lighten the mist that clouded her mind, and she was able to think more clearly. "Are you a real person, or something else?"

"Once, a long time ago, I was as real as you are, the same as you are. Now? I'm not sure I know anymore. People do what they must to survive. We are forced to become things we never dreamed or asked to become. We live long enough to see things we never thought or wished to see." His voice was subdued as he spoke, and then he took a breath that seemed to tremble over the phone line, so that Barrie would have sworn she felt it against her cheek. For an instant, she thought he was sitting beside her, but when she looked, he wasn't there.

"What time do we go over tonight?" he asked.

"Not tonight." Nervously, Barrie traced the carved pineapple on the mahogany bed frame with her finger. "Tomorrow at eleven thirty. That was the best I could do, and I hope you can manage to find a boat, because I'm not planning to dog-paddle across that river ever again."

He was silent long enough that her heart gave a familiar panicked flutter, and then all he said was, "Fine. I'll meet you on the dock."

Barrie hadn't realized her shoulders were clenched until they suddenly relaxed, and then partly because she had already scared herself and partly because the silence was unnerving, she dared to ask what she'd been wondering ever since Cassie had brought it up.

"When you mentioned that the Colesworths had a debt to pay, did you mean the Union gold?" she asked.

She waited, but he didn't answer. There was no click and no dial tone, either, only silence on the phone and a pause long enough that she gradually became aware that Obadiah wasn't there. She wondered if he ever had been, and she peered around the room, wondering if he was hidden somewhere, playing games. But the *yunwi* were watching her with their eyes burning steadily in their faces and their bodies unusually still. They would have been more agitated if Obadiah had actually been in the room.

"God, I wish I knew what was going on," she said to no one in particular. She tossed the phone down onto the white embroidered quilt, and only when both her hands were empty did she realize that the green disk with the raven was gone again.

Gone.

She scowled at her hands, as if—if she stared hard and menacingly enough—the disk would simply reappear. . . . Because, who knew? It could. It might. She went hot, then cold, then hot again, shaken by fear, uncertainty, and determination, her body swinging through the emotional pendulum until she couldn't sit still any longer. Air. She needed air.

She ran to the balcony door and let herself out into the sticky night. She half-expected to find a raven standing on the balcony railing, but air and sanity slipped back into her lungs as she stood, shivering and barefoot. Clouds were gathering quickly, but between them the stars shone brightly. Out there, ripped-from-the-universe magic like Obadiah's wasn't only plausible; it was inevitable.

Possibly like Obadiah himself, some of these stars weren't even real anymore. They were suns that had long since died, leaving ghostly echoes shining through years and galaxies. How could there *not* be magic in a world where stars echoed through centuries and millennia?

Magic itself wasn't good or evil. Watson's Landing was magic at its best. Barrie was safe there; Watson's Landing would keep her safe, and she would keep it safe.

Across on the opposite bank, butterscotch light shone warmly from Beaufort Hall, and a figure stood in an illuminated window on the second floor. Eight. For all his resemblance to his father, Barrie could not mistake him. Her heart recognized the beautiful, sane shape of him even across all the distance. She raised a hand to wave, and he waved back, then turned and walked away. The light in the room winked out.

Elbows braced on the balcony railing, Barrie turned her head downstream to where the houses of the subdivision glowed against the skyline and spilled yellow onto the Santisto's darkling water. A pair of motorboats floated below the narrow creek that flowed into the wider river across from the Colesworth woods. She couldn't make out who was in them, or what they were up to, but a minute or two later, her curiosity diverted to a wavering beam of light threading down through the Beaufort garden to the river—Eight holding a flashlight and carrying something large, bulky, and awkwardly shaped. He threw the object onto the floor of the sailboat, cast off the *Away*, and puttered slowly toward Watson's Landing.

It never even occurred to her to move; that's how strange the whole day had been. Later, she would blame her inertia on moonlight or an entirely different form of magic, but she stood mesmerized by Eight's progress until he had docked and walked through the Watson garden to stand beneath her balcony and look up at her.

"I brought you something," he called. "Are you going to come down, or are you going to make me pull a Romeo?"

"Shhhh." Her voice broke along with her heart and the light from Juliet's balcony window. "Of course I'm coming down."

She listened at Pru's door and, after hearing nothing, raced down the stairs, out the kitchen door, and through the garden. At the back of the house, she veered off onto the section of lawn protected from the maze by a series of low boxwood hedges.

Her footsteps stuttered when she saw Eight again. The

sun loved his features and his coloring, but the cloud-drawn moon bathed him in shadows that were as much a part of him as his warmth. He held his arms out to her in the moonlight with an old car tire propped against his leg, and she knew she always—always—would love him at least to some degree. Some wants would never fade.

"Nice tire, baseball guy," she said, walking into his arms. "Not sure it's exactly the kind of *GQ* look you normally go for."

"*GQ*? Seriously?"

"Maybe I'd be more impressed if I knew why you had lugged it all this way?" Barrie said, but she could feel herself smiling.

"When we were in the chapel yesterday, I happened to notice there was something missing."

"That was only yesterday?"

"Yesterday and a lifetime." Eight picked up the tire and held his other hand out for her. "Come on. Let me show you."

He pulled her toward him again for a lingering sideways kiss. The warmth of his lips seeped into her. Savoring the moment, she couldn't help melting against him. Maybe his was the best approach, not to question, not to doubt.

She did doubt, though; she couldn't help it. And she didn't want her uncertainty to sour their relationship, which it would eventually. How could it not?

Most of all, she was determined not to let her insecurity

make Eight doubt himself. She pulled her hand out of his and reached up to cup his jaw, holding him, bringing him down until he could see her eyes in the clouded moonlight. "I'm sorry I doubted you," she said. "I'm sorry I doubted *us*."

Eight caught her hand in his cooler one and pressed a kiss into her palm before pulling her with him across the lawn and to the other side of the house. Shadows scampered alongside them like barely visible knee-high guardians.

Eight didn't say a word as they passed through the gate into the cemetery. Barrie tried to tell herself he had a reason for not acknowledging what she'd said, but it grew harder with every step.

"That's it?" She dug her feet into the grass and stopped. "I tell you I'm sorry I doubted, and I get total silence?"

"You want to have this conversation while I'm holding a dirty tire, or you want to have it when I can give you a memory that you can dust off and hold on to whenever you're pissed at me for something else?"

"You're thinking about creating memories?"

"Some moments are going to be memories no matter how we make them. This is one of them."

Was it possible to secretly smile so big inside yourself that your chest exploded from happiness? Barrie waved her hand at him with a surprising lack of care. "All right, fine. You may commence with the memory-making anytime you're ready."

His answering grin made her stumble. "In case you've forgotten, I'm limited in what I can say, because you told me not to use the word. I'm just going to have to show you." He turned on his heel before she could answer, and sauntered off whistling "Build Me Up Buttercup," as much as any guy could saunter while carrying a giant rubber tire.

CHAPTER TWENTY

Eight removed a rope and a powerful flashlight from the cavity inside the tire and propped the latter on a thick branch of the tree that grew inside the chapel. Once the area was better lit, he threw the rope over a high branch, then lashed it around the tire in multiple loops before pulling it taut and testing his weight on the rope to make sure it held. With a sudden movement, he dove to his waist through the opening of the tire and hung suspended off the ground with his arms on one side and his legs on the other.

Barrie's heart ricocheted off her ribs at the unexpectedness and the Eightness of it. "A tire swing?" she asked. "You didn't seriously make me a tire swing in the middle of the night?"

"Is that a good thing or a bad thing?" Eight let his legs drop back to the ground and backed himself out of the swing, looking uncharacteristically uncertain.

"That depends on why you did it," Barrie said cautiously.

"It seems like all we've done is fight lately, so I wanted something we couldn't argue about. Also, after the one driving lesson I gave you, you said there were too many things you hadn't done yet. You were going to give me a list so we could do them."

"I haven't had a chance to make a list."

"Have you ever swung in a tire swing?"

"Not yet."

"We'd better change that, then." He caught her waist and lifted her into the swing. His face was shuttered as he steadied her, and then he stood in front of the swing and put his hands on her shoulders across the top of the tire and pulled her close. His eyes were focused on hers so intently, she thought he must see every neuron firing in her brain, every nerve cell jigging breathlessly at his proximity.

"Even if I go to USC and I date every girl in Southern California," he said, "I'm not going to find another girl like you. Not in a year, or ten, or even a hundred years. I'm not stupid enough to let that go without a fight, so whatever assurances you need, I'll figure out how to give them to you." He tossed her one of his careless smiles. "I've been out with enough girls to know what I want. I *know*. You and me together? We're not the same plain vanilla let's-date-while-we're-in-high-school, let's-go-to-prom, let's-promise-we'll-talk-in-college relationship. We're more like those fireworks on the Fourth of July that keep exploding with new bursts every time they're done. Before we know it, we'll be in rocking chairs side by side on the porch, holding hands and watching a houseful of great-grandchildren chasing blue ghost fireflies on the lawn."

"Blue fireflies?"

"They're real and they're rare, which is the point I'm trying to make." Eight pulled the tire swing even closer, his head tipped forward until his mouth was less than an inch from hers. "You asked me a while ago what I really want. I want time to learn to understand you, every insecurity in your brain, and every gallant, aggravating impulse."

An imaginary orchestra had begun to play inside Barrie's head, some golden, epic song with drums and crashing cymbals and joyful violins. She wished she could tell Eight what she was planning, tell him about Obadiah and the lodestones and trying to break the Colesworth curse. Mostly, she wished she could tell him there was a chance to give him what he wanted. But what if it didn't work? She couldn't bear it if he was disappointed.

"I'm a girl," she said. "You're not supposed to understand me."

"Most girls are all too easy to understand. People usually want the same petty things, for the same boring reasons." He leaned even closer until the words were whispered against her lips. "The fact that I don't understand you may be what I love about you. I'm not going to change my mind about that. Give me credit for having a few brains in my head to go with my undeniable good looks and charm."

"There's that self-confidence deficit disorder again."

"But you believe me now."

It was starting to rain, and Barrie tipped her head up to the sky, hoping it wasn't going to be a long or heavy shower. They couldn't end the conversation here. She didn't want the night to end.

"Lift up a bit. Hold on to the top of the swing." Eight reached back into the space inside the tire and, with a flourish, pulled out a red umbrella. "You see? I came prepared. I should have been an Eagle Scout."

Barrie laughed; she couldn't help it. "I have to admit, you don't seem like a red umbrella kind of guy."

"But *you* are exactly the kind of a girl who needs a red umbrella."

"What kind of a girl is that? The kind who doesn't want to get wet?"

"The kind who ought to come with a warning label."

Barrie opened the umbrella high above her head, liking the image of herself as a warning-label sort of girl. "So are you going to push me," she asked, "or what?"

Eight's teeth flashed in the beam of the flashlight, and he

took several steps back, pulling her higher, until he let her go with a shove so that she flew, not too hard and not too fast, but just enough to be a little exhilarating, a little wild, flying high in a tire swing in a cemetery in the dead of night with an umbrella she had to balance to keep right-side up. She flew, and Eight pushed her higher, but never so high or so hard that she was afraid he wouldn't catch her, rocking her physically the way he always managed to rock her emotions.

The thought sobered her, and she grew aware of the stillness, the silence broken by the distant mumble of the river and the hushed rustle of rain on leaves and stone. With that unerring sense of time she was starting to recognize, she knew it had to be close to midnight, close to the witching hour.

"Stop," she commanded.

"Had enough?"

"Yes, and no, and never," she said. "But let me down."

He stopped the swing, leaned on it with both elbows, and kissed her again, slowly and carefully, as if she were made of sugar that might slip away through his fingers.

He took the umbrella and held the swing steady while she shimmied out onto the ground. Then he strode beside her when she hurried out the arched doorway of the roofless chapel and out into the cemetery, past grave after grave after Watson grave until she could see the river.

The Fire Carrier hadn't reached the water yet. Already,

though, the orange glow seeped through the trees and lit the low-hung weeping clouds, and whoever was in the two boats on the river had moved in closer, one of them standing up in the prow of the boat and seemingly in danger of tipping over. Barrie stopped beside a tombstone guarded by a sleeping lamb, and watched the witch's flames wend through the trees.

"What are you doing?" Eight asked.

"Do you see him?" She nodded toward the Watson woods. The glow was so clear to her, it was inconceivable that it wasn't visible from miles away. "The Fire Carrier is coming."

"I see a faint light. But we've talked about this." Eight watched her with that heart-piercing, breath-stealing intensity.

She turned away from the questions, the sympathy in his eyes.

The rain was still coming down, drops plummeting through the trees and smelling inexplicably of licorice. In the beam from the flashlight, they looked like liquid moonlight clinging to Eight's eyelashes and collecting in his hair. The red umbrella seemed to hold the only color, making the night black and white and red.

"I've thought of something else that ought to be done at midnight when it rains." Eight slipped his arm around Barrie's waist and drew her closer. "You should put it on your list."

"I think you've seen one too many old movies. You're not going to sing, are you?"

"*We* are going to *dance*. It's an imperative. You have to waltz in the rain once in your life, and neither of us has done it yet."

His chin fit neatly on the top of Barrie's head. She knew the steps; Mark had loved to dance, and Eight swept her into the movements with all the authority of a hundred cotillion lessons.

It occurred to her that all the bad parts of life, the sad parts, the frightening ones, were meant to be offset by moments and memories like this. She had to be present in it, right here, right now. Too often, people didn't have the opportunity for even a single one.

Mark hadn't.

"*We* will, Bear," Eight whispered. "We'll have a lifetime of them."

Barrie wanted to believe him. In that moment, the urge to tell him about Obadiah was overwhelming, but the dry mouth and painful stickiness in her throat at the thought of Obadiah's name reminded her that she had made a promise. Whatever it took, she decided, even if it meant doing what Obadiah asked of her, she was going to find a way to make him break the Beaufort gift while leaving hers intact.

Eight drew back and studied her, as if he'd caught what she was wanting. She concentrated very hard on only wanting *him*, wanting his lips on hers, wanting his breath and his skin and his heat and his touch.

His hands slid back around her waist, burrowed beneath her shirt until the bare brush of his thumbs raised goose bumps across her stomach. Just looking at her like that, he produced so much want, it threatened to short-circuit her brain.

Fisting her hands in his shirt, she pulled him closer and stood on her toes to reach him. "Why are you standing there instead of kissing me?"

"Well, when you put it that way." His smile was lazy against her lips, and his kiss began painfully, excruciatingly slow. Barrie's heart thundered so loud, she suspected he had to hear it. She pulled him even closer.

He lifted her, anchored her while she wrapped herself around him as if she could eliminate the last millimeters of distance, because even those were too much. His heart beat fast, loud, and deep, and his breathing was as ragged as her own. He burned a trail of kisses across her jaw and down her throat and every cell in her body came alive beneath these kisses, woke in ways she had never even suspected a person could feel.

And she knew.

She *knew*.

No matter what else transpired, she and Eight deserved to have a chance together.

Whatever it took, she had to make that happen.

CHAPTER TWENTY-ONE

Keeping a grip on that decision was harder once Eight had gone back across the river. Barrie tiptoed back into her room, wondering if he was smiling, too, wearing the same kind of boomerang grin that kept coming back to her as she thought about dancing with him in the rain.

But what was he going to do when he found out they had spent most of the night together and she hadn't told him about her plans or mentioned Obadiah? She hadn't even told him she and Pru had been to the funeral. She could have—should have—told him at least that much. Obadiah had been clever to tie the incentive of removing Eight's gift with the threat of taking away her own. If she told Eight, or even Pru, they would be all too happy to have Obadiah do as he had threatened. They hated the magic and the gifts, but finding things had been a part of Barrie as long as she could remember. The binding, that was new. It had come only once she'd arrived at the plantation after her mother's death—after Barrie had finally started listening to what Watson's Landing and the *yunwi* were trying to say. Neither Pru nor Eight had ever felt that connection to the land, to the *yunwi*, and the magic, so how could they understand what losing it would mean?

The main difference between this second encounter with Obadiah and the first was Barrie's ability to remember. He had to be confident that his threat would work—and that made her even more worried about what would happen if he did take away her gift. And about what he wanted in the first place. She almost wished he had taken away her memory of him again. Maybe then she would have felt less like she was betraying Eight and Pru by keeping what she was doing from them.

Still weighing his motives the next morning, she went downstairs to find Pru and Mary already bickering cheerfully at the kitchen table, their chairs drawn close together. As fast as Pru was writing, Mary was leaning over and scribbling things out.

"No cold soup." Mary scratched out the latest line Pru had jotted in the menu notebook. "Folks'll want good Southern food."

"Not at the prices we're going to have to charge. They'll want something more special."

"Cold raspberry soup isn't special. It's stuck up, and raspberries don't keep."

"They do if we stick to local vendors." Pru carefully erased the scratch marks. "Anyway, there's nothing wrong with a good chilled soup in the summer."

Barrie stopped just inside the swinging door. "You're working on the menu without me?"

"Morning, sweetheart." Pru smiled at her. "You look tired. Did you sleep well?"

Barrie shook herself and crossed to the coffeepot. She poured a cup before turning to brace her hips against the counter. "I thought Eight and I were supposed to be in charge of the menus and the decorations," she said, keeping her voice steady, "and you two were going to do the business stuff?"

Pru and Mary exchanged a glance. "We're just figuring out the framework. That, and all right, we did get excited and carried away with everything. Come sit down with us and help." Pru patted the chair beside her. "Later, though, once Eight gets here, I need you to do me a favor. Mary's granddaughter is going to do the website for us, but she'll need a ride over after she's got someone to watch the rest of the kids."

"Sure." Sipping her coffee, Barrie wondered what parallel universe she'd wandered into where Pru knew about websites, but then she realized the idea had to have been Mary's. She peered over Pru's shoulder at all the lines Mary had scribbled out and did her best to swallow down the feeling that she'd been left out and pushed aside. Of course, she wanted Mary and Pru to be excited. She wanted them to feel the restaurant was theirs. She just didn't want to feel like it wasn't hers or Eight's anymore.

"Eight and I had talked about doing elevated Southern food," she began.

"What kind of a word is that? 'Elevated'?" Mary sniffed as if the word itself were rancid. "Tourists want somethin' that'll make them think of what might've been served here. That's what's always worked in the tearoom."

"But we don't just want tourists," Pru said, then she and Mary both glanced at Barrie and then instantly looked away, guilty as hell of something.

"What have I missed?" Barrie set down her coffee cup. "Is there a problem you don't want to tell me about?"

Pru fidgeted with the pencil. "When I was thinking all this through last night and then talking it over with Mary this morning, it struck me that we don't want to have to rely on tourists. Especially not at first, with all that's going on. But if we do it right, people will come from Watson's Point and Charleston for the romance of dining out here. For special occasions. If it works, we could keep it going all year round."

Pru's expression was both eager and wary, and Barrie tried

to grasp the many decidedly *un*enthusiastic thoughts that were chasing one another through her head. One of them was that it would be hard for something to keep feeling magical when you had to do it day in and day out . . . forever.

But that was selfish, and she wouldn't allow herself to be that petty. "I'll try, but I'm not sure I'll be able to help out as much once school starts."

"We wouldn't expect you to!" Pru swiveled in her chair. "I know Mary and I have taken your idea and run away with it. Of course, you can help as much or as little as you want, and we can hire a chef for most nights of the week."

Barrie felt small and petty for not being able to summon up the enthusiasm her aunt so obviously wanted. She thought of Pru and Mary when she had first opened the door a few minutes ago, their cheeks flushed and the words flying between them.

"No," she said, cheerfully. "It sounds like a great idea." She reached for one of the apple turnovers Pru had set out on a platter.

How had she managed to, once again, lose control? There were too many things going on that threatened to overwhelm her. The restaurant was supposed to be the fun thing. Maybe that was the risk. When going after life with a pitchfork, occasionally you were bound to catch something bigger than you expected.

Dropping into the chair beside Pru's, she made herself concentrate on the list of menu options that were already written down:

chilled raspberry soup

crab soup

tomato, roasted corn, and boiled peanut salad

mesclun salad with goat cheese and candied pecans

fried green tomatoes

pickled shrimp plate

shrimp and grits

bacon and cheddar hush puppies

Those were just the appetizers.

"At the restaurant Mark and I went to, they had only one or two dishes and everyone ate family style. That was part of the fun," she said.

"We'll have Seven and Eight to help us read people to see what they really want to eat. Then we can narrow it down and create a smaller, more permanent menu."

"Seven?" Barrie's head came up. "What does he have to do with it? Having a restaurant was Eight's fallback plan for after he retired from baseball. That was what first got me thinking about having a restaurant at all."

"We're not trying to take that away from Eight." Pru and

Mary shared another look. "Seven just pointed out that Eight won't be here once college starts, and with the delay, we'll barely be getting established by then. We don't want you two bogged down with all this. You need time to enjoy yourselves, and you've said yourself that Eight hates using the gift on people."

Teeth clamped firmly to her tongue, Barrie pushed back her chair. She needed a minute to get her equilibrium back, or she was going to say something she might end up regretting. "I think I'll go get my sketchpad and try to work up the logo for the flyers and the website. "

"You're not upset, are you?" Rising along with her, Pru put her hand on Barrie's shoulder. "I thought you liked Seven. I know he can be a little . . . overwhelming sometimes."

"Sometimes?" Barrie asked.

Pru's cheeks went pink. "Most of the time. But he means well, and he wants to help. We both agreed that we don't want to put too much of a burden on Eight."

"He doesn't want to give Eight any incentive to stick around here, you mean."

"He wants Eight to have some experiences before he's stuck here for good."

"Experiences that don't include me!" Barrie strode toward the door before she said something that opened up a whole big conversation she couldn't have with Pru. Then Pru's words sank in, and she turned back around. "Seven told you about the binding, didn't he? He told you Eight doesn't know, and instead of being mad that Seven's basically doing the same thing to Eight that Emmett did to you and Lula, you're on *his* side."

"There's a world of difference between Seven and Emmett: Seven wants what's best for Eight."

"Too bad he doesn't seem to have a clue what that is." Leaving Pru standing behind her with the door propped open, Barrie stalked down the corridor and up the stairs, feeling more pushed into a corner with every step, and at the same time even more determined.

She would find the lodestone for Obadiah, and when the threat to the Watson gift was gone, when he had proven he could safely remove the curse without hurting anyone, she would do whatever it took to get him to help Eight. She wasn't going to feel bad about Cassie's gold, even if that was what Obadiah was really after. The gold wasn't even there.

What would he do when he realized Barrie couldn't find it?

Pondering that along with all the other questions, Barrie found it hard to feel creative or even patient once she got back to the kitchen. Twenty minutes later, crumpled sketchbook pages spilled over the table and onto the floor, and she'd had enough of Pru and Mary bickering over table placement and the choice of hush puppies or shrimp and grits.

She balled up her latest attempt at drawing a logo and tossed it aside. "You're turning this into something that sounds exactly like every other restaurant. We don't need a menu with fourteen appetizers, or the same entrees that anyone can order up in Charleston. It should feel special. Like a celebration."

"It will," Pru said.

"When I told you about the idea and said it should be more like a private party, I meant the menu, too. We could greet people with champagne on the dock when they first arrive, and serve bite-size hors d'oeuvres at different stations on the path up here to the porch."

"Why the porch? It wouldn't be as magical. The garden has the twinkle lights laced through the trees. . . ."

"There are lights on the underside of the balcony, and we can add more. Not to mention the candles and lights on the water. We could still have dessert and dancing by the fountain, too, but having the tables up here would give people less time to wander around unsupervised."

Pru pushed back her notebook. "I do love that idea."

"It would be like throwing a dinner party three nights a week, instead of serving the same thing every night. We'd get to cook something different all the time. That was what Mark and I loved best about trying out the new restaurant recipes we made. Every meal was a surprise."

Barrie thought of Eight as she said the words. Remembered dancing in the rain with him. Remembered floating through the air not seeing where she was going, not needing to see.

Sometimes, not knowing how things would turn out was half the fun.

A night scene in the garden snapped into focus in her mind: the path, the trees, and the river all lit up. She was hunched over her sketchpad with her pencil, feverishly drawing a logo when Eight and his sister knocked at the kitchen door a scant second before letting themselves inside.

CHAPTER TWENTY-TWO

Kate Beaufort looked very little like Eight or Seven. Her enormous brown eyes filled her narrow face, and her mouth was always on the verge of laughing. Everything about her was edged with barely contained energy, like a coiled-up spring. Her movements, though, had the same athletic grace as Eight's, and like him, she was sun-browned as if she spent innumerable hours outside.

"It's great to meet you finally," she said to Barrie, plopping herself down at the table and picking up the various notebooks to have a look. "Daddy and Eight have been talking about you nonstop. It's like they don't even care that I'm home, and then Daddy spent half the morning calling around trying to find a satellite dish and someone to put it in so you could have Internet. It was starting to give me a complex."

"Ignore her, Bear. Kate's been a natural whiner and a daddy's girl since the day she was born." Eight reached for a plate and scooped out one of the last pieces of apple turnover.

"Trust me." Kate grinned and shook her head. "I'm the last person who's going to whine about Daddy managing someone besides me for a change." She snatched a piece of the turnover off Eight's plate and popped it into her mouth.

He swatted her hand away. "Get your own, would you?"

"Borrowed calories don't count," Kate said. "If I take some of yours, I'm saving you from getting fat, and I'm not endangering my own waistline."

"There's genius thinking for you."

"I prefer to think of myself as a nonlinear thinker."

"That's on the rare occasions when you bother to think." Eight stuffed the rest of the turnover into his mouth to keep Kate from taking any more.

A flutter of envy hit Barrie low and hard. Cassie should have cured her of wanting a sister, but she wondered if she would ever stop feeling a twinge every time she ran into a relationship as easy and trusting as this. But then she remembered that nothing was ever as easy as it seemed. Even before their mother died, Pru must have been in Seven's heart, casting a shadow across their seemingly perfect family.

Was it possible to love two people at once? Or did Seven only remember he wanted Pru when he was near her? Barrie wondered if that was another consequence of the Beaufort gift. Maybe his wife wanting him had made him forget about Pru. Maybe he had wanted to forget.

Or had it been simpler than that? When Lula had run away and Emmett had told everyone she was dead, Seven must have believed Pru was going to inherit the Watson gift.

Had he given Pru up the same way he wanted Barrie to give up Eight?

The thought knocked Barrie back into her chair. Feeling fractured, she tried to consider the implications. Had Seven married someone else because he'd assumed Pru was out of reach?

If that was the case, then there wasn't any reason they couldn't be together now.

Listening absently as Pru and Mary explained the new restaurant idea to Eight and his sister, Barrie found Eight watching her. He edged closer and said, "You all right there, Bear? You look a little shell-shocked."

"Shocked" was a good word for it, and mad, and hurt for Pru. Because Seven had just given up.

But she couldn't say any of that to Eight.

"I'm going to have to give you a quota of how many times a day you're allowed to ask me that," she said instead. "I'm thinking 'none' would be a good starting number."

He laughed and held up his hands. "I promise, I won't bring it up again."

"You keep making promises, and yet no results. . . ." She smiled at him fiercely and climbed out of her chair. "I need a ride into town, baseball guy. Mary wants us to pick up her granddaughter so she can do the website."

Leaving Kate to help Pru and Mary, Eight followed Barrie out into the corridor and grabbed the keys to Pru's ancient boat of a Mercedes off the side table in the foyer. Outside, he caught Barrie's arm, spun her toward him, and pulled her close while her pulse sped up with dread and excitement.

He bent his head and slowly kissed her.

Barrie wanted to fall into him, her lost to his found, her need to his want. Kissing was like the physical form of magic, all potential and the sense that anything might happen. When she was kissing Eight, she felt as if she could fly.

His hands slid to her back, and his thumbs, uneven and warm against her skin, seemed to center all sensation there, as if the slight roughness from his calluses made the contact that little bit more dangerous.

Pulling back, she was glad he was breathing hard, too. "What was that for?" she asked.

"I can't be happy to see you?"

His voice held an odd note. She tilted her head and studied him. "Are you?"

"Of course. I'm also mad as hell that you didn't tell me you were going to the funeral." His eyes deepened to a darker green.

Barrie suddenly found her shoes very interesting. "Gossip on Watson Island is very efficient."

"Our housekeeper is Pastor Nelson's second cousin. Dad's livid that Pru didn't tell him before she went over there." Eight walked down the steps and waved the white peacock off its usual perch on the hood of Pru's Mercedes.

"Seven doesn't know everything—and Pru doesn't have to tell him what she's doing. She's done just fine without him for twenty years."

Something cracked behind Eight's eyes, leaving him vulnerable. He looked away, but not before Barrie saw it. "He does like to think he knows what's good for people. But that's how he is. No one's going to change him."

"Did you two have a fight?" Barrie asked warily, and when he didn't answer, she pressed him again, feeling guilty but, at the same time, justified. Because Seven needed to come clean. "Was it because you asked him about the gift?"

"He's been lecturing me nonstop about going to California. Like I'm too stupid to figure out what's best for my future."

He started to slide his hands into his pockets, then raised them in a helpless gesture of exasperation instead. "All this time he's been pushing me to stay, wanting me to stay, and suddenly he says I need to get away from Watson Island, and I'm supposedly the one who doesn't know my own mind? Sometimes I really hate him."

Barrie laid her palm against his cheek. "I know he doesn't think you're stupid. No one could think that—"

"He told me he won't pay for school at all unless I go to California. Also, he told Pru *he* would help with the restaurant so you can keep it going all year round, since I won't be here."

The dullness in Eight's voice and the brokenness of his expression brought an ache to Barrie's throat. The words all tangled together as she searched for how to explain Seven's motives in a way that wouldn't hurt Eight even more.

"You know what? Do me a favor and don't let's talk about him," Eight said. "I need some time or I'm going to implode— Thank God you, at least, are finally getting it. You are getting it, right? I'm not leaving, Bear. I don't want to. I know I don't want to."

Numbly, Barrie nodded. Eight kissed her palm, then went around to slide into the driver's seat of the Mercedes.

The car had been parked in the sun, and the air inside was scalding. It seared Barrie's lungs, but maybe it wasn't the heat that made it hard to breathe. It was the fact that she had missed another perfect opportunity to tell Eight *why* Seven had changed his mind.

She had to find a way to make Seven tell him.

She and Eight talked about the archaeological dig as they drove, and about Berg, and Cassie's flashback, and the horses and the details of the restaurant plans. Eight told her about Kate arriving back from camp with less than half the clothes and things she'd started with, because somehow people had needed them, or borrowed them and never given them back to her.

"Dad about had a conniption. She's always giving things away," Eight said.

"Didn't she know the people didn't want to return them?"

"Of course, but that's Kate. She doesn't care. She'd give the shirt off her back to anyone who asked her for it. Reminds me a lot of *you*. You're both good at ignoring the fact that people are up to no good, and *you both* insist on giving them the benefit of the doubt."

Flushing, Barrie rubbed her temple and stared out the window as they drove into a part of town she hadn't seen before. The clapboard houses were smaller and closer together, low single-story homes set on pocket bits of lawn shaded by old pine trees that overshadowed the buildings beneath them. Pine needles made the grass spotty and sparse, but lawn sculptures and window boxes of potted geraniums and big clumps of bougainvillea provided bright pools of color against the starkly painted wood and brick.

At the house where they pulled over, the front door opened as Eight cut the engine, and Daphne came out onto the stoop wearing shorts and a loose gray College of Charleston T-shirt. Her smile as wide and elfin as before, she put up a finger to signal them to wait and turned back toward the house, where a girl in a motorized wheelchair waved through the darkened doorway at them.

Barrie waved back, but before she could get out of the car, Daphne was already bounding down the steps in a flash of limbs. "Sorry." She dove into the backseat and shut the door behind her. "Jackson has ball practice, so I had to wait for someone to come and stay with Brit. Also, Eight, Jackson says if you're sticking around, he wishes you'd come coach Little League, because the coach they had last year sucks. That's an exact quote, by the way." Leaning over, she grinned at Barrie. "I've got to tell you, this restaurant idea is brilliant. I haven't seen Gramma Mary this excited since she first heard you were coming home."

Eight backed down the driveway, and after the initial burst of small talk had dwindled into a slightly awkward silence, Daphne pulled a laptop out of her backpack. "So, you have a design you want to do for the website?"

Barrie called up a mental picture of the logo she had

drawn. "I want it to look like a paper cutout. A gray background with dark branches illuminated with fairy lights, and a big, round moon across the banner. And the name 'Magical Nights.'"

Eight glanced at Daphne in the mirror. "I didn't realize you're a web designer."

"A programmer." Daphne didn't look up from the laptop screen. "At least, that's what I want to be if I can figure out how to get through school. Gramma has her heart set on me being the first college graduate in the family no matter what."

Daphne didn't specify, but Barrie suspected "no matter what" had to do with money. That was a legitimate reason for Mary and Pru to push so hard for the restaurant to stay open and be successful.

"What if we opened the restaurant on Thursday nights, too? Would that help?" Barrie asked, feeling guilty for having been selfish.

"I'm not sure anything would 'help,'" Daphne said. "Every time I think we've got ourselves figured out, something else goes wrong."

CHAPTER TWENTY-THREE

At nine thirty, after several hours of debating a thousand details for the restaurant and the website with Pru and Mary and Daphne and all three Beauforts, Barrie closed her sketchbook and stood up from the kitchen table.

"I think I'm done for the night." She beamed a what-I-really-really-want-most-is-to-go-to-my-room vibe at Eight, which was as close to what she really wanted as she could get.

The uncertain success of trying to fool Eight was one of the worst aspects of having him know what she wanted. And she had stupidly told him to keep what he felt from her to himself when what she should have done was test him to find a way to work around the gift. As it was, all she knew for certain was that Eight couldn't tell *why* she wanted something.

"You're not getting a migraine, are you? Or coming down

with a bug?" Pru laid the back of a hand across Barrie's forehead. "It's no surprise. All this stress."

"This planning is making my brain hurt, and you look tired, too, Aunt Pru. What we both need is a good night's sleep." Tipping her head in Pru's direction, Barrie bugged her eyes at Seven, *wanting* him to let Pru go up to bed.

Pru crossed toward the sink. "I'll get you a couple of Tylenol and some water. We should probably all get some rest. It's going to be another long day tomorrow."

"I still think it's a bad idea," Seven said.

"What's a bad idea?" Barrie looked from Seven to Pru and back again.

Pru rounded on Seven, her hands moving to her hips and her gray eyes flashing. "Are you too stubborn to ever stop arguing?"

Seven stepped forward and put both hands on her shoulders. "I know this is important to you, but you can't make up for twenty years in a week. Why don't you give it some more time until things settle in? A month. Thirty days. That's not long to wait."

"What isn't she waiting for?" Barrie asked as Pru pulled away from Seven and filled a glass with water from the tap.

"It was meant to be a surprise," Pru said. She extracted a small bottle of medicine from the junk drawer under the kitchen counter. "You and I have a date in the morning to see Alyssa Evans about a couple of horses."

"Really?" Barrie clapped her hands before she remembered she was supposed to have a headache. Sobering, she took the glass of water and the small white tablets that Pru handed her.

"Yes, really. So you're going to want to feel your best. We've got a solid start on the restaurant, and the rest of these details will keep. As far as waiting goes"—she darted a look at Seven—"I'm through waiting. For anything. Watson's Landing has had horses for three hundred years, and I want to pass that down to you and your future children."

"I thought we needed the stables for when the movers deliver Lula's furniture," Barrie said.

"I've arranged for the auction company to be here again when the movers arrive. They'll take away any of Lula's things we decide not to keep right as the pieces come off the moving truck. The more I think about all this, the more I love the idea of clearing out this whole house and starting fresh without all the dents and history."

Barrie thought it would be both a shame and a relief to let all that history go. The past could be a burden that weighed you down. At the same time, it provided ballast. Amid the scratches and scars at Watson's Landing, Barrie knew who she was far more than she'd ever known in the too-perfect replica of the house that Lula had recreated in San Francisco.

Throwing out all that history was a pity, but in the end,

furniture—things—didn't matter. If letting the furniture go and bringing the horses back was what Pru needed, then Barrie would help make that work.

"Can I come with you to Alyssa's?" Kate splayed her elbows on the table and glanced hopefully from Pru to Barrie. "I know her horses pretty well from the local shows."

Pru's faint smile was shadowed beneath the yellowed bulbs of the kitchen chandelier. "Of course. I was hoping you would help us out here until the horses settle in and everything calms down again."

She nodded insistently at the pills in Barrie's palm. Cornered by her own duplicity, Barrie swallowed them and set down the glass. She looked up to find Seven Beaufort watching Pru with a mixture of pain and sadness that he wiped away when he caught Barrie's scrutiny.

"In theory, Kate is grounded from horses until she applies herself to her schoolwork, but since it's summer—and you need the help—I won't press the point." Seven stopped beside Kate and gently tugged a strand of hair that had escaped from her barrette. "But all right. Let's leave Pru and Barrie to get their rest."

Kate's grin reminded Barrie very much of Eight as Seven managed to herd both his offspring out the door. Barrie stood at the railing waving good-bye as Seven and Kate went down the steps together.

Eight leaned in to her for a quick stolen kiss. "Whatever you're up to," he said into her ear, "don't do it."

"Don't do what?" Barrie asked, thinking, *I want to go to bed. I want this headache to stop. I want to go to bed. I want this headache to stop. I want to go to bed. I want this headache to stop....*

"Anything crazy or stupidly courageous. I know you're up to something."

"I don't have a clue what you mean."

"Sure you don't." Eight's eyes were bright and too intelligent. He cupped both hands at the back of her neck and pulled her closer for a softer kiss, the kind that lingered and made the backs of Barrie's knees soften into noodles.

She waited until he reached the bottom of the stairs, and when she turned, Pru was standing just inside the kitchen. Edging past, Barrie went to gather the remaining plates off the table.

Pru locked the door, carefully set the chain, and punched in the code to the new alarm system that had been installed that morning. "Frustrating, isn't it?" she asked. "I remember that feeling so well."

The stack of plates wobbled in Barrie hands. "What feeling is that?"

"The ache of wanting a Beaufort, and the frustration of knowing that he knows exactly what I want. Go to bed, sugar. I'll take care of the cleanup here."

Upstairs, Barrie waited in bed fully clothed, with the sheets huddled up to her chin, half-expecting the door to open and Pru to pop her head in to check on her. The previous night, it wouldn't have mattered if she'd been caught sneaking out. Tonight it would.

There was only silence in the corridor, and the sound of doubt inside Barrie's head. It had never occurred to her that uncertainty could sound like cymbals crashing, like hearts cracking, while certainty was as silent as a thief. She had no choice about trying to break the Colesworth curse. So why did she doubt so much?

She'd taken the precaution, earlier that day, of unlocking the doors to one of the bedrooms farther down the balcony. At eleven ten, she rolled a batch of winter sweaters inside an extra blanket into a human shape and tucked the bundle under the covers on her bed.

Across the river at Beaufort Hall, a light was on downstairs, but Eight's room was dark. Hoping that meant he was asleep, Barrie slipped out onto the balcony and then back inside through the unlocked door. After creeping through the house, she punched in the security code so the alarm would let her exit and then rearm itself.

Unlike the previous night, no clouds ringed the moon or kept the stars from cutting through the darkness. Recently installed spotlights made the exterior walls of the house shine like a wedding cake trimmed in glitter dust and formed pools of gold beneath the trees.

The *yunwi* milled around Barrie, clutching at her jeans and pulling the orange laces of her hot pink Kate Spade sneakers, trying to pull her back. She half-expected Obadiah to be waiting beside the fountain, but he wasn't there. Nor was he at the dock. She sat at the edge and waited, her legs swinging above the water. Frogs sang, and the occasional splash of a fish or small creature sounded above the shush of the river, but that was all. The two boats still floated downstream—or maybe they were different boats. It was impossible to tell. There was virtually no movement until a flashlight bobbed on the bank at Colesworth Place and Cassie wound her way down the steep bank toward the river.

Fog sprang up from nowhere, billowing from the water and eddying around the marsh. Barrie barely had time to wonder at how quickly it had risen, before a splash beside the dock made her startle.

"The girl is late." Obadiah appeared in a boat that Barrie would have sworn hadn't been there a second earlier. He grasped the wooden post to pull himself the final foot to the dock.

The *yunwi* ringed Barrie in a protective circle. A few darted in to kick at Obadiah's hand, and he drew back as if he felt them, but then his lips twitched with amusement.

"Control your pets, *petite*," he said, "or I shall do it for you."

"Don't," Barrie said, not sure whether she was speaking to him or the *yunwi*.

She shouldn't have been surprised at anything Obadiah did or said, but her heart did its best impression of a jackhammer anyway. With his black dress shirt open at the throat, he looked less formal than he had before, but not by much.

"Is there a special school where you go to learn creepy entrances and exits?" she asked, pretending to be brave. "And why are you wearing a suit to row across a river?"

He bared his teeth at her benignly, light flashing on the gold incisors. "You really will say anything, won't you?" He sounded amused, and his dark skin seemed to absorb the moonlight. "There was a time when people wore suits instead of blue jeans and shorts."

"When was that?" Barrie watched him carefully.

But he gave nothing away. "All these questions will make me think you don't trust me," he said.

"Wouldn't you think less of me if I did?"

"Yet here you are anyway. Why is that, I wonder?"

"Maybe because between the blackmail and the hocuspocus you didn't give me any choice."

"Only because you want both your Beaufort boy and your magic. You'll have to figure out for yourself which is more important." He grinned at her again. "I ought to dislike you, but I find that I don't. You should learn to trust me."

Barrie packed as much loathing as she could convey into a single look, and wished the *yunwi* had something they could throw at him. "Trust is not something you can ask for. It's like faith; you either have it or you don't."

"I don't believe I've done a single thing to lose yours," Obadiah said.

Yet.

The word wasn't spoken, but it rang in the darkness just the same.

Obadiah held his hand out to Barrie, and she lowered herself into the rowboat. A soundless cry went up from the *yunwi*, but she couldn't do anything to reassure them.

Shrouded in the unnatural fog, the Santisto was surreal as Obadiah rowed them across. There was a sense of waiting, of time or motion held in abeyance, and the absence of the common sounds Barrie had come to recognize sent up its own cadence of alarm. Where had the frogs gone? The humming insects? Why was there no occasional leap of a fish or the drum of an alligator's tail? None of those things broke the steady splash of the oars slicing into the water and emerging again dribbling liquid silver.

Despite the fog, Obadiah had a glow that came from his skin and illuminated the boat around him, as if he had dipped himself in phosphorescence. Sitting on the narrow bench, Barrie rubbed her temple and took the opportunity to study his face. How had she ever, even for a moment, thought he reminded her of Mark? Now that she thought about it, though, he seemed younger than she'd thought at first. He rowed with his back and legs, cutting through the water easily, and she felt tired just watching him. Then the strain of the oars exposed a half inch of wrist below the long black sleeve, and a gleam of white drew her eye to a bracelet made of teeth.

Human teeth.

A hiss of breath escaped her. But while she watched, the bracelet vanished. There, and then gone, as if it had never been.

Her eyes met Obadiah's, and his held only an open and defiant measuring, daring her to react. She sat rigid, not even realizing they had reached the other side of the river until the boat ran aground.

The Colesworth dock wasn't entirely derelict; only the last ten feet or so had burned. Obadiah hadn't stopped to tie up there. Instead, he dragged the small craft up the bank. Barrie glanced down at her Kate Spade sneakers, then shrugged and pulled them off before getting out. She shuddered at the squishy mud, remembering Ernesto shoving her down into it, Ernesto's fingers digging into her skin the night of the explosion, his fist slamming her down into the water.

"This is the guy?" Cassie flicked a glance at Obadiah as she emerged from the fog to meet them.

Barrie allowed herself an eye roll to conceal her nerves as she stepped up on the bank and slipped her shoes back on. "No. I'm rowing across the river in the dead of night with a guy who is *not the guy*," she said.

"That's funny. I never realized you had a sense of humor." Cassie stepped back to let Barrie pass. "I guess you're feeling a little full of yourself now that you've killed my father. Was that a boost of self-confidence for you? Do you feel less like a weak little girl?"

Cassie's words slammed Barrie in the chest. She couldn't draw in air, as if her lungs had squeezed themselves shut and refused to re-expand. She wondered if this was how a fish felt when it was dying.

What Cassie said was technically true.

By calling for the Fire Carrier, she had caused the explosion. *She* had killed.

How had that not dawned on her until this moment? She might not have killed them directly, but she had reached for the Fire Carrier, called to him, and all he had done was answer. The flames he had spilled onto the water had shot straight to Wyatt's speedboat from Watson's Landing, and if Barrie hadn't seen it coming and jumped into the water, if she hadn't *known*, would she have been incinerated, too?

Or was she immune to the Fire Carrier's flames because she was a Watson?

The witch's fire hadn't burned her, but she had felt the heat of the explosion, and she still carried the stitches from the piece of metal that had hit her shoulder. What part of it all had been real, and what part had been magic? Or was there a distinction? Throwing a sidelong glance at Obadiah, she had to concede that maybe reality wasn't as simple a concept as she'd thought.

Not that she was sorry Wyatt Colesworth was dead. By his own confession, he had knocked Barrie's father down, left her mother in the bedroom, and set fire to the apartment the night Barrie was born.

Death by fire was justice for him. Wyatt Colesworth had deserved to burn in hell. But why did Cassie assume Barrie had caused the explosion or had anything to do with it?

Cassie couldn't have known. She had to be guessing, prodding at Barrie, hoping to find a wound.

Obadiah strode toward Cassie. When he spoke, he looked down at her along the length of his long, thin nose. "I have no doubt you spent hours working on that accusation," he said. "Did it make you feel better to say it, *chère*? Do you feel smarter? More certain of yourself now that you think you've put your cousin at a disadvantage? Yes, that is how people like you operate, isn't it? Always at someone else's expense. But you have forgotten some crucial things."

"I haven't forgotten anything, and you don't even know

me." Cassie spoke calmly, but her muscles had tensed, and it was costing her visible effort not to retreat from where she stood. "I don't know you, either. You're probably only here for the treasure."

"Do you see me loaded down with shovels and wheelbarrows to transport gold bullion?" Obadiah quirked his eyebrow at her. "I am here because my ancestors laid a curse on your ancestors, who were every bit as unscrupulous and unpleasant as you are. Now, if you want me to remove that curse, I suggest you close your mouth. You need me more than I need you. In short, you are dispensable. Remember that, because it seems to have slipped your mind."

It wasn't nice to enjoy seeing Cassie squirm. It took only one look at Obadiah's profile to remind Barrie that whatever game Obadiah was playing was dangerous.

A comeback parted Cassie's lips, but even she thought better of it as she took in Obadiah's stance. She bit off whatever she had planned to say. Or not planned—that was Cassie's problem. She never thought before she acted.

Not for the first time, Barrie wondered how much of Cassie's seeming self-possession was real and how much was sheer bravado. How much of her impulsive behavior was desperation to convince herself, and the people around her, that she was actually okay even when she wasn't?

CHAPTER TWENTY-FOUR

Obadiah stood at the base of the path, peering through the swirling fog toward the knob-kneed cypress tree that marked the tunnel entrance where Wyatt and Ernesto had hidden the drugs they'd been smuggling. Higher, above the obscuring haze, the slave village of brick cabins that Wyatt had restored stood at the top of the riverbank, screened from the ruined mansion by a rank of oaks.

With an odd warding-off gesture and a grim expression, Obadiah turned and strode up the path as if he knew exactly where he was going. The strange glow that had lit the boat moved with him.

Barrie rubbed her aching head and followed. Memories ricocheted all around her, hurtling at her from the woods between the Colesworth property and Beaufort Hall, where the tunnel Cassie had trapped them inside had one of its two riverfront exits: from the muddy, narrow shore, where she had tried to run from Wyatt and Ernesto; and from the water's edge and the burned-out pier, where they had dragged her toward the waiting boat. She could almost smell the stench of the urine that had been used to mask the sweetness of the smuggled drugs, and her ribs ached from being kicked. Her arms and palms felt sticky with sweat as warm as the river she had jumped into that night to save herself.

She was sick of Cassie making her feel guilty—and tired of letting herself feel guilty—about things that weren't her fault. Cassie dared to accuse her of being responsible for Wyatt's death? To hell with that.

About to stalk past Cassie up the rise, she stopped in front of her instead. "You know, if you hadn't locked the tunnel, I would never have run into your father, and he might still be alive. I don't expect gratitude from you, but you're lucky you're not rotting in jail right now. You should try taking some responsibility for yourself."

She swept past Cassie and continued up the path. Of course, she tripped and had to catch herself. Briefly, she thought that Cassie had stuck her foot out, but it was only a knotted root on the unkept walkway, reminding her to pay attention.

Cassie managed a half-convincing laugh. "Careful there,

Cos. Your Prince Charming's not around to whisk you off your feet this time."

"That's the difference between us," Barrie said without looking back. "I've never believed in fairy tales."

A short way up the rise, they cleared the fog that clung to the river. The moon emerged, but the glow that surrounded Obadiah didn't dissipate. It lit the railroad ties that created footing and stability on a grade that still struck Barrie as too unnaturally steep for the relatively flat coastal area. Once again, she wondered if the Colesworths had deliberately steepened it to discourage unwanted visitors. They'd been smuggling one thing or another in and out of the property for centuries.

She picked her way up the slope. Tangles of wisteria, Spanish moss, and resurrection fern cloaked the trees and structures on either side of the path, draping the hillside in a green mask that hid what lay beneath. It would have been an easy place to hide pretty much anything. Or anyone.

At the top, Obadiah waited for Barrie and Cassie to catch up. Where the mansion had stood before Sherman's long march from Savannah to Columbia, the eight broken columns, a hunk of chimney, and the cracked marble steps were all that remained. Even the stage where Cassie and her friends had performed *Gone with the Wind* had been cleared away sometime after the night Wyatt died.

Obadiah turned to face her. "Where do we begin?"

She studied the lawn and the structures that Wyatt had spent so much money restoring—the icehouse, the cookhouse, the overseer's house and the slave village, the stables and the smithy. Crouched among the trees, there was also the cemetery beyond the church, and the small modern house where Cassie and her family lived. Even without the pieces of land that had belonged to the old rice fields, the property was enormous, and Barrie had no idea what she was searching for.

Presumably the lodestone, though, if it registered at all, would register as something important. Something like the bone-jarring lostness that radiated from beside the ruined mansion.

"This way," she said, letting the Watson gift guide her toward it.

With Obadiah striding beside her, she left Cassie to bring up the rear. Cassie seemed in no hurry to get any closer to Obadiah than was absolutely required, and Barrie wondered whether that was Cassie reacting to his obviously magical glow, or to his equally obvious dislike. Where Obadiah went, a solid dose of fear was probably not unwise.

Reaching the steps and the jutting columns of the mansion, Barrie stopped where the finding sense was strongest. Lostness roiled from the ground and drilled into her temples, making it impossible to feel anything but loss—the kind of loss she had felt in the Watson tunnel where she'd found Luke and Twila. The kind that said, whatever was buried there had mattered to someone, and had mattered with devastating consequences.

"There," she said, pointing to the spot.

Obadiah squinted at the patch of ground covered by grass. In the moonlight and the dimmer but still visible macabre glow that seemed to seep from the very darkness of his pores, the small lumps of broken bricks and charred chunks of mortar that occasionally protruded from the ground stood out in colorless relief.

"You're sure? What do you feel?"

"Don't *you* feel anything?" To Barrie, that seemed strange, when for her the sense of loss was so very clear. But seemingly, magic was specific, like eye color or hair, and no matter how much Obadiah had, and how little she had, it was not the same.

She was watching Obadiah, still thinking about magic, so she yelped softly as Cassie came up and dug her fingers into her forearm. "What kind of a joke is this?" Cassie demanded. "The collapsed tunnel is over there, and the foundations of the mansion are way over there. The tunnel has to lead back that direction." She gestured toward the river. "Why would there be anything over here?"

Cassie's face was hollow-cheeked and tense. She had lost weight in the past days, and she seemed to be perpetually cold, or maybe she was trying to cover up the ankle monitor again by wearing the heavy jeans she had on now despite the heat. In Barrie's case, it was a fear of snakes that prompted her to cover herself, but Cassie wasn't afraid of anything.

"I've felt something lost here since the first time I came. Apart from Charlotte's grave, this is the only big loss, the only *important* loss on the property. Sorry if that's not convenient for you." Barrie shrugged out of Cassie's grasp.

Cassie held up her hands. "Fine. Just find the damn rock and make him remove the curse." She hooked a thumb at Obadiah, and then crossed her arms. "And hurry the hell up before my mother wakes up and sees us."

Obadiah's answer was deceptively quiet, but there was ice underneath. "Magic can't be rushed, and not every spirit here is friendly. Show some respect, or you're liable to find that there are things worse than curses."

Cassie fell silent briefly, then her chin came back up. "I know people like you. There's a catch here somewhere. You figure that we're desperate, so you're going to ask for money. Blackmail us." She pulled a packet of folded bills out of her back pocket. "This is all I've managed to scrape together. Five hundred and seventy-five dollars. That's it. There isn't anything else. We're going to lose this whole place and everything in it, so don't plan on holding out for more at the end of this. And don't assume I'm giving you any money at all until you can prove the curse is gone."

"You think I want your five hundred dollars?" Obadiah asked.

The words were so soft that Barrie barely heard them, but the sound shuddered up her spine like a knife scraping stone, leaving the nerves exposed. Even Cassie stepped back with her face drained of color by fear and moonlight.

"You do not buy magic with a fistful of dollars," Obadiah said. "You buy it with blood and bone and desperation, with revenge and fury and prayers. I want many things from your family. Five hundred dollars doesn't begin to cover it."

"Five hundred and seventy-five," Cassie whispered. For twenty seconds or so, she looked like a frightened child. Then she flicked on the secret switch inside herself that allowed her to become someone else, someone in her own way nearly as magical as Obadiah. Pushing a long strand of dark hair behind her ear in a deliberately sensual motion, she kept her eyes locked on his and raised her head. "If money's not enough, then what is it you want?"

"More than is in your power to give, and it isn't about what I want at all." His eyes fixed on her, but to his credit, they stayed on her face and didn't take up the flirtation. She blushed darkly and wrapped her arms protectively around her waist. Glancing at Barrie, she blushed even harder.

Obadiah moved to the spot Barrie had pointed to on the ground. After removing a pouch of white powder from his pocket, he sprinkled the substance onto the ground in the shape of a cross. Moving counterclockwise, he connected the ends of the cross in a circle, and then made a smaller circle within the other. He stepped inside and toed up to the centerpoint of the cross, angling his hands away from his body, palms turned upward. He went still, so still that he was scarcely breathing. A shudder wracked his body and he appeared to grow smaller, energy draining from him so that he was diminished, or the night was getting larger and dwarfing him.

Cassie backed away. "What are you doing?"

"Trying to bind the spirits of my ancestors before they wake and discover we're here to break the curse. Be quiet and let me concentrate."

The tendons on his neck stood out with strain, his fingers contracted toward his palms as if in spasm, and he rocked forward onto the balls of his feet. Then he drew back on his heels again, as if something was pulling at him and he was fighting against it. At last, his eyes flew open. Stooping, he raked up two handfuls of grass and rolled the roots between his hands, releasing the dark earth speckled with charcoal and crumbled brick and letting it rain onto the ground before he dropped the grass as well. Arms raised, he tipped his face to the sky.

The air filled with the rush of wings. Darkness blotted out the stars and swept across the moon. The raucous caw of a raven made Barrie exhale sharply as ten or eleven birds, all soaring and diving, circled above them. Obadiah kept his eyes closed and his face skyward as if absorbing the birds' movements the way a sun-worshipper absorbs heat from the sun. He brought his hands forward, one wrist held slightly higher than the other, and a dark bird immediately landed on it.

Stroking the bird's head and back with two broad fingers, Obadiah began to speak in a rhythmic chant loaded with long vowels and harsh consonants, sounds like light and shadow. Feathers ruffling as if it were going to go to sleep, the raven settled itself and closed its eyes.

Obadiah kept stroking, and then his hand snapped closed, twisted, and broke the raven's neck. Sweeping his arm upward, he threw the limp body into the air.

A scream seared up Barrie's throat. The sound spilled across her tongue and then cut off with a gasp of surprise.

The bird had vanished.

She had seen it thrown. She had seen it hover at the point where it had stopped ascending, but it never fell. Instead, feathers drifted toward the ground like oversize black snowflakes, each different and unearthly.

Both hands pressed to her chest, she covered Mark's watch and held it like a talisman while she pushed herself through the familiar steps of averting hyperventilation and warding off a panic attack. Trying to, anyway. It was easier to focus on the mechanics: exhale before inhaling; breathe out, then in, out and in. How easy it was to forget how to do what every infant knew automatically.

Obadiah had killed a bird.

Killed it.

Or had he?

Because the body still had not appeared. Feathers drifted to the ground in abnormally slow motion, and they didn't stop at the surface. They sank beneath the grass and continued sinking until they disappeared, absorbed as if the earth inside the circle had turned to liquid and the feathers had developed weight.

Barrie wanted to race back to the boat and across the river to Watson's Landing, but her feet had welded to the grass. She doubted she could have moved if she tried. Needing something to hold on to, she stretched her fingers toward Cassie. But Cassie stepped forward and snatched the last handful of feathers out of the air.

Wrapping her fist around the feathers, Cassie crumpled them, and the largest snapped in two. "Was that real?" she asked, her words echoing Barrie's thoughts. "Where's the bird?"

Obadiah's eyes snapped open. He spun toward her to stare in horror at the feathers in Cassie's hand. "What have you done?"

Lightning flashed. The ground rumbled and shook with

a blast of energy that pushed Barrie off her feet and sent Obadiah flying backward, thrown up and away by an unseen force from below the ground. Cassie fell to her knees.

Whatever had happened, it hadn't been any kind of traditional explosion. The ground wasn't split open. There was no fire. But above them, the night sky turned to daylight blue, and the moon became a sun alternately hidden and revealed by clouds racing as quickly as a stop-motion video.

A flicker behind Barrie made her turn. On the foundations of the old mansion, a white-gabled house sprang to life. Three stories rose to form the central wing, and the eight columns in the portico matched exactly the ruined columns of Colesworth Place. Apart from an opalescent shimmer, the image was perfect in every detail, from brick to glass to mortar.

CHAPTER TWENTY-FIVE

Barrie sprang to her feet and took a step toward Obadiah. Only it wasn't him lying where she had seen him fall. Whoever lay there was ancient, a leathered husk of a man, his face shrunken, his cheeks gaunt, and his eyes hollow and sunken so deep his appearance was nearly skeletal. Before Barrie had taken a second step or processed what she was seeing, the mansion in front of her shimmered again, winked in and out of existence like a lightbulb deciding whether or not to die.

The front door opened.

Three abreast, soldiers clad in Union blue slouched down the steps, their half-derelict uniforms unbuttoned. Two more men dragged a dazed, stumbling woman and two girls behind them. One of the girls was white and blond, maybe fifteen or sixteen years old. The other girl was black and younger, probably a slave child, judging by her cheaper dress. The soldiers shoved all three out into the yard, where the woman stumbled to her knees with her wide hoopskirt belled around her. The soldiers pushed the girls down, too, and kicked the black child until the other girl crawled over and pulled her away.

Barrie had already started running forward, shouting, "Stop it!"

No one looked up.

She reached the two girls, but they crab-walked backward *through* her, leaving Barrie between them and the soldiers as if she weren't even there. As if *she* were the ghost and they were real. Except they weren't real; they couldn't have been.

Clinging to each other, the two girls huddled beside the woman, who didn't seem to even be trying to get up. Her eyes were fixed on the house, where more soldiers filed out the door, carrying chests and clanking bundles of looted candlesticks, plates, and silver wrapped in tablecloths and sheets. Two soldiers angled a life-size painting of a young debutante in a pale blue dress through the front door, and put it into a cart drawn up to the base of the steps.

Beside the cart, another man, an officer with gold epaulettes on his shoulders, opened the bundles and looked inside, his frown nearly hidden by a thick mustache and heavy sideburns. Banging his fist on the side of the cart so hard that the horses twitched in their traces, he barked an order at two men trudging up the steps. The men broke into a jog and disappeared through the door.

Hand on the hilt of his sword, the officer marched to the woman and stopped in front of her. She shrank away and pulled her daughter closer.

Barrie couldn't help remembering Twila Beaufort's ghost, who had been stuck in Emmett's bedroom, repeating the last moments of her life on an inescapable loop. Were these ghosts reliving the night they died? Or was this something else? Something that had to do with whatever ceremony Obadiah had performed?

The place where the husk of Obadiah had lain on the ground was now empty. Obadiah himself had disappeared.

The ghosts continued to move around Barrie—but were they ghosts? Could a house become a ghost? More likely she was seeing a scene from the past, an echo of some kind. An alternate reality? Maybe she was the one who had been transported somewhere else.

Barrie rubbed her aching head. None of it made sense.

Wherever she was, past or present, Cassie was there as well, standing a few steps back, still clutching a fistful of raven's feathers. And beneath the trees along the road toward the church, the bulb of a lamp glowed yellow beside the front door of the small house where Cassie and her family lived.

The sight grounded Barrie, assured her the mansion wasn't real, wasn't *now*. But a few feet from where she stood, the officer abruptly pulled out a pistol and pointed it at the woman, shouting words that Barrie couldn't hear. The woman shook her head and shouted back at him equally soundlessly. He asked again. Again the woman shook her head, and he aimed the gun and pulled back the hammer.

The woman was crying, her shoulders trembling, her head shaking no, no, no, and her mouth seeming to repeat words over and over, too. The blond girl stood and dusted herself off, then stepped between her mother and the gun.

"God, no. Please!" Hands to her mouth, Barrie backed away. "Please don't."

She couldn't bear to see another person die, much less a child. It didn't matter how long ago the death might have happened—didn't the fact that she was seeing the echo at all mean someone had died? Were all these people trapped in someone's final moments?

The officer turned the gun on the blond girl and repeated whatever question he'd been asking. The girl answered calmly. Her mother gave another silent scream, but continued to shake her head.

Gesturing with the gun, the officer waved a soldier over and pointed to the other girl. The soldier's eyes widened, and he said something, but the officer snapped another order.

Seizing the black child by the arm, the soldier threw her back down on the ground, then yanked on the cord that held up his blue-gray trousers.

The slave girl couldn't have been more than eight or ten. Her eyes were wide and rimmed in white, and now she was screaming, too, her mouth open and her throat working, but no sound spilled into the freakishly silent night.

Barrie's blood stopped—everything stopped—the world stopped—it *should* have stopped.

She launched herself at the soldier who was pulling down his trousers, but she connected with nothing.

Nothing was there, nothing and everything that was wrong with the world. Everything that was warped and awful.

She fell through the ghostly body and landed on her knees. Beside her, the blond girl grabbed for the officer's gun, and he hit her, knocking her away so that she fell sideways and landed only a few feet from the child. Both girls were close enough to Barrie that the desperation on their faces burned into her memory.

The officer turned the gun back on the woman. Grasping her face between the thumb and forefinger of his other hand, he forced her to look. The child lay on her back, panic-stricken and screaming at the soldier who stood with his boot on her stomach to hold her down. The woman tried to pull away, but the officer pointed at the blond girl in what was clearly a threat. The mother sagged, shaking her head, pleading instead of screaming:

Please, no. I don't know anything. I don't know.

The words were clear, mouthed over and over. Barrie needed no sound to hear them.

The officer reached forward and yanked the woman to her feet. She kicked to break free, crying, cursing unheard curses, clawing at his arm. Finally, she spit on him, and he cuffed her across the cheek hard enough for her head to snap aside. She would have fallen, but he jerked her up.

The pain, the injustice, the fury ripped Barrie apart like shards of glass scraping at her stomach, at her chest. And there was nothing she could do.

These were the men who'd been meant to fight *against* slavery. That's what she'd been taught. These were the saviors. If they weren't, then who was? Because they were raping *children*. Hitting women. Stealing. Extorting.

Barrie wasn't naïve enough to believe there was good in war on either side, but this . . . How did anyone justify this?

The blond girl looked at the officer and screamed something, her lips moving too fast for Barrie to read them. Pants halfway to his knees, the soldier stopped to see what was going on. The officer shifted his grasp from the woman's face to her shoulder and asked the blonde a question. She answered, but her mother sagged, shouting, "No!"

Shoulders hunched and heaving, the woman sobbed, and her daughter looked confused.

The officer studied them both, then snapped something to the soldier who loomed over the slave girl. Pulling up his trousers, the soldier returned to the house, taking several other soldiers with him. They disappeared inside.

Barrie slumped in relief, but she had no breath. She dropped to the ground and hugged her knees. But only minutes later, the soldiers came back out of the house and shook their heads.

Without releasing the woman, the officer barked an order across his shoulder. The woman wrenched away. The officer slammed his fist into her cheek. She fell to her knees, crawled to where the black girl lay curled in a heaving ball, and gathered the child to her. Looking up at the man almost calmly, she rocked the girl in her lap, trying to offer comfort while her own tears streamed.

The officer studied her, then turned away. The blond girl had snuck over, too, and sat beside her mother, stroking the black child's head. All three were crying. The officer turned his back as if they didn't matter and moved toward the loaded cart.

The woman paid him no more attention. It wasn't until smoke rose from the burning mansion—Barrie could smell it—actually *smell* it—that the woman's head snapped up.

Three soldiers ran, crouching, out of the house with flaming torches, which they threw up onto the portico roof. Smoke billowed from inside the open door. Faster than Barrie could have imagined, fire licked the walls and paint peeled off the bricks. The glass in one of the downstairs windows shattered.

The woman bolted toward the house. A soldier snatched at her skirt, but she twisted free and raced up the mansion steps. She darted inside as the portico ceiling caught fire and flames bit through the wood in a shower of sparks.

"Go after her!" Barrie screamed, running herself even though part of her knew it wouldn't do any good. None of this was real.

She couldn't stop it.

The scene all played out in slow motion, as if time had slipped from its moorings and cast her out of the universe she knew. Barrie's rational mind kept telling her none of this was happening. It had already happened, so it couldn't be happening now—again. Yet it was.

Barrie passed the cart and reached the steps. The soldiers ignored her. Reacting to something behind Barrie, they whipped around in unison to face the woods by the slave cabins. The officer snatched a rifle from the cart.

A big man in a long black coat and burgundy waistcoat raced toward the house. The officer raised the gun and fired.

A bullet hit the man in the shoulder. He jerked. Stumbled.

Kept running. Racing past as the officer was reloading, the man swerved to avoid three soldiers who sprinted to intercept him. He passed the steps as other men snatched up their guns. With blood spreading across his shirt and coat, he made it ten more feet before another shot hit him in the back. He fell. Got up. Ran on.

Off to the side of the house, where Obadiah had drawn the circle and the raven feathers had disappeared into the ground, the man in the waistcoat collapsed to his knees. Another bullet hit him, and then another. He dragged himself forward, bare fingers digging into the dirt, scrabbling at the ground as if he had something buried there he had to reach. Another bullet hit him, in the neck this time.

Windows exploded around the mansion, ceilings collapsed, floors buckled.

The two girls clutched each other, their eyes clinging to the door where the woman had disappeared.

The second floor caved, throwing up a fresh burst of flames and sparks. The officer walked to the man, who was still furiously clawing at the dirt. Placing the pistol to the man's head, the officer pulled the trigger.

Then nothing.

Nothing at all except the ringing in Barrie's ears and the cold—the bitter, biting cold that made her shake so hard that her stomach heaved and heaved, long after there was anything in it. Finally, she let go of her hair and braced her forehead on her knees. She felt empty, as if seeing the horror or its echo had stripped her of some portion of her own humanity and left her diminished.

How could people do that to one another? Threaten a child with rape and watch a woman burn?

The rape of a child was the ultimate act of selfishness, the mark of a person who had divorced himself completely from the empathy that bound humanity. Had these soldiers not had children? Sisters? Mothers? Was there some convenient door in their minds they could slam shut on their ability to put themselves in another's shoes?

Barrie wiped the cold sweat that had beaded on her forehead. Around her, the mansion had vanished. The flames were gone—no, they were different. The air filled with the sweet scent of burning sage and the fire on the river crackled magical and blue.

Across the river and barely visible, the Fire Carrier stood thigh deep in the water. Barrie couldn't tell where he was looking, whether he was aware of her, whether he had seen or felt the events playing out or felt the explosion that had sent Obadiah flying backward.

Obadiah.

Barrie spun, wary and confused. Furious. But he was still nowhere. Not lying on the ground, not standing nearby.

Maybe he had escaped the vision, the ghost house, the horror. Maybe it hadn't happened.

"Did you see it?" Barrie moved back to Cassie, her voice a whisper.

Cassie didn't answer. She lay curled in a ball, hands wrapped around her knees, shivering so hard that her teeth rattled. Her breath was shallow and ragged, and her eyes stared, glassy and unseeing.

If this was a flashback, if it was real, then it was worse than the one in the cemetery. And if it wasn't real—why would Cassie bother? There was no one around to be impressed by her performance. Even Cassie wouldn't—couldn't—fake this.

"Cassie." Barrie shook her gently, then pulled back when Cassie flinched. "Look at me. Listen to me. You're all right."

Remembering what Berg had done, she kept talking even though Cassie didn't seem to register the words. She had no idea what she was even saying, though. Her mind kept skittering off to think of other things: the house, the girls, the thing—Obadiah?—she had seen lying on the ground that might have been Obadiah, a mummy of a man shrunken so that he was dwarfed by Obadiah's black silk suit.

She thought back to what Obadiah had said about how once he had been like her. How long ago had that been? How old *was* he? But none of those questions mattered as much as where he had gone and what had happened. What was it that

Barrie had seen, and what had Obadiah done to the curse?

Across on the other bank of the river, the Fire Carrier was moving back to the woods, the orange reflection off the water fading as he retreated, and it finally hit Barrie what that meant. It had been eleven thirty when Obadiah had rowed her to the Colesworth dock. The Fire Carrier always came at midnight.

Whatever had happened had the weight of an hour, at least an hour, but it had taken place in the span of minutes, as if ghost time ran at a different pace.

What else had changed in that time? Anything?

The pull of lostness still called to Barrie from beneath the ground. Whatever had happened with the curse, that hadn't changed. If anything, it seemed worse. More alive, more raw. Deeper slashes of darkness marked the spot where the man had died. Torn grass and gouges in the dirt exposed fresh chunks of blackened bricks, the damage far more extensive than anything Obadiah had done. The chalk cross and circles had all but disappeared.

A flash of light, a flashlight, from down near the river in the woods between Colesworth Place and Beaufort Hall pulled Barrie around, her heart kicking in her chest like a drowning swimmer at the memory of Ernesto and Wyatt . . . at the thought of facing anyone who was wandering around at midnight.

"Cassie. Get up. We have to go." She tried to shake her cousin out of the stupor, but Cassie flailed at her touch, rolling away and scrambling backward with her eyes wide and panicked. Cassie's mouth opened as if to scream, though no sound came out, just sobs and whimpers. She was still shaking, and sweat had beaded at her temple and on the tip of her nose.

Barrie wasn't calm. She didn't want to be calm.

She wanted to run. Her own heart was beating a retreat, the rhythm so fast that she could barely breathe, but she couldn't leave Cassie. Searching for a weapon, she scooped up a fist-size piece of brick that had been gouged out by the murdered ghost. She forced herself to look back toward the woods.

The light was bobbing closer, weaving in between the trees like a weaker, bleached-out version of the glow from the Fire Carrier's flames. Whoever was carrying it was moving fast.

"Cassie. Get *up*!" Barrie reached for Cassie again, then thought better of it, and instead of grasping her, slapped her, not gently, but not hard, either. "You're safe, Cassie, but you won't be unless you get up. Come on. You have to go home."

Cassie blinked. Shook her head. Shook herself and looked back at Barrie with dead, flat eyes. "D-did you just h-hit me?" she stuttered, climbing to her feet.

"There's someone coming up from the river through the

woods with a flashlight. It's after midnight. There can't be any good reason for that. We have to leave."

She reached for Cassie to pull her along, but Cassie had wrapped her arms around herself and stood shivering, the tears spilling even more freely and the words so full of snot and water that they were barely recognizable. "Shit. Did you see? They were going to— She was a little girl. A k-k-kid . . ."

She broke down sobbing, taking deep gulps of air. Barrie wanted to throw up all over again. "I know."

"Men are *pigs*. You think you know them—you think you can trust them. You can't. None of them." Cassie turned her face toward Barrie's, and her knees buckled so that Barrie had to reach out and hold her up. "What *was* that? Did that really happen?"

"I don't know," Barrie said, her throat filling with tears at Cassie's words, and her heart breaking even more at the sudden cold suspicion that her cousin's opinion of men had as much, if not more, to do with Cassie's own experience as with what she and Barrie had just witnessed.

"Where's the raven's body?" Cassie raised her hand, which was still wrapped around a fistful of feathers. "Maybe it was all a trick. The whole thing. Just feathers without the bird, and the rest was some kind of hallucination. It would be nice to have something turn out to have been nothing more than a nightmare. No, a dream," she said mournfully. "Nightmares hurt."

"Cassie! Come on, speculate later. We have to go!" Barrie slapped her cousin again, harder.

Cassie slapped her back. "What are you hitting me for?"

"Because you need to snap out of it and MOVE." Barrie turned to look behind her in the direction of the woods, but the flashlight had already cleared the trees.

CHAPTER TWENTY-SIX

Barrie's hands shook, and she searched the ground for another weapon, something more substantial than the crumbling piece of brick she was crushing in her fingers. There was nothing, though, not unless she left Cassie.

Turning, she blinked against the beam of the flashlight. Recognition swept over her, followed by slack-shouldered relief. Even obscured behind the light, there was a certainty about Eight's figure that made her calm. Calm*er*. Because "calm" was a relative term. Barrie wasn't sure she would ever see the world in a way that would let her be calm again.

She sprinted past the carcass of the Colesworth mansion toward Eight, and he started jogging, too, the white beam of light bobbing over the grass, fracturing into a thousand prisms inside her tears. He caught her as she threw herself at him.

"What is it, Bear? What happened? What did Cassie do to you?"

His arms closed around her, and that was enough. The last of her self-control shattered, and Barrie slumped against him, waiting to feel warm again, burrowing into his chest to inhale his steadiness.

"It wasn't Cassie's fault." She forced her head up, but as she spoke the words, handfuls of feathers drifted through her mind, an image of the sky filled with black feathers falling like charcoal snow. Black feathers on the pale skin of Cassie's palm, like the contrast of two hands clinging to each other, the callused fingers of the slave child entwined with the soft, white fingers of the older girl as they huddled together on the ground.

She began to shake again, looking past Eight's shoulder to the river because she couldn't bear to see his expression change to disappointment or anger instead of worry. "I started something, and I'm not sure what happened," she said. "Or what's going to happen next."

"What did you do?" Eight stepped in front of her so she had to look at him. "What happened? Why are you so upset?" His voice grew more gentle. "You scared the crap out of me. I felt something explode. Although 'explode' isn't the right word, exactly. It was more like a sonic boom without any sound. And what's wrong with her?" He nodded to where Cassie stood.

Cassie was still looking fixedly at the raked-up patch of ground, but she didn't seem to be shaking anymore. Or crying. Still, there was something bruisingly vulnerable about the bowed line of Cassie's neck. Barrie wished she knew how to help.

"What are you doing here, anyway?" she asked Eight, not exactly avoiding the question, only giving herself a bit of additional time to answer.

He was staring at Cassie, too, and answered almost absently, "For future reference, if you want me to believe that you want something, you have to want whatever it is more than you want me to believe you want it. I figured it had to be something to do with Cassie, or you would have told me."

Barrie's eyes slitted. "So you were spying on me?"

"Watching over you. From a distance. To give you space. Although with the fog, I clearly did a lousy job. Jesus, you're still shaking." He moved closer and rubbed her arms, as if that would warm her up. "Now, do you want to tell me what's going on? One minute you were alone on the Watson dock, and the next minute there was a fog on the river so thick that I couldn't hear anything or see my own fingers in front of my face. Then a minute later, boom. The air shook and the fog was gone, and now you're trembling and the Wicked Bitch of the Obsessed is standing over there like someone took away her favorite toy."

"Be nicer to her. She's not what you think." Barrie checked behind her, but the ground where Obadiah had disappeared was still as bare as before. "You didn't happen to see anyone besides me and Cassie around?" she asked. "No one down by the dock earlier?"

"Who else was with you? You don't know anyone else well enough to talk them into— Oh no. *Shit.*" Eight shoved a hand through his hair and glared at her. "It was that guy, wasn't it? The one from the flower bed. You've been secretive since you saw him. Pretending you couldn't remember him . . . I should have known—you went out to meet him, didn't you? That's why you were so evasive about him all along. Who is he?"

He waited expectantly for Barrie to answer, but her brain wouldn't engage. Trying to think of words was like trying to push a car uphill. She looked back with tears in her eyes, wondering why people ever thought you could explain when they stared at you like that, when they had to know they weren't going to like anything you had to say.

Feeling light-headed, she sank to the grass and laid her head on her knees.

Eight squatted down beside her. "I'm sorry, Bear. Christ, you're horrible for my health, you know that? You could have been there with half the drug smugglers in Columbia, and I wouldn't have been able to do anything about it. And that weird fog. It came out of nowhere and felt like it was there for only a minute, but it was almost half an hour when I looked at my watch. I know I didn't fall asleep, so I don't understand what happened."

He was watching her again, waiting for an explanation. But what could Barrie say that would make it past whatever spell Obadiah had put on her and keep from violating the bargain she had made with him? But hold on. Thinking about speaking Obadiah's name didn't come with its usual accompanying tightness in her throat.

"The fog was Obadiah's doing." She tested the name as calmly as she could, waiting for her lungs to seize and her ability to breathe to vanish.

Nothing happened. Nothing, as if whatever Obadiah had done to himself when he'd flown backward had short-circuited any spells or mind games he had put on her. Slowly she filled her lungs, and let out a sigh. "He's got a lot of different ways to make himself disappear," she said.

Eight's face took on an ominous stillness. "Are you trying to say that you've seen him multiple times and never told me?" He waited for her to give a reluctant nod, and then he shifted his weight back onto his heels. "Dammit, you can't keep charging off on your own. That guy could have been anyone—a stalker, a murderer."

Barrie remembered the way Obadiah had wrung the raven's neck, as if the motion had been practiced and familiar.

"Hold on. You think the guy actually killed someone?" Eight asked.

"No! Well, not a person. A raven. Maybe." Barrie shook her head. She put a hand on Eight's arm as his nostrils flared, needing him to understand so much that it made an empty ache in her chest. "It might have been part of the spell."

Eight's jaw clenched. "What spell?" he asked. "Why don't you try starting at the beginning?"

Barrie buried her face against her forearms, bracing herself for him to start yelling. Only, he wasn't Lula. He didn't throw Lula's tantrums. Swallowing painfully, she raised her head.

What had Obadiah warned her about? He had told her not to tell Eight about their bargain. But he had never made her promise not to tell about the curse. Maybe he had counted on his spell for that. Hell, for all she knew, maybe he was dead, and she didn't need to worry about any of it.

He couldn't have been dead, though. Not dead-dead. There was still some kind of magic at work, or his body would have remained where it had fallen.

"Obadiah's ancestor was the slave who helped trap the Fire Carrier," she explained. "He was also the one who put the curse on the Colesworths, which makes more sense than the Fire Carrier cursing them, when you think about it. But since the curse is bad magic and multigenerational, Obadiah says that his family has been paying some sort of karmic debt for it ever since. He wants to remove the curse, but he needs me to find a rock that's been buried here all these years. If I find that lodestone, he can remove the magic anchored to it. He might even be able to remove your gift."

"My gift? You were going to let him take away the *Beaufort* gift without at least talking to me about it?" Eight stared at her as if she'd grown a second head.

"I was going to see what happened with the curse, and then—"

"How could you not tell me?"

Disbelief and disappointment settled onto Eight's features, and the expression was worse than Lula's screaming. Barrie fought to keep her lip from trembling.

"I figured I would find out more before I got your hopes up," she said. "I don't even know if he's telling the truth."

"You don't know." Eight shook his head. "That's kind of the problem, isn't it? *You* don't know, but I *would* know—and here you are, putting yourself in danger without me." He stood up. His eyes had grown bleak and so full of hurt that Barrie couldn't stand it. "I can't believe you didn't trust me enough to try to let me help you," he said. "Give me credit for having some intelligence. You don't need to do everything on your own. Any relationship is a two-way street. You want to be loved so badly, but at the same time, you're afraid you don't deserve it. You aren't giving us any kind of a chance. You were mad about me not telling you about the tearoom. But you danced with me outside last night when you already knew you were going to do all this." He swept his arm around the lawn and up toward the broken columns of the house.

"That's not how it was." Barrie was shivering uncontrollably now, but not with cold.

"It's exactly how it was! Don't you think I wonder if you want me for the same reason that you can't let Mark's ashes go? Because you need something to hold on to? You're wounded and vulnerable, and I'm here and convenient. I know all that, and yet I'm still here. I'm willing to trust that we have something that will grow. I'm willing to give us time to find out what we could be together, and you aren't willing to give me five minutes of explanation because you don't give me credit for thinking things through."

Every word Eight said was a barb dug into Barrie's skin. The dread feeling that he was right about her fear left her no room for reaction, and she stood up slowly, numb, aware of his growing disgust but unable to think where to start in her own defense.

He shook his head when she didn't answer, and shoved his hand through his hair again as if she made him want to tear it out. "Jesus Christ, Bear. What am I supposed to do to make you understand?"

There were so many things she needed to say to make *him* understand, but his anger made her numb and stupid. She stood there trembling.

Eight finally gave a sigh. "Where is this Obadiah guy anyway?"

"Something went wrong, and then he disappeared."

"What about Cassie? What's wrong with her?" Eight gestured behind Barrie to where Cassie was walking back toward the small house, without looking back, without stopping to talk about what had happened, without anything.

Then again, Cassie didn't like to talk about things that were real. Maybe that was why she made things up. Barrie had a feeling Eight wouldn't understand that, though.

"Cassie is complicated. Let's go back to Obadiah first."

Carefully, she explained the ceremony, the explosion, and the horror of what she'd seen, without mentioning the threat to the Watson gift. She finally told Eight about the spell Obadiah had put on her, but that didn't make him any calmer.

"You think the explosion and the ghosts were related to Cassie taking the feathers? Or was it something to do with the curse?" Eight stooped to examine the raked-up patches of grass—more than the two handfuls that Obadiah had pulled up himself—and the faint remnants of the chalk.

"I'm not sure," Barrie answered. "Obadiah told me he needed to bind his ancestors before they woke up and realized we were trying to break the curse. I would guess they're awake now. It looked like he was fighting something—or someone. Maybe Cassie distracted him. Or maybe the feathers were part of the magic and her taking them changed something. I don't even know if the curse is still there. Maybe nothing has changed."

That was the worst kind of wishful thinking, though. Whatever had happened with the curse, Eight was still looking at her with his eyes turned as sharp as oyster shells, and his cheekbones standing out like scars beneath his skin. There was an absence of softening in him that said Barrie had broken whatever it was that had been trying to grow between them.

Was there any way to repair that kind of damage? Barrie's eyes stung as she realized she didn't know that, either.

CHAPTER TWENTY-SEVEN

There was an exquisitely painful aloneness in sitting next to someone and knowing they were too far away to reach. Buckling herself into the passenger seat as Eight settled behind the steering wheel of Pru's car the next morning, Barrie had no idea how to begin to bridge that distance. With both Pru and Kate in the car, she couldn't even bring up what had happened at Colesworth Place. She suspected that Eight was counting on that. He hadn't answered her calls or texts that morning, and he and Kate had shown up at the last minute for the trip to see the horses, leaving no time to talk.

Sneaking a glance at his profile as he steered the car between the double row of oaks in the direction of the gate, Barrie noted the shadows smudged beneath his eyes as if he hadn't slept. There was a tightness about him, too, that only added to the sense of distance. Not for the first time, she wished that Pru hadn't insisted on sitting in the back with Kate and having Eight drive. At least in the backseat, Barrie wouldn't have had to see Eight's anger as well as feel it.

"Are you two fighting?" Kate scooted to the center of the backseat to peer forward at them with an innocent expression that made Barrie want to kill her. "When did you have time to fight?"

Pru's eyes had also quickened with speculation. Which was awesome, because it wasn't enough to have Eight furious. Now Barrie was going to have to manufacture a reason for his anger that had nothing to do with the truth. Why hadn't he just stayed home?

"We're not fighting, Frog Face." Eight squinted his eyes at his sister in the rearview mirror. "And why don't you have your seat belt fastened?"

"God. Shut up!" Kate said, flouncing back against the seat and fumbling for the latch.

"Frog Face? Seriously?" Barrie said. "That's awful."

"Well, she was an ugly baby. You should have seen her."

Kate shook her head at Barrie and rolled her eyes. "I made some unfortunate choices when I was a poor, orphaned child. I've been paying for them ever since."

"She went around everywhere sticking her tongue out as far as it could go every few minutes. The kids at school still call her Frog."

"In my defense," Kate said, leaning forward to punch him in the shoulder, "Daddy told me that being able to touch your nose with your tongue was a genetic trait. Since he and Eight could both do it and I couldn't, I convinced myself it meant that they weren't my real family, and with Mama dead, I didn't want to be a total orphan, so I convinced myself I just had to practice."

Barrie could picture them, the whole broken family. Eight huddled in his closet so no one would see him cry over losing his mother, Kate wandering the halls at school, sticking out her tongue like a frog, and Seven holed up in his office with a combination of guilt and helplessness. How had Pru felt? Had Pru hoped Seven would come and see her? Had she stared across the river and waited for him to come?

"You still haven't answered my question," Kate said, scrunching her nose at Eight. "And stop trying to distract me. You only call me Frog Face when you want to start an argument. Which is ironic, because you want to argue so that you don't have to talk about why you and Barrie are fighting."

"For the last time, we aren't fighting!" Eight slammed a hand on the steering wheel.

The sun outlined the swags of Spanish moss dripping from the live oaks overhead. Beneath the trees, the light turned green and misty, and along the verge of the grass, shadows raced the car.

Eight's jaw did its best impression of being chiseled out of granite, and he leaned over and cranked the dial on the stereo volume, his usual method of avoiding conversation. "Stay" by Maurice Williams and the Zodiacs was playing. The high falsetto begging, "Come on, come on, come on, stay," made Barrie wince, but Kate and Eight both took up singing.

"Sing with us," Kate said. "Please? It'll cheer you up."

Barrie glanced at Pru, who was looking back a bit too intently. She decided Kate was right. Singing was better than explaining. And if she was really lucky, maybe singing would help pause the unending replay in her head. Every time she blinked, she saw the black child huddled in the dirt with the soldier standing over her, the woman running into the burning house, the man scrabbling at the dirt, trying to reach something. . . . Eight's accusations, too, echoed on a constant loop.

And where had Obadiah gone? More importantly, had she done what he'd told her so that now his threat was over? Or did the fact that something had gone wrong last night mean she wasn't off the hook yet? Had she broken the bargain by telling Eight what she'd already told him? She'd spent half the night trying to figure out what she should safely be allowed to say, what she shouldn't, and how much would change if she told.

Still singing, Eight nosed the car off onto a side road before reaching Watson's Point. Occasional weathered houses straggled beside a river of marsh grass on their left, and on the right, the ground sloped gently into a pasture with a series of low jumps set up. A trio of muddy horses had clustered around an old bathtub that doubled as a water trough in the far corner, while a mare ambled away, lashing her tail at unseen flies. At the end of the driveway, a blue-and-white barn sprawled cheerfully beneath a clump of trees, and a woman emerged from it before Eight had even stopped the car.

The woman was rectangular; that was about the only way to describe her. Her body was short and broad and lean, crammed into a tank top, riding breeches, and black knee-high boots. Even her hair was cut bluntly across the bangs and square beneath the chin.

"Hello!" She pulled Pru in for a hug the moment Pru emerged from the car. "Am I ever happy to see you—and I'll be even happier once I get you on a horse again."

Pru disengaged herself and rubbed absently at her ribs. "Bet you never thought you'd live to see that happen."

"I can be magnanimous and say I missed you, can't I? Especially with twenty years of show ribbons hanging on my walls, thanks to your absence." Alyssa smiled without self-consciousness, deepening the sun creases around her eyes. "Also, to be honest, nothing pushes a person to improve as much as the desire to beat out someone who's always that little bit better."

Alyssa greeted Eight and his sister before turning to Barrie and giving her a slow appraisal. "You must be Lula's girl. Pru says you're not much of a rider?"

"Not a rider at all," Barrie said. "The horses should probably run when they see me coming."

"At least you're not afraid. I've heard that about you. Come on inside, then." She glanced down at Barrie's pink sneakers with a frown. "You're going to need some boots. That's the first thing. I've probably got an old pair of my daughter Amanda's around here somewhere that'll fit you. And I've got a couple of sweet mares and a nice gelding for you both to look at, although half the battle is won in the stall, I always say. You need to be the one putting down the hay and raking through the shit, all the day-to-day unglamorous things, or you miss out on half the good stuff with a horse. The riding is the least of it."

She disappeared into the tack room on the left of the barn entrance, with Pru and Kate following close behind her. Eight stood with his hands shoved deep into his pockets, waiting to fall into step with Barrie. As usual, the tail of his shirt was loose over his shorts, and unlike Kate, who wore high boots over fawn-colored riding breeches, he wore just his usual boat shoes.

Barrie ignored the fact that he was gorgeous, and concentrated on the fact that she was mad at him. "You're being a complete ass. You know that, right?"

"Me?" He stared at her blankly for a second. "*I'm* being an ass? The more I think about what you did last night, how stupid it was to go off with Obadiah by yourself, not to mention Cassie, the more I realize I let you off easy. You didn't trust me enough to tell me."

"I told you, my throat closed up every time I even thought about saying his name."

"Did you try writing it down? Hell, you could have transmitted it in smoke signals. Or here's a thought. You could have tried not working so hard to convince me that nothing was going on." He brushed past her and stalked into the building.

The barn wasn't as luxurious as the one at Watson's Landing, but blue ribbons and championship sashes covered the walls of the tack room from floor to ceiling. Pads lightly limned with dirt and sweat had been turned bottom-up to dry on top of their corresponding saddles, and the scent was alive with hay and horse.

After removing her sneakers, Barrie tugged on the boots that Alyssa tossed her, then trailed down the aisle toward a box stall where the others were clustered around a sweet-faced chestnut with deep grooves around the eyes. Still, it was the stall before his that called to Barrie's finding sense.

"Oh, not that one, honey." Alyssa moved over to where Barrie had stopped, and they both looked down at a pure black mare with an impossibly long mane and feathered legs who was lying down in the straw.

"What's wrong with her?"

"Nothing, really. Miranda just doesn't like people much."

"Sometimes I don't, either." Barrie threw a meaningful look in Eight's direction.

Alyssa laughed. "Come meet Cumberbatch, then. He, at least, is a perfect gentleman." Tugging Barrie's hand, she nudged her toward the chestnut gelding. "And before you laugh, his registered name is Graff Benedict. We call him Batch for short."

She slid open the door, pulled a halter over Batch's ears, and walked him down the aisle so that Pru and Kate could check his conformation and the evenness of his strides. While the three experts descended into a long discussion about hocks and backs and shoulders, Barrie went to stand beside Eight, who had leaned against the front of the stall and wrapped both hands around the iron bars above his head.

"For the record," he said, "I'm still not convinced that you on a horse is the best idea."

"Can you at least pretend you aren't mad at me while we're here? You're making Pru suspicious." Barrie wandered back the few steps to Miranda's box. "Hello, pretty girl."

"It takes two to have a fight," Eight called after her. He peeled himself away from the wall and followed with his expression set into bitter lines. "If it helps you any," he added more quietly, "I probably can't stay angry for long—not if you don't want me to be. But right now I don't know how not to be furious. You didn't trust me. You deceived me. You made choices for me without giving me a chance to choose for myself. Those aren't things I can forget. Even if the anger fades, what you did is always going to be there between us."

Moisture blurred Barrie's eyes. The mare in the stall pushed out her front legs and heaved to her feet. She stood with her withers quivering a moment, then minced forward, her head slightly lowered as she came to stand at the bars. Barrie held her hand out, wishing she'd thought to bring some sugar or a carrot for the horse. Or maybe something sweet for Eight would have been better, something to bribe *him* into letting things go back to the way they had been before. Into trusting her.

"I never meant to hurt you," she said.

"I know." Eight pushed his hair out of his face and swallowed. Then, so abruptly it was clear the subject was over, he said, "I've been thinking about Obadiah, and I've decided I want to meet him."

Barrie looked over with a frown. "Why?"

"So we know what he's really after. If all he wanted was to remove the curse, he could have removed that whenever he first figured out it was hurting his family."

"He needed a Watson to find the lodestone, but Pru barely has the gift at all. Lula wasn't here, and Emmett was housebound for twenty years. Until I arrived, there was nothing Obadiah could do." A suspicion about Obadiah's true age intruded there, but she pushed it away again and went on. "Anyway, if he *was* after the gold, what was he going to do, raise it up through twelve feet of dirt and rubble and levitate it away while Cassie and I stood and watched?"

"Not while you watched, no," Eight said. "But he knows how to make you think he isn't there, apparently. And now he knows exactly where the gold is. What's to stop him from going back, creating more of that fog, and hauling it away whenever he wants?"

"First, because he never asked me whether it was the gold buried down there. Second, whatever *is* buried down there isn't money. Anyway, the gold is not our problem. Did you ask your dad about the Beaufort lodestone? If it isn't lost, then Seven knows where it is—along with a lot of other things you deserve to know."

"Yes, I asked. And no, he still won't talk about the Beaufort gift—and I don't want to talk about him. You're good at not talking, so can you please do me that little favor?"

Eyes stinging and ears reddening, Barrie reached through the bars to stroke the black silk skin of Miranda's nose. The mare's lower lip went slack and soft, and a warm, lovely energy soaked into Barrie, calm energy that made her feel like she'd tipped her face toward the sun. The cold that Eight's anger had been making her feel inside lessened marginally, and the headache that had been plaguing her since they'd left Watson's Landing pounded through her a little less.

"Do you remember when we first went down into the tunnel," she said to Eight, "and you found the bag of silver that Emmett had put there so he could pretend that Luke had run away with it? That bag felt lost, but it was lost in a completely different way from how Luke's and Twila's bodies felt lost. Do you understand what I'm saying? Some things *feel* more important than others."

"Of course."

"Doesn't your gift feel stronger when someone needs food to feed their kids versus wanting the latest pair of jeans?"

"Sometimes. But some people care more about their jeans than others care about their kids." Eight moved closer. "Bear, I get that what you saw last night was awful, but that doesn't mean it was real. It doesn't mean it happened. It's too convenient. Think about it. Obadiah performed his magic, and, next thing you know, you're seeing the Union soldiers hunting for the gold. Obviously, you were meant to realize that the gold had to be what Alcee and his wife died protecting. It could all have been an elaborate hoax, some kind of hypnotism to trick you into using your gift to find the gold for him, and everything he told you about the lodestone could have been a lie. Even if what you saw was real and the events happened just that way the night the mansion burned, I can't figure out why Obadiah would have wanted you to see it."

"I'm not sure *he* did," Barrie said.

"Then who?"

That was the sixty-thousand-dollar question to which Barrie didn't have an answer. "We need to find out more about what happened the night of the fire. If we're assuming the man was Alcee Colesworth, what happened to the girls? Cassie said Charlotte disappeared that night and no one has ever found her."

"Why do you think anything happened? You didn't see them die."

"Not then, but at least Charlotte must have, if not both of them. That angry angel in the Colesworth cemetery is the marker for her empty grave. No one knows what happened to her that night, so maybe the same way I was supposed to find Luke and your great-aunt Twila, I'm supposed to find Charlotte and the little slave girl. I can't imagine how they could be buried by the ruins, but there has to be a reason I saw the echo from that night. Maybe someone other than Obadiah wanted me to see it."

Barrie felt the truth of that as she said it. Increasingly, her gift was growing to be less about what was lost and more about finding answers. It made perfect sense, she realized as the mare nudged her hand again and blew out a warm gust of breath. The mare was another example. Although the gelding was beautiful, there hadn't been anything special about him. Touching the mare, though, looking into her liquid brown eyes, Barrie had a feeling of rightness, of *foundness*, as if the mare was an answer to a question Barrie hadn't even known to ask. It reminded Barrie of the way she was drawn to Pru and Eight. Of the way she felt deep down that she and Eight were supposed to be together.

Maybe that was why, out of almost everything that had happened at Colesworth Place the night before, the thing she found hardest to accept was Eight's accusation that she wanted him only because she had lost everything else. Losing everything made a person recognize the value of what they'd found. It didn't make them cling to things they didn't want.

Outside in the baking sun of the Evans paddock a little later, Barrie was still thinking about the relationships between want and need and lost and found. A chip of paint peeling from the fence dug into the skin beneath her nail, and she flinched and popped the finger into her mouth while she watched Alyssa tightening Miranda's girth.

Her face shining with joy, Pru eased Batch from a rolling canter to a leisurely walk. "What did you think, sugar?" She came to a halt in front of the fence where Barrie, Eight, and Kate were standing. "Did you change your mind yet? Want to try him?"

"No, I'm fine. I think he's definitely yours. In fact, I *know* he is."

In some way, she and Pru both needed the horses. Maybe Miranda and Batch were questions, the same way that Obadiah, Charlotte and the slave girl, and even the Fire Carrier were questions. Or maybe they were answers to something that Barrie didn't even know she needed yet. She had to learn to trust her gift. So many of the things she had found lately hadn't been precisely *lost*. But she wasn't found without them.

CHAPTER TWENTY-EIGHT

Back at Watson's Landing, the *yunwi* circled around Barrie as she and Eight approached the stables. But the brooms and the box of cleaning supplies that had been her excuse for spending some time alone with Eight turned out to be superfluous. Eight pulled open the double doors, and the building was spotless. All the dust and grime had been removed as if by magic. *Yunwi* magic, Barrie assumed, since the shadows were practically dancing around her looking giddy and expectant and *happy*. They darted in and out of the stalls, inviting her in to inspect one after another.

A feeling of possessiveness washed over her. "Thank you," she whispered.

"Who are you talking to?" Eight asked her.

"The *yunwi* cleaned the place out for us. I think they're excited to have the horses coming."

"Good. Thank them for me, too. I'm so damn tired, my eyes are crossing, and the last thing I wanted to do was sweep out dust bunnies and cobwebs." Eight yawned for the third time in as many minutes. "Maybe for a little while we could forget about the stables and the restaurant and focus on the actual problem. What do you think? Between you and Pru, I feel like I've been caught inside a tornado." He nodded toward her pink tennis shoes and gave her a narrow smile. "You're even wearing the right shoes for it, Dorothy. Slippers, sneakers. Not much difference."

"Tell that to the Wicked Witch. I doubt she'd agree with you," Barrie said, but the joke made her hope he might be ready to forgive her. She hated that she was going to have to make him mad all over again.

She wandered out of the stall and stood with her back to the sun. "So, I've been thinking over what you said about wanting to talk to Obadiah."

"Did you figure out how to find him?"

"There are things your father hasn't told you about the Beaufort gift. About the bargains and the binding—"

"I thought we agreed you weren't going to nag me about this anymore?" Eight's shoulders were as tight as bowstrings. "Look, I can't push Dad. Not when I'm already pushing him about school and things are ready to blow up. So why don't you just concentrate on finding Obadiah? If he is telling the truth about anything, we can get answers faster out of him than we can anywhere else. And if he can break the Beaufort gift, then none of this will matter."

Eight came toward Barrie, his hands rising and then stopping awkwardly above his waist as if he'd started to reach for her and then changed his mind. "Think how much simpler everything would be if you didn't have to worry about whether my motives were tangled up with yours."

There was no denying that.

Marching around Eight, Barrie exited the building.

"Where are you going now?" he asked, jogging to catch up as she headed down the path toward the ruined chapel and the cemetery.

"I've got something else I want to try. The Watson gift has been getting stronger since Lula died, and I'm feeling things that aren't actually lost."

"You think you can find Obadiah?"

"Who knew you had such a one-track mind?" she said. "I'm not sure what I will find, but there's something there."

"So tell me what you mean."

This new form of the gift wasn't about finding as much as it was about intuition, which was a big word for something that came down to a leap of faith. Eight had been right about that from the beginning. Barrie hadn't realized how little she trusted anyone, especially herself.

The gate around the cemetery was locked, and Eight leaped over it and held his hand out to steady her so she could climb over the fence. His touch warmed her skin, and she clung to the heat and the temporary sense of rightness, but he let go too quickly and pushed both hands into his pockets, as if reminding himself not to touch her.

Barrie suppressed a sigh. "Do you still have the keys from the library? You took them home by accident, but the key to this lock is probably on that ring as well."

"I didn't want you wandering around the house with Mark's ashes after I left."

"So you did take them on purpose?" Barrie heard her voice rising at the end of the sentence, and she closed her eyes a moment, needing to refocus. It wasn't even worth getting mad at Eight. Both of them kept trying to do things for the other, and what they needed to do was work together.

Spotting a stone bench beside a grave, she headed toward it. The tombstone had a stone dog lying at the foot and a gray cat perched on top, and it never occurred to Barrie that the cat was real until it turned to look at her with a lazy wink of pale green eyes. Moving to pet the cat, she couldn't help wincing at the inscription on the grave. A child. Another child.

She shuddered as a raven launched itself out of a tree and cast a shadow over her on its way toward the river. Two more sat on a branch nearby, like vultures waiting for someone's misfortune. Barrie sank down on the bench.

She spoke to Eight without looking at him. "How common are ravens down here? Do you see them often?"

"Not sure I can tell them from crows, to be honest." Eight lowered himself to the bench beside her and watched the bird fly away. "You think that was Obadiah?"

"Or one of his spies, maybe. I don't know."

"Can't you just call him again?"

"I didn't *call* him before. There was never any ringing, and he never hung up. I think the phone was his idea of a joke." Barrie pulled the phone out of her pocket and scrolled to the call history. "See? His number isn't here. Is that technology or magic?"

Eight sidled closer on the bench to look at the call history. Body heat radiated off him, and despite the blistering outside temperature, Barrie had been craving warmth all day. Having him furious with her made her feel cold inside, and empty.

"Can you please stop being mad at me?" she asked.

"How can I not be mad at you?" He braced his elbow on his knees. "In what universe was going to Colesworth Place with Cassie and some strange voodoo guy ever going to be a good idea? You aren't Buffy the Vampire Slayer."

"Maybe I want to be *more* like Buffy."

"Meaning homicidally brave? Or criminally stupid?"

Barrie thought about the two children and the mother at Colesworth Place, and Alcee Colesworth, if that was who it had been, hiding in the woods like a coward.

"Meaning *strong*," she said. "With a kick-ass superpower so I wouldn't have to worry about whether Obadiah was good or evil."

"How is that even a question?" Eight's eyebrows rose. "Oh, wait. I forgot. You're the one who went off for a night of fun and voodoo, live animal sacrifices optional, with a Raven Mocker *and* someone who you knew had already tried to kill you. Your judgment of evil isn't exactly—"

"What did you just call Obadiah?" Barrie grabbed his arm as the words sank in. "What's a Raven Mocker?"

"Something I found on the Internet this morning, a different kind of Cherokee witch. No one knows exactly what the Fire Carrier is or where he comes from, but Raven Mockers start off human. They eat people's hearts while they're still alive and steal whatever years the victim would have had left to live." Eight rubbed his palms on his knees, as if even saying the words had made him sweat.

"You want to go find Obadiah thinking he's one of *those*? And you call *me* criminally stupid. Hah! Have a look in the mirror, baseball guy."

Eight frowned at her with a shake of his head. "If there's

a chance he's telling the truth, I have to talk to him. You don't get how much I hate this gift. Knowing all the petty things that people think they can't live without—"

"In which case—ding, ding, ding—the crazy-nutjob award goes to you." Barrie hoped her voice wasn't shaking as badly as it sounded, but her brain was starting to feel numb. "Because living like that would still be infinitely better than having your heart eaten out of your body. Not that I believe for a minute that's what Obadiah does." She paused to analyze that statement, then nodded. She didn't think she could be *that* bad a judge of character. Obadiah might not be *good*, but he wasn't pure evil, either. "Also," she said, "Obadiah isn't Cherokee."

"Native Americans were slaves, too. They married." Eight didn't look the least deterred. "And the Savannah Indians sold a bunch of Cherokee into slavery in the West Indies about the time John Colesworth was buying slaves from there."

"You think John bought them? That would be a hell of a coincidence."

"Less than the idea that a slave who knew voodoo would randomly also know how to communicate with the Fire Carrier. That's always bothered me."

Barrie shook her head, but Eight was right. That had been a flaw in Cassie's story about a priest helping trap the Fire Carrier that Barrie hadn't even seen. "I was always more worried about how the slave trapped the Fire Carrier than I was about how they communicated to arrange the bargains they made," she admitted.

"Trapping him would have been the easy part. Didn't you see the bottle trees on people's lawns driving into town? Maybe not. You wouldn't have known what you were seeing anyway, but a lot of people around here still thread bottles on sticks and branches to trap spirits who pass by at night. The spirits get stuck in the bottles, and the sunlight destroys them in the morning."

Bottle trees sounded familiar, but Barrie couldn't remember where she'd heard the term. "That's like a genie and a vampire story all rolled into one," she said.

"Vampires are stakes through the heart. You've circled back to Buffy again."

Barrie grinned briefly, but then she remembered where she'd heard about bottle trees. "Mary mentioned using a bottle tree to trap the *yunwi* the night I almost fell down the stairs," she said.

The thought of that moment, that whole night, tied her into a knot of tangled emotions. It had been the first time she'd realized the *yunwi* were trying to send her a message she didn't understand. And there had been so many other things that night—watching Cassie's performance of *Gone with the Wind* beneath the stars in front of the broken columns at Colesworth

Place, arguing with Wyatt, being *scared* by Wyatt, driving to the beach where she and Eight had kissed. . . . It had been a horrible night and a magical one, but the ugliness had been just beginning. When Wyatt died, she had hoped all that was over.

Now here they were, talking about witches who ate people's hearts.

"I think Obadiah's older than he looks," she whispered, as though if she said it quietly, it might not be true. Or maybe in case he could hear her. "*Old*-old," she continued, "as in old enough to want to wear a suit because it was proper to do that back when he was young, even though he looks like he's in his twenties. After seeing the way he looked when the spell went wrong last night, I'll bet he's even older. Either the explosion sucked the life out of him and made him look like that, or—"

"It made him look his actual age?" Eight asked. "Told you. He's a Raven Mocker, or something like it."

"In which case, I repeat: Why would you want us to go and find him?" Jumping off the bench, Barrie stood with her back to Eight, looking toward the tree with the ravens in it.

It was so hard to know what to do. Her intuition, whether it had anything to do with her Watson gift or not, said Obadiah wasn't evil, but that didn't mean she was eager to go poking the hornets' nest. She'd done what he'd asked of her. She hoped that meant her gift was safe.

Obadiah himself had said that she needed to choose which was more important, Eight or her magic. That was an impossible choice.

Closing her eyes, she pushed at her finding sense and tried to feel Obadiah among the row of ravens. Then she spun slowly in a circle to search the cemetery.

"What are you doing?" Eight asked.

"Concentrating."

All she felt was peace pressing in on her, peace and the too-muchness of Watson's Landing that always swept over her when she opened herself to it. The timelessness and familiarity of the plantation sank into her bones. She still didn't fully understand what the water spirit had meant about a binding, but she belonged to Watson's Landing, and it belonged to her. The dead in this cemetery were hers to protect from Obadiah and anything else that threatened them. Good or ill, right or wrong, they were hers. They were family.

Thinking of family made her think of Mark, and what she was searching for changed there in the stillness among the dead. Wherever Obadiah was, he wasn't in the cemetery, but Mark should have been. Mark was her true family more than any of the people in the graves around her.

She thought back to what she had seen the night before, to the ghostly echo of a young girl being used as a bargaining chip, as a demonstration of strength meant to intimidate. Barrie could imagine the fear and sense of powerlessness the girl must have felt. It didn't require much imagination. Barrie had been helpless to stop what was happening as she'd watched.

The past was fixed. Barrie couldn't help the child or alter the existence of slavery, or even make up for the fact that her own family had owned slaves. She could be outraged, though. For that girl, for Mark's ancestors and presumably Obadiah's, for the girls and women she saw in the news from all around the world. For anyone who couldn't defend themselves.

She could try to make sure they weren't forgotten. She would begin with Mark.

Opening her senses, she searched the rows of tombs and graves for an empty space to hold Mark's ashes. What drew her didn't feel like the Watson gift. There was no ache or pressure, only that same sense of rightness, of brightness, leading her toward a spot near the back wall of the chapel. She threaded her way through the rows of cherubs, angels, and weeping children, past gracefully arched headstones and chiseled marble obelisks. She stopped where a thick branch of the oak tree that grew inside the ruined chapel had stretched across the roofless wall and cast kaleidescope shadows on the grass beneath her feet.

"This is where I'm going to bury Mark," she said. "And I think we should bury Luke and Twila here, too. I know Twila is a Beaufort, but she should be with Luke. They were meant to be together."

CHAPTER TWENTY-NINE

"Well, there you are," Pru said as Barrie and Eight came into the library a few minutes later. "I hope you two have settled your differences. I hated that you were fighting."

Barrie cast an embarrassed glance around the room. Thanks to Seven's militant organizational skills, the library had been transformed into an operations center. Two brand-new laptops had been delivered to the house that morning, and workmen had installed an Internet connection via satellite with very little fuss. Pru and Mary were confirming the list of farm-to-table suppliers while Daphne set up the core of a website using Barrie's stark white design on a gray background.

"Like it so far?" Daphne asked as Barrie peered over her shoulder.

Black trees, draped black moss, and a round white moon.

Daphne had taken Barrie's logo idea and digitized it perfectly. She'd even made the fairy lights on the trees look as if they were glowing.

"It's wonderful."

"Oh, good." Daphne grinned at her. "You never know if people are going to be the kind who pick at every tiny detail or if they are the kind who see the big picture."

"Forest or the trees?" Eight suggested.

"Something like that," Daphne said. "Would you two mind doing the text for the website? Pru said to leave that for y'all, but I'm at a point where it would be good to have it."

Pru slid a laptop across the heavy mahogany desk, and after a moment of hesitation Eight pushed it at Barrie and dropped into a chair with his feet planted on the floor and a mulish cast to his jaw that said he wasn't happy. The expression was uncharacteristic enough that it took her a moment to remember his dyslexia. Was he reluctant to read in front of her?

She thought about all the things he must have looked up—the *yunwi*, and Cherokee witchcraft, lodestones, Raven Mockers, Cherokee history, slavery, voodoo. How long had it taken him to read all the different articles and posts online in the course of the night?

She wanted to slip her hand into his, but his arms were crossed self-protectively over his chest. Settling the computer on her lap, she scooted her chair closer to his and opened the new home page for the restaurant website and started to type while Eight watched over her shoulder with his lips moving silently.

Come experience culinary magic amid the beauty of the magnificent plantation gardens of Watson's Landing. Join us for a unique dining experience, eating family-style on the beautiful terrace overlooking

"Don't use that twice." Eight touched the screen to point to the text Barrie was typing on her laptop. "Maybe try something about stepping into the past."

"I don't want this to be about the past," Barrie said.

But Eight was still concentrating on the text. "Also, mentioning magic when it's already in the name of the restaurant is too much. We don't want to make it seem like an invitation for the crazies to come out. Half the guests are going to refuse to leave before midnight as it is."

"Might be worth lettin' folks stay to see the Fire Carrier, so long as they want to pay for it." Mary dropped the notebook into her lap and looked from Pru to Barrie. "It's not like most of 'em would see anythin' anyway."

"God, no," Barrie said at the same time that Pru and Eight both said, "Absolutely not," and the phone rang on the desk.

Setting aside the recipe book she'd been thumbing through, Pru reached over and picked it up. "Hello? . . . What? No."

Her posture stiffened as she listened to whatever the caller said. She turned to Barrie, her fingers twining the cord attached to the black receiver, while the caller continued speaking. "Yes," she said finally. "I suppose she's here." She held the phone four inches from her face and stared at it with a dazed expression as if she didn't quite know what it was. Then she slowly shook her head and held it out to Barrie. "It's your cousin. She says she needs to talk to you."

Barrie leaned across the desk and took the phone. Eight's face had been wiped clean of any trace of softness, and Mary sat forward in her chair, her eyes lit with the kind of horrified gleam that people got watching a disaster unfold.

"Hello?" Barrie said.

Cassie's voice held no pretense at civility, much less friendliness. "You need to get over here. Right now."

Barrie resisted the urge to whisper in the hope the others wouldn't hear. They couldn't avoid hearing. "That's not possible."

"I don't care what's possible," Cassie said. "Whatever ghosts you and your tame witch doctor let loose last night are messing with the equipment over here. The archaeologists have been trying to set up all day, and they're about ready to quit, so you need to get over here and fix it."

Barrie hoped her voice came out sounding reasonable. "We're in the middle of something—"

"I don't give a crap what you're doing. You figure out how to get here, and bring the creepy witch doctor and get him to undo whatever he did. Do it fast, too, or you're going to wish you'd never let me out of jail. I'll announce your little voodoo sacrifice all over the Internet and call every tabloid paper in the country until I turn your life into a living hell. I'm betting your aunt doesn't know anything about that yet. I don't expect she'd like it."

"I'm sorry. I am. But I don't know what I can do."

"Figure something out. You fix this or else. My reputation is shot to hell already, so I don't care what I tell people. But Andrew and Dr. Feldman are the only ones who can dig out the tunnel without the columns coming down—at least the only ones willing to work for free. I don't have time to find anyone else if they give up, and I need to find that gold."

Turning her back on Pru's tight-lipped disapproval and Mary's evil eye, Barrie couldn't think what to say. She couldn't mention Obadiah, and she'd already tried to explain to Cassie several times that whatever was buried at Colesworth Place was more sentimental than gold or money. Her cousin refused to listen.

Eight pried the phone out of her hand. "What is it you want now, Cassie?" he snapped.

Barrie couldn't hear what Cassie answered, but Eight's expression grew progressively darker until he seemed to recall he had an audience. Relaxing visibly, he glanced at Pru and Mary.

"It sounds like fun," he said, emphasizing the last word enough that Barrie caught the sarcasm. "Maybe we'll try to make it over in a little while." He put the phone down without slamming it, but Barrie suspected that was a close call, too.

"I'm surprised at you." Mary sent a scowl at him to show he hadn't fooled her. "I can't believe you're goin' to let that girl drag you into more of her mess. I figured you, at least, had a lick of sense."

CHAPTER THIRTY

Cassie had lied again. That shouldn't have been a surprise to anyone.

Of course the archaeologists weren't ready to leave Colesworth Place.

After following Eight up the path leading from the burned-out Colesworth dock, Barrie paused at the top of the rise and took in the domed tents that had sprouted in front of the restored slave cabins like lime-green and yellow mushrooms. Two male college students in cargo shorts and hiking boots staggered from a Prius to the old overseer's house, their arms laden with picks and sieves and things Barrie didn't recognize.

"Not over there, Jerry! Set the digging equipment in the corner, and go get the printer for me." A blonde with a long braid swinging from beneath a straw cowboy hat followed them as far as the doorway, wiping her hands on her shorts.

Closer to where the tunnel had collapsed, two more students were pounding stakes into the grass. After marking each stake with fluorescent tape, they connected them with string to create a gridline of carefully measured squares. Beyond them, where the grass was still torn up from Obadiah's ceremony and its ghostly aftermath, Cassie stood beside the grad student Andrew Bey. Andrew, his face shielded beneath a Yankees cap, held a laptop computer in one hand and tapped the keys with the other, and did his best to ignore her. Cassie alternated between fussing at him and watching Berg Walters a few feet away.

Berg was wrestling with something that looked like a lawn mower with a computer display on the handles. After pushing it slowly along the grass another yard or so, he stopped abruptly and tapped the screen with his fist. "I'm still alternating between void and static, and the static is spiking the way it did on the other machine."

"I see it." Andrew Bey looked up from the computer screen, pushed his hat back, and wiped his forehead with the back of his wrist. He cast a narrow glance at Cassie before turning back to Berg. "All right. Shut it down. We can't risk a second machine frying out if there's another pulse. This whole area was a long shot anyway, so we'll concentrate on the tunnel the way we'd planned."

Cassie glared at him with her hands on her hips. "You

can't stop. This is where the gold is buried. I know it is—"

"*How* do you know?" Andrew put his cap back on. "I've done my best to check your theory, but without the equipment working, we can't tell what is down there, *if* there's anything down there. Yesterday, you didn't even want to tell us the gold existed. Now today, you know where it is, but you can't tell us why? Give me some evidence, because common sense says the gold should be over there in the tunnel somewhere." Swinging around, he pointed to where the two students had set out the gridlines.

Despite the sweltering temperatures, Cassie was wearing jeans, and the chipped red-polished toenails peeking from beneath her sandals and the heavy fabric managed to seem both defiant and pathetic. Barrie couldn't help seeing everything about Cassie differently now, but even the suspicion that Cassie had been through more trauma than anyone suspected didn't make her any easier to like.

"Could you at least try digging a little bit right there?" Cassie leaned in close to peer over Andrew's shoulder.

He shut the laptop and spoke with a show of exaggerated patience. "Archaeology is a careful process. We don't just take a pickaxe to the ground. Dr. Feldman's already going to kill me for breaking one radar unit, so I can't risk even wasting the time to do a shovel test unless you can give me something concrete to go on."

Tucking the laptop under his arm, he turned to head in the direction of the overseer's house. That brought him almost face-to-face with Barrie. "Well, hello." Stopping abruptly to avoid running into her, he broke into a smile. "I saw you the other day, didn't I?"

"Barrie, tell Andrew this is where he needs to dig," Cassie said impatiently. "You know there's something buried here. Tell Andrew it has to be the treasure."

Where Cassie pointed, loss billowed from the ground like smoke, pressing on Barrie's temples. Berg Walters had the machine positioned only about a foot to the left of the claw marks in the grass. The memory of what had happened there was a cold, sharp ache like a knife that pierced Barrie's lungs.

Eight stepped closer and slipped his hand in hers. "I think the archaeologists know their jobs, Cassie."

Cassie's eyes narrowed even further. "Tell them," she said to Barrie. "Or remember that thing I said on the phone? I'll make sure it happens."

Behind Andrew, two black feathers still lay like smudges on the ground. Barrie stooped to pick them up. Her fingertips brushed the tips of the vanes, testing their smoothness, as soft as a sigh riffling against her skin, the fingernail texture of the hollow shafts, the stiff tiny barbs as taut as harp strings, the downy afterfeathers.

Examined by itself, a feather was a miracle of design and beauty. The sheer impossibility of a bird held aloft by something this ephemeral made Barrie think of magic. Yet the miracle of a feather was the most believable of all the things that had happened in the past several weeks.

Except the feathers, these feathers, by the very fact of their existence, made the rest impossible to deny.

She searched for something to say that would satisfy her cousin without . . . what? Admitting to the Watson gift in front of Berg and Andrew? Mentioning Obadiah? Barrie wished he were there to explain what was happening.

With a sigh, she rubbed her head, and then stiffened as she recognized the tug of pressure making her ache. Turning with a chill crawling up the back of her neck, she found Obadiah standing in the shadow of the old kitchen building.

He'd been watching her, and he smiled when her eyes caught his.

The feathers dropped from Barrie's nerveless fingers and drifted to the grass like a plume of shadow.

Had Obadiah been there all along? Or had her wish conjured him from somewhere else? She nudged Eight with her elbow, but before she could tell him to look, Berg gave a shout. "Hey! Hold on. I've got a steady reading."

"I told you to turn it off," Andrew said.

"I did turn it off. It turned itself back on." Berg studied

the display on the ground-penetrating radar unit a moment longer, then pushed the machine forward again.

Andrew reopened the lid of the laptop, typed in the login code, and switched into a program Barrie had never seen before. With blurred red, green, and yellow areas marked against a blue background, it looked vaguely like a map of the continents, until Andrew clicked a few buttons and it separated into four distinct images marked at different depths. He bent closer.

"Stop!" he called. "Back up." He shouted directions at Berg about where to move the radar unit, growing more and more agitated, until he was pacing ahead of Berg and turning to walk backward while he stared down at the computer screen.

"What's he doing?" Barrie asked. "Did they find something?"

"I don't know. He must have found something. The radar is sending back reflections from whatever's underground," Eight answered about the same moment that Andrew bounded back over to them.

"There is definitely a room down there. And things inside the room. See this?" Andrew pushed the computer screen toward Cassie and traced the outlines of the red and orange areas on the screen.

"I told you there was," Cassie said, without looking at Barrie.

Andrew frowned first at her and then at the computer screen, as if it could explain Cassie to him. "I've at least skimmed through everything I could get my hands on about the history of this house. I never saw a reference to another section that would correspond to anything like this."

Barrie was less worried about the find than the timing. She looked beyond Berg and Andrew to where Obadiah still stood in the twilight shade of the kitchen building.

No one else seemed to have noticed him. He looked like he had before—strong and healthy, the neck of his navy shirt unbuttoned. The whites of his eyes and the gold in his ear and on his teeth were the only relief from the strange darkness that reflected light instead of swallowing it. If anything, he seemed even younger than the first time Barrie had seen him in front of Watson's Landing. She remembered that moment now with perfect clarity.

She remembered everything: Obadiah leaning against the wall, one knee bent while he watched her. He was different, though. Bigger than he had been. Bigger and broader and not remotely like the old man Barrie had seen lying with his eyes closed on the ground, his face all hollow and cadaverous. But there was another change, more subtle and indefinable.

He wore the same kind of clothing, another dark oil-slick suit. His dreads were the same, although he'd gathered them into a ponytail that fell to the middle of his back. The bracelet of human teeth was back around his wrist, and he made no move to hide it as he had when he'd rowed them to Colesworth Place the night the ghost house had sprung to life.

Barrie couldn't suppress a shudder. "While you were doing your research, did you find anything about the night the house burned down?" She tapped Andrew on the shoulder. "Anything that explains why the soldiers burned it? Or what happened to the people who lived here?"

"They died," Cassie said. "That's what happened. The soldiers killed them."

CHAPTER THIRTY-ONE

"Not all of them died." Andrew Bey looked up from the computer screen. "Caroline, the younger daughter, survived. Her diary turned up in the library of the Hampton House this morning as part of our records search—the Hamptons were her husband's family. I assumed you knew all that, since she would have been your grandmother seven times removed. It's an interesting custom, by the way, having the husband take the Colesworth name when there's no direct male descendant. You don't see that very often."

"Charlotte had a sister?" Barrie asked. "Where was she that night? Do you have the diary? Can I see it? Does it say what happened to Charlotte? Did you find anything else about her?"

"Berg, back up a few feet and go to the left." Andrew

tapped the computer again. "There's nothing that explains where Charlotte went, although that's not to say there might not be information somewhere—we're still sifting through various records. I have photocopies of the diary on a USB drive if you want to see it, but I haven't had a chance to do more than scan it for mentions of the tunnel, the gold, and the night of the fire. Caroline doesn't say much about any of these, I'm afraid."

"I'd love to see it," Barrie said, "if you wouldn't mind."

Andrew nodded vaguely, and his attention shifted back to the computer. Barrie looked up to find Obadiah walking toward her.

Two ravens flew above him, circling around the columns before alighting on the broken masonry. Slowly, more arrived. They landed one and two and three at a time, until the columns were full of large, black birds.

The feathers Barrie had dropped had drifted back to the ravaged grass, where the man from the woods—a ghost, a projection, an *image* who couldn't physically have really been there—had left raw, physical gouges in the dirt as if someone had torn the grass away with fingers turned to claws. All traces of the chalk cross and circles had disappeared.

Stepping between Eight and Andrew Bey, Obadiah gave Barrie a feral flash of teeth. "I was hoping you wouldn't take long to return, *petite*, but I assumed you would come alone."

He gave a curt nod at Eight. "I was under the impression you and I had a bargain."

No one looked up when Obadiah moved or spoke. Not Andrew. Not Eight. It was as if he weren't even there. He was using some kind of magic again. But on who? Her or the others? Unable to decide, she turned her back so the archaeologists wouldn't see her seemingly talking to herself.

"We *had* a bargain," she said. "I finished my end of it. I found the only powerful thing there was to find around here, which I'm assuming was the lodestone. That was what you asked me to do. Now I have a question for you. Last night . . . the house burning . . . Did any of that really happen?"

"Really happen?" Obadiah repeated the question thoughtfully. "Reality isn't that easily defined. Spirits are no less real than you or I. They simply exist in a different state. The spirits here are powerful because they have something important they wish to protect. That same purpose keeps them locked here in this reality."

"But what happened last night?"

"What happened? Your cousin stopped me from binding my ancestors when she interrupted the conjure before I'd finished."

Barrie had reached back and grabbed hold of Eight's hand and inadvertently squeezed too hard. He turned her around and loosened her grip. "What are you doing?" he asked.

Barrie's eyes widened. "Obadiah's here. Can't *you* see him? Hear him?"

Eight peered around, then turned back to Barrie. "Where?"

With his index finger extended, Obadiah reached to touch Eight's throat. Barrie brought her arm up to block him. It was too late, though. He'd made contact.

Eight blinked, then hastily stepped in front of Barrie. "Is this him? Where did he come from?"

Refusing to be pushed aside, Barrie moved up beside him again. Eight didn't argue, only slid his arm protectively around her waist.

She fixed Obadiah with a determined glare. "Now that we're all here," she said, "explain what happened last night. Was that the lodestone I found? Did you remove the curse? Is it over? Were those actual ghosts? But houses don't become ghosts, so how could we see the house burning and being looted—and why can't Andrew and the others hear us? Who were the girls we saw, and what happened to them?"

"Slowly, *chère*. *Doucement*. The others can't hear us because I don't wish them to hear, and yes, you located the lodestone. But the curse isn't broken. As for the house burning, that was not my doing." He spoke to Barrie, but crossing his arms over his chest, he returned Eight's scrutiny with a careful appraisal of his own.

They stood comparing testosterone, Eight looking combative and Obadiah looking resigned, until Eight finally shifted his feet and dropped his eyes.

"The guy's a hustler," Eight said to Barrie. "He's after more than the lodestone. I just can't tell exactly what." He seemed puzzled by that, as if it was some sort of surprise that Obadiah's magic was stronger than the Beaufort gift.

Obadiah's jaw relaxed fractionally, and if he had taken offense, he didn't show it. "At the moment, I want many things." He pointed toward Cassie and the archaeologists. "For example, I'd like to keep those fools from blundering into disaster. But you'll have to decide who to believe. I've told you what I want. The boy has told you what he thinks. Your instincts tell you what you feel. Ultimately, you have to face the hardest question."

"What question is that?" Barrie asked.

Obadiah was silent a beat or two, as if debating how to answer her. His mouth twisted into a close-lipped smile. "Whether you believe in your own gift more than you believe in the boy."

He was twisting things, Barrie knew that. Shaping his words to distract and confuse her. At least his weapons were words this time instead of some sort of spell. Her mind didn't feel muzzy the way it had the times she suspected he had tampered with her thoughts.

Obadiah swiveled his head to watch Berg and Andrew

wrestling the radar machine over the grass. When his interest returned to Barrie, there was something about him that looked both strained and urgent, and that current of extra energy lent a growl to his voice. "You have to believe *in* something, *petite*. Listen to your gift if you won't listen to me. There was a time when we could have turned back, but the spirits are awake and angry now, and as you saw last night, their power is immense. They don't want the curse broken."

"Sounds like a good plan to me. Let's not argue with them." Eight drew Barrie closer. "Come on, Bear. Forget I ever wanted to talk to this guy."

"Wait." She pulled away and looked from Obadiah to the dig site. "If you're saying it's dangerous for the archaeologists to excavate," she said to Obadiah, "then you have to make them stop. Cassie won't, and if Eight and I try to talk to them about ghosts and curses, they'll think we're crazy. Can't you *hocus-pocus* them away?"

"Why would I make them leave, when I need them to uncover the lodestone for me?"

"Then why were you keeping the instruments from working?"

The tell was minor, almost invisible. A tightening around Obadiah's lips and the slightest evasive shift of his eyes. But it was enough to let Barrie know she had it backward.

"It wasn't you, was it?" she guessed. "Your ancestors were

the ones making the instruments fail, and you stopped them so the archaeologists would find the buried room." She thought back over the sequence of events, and that made sense. Yet there was still another conclusion she couldn't escape. "You wanted the archaeologists to dig, and you wanted me to know they would be in danger. In effect, you *put* them in danger. Why? What's the *point*?"

Obadiah drew his head back like a snake preparing to strike. There was a disturbance of air, like a rattle or a hiss of scales, and then he hunched his shoulders, the motion barely visible inside his tailored coat. He looked off to the excavation site, and although Barrie couldn't see anything different there, something held his attention. He answered her almost absently. "You see, now?" he said. "You're asking the proper questions."

Barrie hated how out of her depth he made her feel. "Don't play games."

"I know better than you how serious this is," he said, still not looking at her. "I promise you I'll do my best to keep your archaeologists safe, but you saw the power of the spirits. Controlling them will take all my concentration, especially at night, when they are strongest. If I leave even briefly, anyone nearby could be in danger."

"Danger?" A dull ache squeezed Barrie's temples, more even than the usual pressure of being away from Watson's Landing. Eight tried to tug her away again, but she locked her knees and stayed firmly planted opposite Obadiah.

"Why are you even listening to him?" Eight grasped Barrie by both shoulders, bending his knees until their eyes were level. "Look at me. I'll talk to Cassie—or we'll get her sent back to jail, and the dig will have to stop."

Barrie looked back at him somberly, willing him to understand that she couldn't just let it go like that. It was almost impossible to turn from Eight to Obadiah, but she did. "You already know where the lodestone is," she said. "So what more do you want from me?"

"Very little." Without having moved, Obadiah seemed to stumble. He put a hand on her shoulder to steady himself. "Protection magic is draining work," he said. "I'll need food and a cup of coffee now and again. Morning and night, that's all I'm asking."

Despite the near-hundred-degree temperature, Barrie's arms broke out in chills at his touch. Something had altered subtly in his face, as if the bones were more prominent, as if the moisture had leached from his muscles and skin in a way that reminded her momentarily of the way he'd looked lying on the ground like a mummified corpse.

The impression was fleeting, and once again, Barrie had a sense of reality distorting like a broken mirror with pieces missing. What was real and what wasn't? Nothing was as simple as Obadiah made it sound.

But if he was telling the truth . . .

"Decide, *petite*." Obadiah let his voice grow softly menacing. "Or I can always make you the same promise we discussed before."

"The same threat, you mean," Barrie snapped.

Part of her still hoped it was an empty threat. Her gut said Obadiah wasn't wholly evil. As Eight had said, everyone came in shades of gray, and Obadiah was simply grayer than most.

But that meant she had no way of guessing what he would do.

She had always been inclined to put her trust in what she hoped others would be, and when she found she was wrong, she was bitterly disappointed. That's where she and Eight were different. What people wanted most said a lot about them, but Eight didn't rely exclusively on his gift. He claimed that he took a lot on faith. He also looked things up, reasoned through them. Maybe that was an approach he'd learned in dealing with his dyslexia, maybe it was because he fought his gift, or maybe it was just who he was. Barrie needed to be more like that.

Her gift told her the gold wasn't what was buried at Colesworth Place. And logic said that any spirits strong enough to fling Obadiah on his ass could do a whole lot worse to the archaeologists and to Cassie and her family.

Obadiah's threat aside, when it came down to it, she had no choice.

"What kind of food do you want us to bring?" she asked.

"Bread," Obadiah said without a flicker of emotion. "Two whole loaves in the morning and again at night. Apart from that, I'm not picky about what you bring, so long as it isn't peanut butter. I never did learn to like peanut butter."

Barrie felt like nothing was going to surprise her anymore. She nodded without looking at Eight, but she didn't need to see Eight to feel the waves of fury emanating from him.

CHAPTER THIRTY-TWO

Eight didn't start arguing with Barrie immediately. The fight brewed between them in silence while they descended the path toward the Colesworth dock. She darted a glance at him, then bit her lip and concentrated on keeping her footing. They both came to a startled stop when something large rustled and thrashed on the hillside to their right.

"What's that?" Barrie scanned the overgrown mixture of wisteria and kudzu that blanketed the hillside.

"A deer maybe. Or a gator."

Whatever it had been, the sound wasn't repeated. They resumed walking, and the grim set of Eight's features reminded Barrie of something he'd once said about Cassie needing to be defused before she exploded.

"You're the one who wanted to go see Obadiah in the first

place," she said when they reached the river. "I didn't want to go, so you don't get to be mad at me."

Eight stepped onto the surviving section of the Colesworth dock. Holding Barrie's elbow, he moved cautiously to where the *Away* tapped lightly against the pilings in the current. For once, the river was deserted. There were no other boats in sight.

He unwound the rope and held it taut, gesturing for her to jump into the boat. "What promise was Obadiah talking about?" he asked. "What threat?"

"Your gift." Barrie wished as hard as she could that they were already across the river and her head wasn't pounding. "If I help him, then he'll help you. Or not."

Either her attempt at evasion worked, or Eight let it pass. "I'd trust an alligator to guard a poodle before I'd trust that man with my gift," he said.

"All the more reason to keep an eye on him, don't you think? Still, he could have made you trust him. He's done it to me before. The fact that he isn't messing with either of our heads right now should tell us something."

As she said it, though, Barrie wondered if it was Eight's gift that had somehow kept Obadiah from manipulating Eight's mind the way he had played with hers. The Beaufort gift had probably been the reason Obadiah hadn't wanted Eight involved in the first place, and when Eight had said he couldn't read Obadiah, Obadiah had seemed relieved.

The problem—one of many problems—was that Barrie didn't understand how Eight's mind and his gift intertwined. She didn't even understand her own gift well enough for that, which was one more reason why she had to be careful about the possible side effects of Obadiah's threat.

Eight cast off as Barrie put on her life vest. "There's a catch somewhere. If all Obadiah wanted was food, he could order up a pizza."

Barrie snorted and settled onto the seat. "Think that through a minute. It'll come to you."

"He's manipulating you. Some sort of smoke-and-mirrors enticement to lure you back in. Now that you've agreed to this, he'll ask you for something else. The question is, what's he ultimately after? It's strange not knowing what he wants." Eight pulled the cord on the outboard motor perhaps a little more forcefully than was strictly required. "It's like I'm partially blind. I hate the gift, but being without it is disorienting. I might miss it a little."

"You can't read him at all?" Barrie raised her voice above the motor's rumble, and lifted her face to the heavy air stirred up as the boat got under way.

The wind teased Eight's hair and made him look younger. More vulnerable. "All I feel is a tar pit of wants with everything dark and bubbling, and every now and then a shape approaches the surface. I get a hint, and then it submerges again. I'll tell you this much, removing the curse is only part of what he wants—and he doesn't want me to know what he's really after."

"Not everyone is comfortable laying themselves open for examination," Barrie said mildly. "Not that his motives change anything. We don't have a choice. Sending Cassie back to jail isn't an option, and the last thing we want is anyone even mentioning ghosts. If the archaeologists are going to dig, we can't leave them vulnerable. You didn't see the way Obadiah was blown backward last night—"

"You didn't give me a chance to see it."

Barrie blinked at him and blew out a long, slow breath. Her voice was small, swallowed by the sound of the motor, not even really intended for his ears. "Are you ever going to let that go?"

He surprised her by answering at all. "Maybe. Eventually. If you want it bad enough," he said with a halfhearted *almost* smile. Then he closed his eyes. "Oh hell, Bear. I lied earlier. Or I was fooling myself. I wouldn't miss this gift. I'd give anything—*anything*—to be rid of it. Wouldn't you rather have a normal life?"

Bending over the side of the *Away*, Barrie averted her face, trailing her fingers in the water, torn about too many things. The river spilled through her hand, and she knew the moment she had crossed the midpoint, not only because her headache was gone, but because the current of energy that connected her to Watson's Landing instantly returned.

She wasn't used to having to explain herself. She'd only ever had Mark, and the two of them hadn't been like separate people when it came to decisions or secrets or even thoughts. They had spent so many years being on the same side against Lula that Barrie couldn't remember a single time that she had wanted something other than what Mark had wanted, or vice versa.

Obadiah had as much as said she had to choose between her gift and Eight. How could she?

The boat bumped against the Watson dock, and she took off her life vest and tossed it aside. "You don't have to come to the door with me," she said as he started to tie the boat off. "I'll be all right."

His face blank, Eight straightened slowly. "We're supposed to work on the restaurant today, remember?"

It was on the tip of her tongue to retort that Pru and Mary didn't need any help. The restaurant was the only thing that seemed to be going right. Everywhere Barrie turned, something needed to be fixed, and whether that was because it had all been brewing before she got there, or because she had somehow stirred it up, it felt as though most of it was her responsibility.

After crossing the garden in near silence, she and Eight climbed to the top of the steps, crossed the porch, and reached for the doorknob simultaneously.

Inside the kitchen, the table looked like a flower shop the day before a wedding, strewn with bows and flowers and silver ribbons being crafted into an assortment of experimental centerpiece arrangements. Pru and Mary had been laughing when the door opened, but their smiles slipped into almost comically identical expressions of suspicion on seeing Eight and Barrie.

"Well?" Mary said. "What'd the Colesworth girl do this time?"

Pru scrutinized Barrie almost frantically, as if checking for wounds or blood. "You look upset, sugar. Everything all right?"

"Of course." Barrie shot Eight a silent plea for help. "The archaeologists have already found a hidden room using some kind of ground-penetrating radar. It was fascinating," she said too brightly.

"Fascinating," Eight echoed unconvincingly. He tucked his hands into his pockets. "I can't wait to see what they find."

"What do you mean 'see'?" Pru stopped in the act of lacing a strand of ribbon through a basket of white hydrangeas and roses. Her hands went still, and the last pink-cheeked traces of laughter faded from her face. "You said you were going over for one quick look."

Barrie took two tall glasses from the kitchen cupboard. "But now that they've found something—"

"I don't care if they've found three-toed aliens from outer space, you aren't going back there. I'm counting on you and Eight both to help with the furniture when the appraiser and the movers come, and then there's the horses arriving tomorrow. The feed and the shavings for the bedding will be here in the morning, not to mention that the tack and grooming supplies I ordered should show up. All that will need to be put away."

"Going to Cassie's won't interfere," Barrie said, hoping the *yunwi* would help with all that, too. She went to the refrigerator to pull out a pitcher of lemonade. "We'll just run over to the dig a couple of times and see what they're up to. There's a whole crew working over there, so you won't need to worry."

Pru set the flowers on the table and sat back in her chair. "I suppose you and Eight are going to do what you want to do anyway, so I might as well save my breath. In some ways, you're too much like your mother."

Barrie whipped around from the refrigerator to protest, but Pru held up two fingers in a *Hold on* gesture. "You didn't know Lula like I did. . . ." She flushed and dropped her hand. "Oh, sugar. That came out wrong. I meant you didn't know Lula back when she was your age."

Barrie didn't know why that hit her so hard, but it did. Her stomach twisted as she felt all over again, as if for the very first time, that her mother was gone—truly gone—and she had never really known her at all. She hated that the curse and the gifts, and Emmett and the Colesworths, had taken so much away from all of them.

Eight watched her, then took the lemonade and poured her a glass. "You know," he said, turning to Pru, "it would be a shame to waste these centerpieces. We should do a trial run of the restaurant. We could use Dad and Kate and Daphne as guinea pigs."

"Daphne's goin' to be helpin' me serve," Mary said. "But that's not a bad idea. It'll be different from settin' up in the tearoom, and if you two want to help cook . . . It'd be a chance to take pictures for the website and the advertising. Then we wouldn't have to wait an extra week."

Pru gave Mary a brief, keen appraisal. "We'd have to do it tomorrow night, since we have to deal with the appraisers and the movers. Can we make that work? Or is it too soon?"

"We can manage," Mary said.

"That's settled, then. In which case . . ." Pru turned to Eight and Barrie. "Would you two go by the hardware store for me? I talked to Darrel about the submergible lights you wanted. If we're going to take photos, we'll want to have that set up for effect."

The last thing Barrie wanted was to be alone with Eight anymore.

"It shouldn't take you long," Pru said.

Eight poured himself a glass of lemonade and drank it with his back to the room and his shoulders stiff. Then he went to retrieve the keys to the Mercedes and stood jingling them while Barrie put the pitcher back in the refrigerator. Glancing at him worriedly, Barrie wondered if he'd read her—if he was hurt. Of course he was hurt.

She really needed to figure out how to keep her wants to herself. She also needed to learn to drive a car so he wouldn't have to cart her around like a five-year-old. And a boat would be nice. Probably she needed to learn to swim, too, and she definitely needed some friends of her own, because how pathetic was it that the only person who was available to teach her any of those things was Eight? *He* was the reason she needed to learn them in the first place, so she *wouldn't need him for every last stupid little thing*.

"Damn, I think I need a twelve-step program. Or a shrink," she muttered.

"Tell Darrel you've come for the fairy globes, and don't forget to get some fishing net and sinkers to keep them from floating away," Pru called after her as Barrie followed Eight through the swinging door into the corridor.

CHAPTER THIRTY-THREE

Not wanting to argue with Eight when they got in the car, Barrie concentrated on thinking how happy Pru and Mary had looked working on the flowers. "That was a good idea about doing the trial run," she said. "For Mary's sake, maybe we can open next week, if we can book some customers."

"Dad can take care of that. He'll bully people into coming, if necessary. He's good at it."

They passed the turnoff for Alyssa's barn and continued on to where the first straggling houses of Watson's Point began, and Eight pointed across Barrie to a tiny patch of lawn on her right. "That's a bottle tree over there, by the way. In case you're interested. That looks like it was a dead magnolia someone made over, but people make them out of old boards and nails, or wire, or plastic. Virtually anything."

The ten-foot tree looked like it was still rooted in the soil, but in place of leaves, a blue wine bottle had been stuck upside down onto the end of every branch. Eight veered onto one of the more residential roads and pointed out another example where the bottles had been threaded onto the branches like oversize Christmas ornaments. Not just trees, either. Bottles hung from the roof of a porch like wind chimes, and someone else had used old Coke bottles to make a chandelier. One house even had a multicolored garden of jelly jars staked along the walkway.

"Clearly," Barrie said. "People aren't superstitious at all on Watson Island."

"It's not superstition if you know magic is real and dangerous." Eight took his hand off the wheel and waved it at the houses along the quiet street. "Around here, we've all lived with the Fire Carrier and the *yunwi* and the devil digging for lost shoes a lot longer than you have. If you'd ever heard some of the local Gullah stories about boo hags, you wouldn't blame them."

"Boo hags?"

Eight sent her a sideways glance. "Ghosts that steal energy and borrow a person's skin to be able to walk around. I thought about Obadiah being one of those, too. Still not convinced he isn't something like that."

"A ghost or a witch? Because that sounds a lot like the

Raven Mocker, doesn't it? Hell." Barrie shook her head too hard then regretted it, as that made the throbbing headache behind her eyes even worse. "It's all starting to sound alike," she said.

Turning back down toward the main road, Eight said, "That's not surprising. You throw slaves from all sorts of places and religions all together, and you get a melting pot of folklore and magical systems: hoodoo, voodoo, obeah. A few people here still believe in root medicine and using spirits to help with everything from curing coughs to casting curses. Mostly, it's because they can't afford doctors—or don't trust them, or because their parents used root, and their parents before that."

Barrie stared out the window, searching for more bottle trees. "This root medicine traps spirits like Obadiah was trying to? Like John Colesworth's slave trapped the Fire Carrier?"

"I think medicine is more about asking than trapping, and I don't know what Obadiah was doing with the raven. Something a whole lot darker."

"If it was real," Barrie said. "I'm still not sure."

Then again, she wasn't sure about anything when it came to Obadiah. Something, whether it was intuition, or her gift, or something else entirely, had been telling her he wasn't that bad—she couldn't get past the belief that beyond his threats and the promise of removing Eight's gift, there was more. But maybe that was wishful thinking more than anything else.

Her gift was definitely growing, changing. She wished she understood that better, too.

Attempting a practical application, she closed her eyes and tried to sense where Darrel's Tools and Tackle might be located. The slight tug on her finding sense was instant. Even before Eight turned on the blinker, she knew that the store was down the street to the left and that the turn after that would be a right. As soon as she walked under the brown-and-gray-striped awning hung with potted begonias and entered the crowded little shop, she knew where to find the boxes of small pillar candles on the shelves. Knew without having any way of knowing except that they were something she needed.

Darrel, the store owner, was a whip-thin man with a sun-burned, balding head and a pleasant smile. Unlike everyone else Barrie had met on Watson Island, he didn't seem curious about her, or at least he kept his curiosity well contained. As Barrie and Eight walked up, he wrestled a stack of medium-size cardboard boxes out from behind the register and set them on the counter beside a display case of chewing tobacco and a box of fishing lures.

"Like I told Pru, I'm happy to get rid of these. I've got twelve cases taking up room on my shelves after a tourist ordered them and never picked them up. Still, I got to thinking after I hung up with Pru, and I'm wondering if y'all might not do better with the AquaLeds we got in for the Fourth of July celebration a few years back. The mayor never used the orange ones 'cause he figured folks would think something was on fire, but that might be just what you're looking for to make folks think they've seen the Fire Carrier, if that's what you're after. I'd charge admission, if it was me. Throw the gates open at midnight, take the money, and run—and keep running with it as long as I could. Said so to Pru when she called."

"You never know who would come prowling around if Pru and Barrie did that," Eight said.

Darrel pursed his lips, thinking it over. "I reckon that's true enough. Wouldn't be safe, would it? Say, did Beezer get that new security system put in yet?"

He and Eight started discussing microwave barriers and perimeter detection, and Barrie excused herself. Letting the finding sense guide her along the shelves, she gathered up the candles and lead sinkers that she wanted, but the finest-gauge fishing net she could find still seemed too big to hold the fairy globes securely. She grabbed some fishing line and, with her arms full and the box of sinkers balanced between the candles and her chin, headed back to the counter.

"Is there a fabric store around here anywhere?" she asked.

Eight came and took the stack of packages from her. "There's Alice Loly's place, Threadbare Crafts. It's just down the road."

"Would they have netting? Or cheesecloth maybe?"

"My wife bought some of that stuff they use to make ballerina dresses there last year for my granddaughter's dance recital." Darrel steadied the boxes Eight set on the counter, and then went back to ringing up a stack of word search puzzles Eight had taken from a carousel of audiobooks and travel games.

"What are the puzzles for?" Barrie asked.

Eight's grin was uneven, a little sheepish, and too charming for Barrie's equilibrium. "I figured, since you wanted practice looking for answers," he said, "they would come in handy."

Every time Barrie ever started to doubt, he showed her exactly why her intuition had chosen him. She stood on her toes and kissed him on the cheek.

After she had paid for the lights and supplies, Darrel helped them carry the boxes out and stack them in the trunk. Instead of getting in the car when they were done, Eight took Barrie's hand and headed down the sidewalk. "Threadbare Crafts is only about eight doors down," he said. "We might as well walk."

His long legs made his pace faster than strictly comfortable, and Barrie had to hurry to keep up. "I keep forgetting that you know what you know," she said. "There are times when I hate your gift, but then you do something like this. . . ."

"I know exactly when you forget because that's when you

stop trying to convince me you want something other than what you really want." Eight's lips twitched, and his head cocked to the side as he looked at her.

"I'm sorry." In her head, Barrie made the apology a blanket statement, covering everything from going to Cassie's without him to not telling him about his father or Obadiah. Hurting Eight was the last thing she would ever want to do, but her gift was part of her. She couldn't give it up.

Eight stopped walking. "I lied earlier when I said that I wouldn't stay mad at you if you didn't want me to be mad," he said. "That's only part of it. Mostly, it's hard to stay mad at you when what you want most so often has to do with making someone else happy. I know you agreed to look for Obadiah for me today. I wasn't fair earlier."

"I'm trying to do the right thing," Barrie said. "I just wish I knew what the right thing was."

A beige Ford that had been driving by suddenly pulled to the curb, and the passenger window descended. Eight caught Barrie's elbow and started walking again even faster than before.

The car followed them, keeping pace, the red-faced driver leaning across the passenger seat to shout out the open window. "Hey, aren't you Barrie Watson? I recognize you from your picture—I'm Carl Abrams from the *Journal of Parapsychology*."

"Keep walking," Eight said to Barrie.

The driver stayed with them. "Hey, no. Please. Can't you give me just a minute? I've been trying to get ahold of you or your aunt to ask if I can set up some equipment at Watson's Landing. And I'd like—"

Whatever else he'd been going to say was lost in the jangle of a cowbell above the door of the craft shop as Eight pushed Barrie inside. She looked back through the glass. The reporter had been leaning across the passenger seat with the window rolled down, but already he was straightening and throwing the car into park to come after them.

Eight propelled Barrie past a startled-looking white-haired woman wielding a pair of scissors at a fabric-cutting table. "Hey, Alice. Reporter." He hooked a thumb behind him at the sidewalk. "Can you head him off while we duck out the back?"

To the left of the fabric counter, a curtain made of long strings of buttons marked the entrance to a back room. The strands clanked gently as Barrie followed Eight through, and then settled back into place behind them. They had only just fallen silent when the cowbell rang out in the shop to signal that the front door had opened.

Barrie hated running away. Part of what she loved most about Watson Island was the sense that she didn't need to hide anymore, not her gift and not herself. But wasn't that exactly

325

what she was doing now? Hiding herself at Watson's Landing. Hiding the Fire Carrier. Hiding what she was doing and what she knew. She didn't want to live like that.

As she and Eight ducked back through the hardware store on the way to Eight's car, she stopped long enough to buy every box of orange AquaLeds that Darrel had. If she and Eight were going to have to keep Obadiah fed, they would need to shuttle between Watson's Landing and Colesworth Place. Eight would be back and forth from Beaufort Hall. They would all have to come into town to shop for supplies. None of that was going to be possible with ghost hunters watching them and reporters jumping them at every opportunity, so she had to do something about them once and for all.

She hadn't changed her mind about what she'd said to Darrel. She had no intention of trying to fool anyone by re-creating the Fire Carrier's flames in the water around Watson's Landing. At least not for money.

CHAPTER THIRTY-FOUR

The reporter from the *Journal of Parapsychology* remained on the sidewalk looking after them as Eight drove away. He made no move to follow, and Barrie let herself relax against the seat.

"Okay, you can slow down," she said. "Before we leave town, can we loop back around to the QuickMart and park without being too obvious?"

"Why, exactly?"

"To pick up a cooler and sandwiches so you can drop them off for Obadiah. It'll save me from having to sneak something out of the pantry."

"So *I* can drop them off? You don't give up, do you?"

"Not when it's important, no. And can you stop on your way home tonight? Please?"

Eight left the car in the street behind the QuickMart, and

they ducked through a driveway and a low hedge to reach the small parking lot behind the store. Inside, the aisles were narrow and crammed full of everything possible, most of it geared more toward tourists than regular residents. Exactly what Barrie had hoped to find.

Her finding sense led her toward the carousel of thin, neon-colored beach towels in the back corner, but she nearly barreled into a pyramid display of toilet paper on the way. Swerving around it, she knocked a bottle of Cheerwine off the shelf onto the yellow-gray linoleum, where it bounced, rolled, and finally came to rest against a bottom shelf of dusty camp stoves and generic look-alike NyQuil bottles. Eight stooped to pick it up.

Three sun-faded Styrofoam coolers stood on the shelf beside the window. Even better, a deli in the back of the store made sandwiches to order. Barrie bought two chicken salad and a couple of roast beef, as well as two loaves of Italian bread, a package of ham, a box of Pop-Tarts, and a gallon jug of drinking water. Finally, she found a thermos and filled it with viscous coffee that looked like it had been warming on the burner most of the day.

"Also a bag of ice, please," she said to the guy behind the cash register as she pulled out her credit card again.

"You can pick that up from the freezer in the parking lot." The kid, wearing his ball cap backward on his freckled forehead, had his eyes glued on her and his elbows splayed across the counter. He shifted the toothpick in his mouth to the other side and flicked a look at Eight before ringing her purchases up.

All told, the shopping spree had taken less than fifteen minutes, but Barrie stopped to check the street before she stepped back outside. "Hey, what's parapsychology anyway?" she asked.

Eight, too, stepped out onto the sidewalk and looked both ways. "Some kind of ghost hunter thing," he said. "The coast is clear."

"Thanks." Then she had to smile. "This is stupid, right? I feel like I should be wearing a dark trench coat and practicing my code words. 'The night is dark and full of terrors.'"

"I'm not sure anyone uses *Game of Thrones* quotes as code words," Eight said, laughing out loud. "But if you're so worried about ghost hunters, why'd you change your mind about the AquaLeds?" He headed around toward the parking lot.

"Because Darrel had the wrong motive, but the right idea. I'm tired of worrying about people going into the woods or seeing us go back and forth."

"We can always use the tunnel. Dad had someone out to brick up the piece we tore out and put a new grate on, but we have keys, and it would be less conspicuous. And the first diners at the restaurant will all be people who grew up hearing

329

stories about the Fire Carrier. Dad will make sure of that."
Eight stopped at the blue-and-white self-serve ice freezer and
handed the cooler full of sandwiches and drinks to Barrie to
hold while he grabbed a bag of cubes.

"I don't want Pru worried anymore," Barrie said. "All this
ghost stuff, the people watching us from the river . . . I want
our privacy back."

"What's that got to do with the lights you bought?"

Rubbing her head, Barrie stepped around a melted ice-
cream cone someone had dropped onto the asphalt. "I want
to try putting the AquaLeds around the dock and shoreline.
If we're lucky and we can make it look like we're trying to
make the river *seem* like it's burning underwater, or at least
as if someone seeing it from a distance could *think* that was
what was happening, maybe people will assume the rumors
of the Fire Carrier have been a hoax all along. At the very
least, maybe we can create enough light and confusion that
people like the reporter will give up or focus their attention
somewhere else. The fire runs all the way around Watson's
Landing. Let them watch from the other side of the river, if
they want to. Or from the bridge over the creek. As long as
they aren't parked out behind the house. Starting tonight, I
want our privacy back."

Eight stared at her for what seemed a very long time.
"Well, I admit the idea is no crazier than anything else you've

come up with lately. Which, I'll admit, isn't saying much."

Barrie had to give him that, so she just smiled. The more she thought about the AquaLed idea, the more she was able to convince herself it might actually work.

It had to work.

She couldn't bear the thought of having more articles published, bringing more ghost hunters, more people staring.

Thinking of the Fire Carrier also reminded her that she'd been ignoring him as a source of information. He was the only one who knew the truth of what had happened with John Colesworth, Robert Beaufort, Thomas Watson, and Obadiah's ancestor. If Barrie could find a way to communicate with him, he might be able to help her navigate through any danger that Obadiah posed to Watson's Landing.

The Fire Carrier wanted something from her, and it was past time she found out what that was. At the very least, if she could find out more about the lodestones, maybe she could move the Watson lodestone somewhere else.

CHAPTER THIRTY-FIVE

They reached Eight's car, packed the cooler with ice around the food, and headed back toward the highway.

"The more I think about it, your idea with the lights isn't totally crazy," Eight said, pushing his hair back out of his eyes. "At the very least, it will be a nice effect for people coming to the restaurant, and it will probably look great for the photographs. We can set it up tomorrow."

"Why not tonight?" Barrie took in the sudden tension in his jaw and instantly tensed herself.

He looked away with an embarrassed flush. "I have to go out to the University of South Carolina for a baseball team thing. They finally wrote and said they want to meet with me about a spot. I was supposed to ask you earlier if you want to come with me."

"Supposed to?" Barrie turned more fully in her seat, and the seat belt felt loose, as if she had grown smaller or lost all her air. "But you didn't ask."

"There's been a lot going on today. So do you want to come?"

Anyone who said they were *supposed* to do something wasn't looking forward to doing it. Not that Barrie could blame Eight if he hadn't completely forgiven her yet. Talking to the Fire Carrier might be a step toward finding a permanent solution, and she needed the boats gone for that.

"Would you mind if I don't come?" she asked, fidgeting with her watch. "I'd really like to get this done, and you know how much I don't know about baseball. I'd embarrass you the second I opened my mouth."

"I wanted you to see the campus and see Columbia. I thought maybe we could get away from here for a change. Go somewhere we can be just ourselves and not all the things that come with being Watsons and Beauforts."

Barrie reached for his hand instead, because that was all she could reach, and she wound her fingers through his and took simple pleasure in the warmth of his skin on hers for a moment before she spoke.

"Your dad's not coming?" she asked.

"I didn't ask him to."

Barrie wanted to go with him, and have a real date, and

celebrate with him if the coach said they would have him, and commiserate with him if the team turned him down. She wanted to say, *of course* she would go. But if she even asked what time they'd be home, he would become suspicious.

"You should ask your dad instead of me," she said instead. "You and I can go another night—I'd love to do that—but you two need to figure things out. You need a chance to talk."

Eight took his eyes off the road long enough that the old boat of a car began to drift across the yellow-painted line in the road. "You're trying to mask what you want again. What are you up to now? Or should I even ask? Why is it so important for you to do the lights tonight?"

Widening her eyes, Barrie gave him a ghost of a smile. "I just want everything to be perfect tomorrow night. For Mary's sake, but also because I thought we could try a bit of match-making. As stubborn as your dad is, he and Pru might never get around to having a date if we don't give them a push. Also, Pru tends to make him more human, and . . . I don't know. 'Nice,' I guess, is the word I'm looking for. I was going to suggest you and I do the cooking tomorrow and let him and Pru have an 'impromptu' romantic dinner."

"By which you mean that Mary will be in on it?" Eight considered, and after a beat, he nodded. "I like it."

He helped her carry the bags and boxes into the kitchen, where Pru and Mary had moved from flower arrangements to folding stacks of linen napkins into complicated roses and designing a short and elegant menu that could also work as a souvenir. After retrieving the cooler and the bag of bread, Pop-Tarts, and coffee, Eight caught Barrie's hand.

"Walk me to the steps."

Barrie's heart skipped a beat as they ducked out the back door, but then she grimaced as she spotted two boats on the river, closer to the dock than boats had ever ventured before. Something glinted in the sunlight—a camera or binoculars.

Eight muttered under his breath and then caught her elbow. "Come downstairs."

"I thought you were in a hurry to leave, baseball guy."

"Soon," he said with a grin.

He descended faster than she did and stopped at the bottom beside the rosebush where he had offered her a rose not long after they had met. Out of sight of both the kitchen and the river, he put the food down and slid his hands up slowly, bringing them to rest on her waist. Their eyes were level while she stood a step above him. Barrie couldn't stand to look at him that directly for fear that he would see inside her too deeply.

"I wish you were coming tonight," he said, "but you're probably right. You wouldn't want to sit around waiting on me. It'll be more fun another time. Just promise me you don't intend to go over and see Obadiah in the middle of the night. Or anything equally ridiculous."

335

Barrie wiggled her little finger. "Pinky swear. I promise I'm not going over there alone."

He didn't look away until after Barrie had blushed beneath his scrutiny. "Before you say it, yes, I know I was the one who said we'd go over there today. But that doesn't mean we have to keep digging ourselves deeper." He pointed to the cooler and the bag of food.

"You don't really believe the Raven Mocker or boo hag thing, do you?"

"Do I think that he's going to borrow my skin and wear it like a suit? Or that he's going to eat my heart? No, not really," Eight said. "But if he's as old as you think, he's getting those years from somewhere. That can't be exactly safe."

Barrie tried to ignore the chill that ran through her at the idea of Obadiah's age.

"I'm not telling you this to get you to change your mind about taking the food. Whatever Obadiah's up to, it won't hurt to watch him. What I'm trying to say is that I don't want to fight anymore. Especially not over this. Part of the reason I got so mad last night didn't have anything to do with you. I've had to fight my dad for years just to get a vote in my own life. He's always wanting me to do things because he thinks he knows what's best. I know you meant well, but making a deal with Obadiah that involved my gift, that hit a trigger point. It's too similar to what Dad's always done."

If guilt had a taste, it was the copper-penny tang of blood in Barrie's mouth as she bit her lip. Eight was apologizing, and she was the one who had put her own gift ahead of his, her own opinions ahead of his. And she was still doing it. She had to keep doing it. She was worse than Seven. Or at the very least, just as culpable, since she was keeping Seven's secret.

"You have to talk to your father about the binding," she said. "Take him with you tonight, and use the time in the car to make him tell you everything he knows."

Eight pulled her close, and she rested her forehead against his. "What are you thinking?" he asked.

"Would you rather know what people think than what they want?"

"At this moment, no." His brow furrowed, and he looked her straight in the eye. Then he sighed and slid his thumb across her cheekbone, pushing back a strand of hair that had escaped her elastic band. "You're torn between wanting to be closer and wanting to push me away," he said, "so I vote for closer. I'll always vote for closer."

He dropped his arm back around her waist, and the strength of him flowed around her, but it was more than bone and muscle. Standing within the circle of his arms, Barrie was both stronger and weaker than she'd ever been. It took vulnerability to forge strength, the way true courage required fear.

She craved the closeness of honesty, but she wasn't convinced she had the strength for it. She kissed him instead, wanting to breathe him in, wanting to make every moment count. He stepped closer, pressing until her back was against the post.

"You have no idea what you do to me," he said, his voice so deliciously rough it left her dazed. "I can barely remember my own name when you touch me, but at the same time, you make me think. You make me better. When I'm with you, for the first time in my life, I feel like someone sees *me* and thinks that I'm enough."

Barrie pressed her chin into his shoulder and took a shuddering breath. How could she hurt him after that?

CHAPTER THIRTY-SIX

So long as the boats were on the river, Barrie couldn't do anything about setting up the lights, but she assumed they would eventually disperse for dinner the way they had the past few nights.

In the kitchen, Pru and Mary had been working like whirlwinds on the restaurant, and there wasn't much left for Barrie to do. After quietly pulling Mary aside and filling her in on the change of plans for the trial run dinner, Barrie ducked into the butler's pantry. Feeling the need to accomplish something of her own, something visible and tangible, she retrieved a box of canning jars she had seen in one of the cupboards, and collected a box of the LED Fairy Globes, some fishing line, and some of Pru's silver ribbon.

"What on earth are you going to do with those old Mason jars?" Pru asked.

Mary slid her glasses down her nose. The glow from the computer screen turned them an eerie shade of blue.

"It's a surprise. You'll see." Barrie grinned and pushed out through the swinging door, pausing only long enough to grab the toolbox from beneath the stairs before she walked up the two flights to the attic accompanied by a group of curious *yunwi*. The antique stroller she was looking for was still in the corner behind the trunk of old quilts. It was perfect.

If only her first DIY project had involved red satin instead of silver ribbon, Mark would have approved. Hell, he would have cheered.

The reminder that Mark wasn't with her, that Barrie couldn't run into the next room to spill all her problems in a rush of words, made her eyes fill so suddenly she had to stop to wipe them. It still surprised her that memories could cause such physical pain.

She wasn't weak. She was starting to discover that. Still, her life had changed so much, and she missed Mark so much . . . Lula's death, too, was starting to hurt more and more. A shrink would probably have told her it wasn't healthy to want to push her feelings about her mother into the locked recesses of her brain, but right now she didn't have the emotional strength to deal with them.

With the *yunwi* dispersing to rifle through trunks and boxes, Barrie retrieved the stroller, turned it upside down, and tried to unscrew one of the large, old-fashioned wheels, which resulted in scraped knuckles and choice curses more than in any form of success. She sat back on her heels and blew her hair out of her face.

She felt a brush of air on her cheek as one of the *yunwi* reached up to touch her. Another took the screwdriver from her hand, and then several worked together to pull all four of the wheels from the stroller. They looked absurdly pleased when they had finished, their eyes burning and faces turned to Barrie for approval. She laughed and slid one of the wheels toward her.

"I should have remembered that you guys are geniuses at taking things apart. Now if you could fix everything else that's broken, we'd be in business." Tapping her chest over her heart, she settled herself in a cross-legged position. The *yunwi* gathered around her, and a couple pressed close enough for the strangely cold-warm sensation of their bodies to dispel some of the stifling attic heat.

Barrie worked quickly, removing the tires from the wheels, dropping three Fairy Globes into each Mason jar, wrapping a loop of fishing line around the lid, and hiding it with silver ribbon and a bow. When the miniature lanterns were finished, she spaced them evenly along the rim of the stroller wheel and attached them with more fishing line to create a chandelier. After going around the house from the front and climbing back up the steps to the porch to avoid being seen, she hung the chandelier from the underside of the balcony above one of the two tables Pru and Mary had set out.

From inside the jars, the bright glow of the Fairy Globes picked out the metallic threads in the silver bows. The sparkling effect made Barrie think of the kind of picnics she might have had if she'd grown up on Watson Island, catching fireflies after dusk. It made her think of Eight's blue ghost fireflies, and ghost stars, and ghost girls, and ghost smiles.

She was struck again by the sense that time moved at a different pace on Watson Island, or at least that the past was never truly past. It bubbled to the surface like the wants Eight had seen in Obadiah's tar pit of a heart.

The boats were still out on the river, so with a growl of frustration, Barrie went back upstairs to the attic. She made a second chandelier, and was standing on the table to hang it when Pru poked her head out the door. The Mason jars swayed on the fishing line with a soft clink of glass.

"Mind if we come and have a look?" Pru asked.

"You've got 'em upside down," Mary said, stepping out to stand beside the door. "The holes need to be on the bottom, if you're lookin' to catch the pests."

"There aren't any holes, and I'm not trying to catch anything." Barrie seethed at even the idea of anyone trapping the *yunwi*.

Pru came to slide an arm around her waist. "The chandeliers are beautiful. People are going to love them. And they're the perfect finishing touch of whimsy for out here."

Barrie smiled at that. Mark had always said that life demanded whimsy.

She imagined him beside her, hooking his arm through the crook of her elbow and giving her one of his wide, wide grins.

Look what you did, baby girl, he would have said, and they would both have known that even if the chandelier wasn't brain surgery or even art, it was something. Making a place more beautiful was always something.

"I'd like to bury Mark in the cemetery," she said to Pru. "There's a spot beside the wall of the church. I think we should bury Luke and Twila there, too—whenever the police release their bodies. What do you think?"

"I think it's a wonderful idea," Pru said simply. "I'll speak to Seven about Twila, and do you want me to talk to Jacob about doing a service for Mark?"

"Give me a bit to think about that first," Barrie said.

The boats stayed out on the river until after nine, and she worked on laying out the ads for the restaurant, checking the window now and again until she saw that the boats had gone.

Lying flat on her stomach at the end of the dock a few minutes later, she dipped one of the AquaLeds into the water and studied the effect. The orange glow spread beneath the water, rippling as the current passed around it. Pretty enough, but still a pale shadow of the real thing. There was something missing that Barrie could not define. Magic, she supposed.

A squadron of brown pelicans flew by, low above the water, their prehistoric shapes like awkward old airplanes flying in tight formation. Barrie turned over onto her back to watch them fly out of sight, then set to work tying the rest of the AquaLeds to varying lengths of fishing line, weighting them, throwing them out into the river, and anchoring them to the dock at staggered points. The current did the rest. When she had finished, the lights glowed downriver to the creek across from Colesworth Place, and she sat dangling her legs with the *yunwi* around her until the sound of an approaching outboard motor broke the temporary peace.

She scrambled to her feet, gathered up the empty boxes, and hauled them back to the house. At the top of the terrace steps, she stopped to look back. The boat had docked at Colesworth Place, and two people had gotten out. There was a big guy, and a smaller one—Berg and Andrew Bey, most likely. Their flashlights and the glow on the river cast them in silhouette as they started up the path.

Mary had gone when Barrie returned to the kitchen, but Pru came outside to look at what Barrie had done. Smoothing her palms down her wash-faded sundress, Pru opened her mouth and closed it again soundlessly, and then she wandered to the edge of the porch and caught the railing.

"Is that what the Fire Carrier looks like to you?" she asked, finally turning back to Barrie. "That intense? That beautiful?"

Seen from the porch, the lights swayed gently in the river current, making the glow shift and shimmer beneath the water. Barrie squinted, trying to consider it from the perspective of someone who had never clearly seen the river on fire. Without the flames dancing above the surface, it was too static, too unwild, too underwhelming.

Alike and not alike.

"The real thing is far more beautiful," she said. "Maybe it's silly to hope that this will change anything. It probably won't even work. But I guess it's my way of claiming the river. I refuse to be afraid to walk down to our own dock because people will be watching, and I hate the idea of people waiting here for the Fire Carrier to emerge from the woods. I just want it to be over."

Pru pulled her into a hug, and while that helped, it didn't solve the problem.

The past was never over. It cast a shadow over the present and the future.

CHAPTER THIRTY-SEVEN

Through the closed French door to the balcony, Barrie tried not to stare across the river into Eight's room while she waited for Pru to go to bed. His window was dark, so he was probably still on his way home from Columbia.

She didn't step outside. There was still too much to do, to think about. In the confusion at the dig that afternoon, she'd forgotten to get the copy of Caroline's diary from Andrew, but the newly functioning Internet let her search for information about the night Colesworth Place had burned. Few of the results were helpful. General Sherman had ordered his Union army to leave occupied houses unharmed, but his troops had taken out their wrath on the entire state of South Carolina for leading the charge of Southern succession. A burned house was not unusual. To generals and politicians, wars were about ideology, but to soldiers they were personal. The men Barrie had seen threatening that little girl with rape hadn't been thinking high-minded thoughts.

Maybe the Union officer had been angry overall, or he'd been sent to get the gold back, or maybe rumors of wealth or buried treasure had sent him scavenging closer to Charleston than most of Sherman's troops had ventured on their way from Savannah to Columbia.

But why hadn't Alcee's wife just told him where the gold was buried, if that was what he'd been after? And why had Alcee been hiding in the woods?

Obadiah claimed that "why" was the most important question, but "who" was always harder to understand. It was people who made things happen, and their decisions were the sum of a million individual experiences. Someone could be ordered to burn down a house, to kill a man, to rape a child. If he chose to follow those orders, it was because of who he was and who his life had made him.

Barrie thought of Cassie, curled in a fetal ball and shivering, lost in her memories after seeing the slave girl threatened. What had happened to Cassie after Ernesto and the cartel had ordered her kidnapped?

Four years ago, Cassie would have been thirteen. *Thirteen*.

How did anyone think that exploiting the vulnerable was a show of strength? The whole idea made Barrie so furious that she felt helpless. She looked up a few websites about flash-backs and PTSD, but they only made her frustration worse. There was nothing she could do for Cassie, but she had to believe there was a reason the ghost house had appeared and the events of that horrible night had echoed into the present.

People assumed there would always be someone around to tell their stories. That wasn't true. Maybe that was the real purpose of Barrie's gift. Every lost object was a story, and every story needed to be heard.

It was nearly midnight. Barrie wound a black scarf over her hair. Despite the heat, she changed into black yoga pants and a dark long-sleeve tee. After easing the door open, she tiptoed out of her room. Downstairs she tugged her feet into a pair of Pru's outsize Wellingtons and let herself out of the house.

The motorboat was still tied to the Colesworth dock, and the speedboat with the canopy had come back again. It lay at anchor closer to the marsh grass near the Watson woods.

To avoid being spotted, Barrie didn't cross through the hedge maze and go down to the dock as she'd planned. Instead, she ducked down low and traversed the lawn far from the river and skirted the edge of the trees.

Ducking into the dark woods as late as possible, she blinked and tried to get her bearings. The *yunwi*, who had run beside her, abandoned her at the edge of the grass, as they always did. She wished she'd brought a flashlight to use, not for illumination but as a weapon.

Hopefully, she wouldn't need it.

After the explosion, she had been too disoriented to pay much attention to her surroundings. Now she picked her way through the concealing woods filled with carnivorous brambles and fallen branches, searching for the place on the bank where she had emerged from the river.

When she finally found it, she retreated to a spot a short distance back from the water's edge and sat on a crumbling cypress log to wait. The passage of time seemed to have slowed to a trickle. Her nose filled with a sensory overload of decay and rich new life, and her ears hummed with frogs, insects, and the occasional disgruntled hoot of an owl.

She had become impatient lately, mostly with herself and how even her best-intentioned decisions seemed to go awry. Not that anything could possibly go wrong with her current plan. *Of course not.* She was only sitting alone in the dark, in the middle of a wood filled with ghosts and snakes and alligators and who-knew-what-kind of human predators.

She had barely experienced the prickle of goose bumps generated by that thought when the first faint hint of sage smoke mixed with the forest smells, and the orange glow lit the trees at the farthest edge of her peripheral vision. Hugging her knees to her chest, she turned her head.

Despite the treacherously uneven ground, the Fire Carrier moved as sure-footedly as if he were floating. He was as real as he had been the night he had saved her, as young and alive, as somber. His red-and-black mask of war paint made the whites of his eyes stand out in the darkness, and the black feathers of his cloak and feathered cap fluttered with every step.

He watched her, but she didn't move to stop him. Instead, she followed while he carried his burning sphere into the river and unspooled threads of fire onto the water like a ball of yarn unrolling across a floor. The flames spread upriver as far as Barrie could see, and downstream to the creek opposite the Colesworth dock, where the fire turned and raced toward the left branch of the Santisto River on the other side of Watson's Landing. Rather than watching the ceremony, Barrie hid in the darkened woods and watched the occupants of the canopied speedboat. The men were drinking beer, their feet splayed, backs braced against each other as if they were too bored to even sit up straight. Once again, nothing changed when the flames sped past them. Despite the fear that leaped into Barrie's throat and tied knots in her lungs, the boat didn't burn.

She had known that. Boats had been here several times during the Fire Carrier's ceremony without burning, and the dock and the marsh grass didn't burn every night when the spirit spun his magic. Seeing it up close was different. Barrie could no longer pretend that the Fire Carrier hadn't changed his spell or changed his intent the night of the explosion, changed it because he'd tried to save her.

She was grateful. And her gratitude frightened her.

The fact of Wyatt's death, and Ernesto's death, two deaths on her conscience, frightened her. Yet looking back at the Fire Carrier, she felt no fear.

He finished his ceremony and recalled the flames to himself, spun them back into a ball of fire, and turned toward the Scalping Tree at the center of the Watson woods. Now Barrie did step out onto the path to stop him.

"Tell me what you need. What do you want from me?" she asked. "I know you want something. I feel it, but I don't understand what I'm supposed to do, and I need to know about the bargain you made with Thomas. All the bargains."

He watched her, and as real as he was, as clearly as she saw the definition of his muscles and the tracing of veins beneath his skin, he was also transparent. Through him, the Santisto rolled inevitably toward the ocean.

His eyes were as sad and solemn as the night that he had saved her, and he remained just as silent. But he raised his hands and blew on the sphere he carried. It split in two, and as he continued to blow, the fire in each hand took the shape of a small person, or a child—no, a *yunwi*. Even as Barrie made the connection, the shapes changed, melted together again, first into a circle of flame and then into a bird. A raven?

"What does that mean?" The tug of frustration that knitted Barrie's brows together was becoming all too familiar. "Are you trying to warn me about Obadiah?"

The Fire Carrier didn't answer. He gathered the flames into a ball again and walked back toward the Scalping Tree.

She ran beside him, peppering him with questions. When he didn't so much as look at her, she reached out to grasp his arm, needing to hold him back. Her hand passed through him, and she felt only a thickening of the air, a slight resistance and a cooling of temperature. She stopped walking, her mind clouding as if the cold had made her lethargic, and by the time she looked up again, the Fire Carrier had gone.

CHAPTER THIRTY-EIGHT

Eight took forever to come over the next morning, long past breakfast. Barrie picked up her phone eight or nine times with her finger poised to press his number. But she chickened out. Because as much as she wanted Seven to have gone with him, to have told him everything . . . What if Seven *had* told him, and Eight was furious that she had kept it secret?

The delivery trucks came with the sweet feed and hay and salt blocks for the horses, and another truck dumped a big pile of wood shavings behind the stables. Barrie waited until the driver packed up. Then she left the *yunwi* happily shoveling the shavings into the stalls.

Back in the kitchen, she concentrated ferociously on washing mesclun greens and prepping shrimp instead of checking her phone every couple of minutes. When she finally looked up through the kitchen window and saw Eight walking down the shallow Beaufort hill toward the dock, she half-hated herself for the surge of relief that ran through her. He was carrying a cooler, and the yellow Labrador retriever bounded happily around him.

The knife slipped, slicing into Barrie's finger. She ran her hand under the tap while Pru fussed at her.

"Hydrogen peroxide and a bandage," Pru insisted. "I don't want to hear any arguments about how it's just a little cut. You don't know where that shrimp has been."

"I'd be more worried about the salad these days," Barrie said, more to distract Pru than out of genuine concern.

"That's true," Pru called as she ducked into the butler's pantry for the cardboard box of first aid supplies. "There's probably a thousand and one different bacteria in organic fertilizer." She bandaged Barrie's finger and paused, looking out the window to where Eight was tying the *Away* to the Watson dock.

Barrie cringed inside, dreading another argument, but Pru only gathered up the Band-Aid wrappers to take to the trash and said, "If you're going somewhere, be sure to be back by three—unless you want to miss the horses."

"We won't be long." Barrie curled and uncurled her finger to take the stiffness out of the bandage. "I want to hear how Eight's trip went, and we're going to run over and see the archaeologists."

Pru tightened her lips momentarily. "You know what I'm going to say, don't you?"

"Yes." Barrie scraped the shrimp from the cutting board into a storage container with the edge of the knife before popping on the lid. "I promise to be careful, and I won't trust Cassie." She kissed Pru's cheek. "Thank you for being a sweetie."

Pru blushed a faint pink, then fluttered a hand at her. "Well, go on, then. No need to have Eight walk all the way up here only to turn around again."

A few minutes later, Barrie met Eight below the fountain. Grabbing the crook of his elbow to spin him around, she dragged him with her.

"Keep walking," she said. "I barely got out without a lecture on the evils of Cassandra Colesworth. I'd like to keep it that way."

"Yes, Highness." Eight inclined his head. "As you wish."

Barrie grinned up at him. "Never mind the *Princess Bride* jokes. What happened with your baseball thing last night? Did you get on the team? Did you take your dad with you?"

The tails of Eight's yellow oxford billowed out behind him as he walked, and his boat shoes crunched in a steady rhythm, a rhythm that was almost in time with Barrie's heartbeat. His smile fell away. "They'll give me a spot on the team, but they've already given away the scholarship they had originally offered. There's a small chance they'll be able to put together something, but I'm not holding out much hope. They're going to try to let me know tomorrow."

"And your dad? Did he change his mind about the money?"

"Dad? He doesn't change his mind when I want something. Which is disturbingly ironic, isn't it?" Eight's sigh held more outrage than resignation. "And it's not like parents don't have enough tools in their arsenals already—guilt, love, and a lifetime of lectures—they get to hold the money card, too. So many different forms of blackmail and all perfectly legitimate just because they're parents."

Pulling him to a stop, Barrie wrapped her arms around his waist and buried her forehead in his shirt, offering silent comfort and at the same time, hiding her shame. She wished she could help him.

"You're helping right now," he said. His breath was warm against the top of her head, and when she tilted her face up, he kissed the corner of her mouth. Then he started walking again. "Come on, let's get this over with."

"So what will you do if Seven doesn't change his mind?" Barrie asked Eight quietly.

"I spent the whole morning arguing with him, and there's nothing I can do except come up with the money myself. I'm supposed to meet with the coach from Charleston this morning to see what they can come up with for me, too, and I'll have to take what works out the best. Trust me, I know how lucky I am. Normally, I wouldn't have a chance of even getting back on the team, much less having them give me any financial help. And I can get a job. If Daphne can do it, I sure as hell have no right to whine."

They both fell silent, and it wasn't until they were halfway back across the river that Barrie scraped up the courage to bring the subject up again. "Maybe you should think about going to California, after all. It's not that I want you to go," she added hastily. "I know you could get jobs, but with your dyslexia you're already working harder than most people—"

"You think I want things easy?" Eight cut the motor to glide in beside the Colesworth dock. "Or are you assuming I can't manage?"

Barrie hid her expression as she stood up to loop the mooring line around the pillar. "I know you can do whatever you set your mind to. All I'm trying to say is that I'm not going anywhere, so maybe it's not worth killing yourself to be closer to me. Four years is a long time, but it's not forever."

Her stomach clenched as she said the words, and even the thought made her feel lost already.

"You should get a chance to be away from this place," she continued. "I've had the chance to see what it's like in other places. All right, I admit I haven't experienced much, but it was enough to know that this, right here, is where I want to be. I think you should have the same opportunity."

"*You* think? Or my dad thinks?" Eight pulled himself up to the dock and held out his hand to steady her. "Because I thought we agreed last night that you weren't going to make assumptions or decisions for me anymore."

He walked up the path toward the top of the rise, his strides long and alive with anger. Not for the first time, Barrie wished a meteorite would fall on Seven's head.

She owed Eight the truth. Telling him was never going to get easier. She hurried after him, but by the time he had stopped to let her catch up, they had reached the top of the path. And Obadiah was sitting cross-legged off to the side of the excavation area with his eyes locked on hers.

Hands on his knees, he looked perfectly relaxed. Even his suit and navy shirt, apparently the same ones that he had worn the day before, didn't seem to have a speck of dirt or a wrinkle on them, and the archaeology crew, Andrew and Berg and all the other students, simply flowed around him like water around a boulder in a stream.

"They don't even know they're walking around him, do they?" she whispered to Eight. "Wait. *You* can see him, can't you?"

"Yes, and he's creepy as hell." Eight shaded his eyes to look around.

As before, a dozen large black ravens were perched on top

of the broken columns of the ruined mansion with their feathers ruffled and their heads swiveling with interest to follow the movements of the dig crew.

The archaeologists had made good progress. They had cut the grass away from some of the squares around the collapsed tunnel and from most of the area above the hidden room, and dirt had been dug out and hauled away in different sections so that the area now looked like a three-dimensional patchwork quilt. Their movements slow and interspersed with yawns as if they hadn't slept much, the students were scraping away the soil with trowels and dumping it into buckets. When those were full, they hauled them toward the side of the overseer's hut, where they ran the dirt through giant sieves to separate out the artifacts. Berg and Cassie, who was still wearing long pants to hide her ankle monitor, were working in adjacent squares above the hidden room.

They were talking, Barrie realized. Or rather, Berg was talking and Cassie seemed to be genuinely listening. Surprisingly, Cassie was also doing as much manual labor as any of the others, despite her lack of experience.

None of the crew looked up as Eight and Barrie crossed the grass. Barrie said, "Hello." But no one answered.

She stopped in front of Obadiah. "Why don't they notice us?"

"The same reason they don't see me," he said. "People see what they expect, and that's not a fraction of what their eyes take in. Most of them are easy to fool, at least while I'm nearby."

"Is that what we are to you?" Barrie flushed hotly and crossed her arms. "Fools to play with? Entertainment?"

"Don't put words into my mouth, *petite*. Both you and the boy are surprisingly hard to fool."

"Meaning what, exactly?" Eight asked, which he did quite frequently, now that Barrie thought about it, as if the world was blurred around him, and he needed his corner of it in clear focus. A realist trapped inside an impressionist painting.

Or maybe what Obadiah was saying was that the world was more cubist than impressionist. That the human mind couldn't comprehend all the layers of time, space, and motion and place them into a harmonious image, so it shut its mental eyes to everything that didn't match its preconceived ideas.

Maybe that was what she'd been doing too.

"Are you planning to stand there all day holding that food?" Obadiah rose to his feet in a single sinewy motion and held his hand out to take the cooler. After rummaging through it and the bag Eight had brought, he extracted a sandwich and both the loaves of bread and took them over to one of the slave cabins. The door creaked open, and he crossed the plank flooring of the narrow one-room building. Prying up a loose board beside the brick hearth, he revealed a makeshift cellar filled with clay bowls and various jars. There were stones also, and piles of cracked, yellow bones and rusted straight pins tied together with what Barrie hoped was string.

Crouched beside the opening, Obadiah unwrapped the two fresh loaves of bread, and lowered them in to replace the two loaves from the previous night, which he removed. At least half of the sandwiches that had been intended for his dinner were also in the cellar, and he tore his current meal in half. After depositing one portion into the hole, he bit into the remaining piece as if he were ravenous.

"You're not leaving yourself much food," Barrie said.

"It wouldn't be much of a sacrifice if I didn't need it myself, now, would it?" He took another bite and wiped his mouth with the back of his hand.

The memory of his ceremony flooded back, and Barrie shuddered, chilled despite the outside heat. "I guess it's better than killing another raven."

"Death doesn't calm an angry spirit, *chère*. Just the opposite. It takes reminders of life for that, and all the spirits here are so far gone that their humanity is hard to reach."

"All the spirits?" Barrie asked with her mouth gone dry.

"My ancestors and Alcee Colesworth and his wife, mainly."

"But wouldn't the Colesworths *want* the lodestone found?"

"Doesn't much matter what they want—they're desperate,

but they don't have much strength. The others, though? They've got strength and rage—and that adds up to trouble." Obadiah finished his sandwich and rubbed his hands together. Then he replaced the floorboards, gathered up the stale bread and half-eaten sandwiches from the night before, and stood up again. "If I knew how to set this right, *petite*, trust me when I say I would. I thought I could bind my ancestors and let them rest while I removed the curse. I'm not sure how to get past them now that they're fully awake. They've been angry so long they won't listen through their hate."

CHAPTER THIRTY-NINE

Emerging from the cold gloom of the slave cabin in Obadiah's wake, Barrie paused, blinking in the sunlight. Her hand automatically sought Eight's for comfort. They rounded the corner of the overseer's cabin and found Cassie coming toward them with a pailful of dirt that needed to be sifted.

Cassie's eyes fastened first on Barrie and then on Eight, where they softened and widened and lit with the gleam that Barrie had come to dread. "What are you two doing here?"

"Just came to see how things were going," Eight answered, at the same time that Barrie said, "We came to pick up the diary that Andrew was going to copy for me. I forgot it yesterday and I can't stop thinking about what we saw."

Cassie's nose wrinkled. "Knock yourself out, if you really want to read about that stuff."

"That stuff . . ." Eight repeated. "That *stuff* happened to people. Your family. You really don't give a damn about anything that doesn't benefit you directly, do you?"

"She cares more than she lets on." Barrie put a hand on Eight's shoulder, but she didn't expect he would understand. Not without explanations about what had probably happened to Cassie that weren't Barrie's to give him. Barrie had to believe Cassie couldn't be that callous, that indifferent. Not with the way she'd reacted to what the soldiers had done.

The same way Cassie was reacting *now*.

Cassie's attention had shifted over Barrie's shoulder to the woods behind the cabin. The bucket fell from her grasp and clanged on the bricks that lined the edge of the path, spilling soil and rubble across the gravel. Her face had been bled of color, and she was trembling, staring fixedly. Her breath had turned sharp and ragged.

"Cassie!" Barrie lightly touched Cassie's shoulder. "Don't disappear on us. Stay here. Can you hear me?"

"What the hell is she playing at now?" Eight asked.

"She isn't playing." Barrie turned to look behind her, following the direction of Cassie's stare. There was only one of the slave cabins and the woods between Colesworth Place and the neighboring subdivision where the old rice fields had been. Nothing looked different.

"You're safe, Cassie." Barrie spun back to her cousin.

"There's no one there. No one is going to hurt you. We won't let them, but you need to snap out of this."

Attracted by the falling bucket, people were starting to converge. Berg jogged to Cassie's side, and Andrew emerged from the overseer's cabin.

"What's going on here?" Andrew asked.

Berg stepped in front of Cassie, shielding her. "Don't touch her. That can make a flashback worse," he warned. "Cassie, listen to my voice. It's me, Berg. You're safe. Everything is all right, and there are people here who want to help you. Nothing can hurt you here."

"What's wrong with her?" Andrew took off his cap and ran a hand distractedly across his head.

"She hasn't been the center of attention in the last few minutes," Eight said. "That's what's wrong. She's faking."

Berg sent him a warning look. "She has PTSD— post-traumatic stress disorder. It's a reaction to something she saw or experienced in her past that she's literally reliving."

"What she's 'reliving' is a lifetime of manipulating people to get what she wants," Eight snapped.

Muscles tightened in Berg's face, squaring his jawline, sharpening his cheekbones . . . making him dangerous. "No one wants to 'fake' this," he said. "Flashbacks are agonizing, debilitating, and humiliating. She's literally feeling something she went through before, as if she's right there all over again."

Eight opened his mouth, but Barrie shook her head at him as Berg went back to soothing Cassie. "Let's leave them alone."

She pulled Eight in the direction that Cassie had been staring—was still staring—even though there didn't appear to be anything to see. Beyond the line of slave cabins and a shallow, shaded gully, the ground sloped down into the narrow copse of the Colesworth woods. Through the trees, the oversize McMansions of the subdivision were faintly visible, crammed onto their tiny lots around a cul-de-sac.

In the trees, something rustled faintly, and a twig snapped. Barrie couldn't tell if whatever was there was animal or human. But a few feet beyond the cabin, where the gully still held moisture from the recent rain, several sets of prints showed the clear impressions of booted feet.

"You think someone was here and that set Cassie off?" Eight stooped to examine the prints while being careful not to damage them.

"I don't know anything about PTSD apart from what I looked up on the Internet. Flashbacks are real. That's all I can tell you. And this is the third time I've seen Cassie have one."

"She was never like this before," Eight said flatly. "You're too trusting, Bear. You're letting her manipulate you again. Cassie has never been scared of anything in her life."

Barrie arched her eyebrows at him. "What do we really know about Cassie's life apart from what we *think* we know?

We all bury the truth of ourselves below the surface. Anyway, PTSD can come on years after an event. It's not just about fear—it's a mix of triggered memories and the mind being tricked into thinking whatever happened is still happening, right then, right that moment. You don't even have to be scared for yourself—you can be scared for someone else, or guilty that you didn't do more to stop something from happening."

"Like locking your cousin in a tunnel, maybe?"

"You're taking all this out of context. Anyway"—Barrie pointed at the footprints again—"those definitely aren't figments of Cassie's imagination."

"They could have been made anytime."

"Not before the rain the other night!"

Somewhere in the subdivision, a car engine fired, and a faint sound of tires on asphalt suggested someone leaving in a hurry. It could have been unconnected, that sound, but Barrie doubted it was. She looked into the trees where the branches had rustled a minute before. It was tempting to try to follow. The chances of finding anything that way were slim, though.

Grim-faced, Eight, too, stared into the trees. Then he set off down the row of slave cabins. "Whoever that was—if there was someone—they're gone," he said. "Let's see if there are any more footprints here."

He and Barrie searched behind the cabins. There were plenty of places where someone could have stood and watched the dig, hidden from the archaeologists. But there was no more evidence to prove someone *had* been there.

"You think it was more treasure hunters?" Barrie asked. "Or reporters?"

"Or kids interested in catching a glimpse of the gold. Whoever it was, we probably scared them off, and they're not likely to be back." Eight turned to head back to the dig.

"I wouldn't bet on that." Berg had come up so silently that he'd given them no warning. His head was down, and a few feet behind Eight and Barrie, he stopped to examine a broken twig that Barrie hadn't even noticed.

Barrie watched him curiously. "Is Cassie doing better?"

"She won't talk about anything, so it's hard to say. Andrew and Stephanie are with her."

Barrie tipped her head at the unfamiliar name, then realized Berg must have been referring to the blond girl who'd been supervising the setup the day before.

"What did you mean about not betting on whoever it was not coming back?" Eight had gone from studying the broken twig Berg was still idly twirling between his fingers to studying Berg himself.

"Come on. I'll show you." Berg led the way back, taking a

slightly different route. "We want to stay clear of the way they went, just in case."

Barrie cut a sharp look at his profile as she walked beside him. "In case of what?"

There was something different about Berg, a quiet sureness that had settled around him. Or maybe it had always been there, and Barrie just hadn't seen it. "We had some grid stakes pulled up this morning. Nothing serious," he said. "We assumed it was kids playing pranks, but based on those footprints, whoever was watching stood here for a while and came back several times. The prints cross over and over each other."

"Maybe it was a lot of different people," Barrie ventured.

"Just two. A small guy wearing a size-nine shoe and a big guy wearing a size thirteen, and there's a bottle of beer kicked under the cabin that hasn't had time for the label to fade or get wet."

Eight's expression took on the familiar stillness that meant his attention was completely engaged. "What did you say you were studying again? Apart from archaeology?"

"I was in the Marines for three years straight out of high school," Berg said, studying him back.

Barrie remembered Berg talking to Cassie down by the angel statue, telling Cassie about his parents taking him to cemeteries, about how much he'd wanted to escape their preoccupation with the past. But whatever he'd seen as a soldier had sent him running straight back to archaeology. Barrie couldn't blame him—it had to be far less painful digging up gravestones than burying your friends.

"That must have been a hard transition for you," she said.

Berg was silent long enough that she didn't think he was going to answer at all. But then he shrugged. "It cured me of feeling sorry for myself, I'll tell you that. My parents never needed much apart from their work and each other, so I convinced myself I wanted to go do something that really mattered. The one thing you learn in places like Afghanistan is that you can't solve problems until you understand how they became problems in the first place."

Crouching beside him to peer beneath the slave cabin, Barrie scanned the ground for another beer bottle, or anything else that shouldn't have been there, but she felt nothing from her finding sense apart from the usual pull of loss that spilled from the hidden room and the migraine that warned her she wasn't where she belonged.

"Do people with PTSD get better?" she asked.

Berg's expression sharpened. "Everyone's different. It can take months or years of thinking you're perfectly all right before you realize you're not. Even longer than that to heal. Other times, by the time you start to experience flashbacks, you're already starting the healing process."

He paused as the crack of a twig suggested someone else

was coming, and Barrie glanced back to find Cassie moving toward them. Berg's voice grew deliberately, if only slightly, louder. "PTSD isn't what most people think," he said. "Anyone can have it, no matter what they've been through. Big traumas, small ones. It's not about what happened so much as what you do to process that event. Too often, people hold themselves accountable for things beyond their control."

"You're psycho-babbling at me again, Iceberg." Cassie emerged from around the cabins. "Stop it. I'm nothing like your soldiers. I keep telling you that, but you don't listen." She stopped beside Berg, the fraying hems of her jeans spilling around her dirty Keds and her face pale and drained. Then she swept a glance from Berg to Eight, and her smile reappeared. A wide, lethal smile that would have seemed like the old Cassie if not for the dead eyes that Barrie was coming to associate with the aftereffects of the flashbacks.

"Now, don't you listen to any of this crap that Berg's trying to sell you. He doesn't know what he's talking about. He wasn't even a shrink in the Marines, he was a sniper. I'll bet he didn't mention that he killed people. Lots of people. Men, and even a pregnant woman with a bomb once."

Her face was carefully schooled, and she had managed to wipe away her tears so that except for the cold emptiness that had darkened her eyes, she looked like nothing had ever happened. She glared at Berg, daring him to contradict her, daring him to fight her or yell at her for repeating something she had obviously been told in confidence.

Barrie recognized what Cassie was doing: pushing Berg away, just like Barrie sometimes wanted to push Eight away. It was always easier to kick someone out than to let them in.

"That was my job, Cassie. I killed people to save other people," Berg said quietly.

He spoke with no trace of self-consciousness, as if he didn't care whether Cassie, or any of them, took his response or left it. Underneath the words, though, Barrie couldn't escape the cold fact that when he'd been looking through a scope, it had been part of a process of deciding whether someone needed to live or to die, to be killed because they were likely to kill someone else.

If Cassie thought Berg was weak or easily manipulated, she was likely to be very much mistaken. And whether through a scope or without one, Barrie suspected he saw a lot more than most people.

Maybe that was exactly what Cassie needed.

CHAPTER FORTY

The whole experience at Colesworth Place left Barrie shaken and unsettled. Eight dropped her back at Watson's Landing, and despite the fact that they'd been at Colesworth Place too long and he was running late, he walked her up to the base of the steps as usual.

"I'm sorry I can't stay to help with the horses," he said.

"Pru and I will be fine." Barrie spoke almost absently. In truth, she had so much to think about that she was almost glad he had to go. Or maybe she was just relieved to be home, to have her headache gone, to have the calm of Watson's Landing wash back over her and push the ugliness of Colesworth Place away. "Go have your meeting. I'll see you later, and tonight will be great. We can celebrate when you get back."

He stepped close and pulled her to him. The wind off the

river blew her hair forward, and he caught it and started to tuck it behind her ear, but then he thought better of it. He wound it into a bun, broke off one of the white roses from the bush at the bottom of the steps, and spiked the stem through to hold it in place.

"I wish I thought you were happier about me going to school here," he said.

Barrie pulled him out of sight of the boat on the river, stood on her toes, and kissed him. Tapping his bottom lip with her finger, she said, "That's a bookmark from me right there, baseball guy."

Eight went down the path whistling, "When Will I Be Loved" by the Everly Brothers, and Barrie winced, because the lyrics about being lied to were truer than he realized.

She caught herself humming the tune when she and Pru stood together beside the stable waiting for Alyssa to back the horse trailer to the entrance a half hour later.

"I have to admit, I'm nervous," Pru said. "I know I want to do this—the horses, the restaurant, all of it—but I've been basically useless for twenty years. . . ."

"Hardly useless. You took care of this whole place." Barrie took Pru's hand and squeezed it as the trailer came to a stop in front of them. "Anyway, every magic garden needs its Sleeping Beauty." Tilting her head, she considered, and added with a grin, "I wonder if that fairy tale is where the idea of a late bloomer came from. And doesn't it feel good to be doing the things that make you happy again?"

"This feels right. Doesn't it? Watson's Landing hasn't been the same without horses."

Dressed in jeans, low boots, and a yellow T-shirt, Alyssa came around the back of the trailer. "You two ready?" she asked.

"Absolutely." Pru went to undo the latch on the other side of the ramp.

They let Batch down first. He backed down the ramp, placid and apparently nerveless, stepping carefully in the green shipping boots that wrapped around his legs for protection. Left alone in the trailer, Miranda whickered anxiously.

"Can I?" Barrie asked as Pru moved forward to get the mare.

"Sure. Go and unclip her lead. She might be calmer with you there."

After scrambling up the empty side of the double trailer, Barrie slid under the partition beside Miranda's head. The *foundness* clicked into place again the instant the mare nuzzled at her hand.

"Hello, sweetie." Barrie released the trailer tie and picked up Miranda's lead rope. "I think you're going to like it here. I wasn't sure at first, either, but the place grows on you." She found herself using the same soothing tone on the mare that Berg had used on Cassie, and she hated that she was still thinking of Cassie even when she was trying not to. She couldn't help it, though. Cassie, like Charlotte and Obadiah, Mark and Pru and Mary, the restaurant and the horses, had somehow gotten all wrapped up in her mind with the need to put things back the way they were supposed to be.

The *yunwi* darted in to pet Miranda the instant the mare was off the trailer. She lowered her head to snuffle at them as they gathered around, blowing hard enough to send them tumbling for a moment. But they came back. Miranda's ears pricked to watch them as if she saw them clearly, and looking at Batch, Barrie realized he saw them, too.

A half hour later, after Alyssa had gone, Pru and Barrie watched the horses in the pasture. There was an electricity in the air that hadn't been there before. The *yunwi* raced the horses along the fence line, clearly happy. Pru didn't notice— she had never truly seen the *yunwi* as anything but shadows, and in the light of midday, Barrie imagined they were even harder to see. But to Barrie they were more *present* than ever. When they tired of chasing the horses, they gave up and came back obviously content.

"I think you were right, Aunt Pru." Barrie linked her arm through Pru's elbow.

"Was I right about anything in particular, or only in general?" Pru asked, as she turned to go back to the house.

"About getting the horses now instead of later."

Pru took Barrie's face between her hands and kissed her on the forehead. "I don't know what I did all those years without you here. It's been a big adjustment for you though, hasn't it? I know you're troubled about something, and I wish you would talk to me about it. But whatever it is, I trust you to work it out."

Barrie couldn't push words past the lump of love, gratitude, and guilt that had wedged itself into her throat. She gave a long, slow nod instead.

They worked companionably together in the kitchen, prepping for the rehearsal dinner. Barrie lost track of time in the soothing task of cooking, then she looked out the window and spotted Eight and Seven bringing the *Away* across. She spun Pru around and untied her ruffled apron from around her waist.

"It's almost five o'clock. No more work for you tonight," she said.

Pru tried to snatch the apron back. "Don't be silly. We've barely even started."

"Mary and Daphne will both be here to help, and *you*"— Barrie pushed Pru through the swinging door to the corridor— "are going to go make yourself pretty, because you and Seven are going to be the guests of honor." She cut off Pru's objection and nudged her aunt to the bottom of the stairs in the foyer. "You and Seven need to pretend to be arriving guests," she

377

called as Pru climbed the steps. "Seven is going to sail you both down to Watson's Point, then phone us when you leave there so we can practice the timing and make sure we have everything ready down at the dock."

"Why don't you and Eight do that?" Pru asked. "It should be you."

"We are going to take the hors d'oeuvres down and greet the guests."

Standing on the dock twenty minutes later, Barrie hid a smile as Seven took Pru's hand and helped her onto the swaying boat. Eight slipped his arm around Barrie's shoulders, and they watched the *Away* grow smaller. As it passed the speedboat down by the creek, Seven stopped to speak with the occupants.

Barrie reluctantly turned away. "We better get back to work."

"As you wish," Eight said, laughing just a little.

They set out some of the stout pillar candles along both sides of the dock and covered them in plastic hurricane cylinders. Next they put tea lights inside paper bags weighted with sand and placed the sacks along the length of the path that led down to the expanse of marsh grass. By the time Seven phoned to say he and Pru were coming back, the candles and lanterns flickered and the AquaLeds glowed orange beneath the water. The fairy lights twinkled throughout the trees.

Eight cupped the back of Barrie's head and brought his mouth to hers.

The river was mercifully empty. Whatever Seven had said to the occupants of the speedboat, they had turned and headed back toward Watson's Point almost immediately. Barrie let herself get lost with Eight, lost in the sensation and the warmth of kissing him, until the *Away* appeared in the distance. Kissing Eight left no room for thought or doubt, but when she stepped back as the *Away* passed the subdivision and neared the Colesworth dock, the doubts flooded in again. As much as she wanted Pru to be happy, after the way Seven had treated Eight about the binding, Barrie was going to hate it if Pru and Seven ever married.

"Tell me again why we're matchmaking," Eight said, "if you don't want them to be together."

"I want Pru to be happy, so it isn't about what I want." Barrie tugged her hand free and turned to remove the wire cap from the bottle of champagne set out in the bucket on the small serving table they had brought down from the parlor.

"But you don't like my dad." Eight caught her shoulders as she tried to turn away.

"I don't not like him," she said.

A corner of Eight's mouth tipped upward. "Is that even English?"

"Sometimes a double negative isn't wrong." Barrie glanced up and couldn't help smiling. With his hair fallen into his face and his eyes gleaming, teasing, Eight was as unconsciously adorable as the dog that lay waiting for him across the river on the Beaufort dock.

"What's your dog's name?" she asked, changing the subject. "You've never introduced us."

"*Her* name is Waldo, and I haven't introduced you because you haven't come to Beaufort Hall yet."

"I haven't been invited."

"In that case, consider this your invitation. Tomorrow morning, I have to go see the coach in Columbia again. I'm not sure when I'm going to be back, but, hopefully, you'll be done with the appraiser. I'll come and pick you up."

"Money. The scholarship. Right." Barrie gave an emphatic nod. "You asked why I don't like your dad. I hate the fact that he would try to use your college education to control you. He—"

"He what?" Eight tilted his head and watched her. "You've been wanting to tell me something for days. What did he say to you the other night?"

Barrie bit her lip, caging the words because once she said them, she wouldn't be able to ever take them back. Just one more try, she decided as the *Away* bumped the dock. She would talk to Seven herself.

Eight grabbed the line Seven threw to him and tied it off while Seven took down the sails. After helping Pru disembark, Seven narrowed his eyes at Barrie. "Any problems here?"

Watching her aunt, Barrie shook her head. Pru's face looked flushed and alive, her hair ruffled by the wind into a cloud of loose curls that framed her face. It was the expression Barrie had been hoping to see Pru wear, she realized, and if Seven could make Pru look like that, she could forgive him a lot. She handed Pru a glass of champagne, and Pru looked at her across the rim.

"Thank you," Pru whispered.

"You're welcome," Barrie said.

Barrie tugged Eight up the path back toward the house. Pru and Seven followed more slowly, stopping to pick up bite-size crab cakes and miniature green tomato tarts from domed serving trays Daphne and Mary had pre-positioned on the tables. By the time they reached the porch, Barrie had the candles lit and the wine all poured.

Hand to her mouth, Pru halted at the top of the steps and took in the candlelit table set for two beneath Barrie's makeshift chandeliers. She turned to Barrie with tears in her eyes.

"You deserve this, so sit down and relax." Before Pru's reaction could get them both crying, Barrie nudged Pru toward a chair. "Besides," she added, "Eight and I wanted a chance to help with the cooking, remember? This is fun for us."

It *was* fun. They worked well together, falling into an efficient rhythm as they cooked, but the proximity made Barrie all too aware of Eight. The work and the heat and the way he watched her made the kitchen seem to shrink.

Barrie turned from the oven with the blue cheese soufflé held between two oven mitts and found him watching her. A shiver of happiness ran across her skin.

"Do you two want to give that a rest for a bit?" Daphne rolled her eyes and came to take the soufflé from Barrie and set it on the counter. "The kitchen's hot enough without you two raising the temperature. Also, some of us are trying to work around here."

"You leave 'em alone, Daphne." Mary smiled indulgently. "They're doin' fine. And that soufflé smells like a slice of heaven. I'd say a little romance didn't hurt it none."

Eight plated the pan-seared duck breast over a swirl of fig sauce and wiped the rim of the serving dish before handing it over for Daphne to take outside. Mary carried out the soufflé, and when they had gone, Barrie leaned against the sink and watched out the window. "They're kind of cute together—Pru and your father, I mean."

"You're feeling virtuous, aren't you?" Eight dropped a kiss on the tip of Barrie's nose.

"Well, look at her." Barrie gestured at the starry-eyed expression still shining across Pru's face. "How can I not be happy when she looks like that?"

"I don't know, but you aren't. I wish you'd tell me what's going on."

Barrie busied herself collecting pans and putting them in the sink to soak. "Not tonight, okay? Let's just focus on one thing at a time."

She waited until dinner was over, intending to speak to Seven, but he grasped her elbow as the others went back inside. Keeping her beside him, he took the plates she had stacked and set them back down on the table.

"I thought we had an agreement," he said, his voice low with a hint of threat. "You were supposed to talk Eight out of staying here, and instead you're making him more determined to stay and more poised for heartbreak."

"You and I never agreed on anything. Anyway, I can 'talk' to him until my face turns blue, but it won't change his mind unless I mean it."

"You *should* mean it. It's your own pain as well as his."

"Pain like you caused Pru?" Barrie picked up a napkin and absently smoothed it flat before looking up to meet his eyes. "Were you eventually able to convince yourself that you loved Eight's mother? Or did you just settle for second best?"

"I loved my wife, and I made her happy."

"Which is as good as admitting you weren't happy yourself. So how can you blame Eight for wanting what he wants? Or me? Knowing we shouldn't be together doesn't change the fact that we want to be."

Seven's lips flattened as he paused to study her. "There's

still the matter of Cassie's hearing. I can tell the judge we object to her being in the pre-trial intervention program."

"I'd say blackmail was beneath you," Barrie said more calmly than she felt, "but you seem to be getting very comfortable with it. I don't think you can really be as heartless as you seem, though. You wouldn't put Cassie back in jail simply because I can't convince Eight I want something I don't actually want."

Seven slowly rubbed his temple. "Do you have any idea what it's like having people's wants thrown at you day in and day out? Hundreds of wants, and everyone thinks they can't survive without them. Fortunately, the only ones that are excruciatingly painful are those of the people closest to me, but I can't give everyone everything. Living with the pain of that hardens you." He picked up the glass beside his own place setting and threw back the last of the dinner wine before he continued. "Look, all I want is for Eight to be happy, and for Pru to be happy. You and Eight going over to Colesworth Place on whatever pretext you're giving us only makes it more difficult for me to be charitable. And the more I see you and him together, the more I realize you're the last person he needs in his life."

Barrie opened her mouth to defend herself, but what was the point? Anyway, starting any kind of a conversation with Seven that could lead to what was going on at the dig would only guarantee disaster.

Maybe Cassie and Seven weren't all that different.

"You're still using your own experiences and emotions to justify ignoring what Eight wants. That only hurts you both," she said. "You have to be honest with Eight. Let him make his own choices. Either you tell him, or I will. Keeping this secret isn't fair, and whatever you say, I don't intend to give him up."

She felt brave once she'd said that, but later that night, lying on her bed with the covers thrown back and the open balcony door creaking gently in the mild night breeze, she wasn't so sure she hadn't made another mistake. She still had little confidence that Seven would come clean, and giving him another opportunity to tell Eight himself just added another day of delay. Unable to sleep anyway, she retrieved her laptop and clicked in the USB drive with Caroline Colesworth's diary. She couldn't help thinking Cassie and Seven were not so different in many ways. Both were such a mess of contradictions, it almost made more sense to believe their toughness, their callousness, was just an act.

In Cassie's case, if you took that out, and threw in the curse on top of it, what was left? A scared girl trying to find her way out of the mess her family had created for her.

CHAPTER FORTY-ONE

There was a certain illicit pleasure in seeing the early entries that Caroline Colesworth, aged fifteen and a half, had begun in 1864. Barrie had never kept a diary herself, and as she scrolled through the start of the scanned pages of beautifully neat handwriting, she couldn't help comparing it to the painful, hesitant script in Lula's letters. It made her feel guilty, and cowardly, for not having made herself read those yet. Other people's truths were always easier than one's own.

> *Monday, December 26, 1864*
>
> *There was scarce anything to celebrate this Christmas, but Mama did her best. Papa gave Charlotte a new silk dress, but Charlotte told me in private that she would have sooner had shoes for our poor soldiers, who, as James writes her,*

must daily march many weary miles on nothing but holes strung together with occasional strips of leather. She is a different Charlotte since James left to join his uncle's First South Carolina regiment. Of course, I am also changed.

It is a relief to finally confess it. Mama says a diary is the place to write all the small griefs and follies you cannot tell another soul. I imagine she writes of Papa's drinking and her worries, which Charlotte and I are not meant to know about, but many are the nights I watch from the upstairs landing as he comes home late and stumbling long after Mama has retired to bed.

I miss James, and I worry for him nearly as much as Charlotte does, although I cannot say so to anyone outside these pages. I know it is wrong to love my sister's beau, but I can't help it. We have heard nothing from James since Sherman presented Savannah to Lincoln as a Christmas gift. Papa urges us to go to our aunt Maddy's now that the vandal has South Carolina in his sights. The neighbors all flee, but Charlotte promised James she would be waiting here until he returned for her, and Charlotte has never broken a promise yet.

Thursday, December 29, 1864
Charlotte has cried herself into a fever, and Daphne and I have spent the better part of the past days sitting at

her bedside while Mama and Mary tend to the house and help with the livestock. There is scarcely anyone left to work, and Papa was gone again the entire day yesterday. Even once he did return, he busied himself with something in the cellar instead of doing anything useful.

The long day had taken a toll, and the small letters of Caroline's narrative began to blur together. To save time, Barrie skimmed the remaining passages instead of reading carefully. There was no reference to the events she was searching for, though. Following the date of the fire, there were only descriptions of the burned-out mansion, and notes about Caroline going to stay with her cousin Ashley in Charleston, and pages and pages about the search for Charlotte. And then, at last:

> *Monday, February 12, 1866*
>
> *I have not had the words yet to write of what happened. I continued hoping that somehow Charlotte would find her way back to us, that Mary and the others would bring her back.*
>
> *Papa swore the Federals would leave the house alone so long as it was only women inside. He said the only danger would be to Charlotte, so she would have to hide. He took Mary and the few remaining field slaves away to wait, leaving only Daphne to stay with us. But the officer—one*

of the deserters and certainly no gentleman—was relentless in asking Mama where we had hidden the gold. I could not think what gold he meant, so when he threatened harm to Daphne, I could not stay silent. I told them I had seen Papa in the cellar! Had Mama told me about the tunnel where Papa had been storing things, I would have kept silent, but I knew nothing until she whispered into my ear.

The Federals had searched and returned emptyhanded, angrier than before. Since they said nothing of Charlotte, Mary, Jackson, or any of the others, I had hope that everyone must have reached safety and continued running. Jackson and Mary turned up a while later, claiming they'd never had Charlotte with them, but we've searched the tunnels and woods a hundred times since for clues. I can't help thinking Charlotte would have been safe if Papa had only left her with us instead of sending her away. If she is alive somewhere, I pray she will yet find her way back to us.

I cannot bear to write of Mama and Papa. My heart has no words for such rage or sorrow.

Barrie set the computer down. Choking on tears, she went to the desk to get a tissue to blow her nose. It seemed obvious now that she'd read the entry, but not knowing that

389

Caroline had even existed until Andrew had mentioned her, Barrie had believed it had been Charlotte with the slave girl and the woman the night the mansion had burned. Since the two girls had survived the fire, she had assumed something else had happened to them later that night, that somehow *they* had disappeared.

But it had been Caroline who survived. What had happened to Charlotte?

The answer was obvious, now that Barrie knew who the girls had been.

Charlotte had never gone out through the tunnel with the slaves, and Alcee had never placed his stolen treasure in the tunnel. He'd built a separate treasure room that no one had known about, and that was where he'd hidden everything he'd thought the Yankees would most likely want to steal.

No wonder the spirits of Alcee and his wife had been trying to reach the buried room beside the basement. And no wonder Barrie had been convinced all along that what was lost in that room was more valuable than gold.

Snapping the laptop closed, Barrie tried to think through what that said about Obadiah's motives. About what he was after, and who he was. To whom he was related.

She opened the laptop again. It wasn't cheating, exactly. Flipping to the end of a book was fully justified when not knowing the ending made sleep impossible.

Saturday, July 28, 1866

Today, James showed me the sketch of the angel he ordered to guard Charlotte's empty grave. It is beautiful and angry, just as he is himself. He asked me for the hundredth time why we stayed even when we knew the Federals were coming. I still cannot bear to tell him Charlotte refused to leave because she had promised to wait for him. Oh, the argument when she told Mama and Papa for the third time that she wouldn't go! But they gave in to her, as they always did. She stayed and so Mama and I stayed as well.

I told James instead that Papa would have sooner been damned than leave while the Watsons and the Beauforts stayed. I said it was the curse that caused it all, and maybe it was.

I can still scarce believe that I shall marry James tomorrow. I tell myself that I am doing it for Charlotte's sake, that she would have wanted me to try to make him happy. But I shall never be the most beautiful girl in three counties the way she was, and James will never love me with the passion he had for her. That sort of love comes along once in a lifetime, I am convinced.

Barrie set the laptop on the desk. She moved to the window and stood looking across the river. Ragged clouds drifted across the moon in much the same way that tattered thoughts and emotions were chasing themselves through her consciousness.

She considered what to do. If Charlotte was in the buried room, the archaeologists couldn't be allowed to break through the ceiling unaware that she was down there. Barrie had to talk to them.

And there was also Obadiah.

She hadn't given much thought to what he planned to do with the gold or how he had planned to get it. Since she hadn't believed it was in the buried room, it hadn't mattered. But eight million dollars was a lot of motive.

Not just for Obadiah. For anyone.

Where were the two men who had stood beside the slave cabin watching the excavations? Who were they?

Barrie needed to talk to both Cassie and Obadiah.

CHAPTER FORTY-TWO

After spending most of the night tossing impatiently, Barrie was coming out of the shower when Pru knocked on her door early the next morning.

"Could you be ready in half an hour?" Pru poked her head into the room. "I've taken care of the horses already, so I thought we could stop at the restaurant supply in Charleston before we take the list and photographs to the auction house. Mary says we're going to need some bigger warming trays, and I've got an address for a place that sells velvet ropes to keep people from straying off the path in the garden. What do you think?"

"I think the ropes will be something for the *yunwi* to play with," Barrie said, smiling. "But would you mind very much if I don't go with you?" Telling herself to be patient was like telling herself not to scratch an insistent itch. The thought of waiting most of the day to talk to Obadiah, Cassie, and the archaeologists was intolerable, and she fiddled with the dial of Mark's watch, trying to think of an excuse.

Pru's expression softened, and she stepped inside the room. "You want to be here when Eight gets back from Columbia, don't you, sugar? It's all right. I understand more than you know what that feels like."

Somewhere in the past days Pru had found time to shop, or at least time to surf the Web, because for once her clothes looked like they'd been bought in the present century instead of the last. Barrie went and gave her an impulsive hug. "You look beautiful, Aunt Pru."

Pru's cheeks turned pink, but she smiled widely enough that the first faint creases came out around her eyes. She seemed to look younger every day, and happier.

She pressed her palm to Barrie's cheek and held it there a moment. "All right. You can stay, but keep the alarm on and the doors safely locked."

"Don't worry about me," Barrie said, which might, she conceded instantly, have been a bit of a tactical mistake.

Pru paused and gave her a hard appraisal. "You're not planning on getting into any mischief, are you?"

"Of course not," Barrie said, making a cross over her heart.

Pru held her gaze a few moments longer before she left,

and Barrie waited to hear the sound of the front door closing before she pushed herself into action. After grabbing a couple of cinnamon Pop-Tarts from the kitchen cupboard and dosing herself with a strong cup of coffee, she dug out the fixings for sandwiches and found a loaf of bread in the pantry. Eight had said he would take things to Obadiah on his way to Columbia that morning, so what she was doing wasn't strictly necessary.

Still, some extra appeasement couldn't hurt.

After stopping briefly to retrieve the keys and a flashlight from the cupboard beneath the stairs, Barrie made her way to the unused wing upstairs and into her grandfather Emmett's bedroom, with an escort of dubious *yunwi* trailing behind her. Twila's ghost was gone, but the room still seemed cold and awful. The *yunwi* grew agitated when Barrie passed through and unlocked the hidden wall panel. She slid it open to reveal the secret room and the staircase that descended to the tunnel that led beneath the river.

"Stop fussing," Barrie said. "I'll be back soon."

They stayed close behind her down the staircase, but hung back when she came to the iron door that had been designed to keep them out.

The tunnel looked much the same as it had when Cassie had locked Barrie and Eight inside. Seven, or someone, had left matches and a modern lighter beside the oil lantern that stood in the niche in the wall, and Barrie opted to use it to save her flashlight batteries. After a moment of hesitation, she shut the outer door and locked it. The *yunwi* hadn't crossed the magical barrier by the water before, but until she knew what the Fire Carrier had been trying to tell her about them, she didn't want to take any needless risk.

The tunnel was cold and dark. Memories swooped in like a cloud of bats, beating at her with leathered wings and sharpened talons. It was claustrophobic, that painful barrage, and it made her want to turn and run. She couldn't help thinking, suddenly, of Cassie locked within her flashbacks. Shaking off the acrid taste of adrenaline, she tried to still the rapid pounding of her heart.

She hugged the wall, trailing her fingers along the bricks, concentrating on counting her footsteps, reminding herself that every stride carried her closer to the exit. Still, the memories wormed their way past her defenses. Right there in that spot, she and Eight had found the bag of silver, and there the remnants of the suitcase. Here was the place where the skeletons of Luke and Twila had lain, with Luke's ghost forever grasping for a Twila he couldn't find.

Barrie blinked away a wet, hot spill of pain for the lives Emmett had stolen in a fit of jealousy. And for Charlotte and James and Caroline, their lives broken by Alcee Colesworth's greed. How could an emotion as selfless as love create so much selfish tragedy?

When Eight returned from Columbia, she would apologize to him. She would say anything she needed to say, want anything she needed to want, to give the two of them a chance to see where they could go together. If there was a lesson in the history of Watson Island, it was that people made their own curses. They didn't need magic for that.

Shadows from the newly installed grating broke the sunlight overhead as she emerged through the renovated doorway that led into the Beaufort woods.

She paused then. Sternly, she told herself the hard part was behind her. There was no chance of running into Wyatt or Ernesto. She knew that. In the daylight, in safety, fear seemed like it should have been a conquerable thing, but it loomed larger than any iron door and slowed Barrie's steps more than any iron grate.

She dropped the grate back into place and locked it, before weaving around the clumps of underbrush and poison ivy, avoiding rocks and fallen limbs where snakes might lurk. In less time than she would have thought, she was clear of the woods and starting up the path toward Cassie's house.

At the top of the rise, she stopped. The archaeological dig had descended into chaos.

CHAPTER FORTY-THREE

Berg, Andrew Bey, and the archaeology students, all of them haggard, bruise-eyed, and raw as if they hadn't slept in days, stood clustered at the excavation area above the hidden room. Cassie's mother and both Cassie and Sydney were with them. Everyone was speaking at once, raising their voices to be heard over each other by two sheriff's deputies, who scribbled notes and shouted back for everyone to talk one at a time.

But it was the excavation itself that made Barrie's footsteps falter. The stakes that had formed the gridlines lay splintered, scattered across the ground like some macabre game of pick-up sticks. Beside the overseer's cabin, the mesh of the two enormous screens through which the archaeologists sifted soil had been slashed into ribbons, and the crate of trowels and digging supplies that had stood there the day before was missing. On the opposite side of the excavation, the iron rebar and heavy block of concrete that had been set as the default point of measurement had been dug up and tossed aside. The effect was surreal, as if a giant had come through and pitched a fit.

In the center of it all sat Obadiah. His face was serene, and his hands lay on his knees, and as before, his eyes were locked on Barrie. Ignoring him, she waded into the midst of the argument and tugged at the hem of Cassie's shirt.

"What's going on?" she asked.

Cassie didn't answer. No one did. No one even turned. Barrie pulled harder, but Cassie only moved her arm as if she was swatting away a pest, and continued shouting to the deputies.

"How can it possibly be my fault?" Cassie demanded. "Try to think that through. How would I do this? That's the first question. Second, *why* would I do it?"

"I don't know why," the taller of the officers said. Reed-thin and stoop-shouldered, as if he spent too much time bending to speak to people or hunched over his notepad, he glanced up to catch Cassie's eye. "Why don't you tell me? You've done a lot of things I don't begin to understand."

Cassie flushed and looked away. "I promise you, I didn't pull up a hunk of concrete bigger than your ass with my bare hands, in case you haven't figured that out already."

"Cassandra!" Cassie's mother gave the deputy an apologetic glance, although she might have had more authority if she hadn't been dressed in a pink beautician's uniform short enough to leave ten inches of thigh exposed.

"We could all be more polite." Berg pushed closer to Cassie, and there was enough quiet command in his voice that even the two officers turned toward him. "There's no point blaming anyone before we have all the facts. That block of concrete weighs a good seventy pounds. It wouldn't be easy to tear it out of the ground like this. Also, the grid stakes were yanked out and thrown aside when we got up yesterday morning. We found some footprints and a beer bottle and assumed it was kids playing around, but maybe it was something more serious. I've still got the bottle. There might be fingerprints on it. That could be a place to start."

The shorter officer seemed to breathe a sigh of relief, looking everywhere but at Cassie. "You might not be wrong about kids. Could be a prank, I reckon. Someone wanting to give the ghost hunters something to get excited about. There's not much in the way of real damage done. Go ahead and give us that bottle, and then why don't you call us back if you notice anything suspicious."

"What kind of suspicious?" Barrie asked, but again, no one took any notice.

Andrew had pushed to the front, his face red and sweating. "To you," he said, "this may seem like 'not much in the way of damage,' but they took all the trowels, shovels, and picks, not to mention slicing the mesh in both the sifting screens." He gestured to where two and a half widths of brick had been cleared in the excavation, enough to suggest that the ceiling of the room had been domed instead of flat. "That's going to set us back most of the day."

Barrie edged over to Obadiah. "Did you do this?" she asked. "Why? What are you up to?"

"Me, *chère*?" Obadiah's expression was smug and calm. "I don't know what you mean."

"How did the equipment get stolen under your nose? Don't tell me you're not the one responsible."

"I have enough trouble tending to the spirits at night. Trust me when I say I have no energy left to pay attention to human thieves and vandals. You want someone to do that, get a German shepherd."

"Funny," Barrie snapped.

"I'm not laughing, either. A couple of trowels and shovels? Those are the last things the spirits care anything about. You see that mess over there?" Obadiah pointed at the piece of iron rebar embedded in concrete that had been torn from the ground. "That's what happens when the spirits aren't happy.

Things get thrown and people get hurt. And they would have done much worse without me here, I promise."

He stumbled as he got up, and Barrie automatically offered him her hand. He seemed brittle and creaky. Thinner, and at least a dozen years older than he had the day before. Their skin touched, and a surge of energy rushed through her, quickening her blood and bringing it to the surface of her skin. It ebbed almost instantly, and it left her weak and cold, deeply cold. She shivered.

"Stop that!" Wrenching herself away, she stepped back and glared at Obadiah, her blood pounding too quickly and too loudly in her ears. "What did you just do?"

"Nothing permanent." He drew himself up and looked at her with a defiant arrogance that reminded Barrie, unexpectedly, of her cousin. "I borrowed a small amount of strength and magic," he said. "Eat and sleep, and you'll be fine. I promised you already, I have no desire to harm you or anyone you love."

Obadiah stumbled again, and without his even touching her, Barrie felt the air around her drain of warmth. She backed away.

"Is that what you're doing to keep yourself going without sleep? You're stealing energy?"

"Only from people who have enough to spare. I'm not taking much."

"That's why the archaeologists all look so tired? That's horrible!"

"They're better tired than dead," Obadiah snapped. "What do you think I'm spending that energy on? If I took what I needed only from the archaeologists, my strength would have failed a long time ago, and the spirits would be doing more than throwing concrete."

"So that's why you wanted me and Eight to come over here, because we have magic? It didn't have anything to do with sandwiches and coffee, did it?"

"A little energy from you provides more power than I can get from all the others combined. It won't do you any lasting harm."

"How am I supposed to believe that, when you haven't told me the truth about anything so far?"

"When have I lied to you?" Obadiah's eyes gleamed dangerously.

"Not lying isn't the same as telling the truth. You never told me you were related to Mary, for instance. But the names aren't a coincidence, are they? Mary, Daphne, and Jackson. And you said your family was cursed. Mary's had more than her share of hardships." Barrie watched Obadiah carefully as she voiced what she'd suspected after reading the diary.

He only shrugged. "You never asked who my relatives were."

"You're not after the lodestone to break the curse. Or, at least, that's not all you want, is it? You want the gold."

"I told you there was a debt to pay."

"Blood and years and lives, you said."

"Stolen lives and years of servitude. Yes, and blood." Obadiah's face lost any veneer of charm. "John Colesworth thought nothing of ordering his slave to trap the Fire Carrier and demanding a *gift* that would always make him prosper while the Watsons and the Beauforts failed. Elijah refused. He knew that kind of magic would have consequences, and John Colesworth bludgeoned him to death for refusing. Elijah's wife, Ayita, cast the curse and buried the lodestone in the treasure room that John was having built."

"So you have known about the hidden room all along," Barrie said.

"I knew it existed. I didn't know where it was, and I couldn't be sure the gold was in it."

"You still don't know that."

"No, I don't," Obadiah said, regarding her steadily and somehow managing to turn the statement into a question.

Barrie had no intention of telling him. Not until she'd sorted through her options.

"Charlotte Colesworth is buried in that room. Did you know that, too?" she asked. "Whether or not the gold is there, whatever happens, we have to get her out and make sure she's laid to rest. That's who Alcee and his wife were both trying to reach the night they died."

"How do you know that?" Obadiah's exhaustion showed in the sag of his shoulders as he studied her.

"I read between the lines in Caroline Colesworth's diary. Caroline never knew about the treasure room, and she never knew about the gold until the night the Union soldiers came for it. Alcee took the slaves and men out through the tunnel, but because Charlotte was beautiful, he locked her in the hidden room where she'd be safe—or so he thought. He must have figured his wife, Caroline, and Daphne would be all right because he thought the girls were too young to be of interest to the soldiers, and he believed that if the house was occupied, the Federals wouldn't burn it. They must have been desperate to reach her when the fire started."

Eyes closed, Obadiah rolled his head on his neck until his spine cracked loudly enough for Barrie to hear it. "They're both still desperate. That must be why they wanted us to see what happened. They can't speak, so they used the burst of power Elijah and Ayita threw at me to show us what happened that night, hoping we—someone—would finally reach Charlotte and set her free."

"What happened to Daphne?" Barrie asked, biting her

lip. "I know Caroline survived, but was Daphne all right?"

Obadiah's expression smoothed out and became inscrutable. "Why do you suppose I would know that?"

"The names can't be a coincidence. Mary, my friend Mary, is your family, isn't she?"

"That's not the family I need to be concerned with now." Obadiah sounded even more exhausted. "Elijah and Ayita have never lost their hatred for John Colesworth and his descendants. Their need for revenge makes their spirits strong, and their hate keeps them from caring whom they hurt."

"But who's to say what the Colesworths who came after John would have been like if they hadn't been affected by the curse? *I'm* half-Colesworth."

"Not like them."

Barrie shook her head. "I can't let you take the gold," she said, before she'd even realized she was thinking it. "It doesn't belong to you, and I can't imagine that Mary would want it if you take it illegally. Stealing won't solve anything."

Obadiah didn't answer her, and in the silence, the sound of car doors slamming and an engine turning over made her turn to look behind her. The police were leaving, and Andrew and Berg were climbing inside the dusty white Prius. From the row of tents, the other students were emerging with towels and bathing suits and racing one another to ride shotgun in an equally dirty Ford Escape and a tiny, battered Fiat. Closer to the house, Cassie's mother hustled Sydney into a Toyota and sped down the driveway as if she was late for work, which she likely was. In less than five minutes, the grounds were empty, apart from Cassie standing beside the excavation site alone.

Barrie turned back to Obadiah in time to see him make a gesture with his fingers. His lips moved, Barrie's breath died, her muscles spasmed, and everything went black.

CHAPTER FORTY-FOUR

The earth shook. Rumbled. Barrie groaned and tried to roll over, but her entire body felt too stiff to move.

"Wake up! Barrie, you have to wake up." The ground rocked even harder.

Forcing one eye open, Barrie pried her brain loose from a deep swamp of sleep that wanted to pull her back. She found herself lying on her side on a wooden floor. There was no earthquake. Someone was shaking her. She was staring at brick, and the planks beneath her were worn, rough, and splintered.

Damn, her head hurt even worse than usual.

And while her mind was cloudy, her body was on high alert. Every heartbeat was too loud and too fast, and her wrists were bound behind her. The pull in her shoulders said they had been fastened behind her for too long already. Her ankles were tied together. What the *hell*?

"Barrie, get UP!"

A shoe connected with her hip in a white flash of pain, and Barrie came fully awake. Awake enough to recognize her cousin's voice.

"Stop kicking me, dammit. Where are we?" she asked.

That was a stupid question, though. Barrie recognized the low ceiling, the two tiny windows, the brick fireplace, and the wooden flooring of the slave cabin where Obadiah had left his offerings.

The thought poured chills down her spine.

She wiggled onto her back, and then turned her head so that she was facing Cassie. Her cousin had tears brewing in her eyes. Lying on her side, hands behind her back, Cassie had been pushing Barrie with her knees and feet instead of her hands because she was tied up, too.

"Stop gawking at me," Cassie said. "Turn back over and let me see your ropes."

Barrie inched her way along the floor and rolled over so that the ropes around her wrists were close to Cassie's mouth. Cassie tried to tug on the knots with her teeth, but that accomplished nothing. Cassie started to tremble, her teeth chattering.

"Cassie, stop. Let me try yours instead." Trying not to

panic herself, Barrie took deep breaths and forced herself to think while Cassie got into position.

Obadiah had used magic to knock her out. And Cassie, too. That was fact number one. He had said he wouldn't hurt her, but he'd lied. Or had he? She wasn't hurt. Even Cassie wasn't hurt. At least not yet.

She and Cassie were in one of the slave cabins. That was fact number two. If it was the same cabin where Barrie had been before, the floorboard was loose. That might be useful. If she couldn't release Cassie's wrists, maybe she could pry up the plank and push it aside and get—what? A pile of bones? A rusted straight pin? A pot?

With a sigh, she tried to find an angle on the rough twine that Obadiah had used to bind Cassie's wrists together behind her back. The knot was tight.

"Ow," Cassie said. "What are you doing?"

"Trying to break the twine. It's too tight to untie, but it's the same stuff they used to create the gridlines."

"Well, quit. It hurts." Cassie pulled away.

Barrie thought of the clay jars in the recess beneath the floorboards. If she could break one, it might be sharp enough to cut through the twine. But how would she pry the floorboard open? Maybe the jagged brick of the fireplace would do just as well.

She rolled onto her side and pushed herself into a sitting

position. Trying to stand up with her ankles bound was harder than she'd expected. With effort, she maneuvered herself into place in the low fireplace, her knees bent, her back wedged along the top so that she could rub the twine back and forth against the corner of the bricks.

"Are you about done wasting time yet? What are you doing now?" Cassie asked.

Barrie sent her a withering glance. "What does it look like I'm doing? Shopping for shoes?"

"You don't have to be a bitch."

"Gee, and you've always been so nice to *me*—" Barrie broke off as a gunshot rang out. One gunshot, and then another.

"What was that?" She tugged frantically against the ropes, working her wrists even faster across the brick. "Go look out the window, would you? Hurry."

Cassie grunted as she struggled to her feet and hopped to the window, and then her muscles seized. She began to shake, and tears slid down her cheeks, leaving fresh dark mascara smudges.

Who wore makeup to an archaeological excavation anyway? Well, apart from Cassie. And Mark would have, too. He had always said it wasn't worth going anywhere that you couldn't go in a good pair of shoes and a great pair of lashes. Which pretty much ruled out where she was right now— Barrie really should have considered that.

But that was beside the point. Barrie recognized that she was trying to distract herself because she was on the verge of being hysterical. Dammit, she needed to breathe. Her chest ached, and she couldn't take in air. Now was not the time for a panic attack.

She made herself take five deep breaths. Exhale, then inhale.

She made herself keep working the twine back and forth against the bricks. "Cassie, what do you see?" she asked. "I need you to stay with me. Tell me who's out there."

Cassie gave no sign that she'd heard.

Barrie doubted that it was Obadiah. He wouldn't have needed a gun. So who had fired the gunshots? The police? Or someone else?

Speculation was pointless. She worked the twine back and forth on the edge of the fireplace, and the rope grew sticky with blood. But eventually it began to loosen.

For her own sanity as much as her cousin's, Barrie talked to Cassie as she worked, trying to bring her back to the present. "Focus," she said. "Come on, Cassie. Tell me who's out there. Who fired a gun and who got shot?"

The possibilities were endless. Barrie didn't even know how long they'd been knocked out. Maybe the police had shot someone, or had someone shot Obadiah? Or had he shot someone else? What if Berg or Andrew Bey had come back?

What if they'd been shot? Any one of them might have forgotten something. Or—and now Barrie's mouth went dry
and her vision darkened until she felt like she was blacking
out—what if Eight had come after her? What had happened
to him that morning? He was supposed to stop and drop off
the food for Obadiah on his way to Columbia. What if he'd
forgotten and then come back? Or what if Pru had noticed
the keys were missing from beneath the stairs?

"Cassie!" Barrie couldn't keep the panic from her voice.
"Dammit, Cassie! You have to tell me what's going on!"

Cassie stood at the window and didn't move.

CHAPTER FORTY-FIVE

The twine finally broke. Barrie felt the release in her wrists and her screaming shoulder muscles, and she sat down in the fireplace and breathed a sigh. Twisting and pulling her clammy hands, she managed to unwind the rest of the rope after loosening it enough to pull her hands back through. The first thing she did was reach into her pocket for her cell phone, but Obadiah must have taken it. It wasn't there.

With a growl of frustration, she fumbled at the twine binding around her ankles, but the knot was drawn too tight. The fireplace would have been impossible, so after hopping to the area where Obadiah had lifted the oak plank, she pried up the board to reveal the shallow root cellar the slaves had used.

The desperation struck her then, the desperation to escape, and the desperate sense of helplessness. The magnitude of the impossible hope that she was investing in a few objects in a hidden cellar. She wondered if that was what Obadiah's family had felt while they were alive, what Cassie had felt.

Did a prisoner ever stop hoping? When people didn't see you as a person, when who you had been or what you did made no difference to their opinion of you, how long did it take for hope to turn to resignation?

Barrie lifted one of the clay urns out and smashed the lip against the edge of the plank. It made a deep thud, and the vibration shook against her fingers. She tried a second time, harder, and a two-inch chunk of the narrow lip broke off.

Two inches was all she needed. She used the broken edge to saw through the twine around her ankles.

When she was finally free, her hands and feet throbbed and burned with the effort, and raw red welts around her ankles showed where the twine had rubbed her skin. She ignored that and scrambled to her feet, ducking low to run to the window. Not that it mattered if she kept out of sight. Cassie was still standing in plain view of anyone who happened to look. Cassie's entire body was rigid as Barrie nudged her aside. Finally in position, Barrie looked out the window.

At the excavation site above the hidden room, Obadiah lay unmoving on the ground. Two men were using a shovel and a pick, swinging them high and striking hard at the brick that had been exposed.

Recognition didn't come until one of the men had turned. Junior Evers, the weedy, straw-haired guy from the funeral, and Ryder Colesworth, the big bull of a guy who had put his finger across his lips at the service to silence Cassie.

Why hadn't Barrie connected that back then?

Because she hadn't known until later about the PTSD, and because Cassie had left out part of the truth.

At the funeral, Barrie had assumed Cassie was exaggerating her grief over her father. Like the police this morning, Barrie had assumed the worst because Cassie was who she was.

Gently, she took Cassie's hand, placed it on the rough cabin wall, and guided it across the bricks. "Do you feel that, Cassie? That's the brick in the slave cabin. You can smell the oak boards on the floor and the air coming in from outside where the door doesn't fit quite right. Outside is right through that door. Outside and escape and safety. I need you to pull yourself together now so that we can go out there together. You have to come back."

Ignoring Berg's warning about not touching Cassie, Barrie stepped in and folded her cousin into a hug. Up close she could hear Cassie muttering, repeating, "Please don't hurt me."

Her own chest aching, Barrie rubbed Cassie's back and kept speaking to her softly. She left one eye on the window where she could see Ryder and Junior digging. It felt like hours before Cassie's shaking slowed, but it was probably only minutes.

Cassie's breathing became less erratic. Feeling her stiffen, Barrie stepped back fast enough to cover Cassie's mouth. The scream pressed against her palm. "Shhhhh!" Barrie hissed. "You can't make any noise. No matter what you see out there— In fact, don't look out there. Just focus on the sound of my voice, Cassie. Nod if you understand what I'm saying." She held her breath until Cassie nodded. "Good. We have to get out of here," she continued. "I'm going to saw these ropes off, and then we're going to make a run for it."

She steadied Cassie and kept her turned away from the window while she went to get the chunk of broken urn. Cassie's tears were still flowing as Barrie worked at the twine, but Cassie tried to wipe them away by hunching her shoulder against her cheek. Pausing, Barrie used the hem of Cassie's shirt to wipe away the mascara smudges. Then she knelt and raised the bottom of Cassie's long pants to reach the twine that bound her cousin's legs together above the ankle monitor.

Barrie stared briefly at the box. Then she darted back to the recess beneath the boards and pulled out two of the rocks she had seen there. They were polished smooth, dark gray and almost metallic-looking. One was round and one was triangular with a point that, if not quite sharp, would at least hopefully do what Barrie needed. After returning to Cassie, she bent down again, and wedged her fingers beneath the band of the electronic ankle monitor.

"Hold very still," she said.

"What are you doing?" Cassie tried to pull away, but with her legs bound, she had to fight to keep her balance.

"Mark and I used to watch that show on television where the thief worked for the FBI. These things are designed to send a signal when they're tampered with. Hopefully, if I can break the plastic around the electronic bit, that will be enough to get the police out here."

"And what are we supposed to do in the meantime? Sit around and wait to be rescued?"

"No. We're going to go and hide. If Obadiah was the one who put us in here, those guys probably don't know we're here. If we slip around the back, there's no reason they would ever look for us, but the last thing we want is to be stuck in this cabin with no way out."

Eyes dark and wide, Cassie stared at Barrie for several long beats of Barrie's heart without responding.

"Don't zone out on me again, okay?" Barrie slammed the pointed end of the rock into the ankle monitor and felt the plastic break.

Cassie's leg jerked. "Ow! Hell, that hurts."

"Hold. Still," Barrie hissed. She inserted the stone back into the hole where she had pierced the ankle monitor and twisted it a few times so the tip of the rock would damage the electronics. "There. Hopefully that's good enough. Who knows how closely they monitor these things. It's probably a long shot anyway."

She went back to sawing at the fraying strands of the twine around Cassie's ankles, and then worked Cassie's hands free, too. When that was done and Cassie was rubbing the chafed skin of her wrists, Barrie peeked back out the window. Junior and Ryder were both still digging. But Obadiah was gone. Junior and Ryder hadn't seemed to notice.

Did that mean Obadiah was conscious enough to do whatever disappearing act he had done before?

Barrie edged over to the door and slowly pressed the latch. It moved, and she eased the door open, waited briefly, and poked her head out enough to see.

"I don't think I can go out there," Cassie said. Her voice was high and panicked.

Barrie infused as much certainty as she could into her voice. "Yes. You can. You have to."

"You don't understand."

"I think I do. I'm afraid I do. They hurt you."

"You don't get it—no one gets it." Cassie slapped her hand against the wall. "You don't until it happens to you. Ryder is Daddy's cousin. Ernesto had him watch me when the cartel took me after Daddy tried to quit working for them. But he was mad because Daddy was trying to quit, so he took it out on me. He said he would do the same thing to Sydney if I told." Her voice dropped to a broken whisper. "I never told."

Barrie decided that "I'm sorry" was one of the most useless phrases in the English language, too easily thrown around and too rarely helpful. She said it anyway.

Cassie only nodded. "I really can't go out there," she said.

"We'll go out together, and you're going to be fine." Barrie squeezed Cassie's hand. "You're going to have to, because if you don't, if you let them take more from you, then they are going to win all over again. And you're not a quitter—you don't let other people win. I don't know you all that well, but I know you enough to realize that much."

Cassie stared back at her, her chin puckering as her lip trembled. Then her face sharpened into determined angles, and she wiped her hands on her shirt. "All right," she said. "We'll go."

"We'll run to the right and hide behind the cabin until someone gets here to help. That way, we can escape through the woods or slip between the other cabins if it looks like Ryder and Junior are coming this way." Barrie smiled encouragingly. "We'll be all right, Cassie. We can do this," she said.

She hoped she was right.

CHAPTER FORTY-SIX

Barrie ran first. She darted through the door and crouched low as she rounded the side of the cabin, then she stopped to wait for Cassie before continuing toward the back. Cassie passed her and ran straight into the woods, ignoring everything Barrie had said.

Barrie's throat closed around a fist of panic. Blind panic, because from where she stood, she couldn't see Ryder or Junior, or what they were up to. Fortunately, Cassie made little noise, maybe because she had grown up playing in these woods, or maybe because she was naturally more graceful than Barrie, or maybe twigs snapping under your feet sounded louder when they were under *your own feet*.

Shaking her head, Barrie edged to the end of the building

and peered around at Ryder and Junior. They were still working. Still oblivious.

Should Barrie try to follow Cassie? If she made more noise than Cassie had made, she was likely to bring Ryder and Junior chasing after them both. On the other hand, if Cassie managed to get away, she could bring back help. Or her ankle monitor would send out an alert, if Barrie hadn't managed to trigger the signal already.

Her head resting against the rough brick at the back of the cabin, Barrie tried to reconcile herself to staying and waiting, to doing nothing in case doing something made things worse.

She couldn't. Her feet itched to run, every nerve ending in her body hummed, and her hands were clammy. Standing still made her breath come too fast.

Testing the ground at every footstep, she began to walk. She moved from tree to tree, pausing to look behind her, poised to run if she needed to. Telling herself she would run like hell.

Patience. If she walked carefully, she wouldn't need to run.

Placing every step where there was the least amount of vegetation, she finally emerged at the far side of the woods and stepped onto a shadowed verge of grass that bordered the cul-de-sac.

The street was quiet. Empty driveways fronted tightly clustered houses, and behind them, shallow yards backed to the woods. Cassie was a ribbon of dark hair and a pale flash of fabric cutting across the shadowed lawns a hundred yards ahead, and then she ducked back into the trees of the Colesworth woods.

Barrie bit off a shout, and wasted a moment looking behind her before sprinting to catch up. Clutching a cramp in her side, she made a mental map of Colesworth Place. From the point where Cassie had cut into the trees, the woods ran into the parking lot near the cemetery, the chapel, and Cassie's house.

There was no help in that direction. Cassie should have kept running. Or started ringing doorbells in the subdivision.

Unless Sydney was at the house.

Barrie's skin broke into goose bumps, and she plunged back into the shadowed woods. She thought of the way Ryder had spoken to her at the SeaCow, the way Cassie had locked up at the cemetery and frozen when she'd seen the two men digging. What if Sydney came out of the house, unsuspecting. . . .

But Sydney had gone with Cassie's mother, hadn't she? Barrie stopped, bent nearly double, sucking in air, her hands on her knees. Yes, she remembered Sydney standing beside the open car door, turning to look back at Cassie and the dig crew. Didn't Cassie remember that?

Gulping another breath, Barrie wiped the sweat out of her eyes and ran on, doing her best to avoid roots and trees and brambles. The stitch in her side had grown into a ripping knife by the time she emerged above the cemetery. Cassie was even further ahead, already slipping around the back side of the fence and circling behind the chapel.

Barrie pushed her body back into a sprint. By the time she cleared the side of the chapel, Cassie emerged from the back door of the house with a shotgun in her hand. A *shotgun*.

Worse, instead of returning to the subdivision, Cassie ran toward the broken columns of the old mansion, where Ryder and Junior were digging.

The angel statue above Charlotte's empty grave blocked Barrie's view as Cassie separated from the trees. Dirt had blackened the face and worn away the angel's features, but the fist still shook in the face of God. Barrie thought of Charlotte in the hidden room, waiting for James all through the war, all through her death. Charlotte, who deserved better than what would happen to her body if Ryder and Junior were the first to reach her.

Barrie forced her feet to move. Running toward danger didn't get any easier, step by step.

Cassie reached the ruins and she circled behind the columns. Behind her, Eight was emerging from the Beaufort woods and running toward them in the shadow of the trees. Barrie's fear suddenly doubled, multiplied. Cassie moved from one column to the next, timing her progress with Junior's movements as he plied the pick. When she reached the last column, she was only a few feet away from him. Eight was thirty yards away. Cassie stepped into the open, pumped the shotgun, and leveled it at Ryder's back. Barrie ran forward, but everything was too slow and disjointed.

Holding the gun steady, Cassie took another step. "Back up and put down the pickax. Move away. Both of you."

Junior dove for a rifle that lay beside a metal detector on the ground.

Cassie's shotgun roared.

There was the sound, and the stench of powder, and a piercing scream. Then blood and flesh sprayed from Junior's knee, and he fell. Barrie saw it, heard it, but somehow her brain lagged behind so it all seemed unreal.

Ryder dug into the waistband of his jeans and pulled out a handgun. He fired it as he spun toward Cassie, barely aiming. The bullets kicked up dirt and grass, and one smacked the nearest column with a ping and a cloud of mortar as Cassie fired again. Cassie stayed standing. Ryder didn't. His leg buckled, and he screamed, but he managed to stay half-upright and raise the gun again.

Cassie shot him again in the shoulder. The gun fell from his nerveless fingers.

Sensation flooded back into Barrie's feet and hands, filling her with pins and needles. And horror. She had lost all sense of time. Eight was closer, but not close enough. Sirens were wailing on the road. She turned toward the sound, and when she looked back again, Cassie had reached Ryder and kicked the gun out of reach. She stood over him. Her face was perfectly blank, her eyes glassy and dark. The shotgun shook as she raised it.

"Don't!" Barrie shouted. She ran forward, but everything blurred. Movements, sounds. Past and present. She already knew Cassie was going to fire.

Cassie was going to shoot again.

Holding the barrel of the shotgun three inches from Ryder's face, Cassie spoke to him. The sirens drowned out both her words and the answer Ryder gave her with his lips drawn back from his teeth in something that was disturbingly like a smile. Eight gave a shout.

Cassie's hands shifted on the gun. Instead of firing it, she swung it at the side of Ryder's head. It connected with a sound like a watermelon cracking open, and he staggered, falling sideways until he caught himself with his uninjured arm and turned back around to face her.

Cassie swung the shotgun a second time. She was saying something—her mouth was moving, but they were whispers or prayers or curses spoken beneath her breath. The weapon came down again. Ryder slumped to the churned-up dirt where he and Junior had been trying to expose more of the brick roof to the hidden room.

Barrie reached Cassie at the same time that Eight pried

the rifle out of Junior's hands. All her focus had been on Cassie and Eight. She hadn't even seen Junior getting up or grabbing the gun. Eight held it pointed at Junior, and Barrie caught Cassie's forearm.

"Cassie, stop. You have to stop. He's down. He's not going to hurt you anymore."

"I was thirteen years old, and he was my daddy's cousin. His *cousin*." Cassie wrenched out of Barrie's grasp and raised the gun again.

Arms outstretched to block the blow, Barrie stepped in front of Ryder. "Killing him isn't going to change that, but it will change you."

"Like he hasn't done that already." Cassie's voice was flat. "He made me turn myself inside out until I didn't know if it was my fault or his, because I couldn't imagine someone doing that to another person without there being a *reason*." The gun was slippery, the weight of the handle pulling the dark barrel through Cassie's fingers. Drops of blood gleamed red against the wood.

Barrie glanced back as the first of two police cruisers turned off the frontage road and raced up the long oak-lined drive. "Cassie, please. Put the gun down. Killing him isn't going to make you doubt yourself any less. It's only going to push you further away from the person you want to be, and you don't want the police to make a mistake when they see you with the gun."

"So they don't shoot me, you mean?" Cassie gave a harsh, dry laugh devoid of humor. "That might not be so bad. Haven't you ever thought about how much easier it would be to have it all just stop?"

Barrie's hands shook so hard that she pressed her fists to her thighs to keep them steady. How was she supposed to find words to say what should never need to be said? That you kept fighting, because as long as there was life, there was change. And hope. There was always hope, even if sometimes it was a wisp so thin that it was barely hope at all.

"If you don't fight to survive, you will never know how strong you are. I think Berg would tell you that. Also, unless we can find a way to break it, the curse and the binding will pass to Sydney if you die. That isn't what you want."

"No," Cassie breathed.

"Then put the gun down and help me figure all this out."

Opening her fingers, Cassie let the weapon fall. Slowly she sank to the ground and drew her knees to her chest, then rocked back and forth while Barrie held her.

CHAPTER FORTY-SEVEN

The police took Cassie aside to question her, and the paramedics came. Ambulances and ambulances, but none for Obadiah, who had vanished.

Barrie burrowed into Eight's shoulder. He was as pale as bone beneath his tan, his eyes darkened to slashes of shadow she couldn't read as he searched her face as if it were his turn to memorize *her*. "Christ, you scared the crap out of me again," he said. "You have to stop this. My heart can't take it."

"I thought you were in Columbia," Barrie said.

"I dropped everything to race back here when your aunt called to say you weren't picking up your phone. I figured you were doing something stupidly brave or insanely stupid, and I was on my way to the tunnel when I heard the picks striking brick. For future reference, next time you see people with guns, try running away instead of running toward them."

The police stayed for what seemed like hours, taking statements and photographs. The procedure felt too familiar. Except that the bodies leaving in ambulances were alive this time, alive and under police escort. Barrie hoped it would be a long time before Ryder and Junior went anywhere that didn't involve armed guards and prison bars.

She sat on the grass leaning against Eight's knees. Berg and Andrew Bey and a parade of archaeologists, police, various people from the university, and even someone from the coroner's office milled around the excavation area, trying to assess the damage, and trying to confirm what Barrie had told them she'd deduced from Caroline's journal. Seven alternately barked into his phone and hovered anxiously nearby. Now and again, he dropped a hand on Eight's shoulder, as if he needed that connection to assure himself Eight was there.

Pru paced, but she barely took her eyes from Barrie. "How much longer do we have to stay?" she said to Seven after Barrie had given her statement and the police had come back several times with additional questions. "Barrie's already given her statement. What more do they want?"

"They haven't finished with Cassie yet," Seven answered, stopping with his hands in his pockets so that he looked eerily like Eight.

"They're not going to arrest her, are they?" Barrie swiveled to look back at her cousin. "That lawyer of hers was crappy at the hearing. Maybe you should help her."

A sharp denial formed on Seven's lips, but he bit it off and shook his head. "I don't think they'll arrest her, under the circumstances," he said cautiously. "You and Eight both explained Cassie didn't shoot until they went for their guns."

Standing with Dr. Ainsley, the doctor who had stitched up Barrie's shoulder, a policewoman, and Mrs. Colesworth on the other side of the excavation area, Cassie looked shaken and bewildered, devoid of her usual bravado. Cassie's mother's car still stood on the grass with the driver's door open and the dashboard lights glowing as if she'd left the keys in the ignition. She looked stunned and unsure what to do for Cassie, or what to do with herself. Cross-legged on the hood of the car, Sydney sat with her elbows on her knees and her chin cupped in her palms, watching everything with quiet but avid interest.

"Someone ought to go talk to Sydney," Barrie said.

She started to get up, but Pru firmly pushed her back down. "Oh no, you don't. You stay right here," Pru said. "I'm not sure how anyone is going to explain all this to that poor child, but leave it to her mama and Cassie to do it."

From beside the excavation site, Berg and the archaeologists went to meet another dusty Prius approaching down the drive. Each of them veered around a nearby stretch of grass seemingly without reason, walking around it as if they weren't even aware they were detouring around. It was the same place Obadiah had been lying before he had disappeared, and Barrie leaned forward, staring hard at the spot, as if staring would let her see what the others couldn't. She had before.

But if Obadiah was still there, he was hiding himself from her now as well as from the archaeologists and police. Maybe he wasn't there at all.

Dr. Feldman, the head archaeologist, levered himself out from behind the wheel of the Prius. He listened to Andrew and Berg talking while he reached in the backseat for a large square plastic case. He handed the case to Berg, and they all walked over to the police and stood in a huddle, talking rapidly. Two plainclothes police led the way back toward the excavation site.

"Watch that spot over there when they go past it," Barrie whispered to Eight, pointing to the apparently empty stretch of grass. "Tell me what you see."

"I don't see anything."

"Just watch."

Dr. Feldman, the police, and the others all walked around the same area again.

Eight sat forward. "You think Obadiah's sitting over there being invisible again?"

"Maybe he was too hurt to go anywhere, so all he could do

was make it look like he disappeared. He could be there sucking up enough energy to make himself strong again. It would
make sense, wouldn't it?"

Dr. Feldman reached the dig. The police, Berg, and
Andrew all pointed out various things, talking over each other.
He gestured for Berg to give him the case, and then he flipped
it open, extracted something that looked like a flexible flashlight mounted to a computer screen, and flipped a switch. Two
LED lights flared up brightly. Kneeling beside the exposed
brick of the roof, Dr. Feldman fed the lighted end of the scope
into the narrow chip that Junior had managed to make with
the pickax. Everyone else gathered around, peering over his
shoulder at the screen.

"What is that? Some kind of camera?" Barrie asked, looking back at Eight.

"Apparently."

An excited murmur rippled through the archaeologists,
and several pointed at the screen, talking at once. Then something happened. They all drew back, exchanged puzzled
looks, and leaned in closer. Dr. Feldman slapped the side of
the screen, and flipped the switch on, then off again.

"I think Elijah and Ayita broke their camera," Barrie
whispered to Eight. "But why did they let Ryder and Junior
dig in the first place?"

"Maybe they were too weak in daylight? Or they'd used

up their strength pitching that fit this morning? Who knows," Eight said.

Berg stepped away from the other archaeologists. He looked first toward Cassie, who wasn't paying any attention, before he crossed to Barrie instead. Worry—or Obadiah— seemed to have aged him five years since that morning. "There's good news and bad news."

"Did they see any details before the camera died?" Barrie asked.

His face sharpened. "How did you know it died?"

"Call it a lucky guess." Barrie shrugged halfheartedly. "What's the good news?"

"We caught a glimpse of a skeleton. And stacks of boxes that could be just about anything. Exactly what you told us we would find."

Andrew Bey, looking equally pale and hollow-eyed, stepped up beside Berg and ran a hand through his hair, managing to look both sheepish and elated. "I wish I had made the time to read Caroline's journal more carefully," he said. "Because Cassie insisted we start the dig so quickly, I had too little preparation. I only took the time to really study the entries around the night of the fire, and I skimmed the rest. I should have considered that children will often write about events without understanding the significance of what they've seen. And I didn't take into consideration that it might have taken Caroline years to finally write about that night."

Barrie's gaze slipped back to Cassie, who had waited four years to speak about her pain. Ironically, she was comforting her mother while Marie Colesworth cried. But maybe needing to care for someone else would help Cassie come out of herself.

Barrie thought of her own mother, and all that Lula had been through. All the things Lula had never talked about. Pru had said Barrie needed to read Lula's letters, but Barrie had been so fixated on finding answers to the questions she needed answered herself that she hadn't been ready. She hadn't had the courage. Watching Cassie, she was starting to understand that courage took many different paths.

"You think she's all right?" Berg asked.

Barrie rubbed her thumb across Mark's watch. "You tell me. How long does it take for someone to become 'all right'?" She thought of her own memories of the night of the explosion, the suddenness that could make her see everything as if she was right there in the moment. And she *was* all right. Relatively all right. What she had been through was nothing compared to what Cassie had been through, or the things that Berg must have seen in Afghanistan, or what Lula had suffered because of Cassie's father. What the Union soldiers had done and what the slaves had suffered. How could human beings continue to do so many inhumane things to each other?

Hands clasped behind his back, Berg dropped into his quiet stance, deceptively relaxed. "There's no easy answer for that. Everyone is different," he said. "The important thing is that she's talking and getting help. Or at least, I hope she'll get help."

"She will." Barrie stood up and dusted off her shorts. Eight stood up with her. "What are they going to do about the room? About Charlotte?"

"We can't risk breaking through from the top with the skeleton down there. We'll get a bigger crew and excavate around the room until we find a way inside. Since we can't be certain whether the Union gold is down there or not, we'll have a guard on-site," Berg said.

Barrie exchanged a look with Eight, but she wasn't ready to bring up the ghosts and the curse, not with Andrew standing there. First, she needed to know if Obadiah was still alive.

"Could you take an extra volunteer to help dig?" she asked. "I want to be there. For Charlotte."

For Charlotte and her mother and father. For Caroline and Daphne.

"Make it two volunteers." Eight waited until Andrew and Berg had gone back to the huddled group of archaeologists, then laced his fingers through Barrie's and pulled her up the marble steps and off behind one of the broken columns of the old mansion, out of sight of everyone.

"What?" Barrie said, her eyes stinging because she was afraid she already knew.

"Several things. First, if we're going to have any kind of a relationship, Bear, I need you to stop deciding things for yourself and then charging off without me. A relationship is about two people deciding. You should have talked to me about volunteering." He threw a dark glance back to where the archaeologists eddied around the bare spot at the excavation area. "It doesn't look like things are going to be any safer here."

"That's why we have to come back. We have to find a way to break the curse. We're going to need to find Obadiah to figure that out."

"You're assuming he's alive—or even willing to help." Eight pushed a hand through his hair, as if he was doing that because he wanted to do something else—like shake her. "I mean it about you not deciding things on your own, Bear. I can't do that anymore. You have to *talk* to me."

"Like you talked to me before you sent the email turning down your scholarship?"

"That's not the same. I knew you wanted me to stay here," Eight said, but then he rocked back on his heels and shook his head. "No, you're right. It is kind of the same. I'm not even going to try to argue."

"That'll be new." Barrie found herself smiling, even though she hadn't expected to want to smile for a good long time. "What else did you want to tell me? You said you had several things."

"There was that one thing," Eight said, stepping closer, "and then there was this."

He cupped her face, his callused fingers both rough and gentle against her skin as he bent to kiss her. They came together like thirst and water, like dark and light. Eight's thumb traced the shape of Barrie's face, the curve of her cheek. Then he groaned and dropped his arms around her waist to pull her closer. Barrie felt found, the way only Eight ever made her feel found.

At that moment, the gifts didn't matter. There was only skin, and breath, and touch. For that moment, in that moment, they were each enough.

Enough. The word echoed through Barrie's heart, leaving a wake of emptiness.

Were they enough? She stiffened, and Eight pulled back to look at her.

"What's wrong?" he asked.

She shook her head. "Nothing."

"I thought we were done with the secrets," he said, pulling away.

And wasn't that the problem? Secrets were never done. Secrets left their barbs burrowed deep within people, within relationships, quietly doing more damage with every passing day. What kind of a chance would she and Eight ever have with secrets between them? Without honesty?

Without trust.

Because that was what it all came down to. Love was mutual. It was give-and-take, and laugh and cry. Love was about sharing, not persuading. Didn't they have enough examples right in front of them about how that went wrong in so many different ways? How was Seven's use of withholding money so that Eight would choose the college Seven wanted that much better than the threat of force the Union captain had used against Daphne? They were different levels of awfulness motivated by different reasons, but a threat was a threat. By the same token, if there was *any* chance Eight's gift was making him want Barrie, or even contributing to it, then wasn't that only a milder version of what Ryder had done to Cassie? Persuasion and coercion came in varying degrees.

"What is it, Bear?" Eight watched her steadily. "What are you thinking?"

She couldn't face him while she spoke. "There's something I haven't told you. Something your father didn't want you to know, and he asked me not to say anything, either." She took a deep breath. "It isn't only the Watsons who are bound to the land. The Beauforts are bound to Beaufort Hall. *You'll* be bound to it after your father dies, if we don't break your gift."

Eight's face closed, his eyes darkening and the pupils

receding as if to underscore the distance that had reared between them.

"That's why you were trying to help Obadiah? Because I was going to be bound?"

"That, and he threatened to take the Watson gift away. He said he knew the Watson lodestone was buried near the Scalping Tree."

"Why didn't you say anything? Why didn't you tell me?"

"He told me not to! And your father begged me not to tell. Mostly, I couldn't bring myself to say anything because I didn't want to hurt you. Your father keeping it from you, making decisions for you. I didn't want to have to be the one to tell you he'd done that."

"So you made decisions for me instead." Eight's voice was so quiet, Barrie scarcely heard him. "You made decisions for both of us, because you couldn't trust me and you couldn't trust yourself." He shook his head in disgust. "How long have you known?"

Barrie caught one of his hands, willing him to, begging him to, try to understand. "Since the night we came back from San Francisco. He wants you to have the choices he feels like he never had. He wants you to go and live while you can."

"That's not any kind of a choice worth having."

"I didn't say I agreed with him!"

"But you kept it from me. That speaks loudly enough."

Eight's shoulders dropped an inch and curled in on themselves, and he took a step away, pulling his hand from hers. "You had opportunities, Bear. Every time you told me you would change, that you would trust me, you were lying by omission." He swallowed, blinking rapidly, as if trying to see Barrie clearly. Or maybe he was trying not to cry.

Barrie couldn't stand it, knowing that she had done exactly what she'd been trying so hard not to do.

Before she could think what to say, Eight rubbed his finger across his lip and briefly closed his eyes. "You and my dad both think I'm not smart enough to make decisions for myself," he said. "How could I not have seen that? Dad trying to tell me what to do with my life. Pushing me to be a lawyer. You starting the restaurant to give me something to do." His head jerked up and his brows lowered. "I even thought it was cute when you called me 'baseball guy.' I thought you were teasing, but what you're really saying each time is that I'm just a poor, dumb jock."

He walked away.

"Eight, wait! Please. That's not what I meant at all. God, I'm sorry. You know I only called you that because I don't like baseball. You're far smarter than I am. You're the one who always thinks problems through, while I jump into them without looking." Barrie ran after him, but he started running, too, and halfway to the trees she realized she wasn't going to catch him.

441

He didn't turn around, and he didn't slow down, and even if he had, she had no idea what to say or what to promise that she hadn't already said or promised him before. Her knees threatened to buckle, as if her body were too heavy for them.

She'd tried so hard, and yet she'd still managed to get it wrong.

Eight dropped back to a walk as he reached the woods, hurrying farther and farther away, growing further and further from her.

This was why she hadn't told him, because she had known this pain was coming. Not her pain; that didn't matter. He was the one who was hurting, and she didn't know how to reach him.

She was going to, though. She had to. She had so many things to fix.

She had barely had the thought when three black feathers drifted from the sky and floated to the grass. They rocked gently a few times, then stilled and sank into the ground. The air above her was empty, but when she looked behind her, the tops of the broken mansion columns were filled with ravens. None of them appeared to have moved, and none was positioned right to have lost the feathers.

"Obadiah?" she asked. "Is that you?"

There was no answer, but her gift gave an insistent pulse, a reminder of more unfinished business.

Acknowledgments

It took *so* many people to create *Persuasion*. This includes, of course, all those named below, but ultimately my biggest thank-you is a general one that goes to the readers, bloggers, reviewers, librarians, and booksellers who have supported *Compulsion*, and to readers who support and live in fictional worlds in general.

Specifically, I am so, so grateful to:

My husband and kids for putting up with me through a debut year and deadlines that had me working on vacations and even holidays. I'm going to get better at juggling all this, I promise!

The survivors who were kind enough to read and share their very personal stories of PTSD, violence, and sexual assault. For obvious reasons, I won't name you, but *Persuasion* wouldn't exist without your generosity, insight, and tremendous courage.

Sara Sargent, my fabulous and patient editor at Simon Pulse, for her keen eye, sensitivity to balance, and the two million other things that she does for me.

Katherine Devendorf, Bara MacNeill, and Amy Wilson for managing the editing and copyediting and helping me make *Persuasion* better than I could have hoped to make it.

Regina Flath and Hilary Zarycky for a fantastic cover and interior book design.

The whole incredible team at Simon Pulse and Simon & Schuster who have worked behind the scenes to make this book possible: Mara Anastas, Mary Marotta, Carolyn Swerdloff, Teresa Ronquillo, Lucille Rettino, Christina Pecorale, Emma Sector, Michelle Leo, Anthony Parisi, Candace Green, Katy Hershberger, Nicole Ellul, Sara Berko, Jodie Hockensmith, Kelsey Dickson, and everyone on the editorial, art, marketing, publicity, sales, and rights teams—THANK YOU! I'm so lucky to have you all!

Kent Wolf and Patricia Burke at LMQ and Jessica Regel at Foundry Media for their savvy and kindness, and for not only doing all the things that let me write books in the first place, but also believing in this series and in my career.

My amazing critique partners, Susan Sipal and Erin Cashman, for their expertise, advice, support, and enthusiasm, and the lovely beta readers from my street team—Amanda Pate, Beth Edwards, Brittany Todd, Karina Romano, Elizabeth Dobak, and Stephanie Habina. Love you ladies so much!

Andrew Agha, who patiently explained the archaeology of lowcountry plantations, took me around Charles Town Landing, and then let me twist what he said to suit my fictional purposes. All those twists and departures are, of course, entirely my own fault.

All the generous authors who blurbed *Compulsion*, came out on the Compelling Reads tour, supported YA series books with me on YASeriesInsiders.com, and/or were kind and patient enough to put up with my newbie enthusiasm and cluelessness while diplomatically teaching me a *ton*. Sending you big hugs.

All the bloggers who reviewed *Compulsion* or helped spread the word through giveaways, with special thanks to Hafsah at *Icey Books* for having been the first, to Jamie at *Rock Star Blog Tours* and *Two Chicks on Books* for doing the blog tour, Andye at *Reading Teen* and Daniel at *RT Book Reviews* for writing my favorite lines about Eight, and Katie from *Mundie Moms* for the Compulsion for Magic tour and a review that made me happy cry.

Everyone on the *Compulsion* street team. You guys! You're wonderful. Thanks especially to Britt for painted shoes and Alice for word search puzzles, and to Becca, Kate, Alyssa, Beth, and the other captains.

My wonderful AdventuresInYAPublishing.com partners, past and present. Thank you for putting up with my periodic absences and making the blog continue to grow as a support system for aspiring authors.

Jan Lewis and Max Kutil, who do their best to make sure what needs to get done gets done.

And last, but certainly not least, Carol Barreyre and Cici Ramirez for being with me every step of the way and putting up with launch week and making it fun! You know how much I love you, but it bears repeating.

Finally, I'd like to add a special note. Post-traumatic stress disorder affects many different kinds of people, from those who valiantly serve in the military and first-response teams to keep the rest of us safe, to those who have experienced trauma in other ways. PTSD ranges widely in symptoms and intensity, and it can come on immediately after or many years after a traumatic event. It affects the families and loved ones of those who suffer, as well as the victims themselves. I'd like to take this opportunity to thank those who are on the front lines of studying and healing the frequently unseen and undiagnosed effects of PTSD.

If you or someone you know may be suffering from post-traumatic stress disorder, the following sources provide various forms of help and information:

https://www.sidran.org/resources/for-survivors-and-loved-ones/
http://www.ptsd.va.gov/public/index.asp
http://www.nimh.nih.gov/health/topics/index.shtml

Turn the page for a sneak peek at
the finale to the
Heirs of Watson Island series,
Illusion!

Bravery isn't born. It's forged in the nightmare places where fear tears the mind apart. For Barrie Watson, her cousin Cassie's plantation across the river from Watson's Landing had become such a place. There, it was all too easy to see how shards of past events could turn into weapons, until one bad choice led to another, and memories became prisons that trapped people as surely as any door.

Between the memories and the migraine that always formed when she was away from Watson's Landing, Barrie fidgeted in the passenger seat of her aunt Pru's old, black boat of a Mercedes. The sun-pinked skin exposed by her sleeveless top stuck to the leather in the sodden Southern heat and plastered her long, pale curls to the nape of her neck. Her traitorous fingers itched to grab the steering wheel and tell her aunt to turn around. Even the sun slanting low through the oaks that lined the winding drive seemed to whisper a warning, transforming the veils of Spanish moss into something ghostly and macabre.

But Barrie couldn't change her mind. No matter how excruciatingly hard she had tried to make the right choices recently, she had kept hurting other people. She had to set that right, and the first step began here at Colesworth Place.

Pru eased the Mercedes to a stop at the edge of the visitor lot closest to where the lane continued on toward the ruins of the old plantation mansion and the smaller, modern house where Cassie and her family lived. Barrie adjusted the foil over the chicken casserole that Pru had hastily assembled and pushed the door open. Pru didn't move. Sitting there with her hands gripped tightly at the top of the steering wheel, her fine, blond curls haloed around her in the fading light, Barrie's aunt resembled a lovely and slightly demented angel.

Barrie hated what all this was doing to her. "Are you all right, Aunt Pru?"

Pru's lips lifted wryly. "Look at us. We're a fine pair, aren't we? I'm trying to talk myself into getting out of this car, and for all your determination, you look like you'd rather turn around and run." She reached out and touched Barrie's wrist. "Let's just go on home, sugar. At least for tonight. You don't owe it to your cousin to break the Colesworth curse, and you certainly don't owe a thing to this Obadiah, or whatever that magician of yours calls himself."

"I'm not sure magician's the right word, exactly. More like a shaman," Barrie said, avoiding the question.

"You know I ought to have my head examined for even considering letting you come over to look for him, don't you? Not that I seem to be able to prevent you from doing anything. I wish you'd just forget all this."

"We can't forget. This isn't about owing Cassie or Obadiah. We can't walk away when the curse is hurting Mary and her family, too. And Obadiah promised he would break the Beaufort binding if I found the Colesworth treasure. If we don't break that, Eight will be stuck at Beaufort Hall when Seven dies, and I'll be across at Watson's Landing, and we'll have no chance of ever being together. Too many things all center on Obadiah being able to help us. At the very least, I have to know whether he's still alive."

"Can you call it living when someone is more than a hundred and fifty years old? I'm still not sure I believe that, but it's one more reason why I ought to be grounding you for a month instead of bringing you over here and letting you get involved with that man again."

Switching off the ignition with an emphatic motion and a jingle of keys, Pru sat there a moment looking so small and defenseless that it made Barrie's heart swell with guilt. But

Pru was stronger than she looked. The more Barrie had come to know her aunt, the more she had seen the quiet core of steel that Pru didn't even know she possessed.

Strength was a bit like courage, Barrie thought. She herself had found both only when she couldn't live without them, and they had come to her when she had needed them the most. But fighting to protect the people you cared for was one thing. Trusting someone you loved to fight for themselves took a different kind of strength and bravery.

Leaning over from the passenger seat, she dropped a kiss on Pru's smooth-skinned cheek. "Thank you, Aunt Pru."

"For what?" Pru looked over, startled.

"For not grounding me. For coming over here to help distract Cassie's mother. For believing in me and not telling me that letting Obadiah take away the Watson gift like he threatened would have been the obvious solution."

Pru's smile was misty-eyed and ephemeral, and she pushed the door open with fresh determination. Barrie, too, got out, and they stood on the brittle and cracking asphalt looking at each other across the top of the car. "I'm sorry I yelled at you when you told me everything. The fact that I did that makes it harder for you to be honest with me in the future, I know that, and I promise you, I'm through with ignoring problems and hoping they'll go away on their own. I'm done with letting life happen to me instead of living it. Obadiah's already had plenty of opportunities to hurt you, if that was what he wanted, and anyway, if he can change himself into a raven and make himself invisible, there's not much you and I are going to do to stop him coming to Watson's Landing. I'm already having enough nightmares about—"

Barrie looked over as Pru cut herself off. "About what?"

"Never you mind." Pru pushed her old-fashioned white patent purse up to the crook of her elbow and slammed the door. "My point is that you were right. As much as I wish we could, we can't leave things the way they are."

They set off shoulder to shoulder through the trees that cut the visitor parking area off from the cemetery where Cassie's father had so recently been interred. Pru's expression was unreadable, but the kitten heels of her shoes clicked on the asphalt in a decisive rhythm. Barrie juggled the casserole, and as they rounded the corner, the shoebox house where the Colesworth family lived came into sight at the edge of the woods between the Colesworth property and Beaufort Hall. Farther on, toward the river, the ruined columns and crumbling chimneys of the old mansion cast long shadows over the kitchen, slave cabins, and other outbuildings that Wyatt Colesworth had been obsessed with restoring. Watched over by a dozen ravens perched at the top of the columns, the archaeological dig area that had recently been torn up by violence was surrounded by yellow police tape, and on the far side of it, two sheriff's deputies sat in their cruiser beneath a thick-trunked oak.

A sickening wave of lostness pulled at Barrie from the dig site, a physical reminder that, regardless of what she wanted, her gift wouldn't let her walk away. Along with the lodestone that anchored the Colesworth curse and the angry spirits who had cast the evil magic—not to mention eight million dollars, give or take, of stolen Union gold—Charlotte Colesworth's skeleton was still buried down there. Somebody had to get her out, and the archaeologists had already made it clear they were going to continue the excavation.

That was the problem with Watson Island. There were too many secrets and dangers lurking beneath the surface, waiting for someone to stumble over them.

All three of the pirates who had founded the planta-tions—Watson's Landing, Beaufort Hall, and Colesworth Place—had built secret tunnels and rooms so well hidden that they'd long been forgotten, the way unpleasant things in a family's past were easier to forget when you shut them away. Their descendants had locked the doors, sealed the rooms, moved to the other side of oversize mansions, or let the grass soften the ashes and crumbled bricks of the families' mistakes. They'd put statues of angels with fists raised against the sky over empty graves.

Hiding things was easier than repairing the damage that they had all left behind them. Barrie had learned the hard way that when it came to emotions, you couldn't heal until you acknowledged what was lost. And thanks to the bindings that came with the magic in all three families, none of the eldest heirs could leave the plantations without suffering migraines that in the past had driven people crazy or moved them to suicide. There was no way to escape.

Thinking of the bindings made Barrie stop abruptly. "Would you mind going ahead without me for a minute, Aunt Pru? I want to try Eight again before I talk to Cassie. I'm worried that he still hasn't called me back."

"Of course." Pru adjusted her purse and took the casserole dish Barrie handed her. Then she patted Barrie on the cheek. "Don't worry too much if he won't talk yet, though. He's got a good streak of the Beaufort stubbornness, but as mad as he may be that you didn't tell him about the binding, you'd only known about it a couple days. His father kept it from him his entire life. Those two have a lot of ground to cover, and I've no doubt that's keeping Eight distracted."

Barrie wished she were as certain of that as Pru. She dialed Eight's number while her aunt walked on toward the small brick house with its too-bright shutters and overly ornate front door.

The phone rang and rang. Then abruptly Eight's voice was there, that soft drawl with a sultry hint of gravel. "Stop calling me, Bear. I'll call you when I can talk."

Eleven little words, that was all, but his voice was raw. Barrie wondered if she'd ever stop seeing him the way he had looked that morning at the dig site when she'd finally told him about the Beaufort binding. A salt-edged breeze from the Atlantic had swept up the Santisto River to stir his hair, and his lips had still been reddened from kissing her. But he'd hunched in on himself as if she'd hit him when he'd realized she had known he was going to inherit the binding that would confine him to the place he'd been wanting to escape from all his life.

Barrie's breath hitched, and she felt stupid and lost all over again. In the time that she had known him, Eight had shown her weaknesses inside herself she would never have explored without him, shown her possibilities she had never even considered. Holding the phone to her ear, she looked out across the excavation area, where the evening sunlight glinted on the plastic sheeting that covered the hole that Ryder's and Junior's pickaxes had made in the arched ceiling of the hidden room that morning. The sight was a reminder of what happened when you tried to keep secrets buried.

"Tell me we can fix this, Eight. Tell me what I can do," she said. "At least tell me you're all right."

"How can I be all right? My entire life has been a lie, and the future I wanted isn't going to be a possibility. You knew that, and you didn't tell me. You made choices for me because you didn't think I could handle the truth—"

"I never intended to make decisions for you. I was only going to help Obadiah break the curse before I told you—I wanted to be sure it was possible and safe before I got your hopes up about him breaking the Beaufort binding—" Barrie cut herself off and sighed. "It sounds like I'm making excuses for myself, and I don't mean to do that. I was wrong. I know I was wrong. I should have told you. At first Obadiah's magic was messing with my ability to tell you anything, and then I thought that if you and your father were ever going to have any kind of a relationship again, he needed to be the one to tell you, but that wasn't fair to you."

"You're still making excuses. I don't need you to protect me. You chose your gift over me, and you didn't trust me to understand the choices you were making. You lied to me. Over and over again, and I always forgave you. This time, I'm not sure I can. All along, you've been worried about my gift making me want what you want and about whether I want you for yourself. I never cared about that, but I don't want someone who can't be honest with me. I don't want to be with anyone who manipulates me. I get enough of that at home. And since my gift makes it harder for me to separate what I want from what you want, at least for now, I can't be with you."

Barrie stared at the ground. There wasn't anything she could say to counter that. All she could do was tell him how she felt. "I should have explained. You're right. I was afraid of losing my gift, and I should have trusted you to understand. I should have known you would. I don't want to lose you, Eight. Don't shut me out. I get that you need some space, but give me a chance to show you that I can do better. I swear I can. I want you to be involved in all the decisions from now on. I'm over here at Colesworth Place, and the archaeologists are coming back to start digging again tomorrow. We still have to get rid of the curse—"

"*We* don't have to do anything. I'm done caring about Cassie, her curse, or her stupid treasure. I have my father to deal with, and I have to go to Columbia tomorrow to meet with the baseball coach again and finalize things at the university for next semester." He paused, and his voice grew softer. "I'm not sure I'm going to come back."

"What do you mean?" Barrie's chest clenched, and for the first time since Eight had walked away from her that afternoon, she let herself consider the possibility that she couldn't fix what she had broken between them. That he was really done. But she couldn't—wouldn't—consider that. "Don't leave," she said. "Running away doesn't solve any problems. You're the one who taught me that. We have to talk—"

"No," Eight said. "We don't. My whole life is up in the air, and I need to figure it out myself."

He hung up before Barrie could say anything else, and she stood with tears burning her eyes and the phone digging into her hand, listening to the silence, as if by some miracle Eight would pick up again and assure her that he'd eventually forgive her. That they could find a way to work things out. But miracles didn't happen, and no form of magic would let her rewind her mistakes. She couldn't make him get over the way she'd hurt him or forget that she hadn't trusted him with the truth.

She had to find a way to fix things. Hurting Eight was the very last thing she had ever meant to do. Losing him had shown her that she couldn't bear to lose him.

She looked up as a bird fluttered out of the lower branches of an oak to perch on the upraised arm of the angel statue above Charlotte's grave. Feathers ruffled and yellow eyes bright, it cocked its head to peer at her. Barrie's heart filled with outrage and dread and hope in equal measure, because it was Obadiah who had pushed her into all of this with his magic and his threats. She reached out toward the bird with her own magic, but she was still too inexperienced, too uncertain of the way the Watson gift had been growing and changing since her mother's death.

The raven wasn't lost. It didn't need returning. As to

whether it was one of the ravens that often accompanied Obadiah or the man himself, on that subject, her gift was stubbornly unhelpful.

Taking a step toward the bird, Barrie held her hand out. "Obadiah? Is that you?"

The crunch of a footstep on the asphalt behind her made Barrie turn, and she found Cassie coming up the path alongside the cemetery fence. Like Barrie, she was watching the raven that stood hunched on the branch above Charlotte Colesworth's grave with its head cocked toward them.

"You think the bird is Obadiah?" Cassie asked. "On the phone, you said you thought he was down by the excavation area, where Ryder and Junior shot him."

The raven opened its beak, but no sound came out. He hopped once on the branch, then flew away. Barrie turned to watch him fly over the excavation area and land back on top of one of the columns that overlooked the mansion ruins. "I'm not sure what I think anymore. All I know is that I noticed the police and the archaeologists walking around an empty spot on the grass where Obadiah was lying the last time we saw him, the way people walk around Obadiah when he's hanging around not wanting to be seen. He may still be there soaking up energy from people and trying to heal, or he may have run off or flown off somewhere, or he may have crumbled into dust for all we know. I want to be sure."

A breeze lifted, raising the scent of tannin and pluff mud from the river and flinging Cassie's tumbled black curls into her eyes. She wore none of her usual sass and bravado. Her beautiful face was bare of makeup, telling its own story about what she'd been through, and it felt wrong to Barrie to have even dragged her back outside after everything that had happened.

She caught her cousin's elbow as Cassie turned back toward the small house where she lived with her family. "If you'd rather not help with this, I can do it on my own. And if you need someone to talk to . . . I know we haven't exactly been the best of friends, but I'm here if you need anything."

"I don't need your pity," Cassie snapped. She stared at the angel statue above Charlotte Colesworth's grave long enough that Barrie began to wonder if Cassie was having another of the flashbacks that had started after her father's funeral, but then Cassie turned abruptly and hurried down the path. Her long, flared jeans swished angrily around the outline of the ankle monitor the police had replaced after Barrie had smashed the first one that morning to summon help.

Barrie walked after her with an inward sigh. "You and I need to find a way to get along if we're going to figure out the curse situation. I was only trying to see how you're holding up."

"How do you think I'm holding up? Why do people even ask that question? Am I supposed to lie to make you all feel better? Pretend Ryder didn't rape me? I hate that everyone knows. You. Berg. The police. My family. People in town. Half of them are wondering if I made it up. Even my mother. She keeps asking me why I hid it, as if I betrayed her by not confiding in her. But she and Daddy didn't want to know. That's why they never asked the question. Even with Ryder's threats, I kept waiting for them to ask. I felt so different that—" Her breath snagged on the last sentence, the way people sometimes struggle with a foreign language, as if it were still impossible to admit what had happened to her four years before.

Barrie's eyes stung at the pain in Cassie's voice. She searched for something to say. There were so many words in the world, so many ways to communicate, and somehow, too often none of them were good enough.

Cassie walked faster, her stride longer than Barrie's so that Barrie had to jog to keep up. Beneath the oak tree at the far edge of the excavation site, the passenger door of the sheriff's patrol car opened, and one of the deputies got out. Adjusting the utility belt that hung low on his hips, he ambled bowleggedly toward the area ringed by police tape, looped around once, stopped, and peered at Barrie and Cassie, before sauntering back to the car again.

"Maybe your mother feels guilty," she said when he had gone. "Not only for what you went through, but for not having seen how you were suffering. She has to be thinking of all the ways she failed you."

"I shot the man who raped me. I shot him, and she's worrying about her own guilt," Cassie said.

"Worrying about having failed you is probably normal—"

"And then she asked me why I shot Ryder, whether it was because of that or because he tried to steal the gold."

Barrie herself wasn't sure that was an "or" question where Cassie was concerned. "The police said it was self-defense," she said softly. "They're not pressing charges after all, are they?"

"Not for now." Cassie reached the front steps of the house, and then she turned with her foot on the bottom stair. Anger crackled out of her every pore, but it was the kind of anger that was a form of armor, a way to hide her brokenness the way that Pru hid hers with quiet acceptance. Maybe everyone in the world was a little broken, pretending to others that they weren't.

"I just want this to be all over with!" Cassie cried suddenly. "Is that too much to ask? The curse, the archaeologists, all of it. If Obadiah's still here waiting to steal the gold, then I want him gone. It's mine. I can't leave, and my family and I need the gold to keep this place. He doesn't get to take it. But if he's here, that means Ryder and Junior didn't manage to kill him when they shot him. So how do we get rid of him? I couldn't even tell the police that he was here. My throat felt stuck whenever I tried to say his name."

Barrie looked out toward the dig site where the police tape fluttered in the breeze that came up from the river. A single raven gathered its wings and took off from a broken column and flew a wide, lazy circle toward the woods.

"I think we just have to take it one step at a time," she said. "Let's see if Obadiah's even here. Most of all, we can't jump to conclusions anymore. We don't know what Obadiah was doing when Ryder and Junior interrupted him," she said. "We don't even know for sure that he was the one who tied us up and put us in the cabin."

"God, how can you still be so naïve?" Cassie's breath was too loud as she climbed the remaining two steps toward the door. "But then you can afford to trust him. It's not your curse or your gold he's after. You've never been poor. You've spent your whole life locked away in your neat little corner of the world where everything's been taken care of for you, and you've never been unsafe or uncertain of anything for a single minute."

Given what Barrie had been through over the past few weeks, what Cassie and her family had put her through, a half-hysterical laugh bubbled up in Barrie's throat. Not that there was any point in arguing. Cassie was never going to see past the preconception of the charmed life she believed the Watsons and the Beauforts led. Maybe that was another symptom of the Colesworth curse, or maybe it was Wyatt filling his daughter's head with poison for too many years.

The door opened behind Cassie, and she stood back out of the way. Pru and Marie Colesworth came out with a pitcher of tea and a tray of sandwiches covered with a blue-checkered dishcloth, and a few minutes later, Barrie accompanied Cassie to the police car with the food. She stopped there only long enough to hold up the earring she had brought and to mumble an explanation about needing to search for its mate.

At the excavation site, the neatly measured squares cleared by the archaeologists had been obliterated by the illegal digging. The soil was a torn mess of dirt and brick chips, and the datum, the piece of iron rebar used to set the measurement standards for the dig's grid layout, lay where it had fallen when the spirits of Ayita and Elijah had thrown it, thirty feet from where they had ripped it from the ground.

Circling around the police tape that cordoned off the circumference of the hidden room, Barrie concentrated on remembering exactly where she had seen the police and archaeologists deviate around a seemingly bare spot of lawn. She searched for a hint—some sign she didn't even know how to look for. There was only the broken soil and the usual headache.

Then something grasped her ankle. Brittle finger bones ground against her skin with a touch so cold that it sank straight to Barrie's marrow. She felt her strength ebb away.

MARTINA BOONE was born in Prague and spoke several languages before learning English. She fell in love with words and never stopped delighting in them. From her home in Virginia, where she lives with her husband, children, and shelter cat, she enjoys writing contemporary fantasy set in the kinds of magical places she'd love to visit. She is also the author of *Compulsion*.

For book club and curriculum-related bonus material, discussion questions, and additional information on the history and folklore of the Heirs of Watson Island series, please visit the author's website at www.MartinaBoone.com.

Discover more about Watson Island online!

Watch the trailer

·

Read reviews and sneak peeks

·

Learn more about the series

At MartinaBoone.com!